WYND™

BOOK TWO: THE SECRET OF THE WINGS

Published by

BOOm! BOX™

DESIGNER
MARIE KRUPINA

ASSISTANT EDITOR
RAMIRO PORTNOY

EDITOR
ERIC HARBURN

Ross Richie Chairman & Founder
Matt Gagnon Editor-in-Chief
Filip Sablik President, Publishing & Marketing
Stephen Christy President, Development
Lance Kreiter Vice President, Licensing & Merchandising
Bryce Carlson Vice President, Editorial & Creative Strategy
Kate Henning Director, Operations
Elyse Strandberg Manager, Finance
Michelle Ankley Manager, Production Design
Sierra Hahn Executive Editor
Dafna Pleban Senior Editor
Shannon Watters Senior Editor
Eric Harburn Senior Editor
Elizabeth Brei Editor
Kathleen Wisneski Editor
Sophie Philips-Roberts Editor
Jonathan Manning Associate Editor
Allyson Gronowitz Associate Editor
Gavin Gronenthal Assistant Editor
Gwen Waller Assistant Editor
Ramiro Portnoy Assistant Editor
Kenzie Rzonca Assistant Editor

Rey Netschke Editorial Assistant
Marie Krupina Design Lead
Grace Park Design Coordinator
Chelsea Roberts Design Coordinator
Madison Goyette Production Designer
Crystal White Production Designer
Samantha Knapp Production Design Assistant
Esther Kim Marketing Lead
Breanna Sarpy Marketing Lead, Digital
Amanda Lawson Marketing Coordinator
Grecia Martinez Marketing Assistant, Digital
José Meza Consumer Sales Lead
Ashley Troub Consumer Sales Coordinator
Morgan Perry Retail Sales Lead
Harley Salbacka Sales Coordinator
Megan Christopher Operations Coordinator
Rodrigo Hernandez Operations Coordinator
Zipporah Smith Operations Coordinator
Jason Lee Senior Accountant
Sabrina Lesin Accounting Assistant
Lauren Alexander Administrative Assistant

BOOM! BOX™

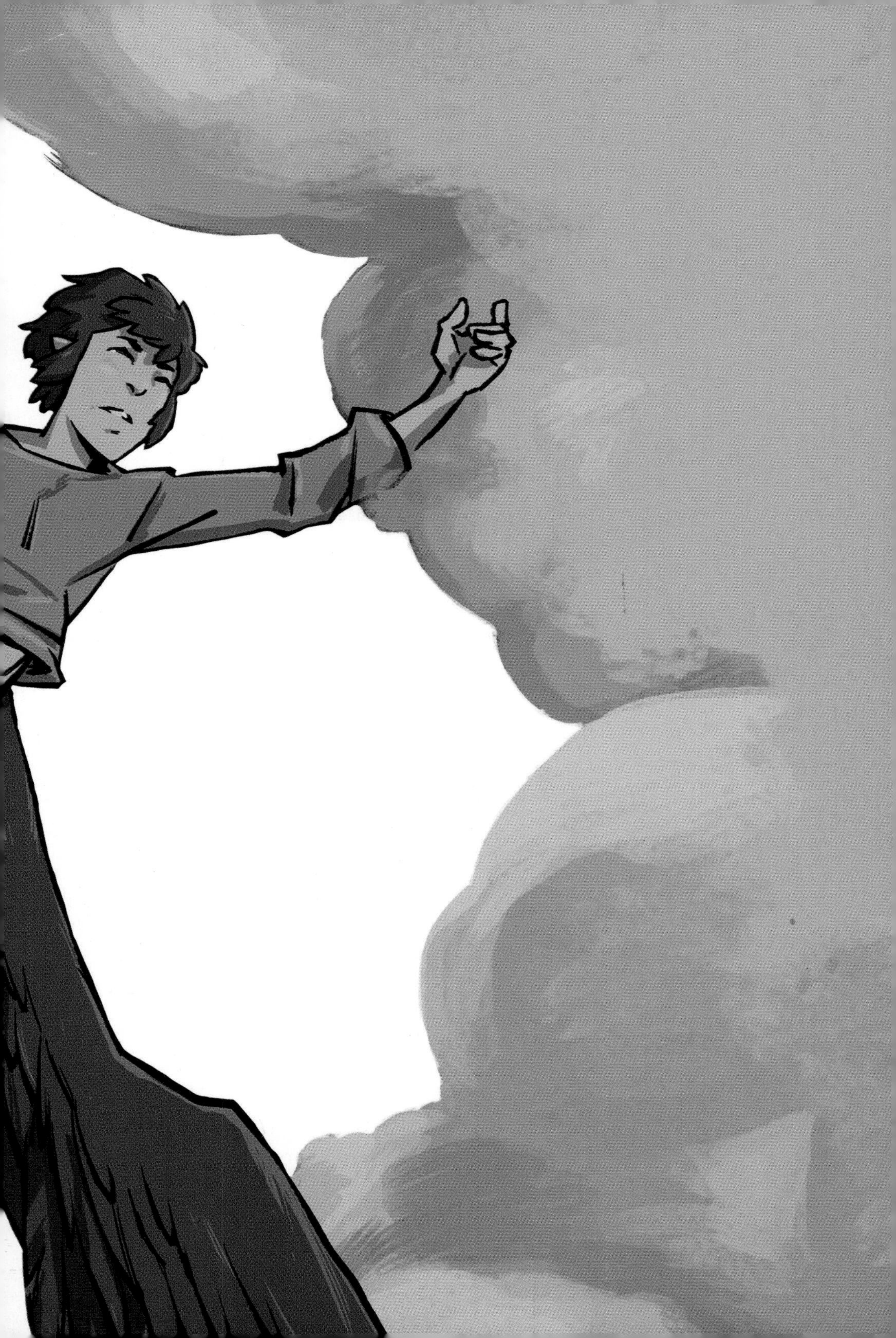

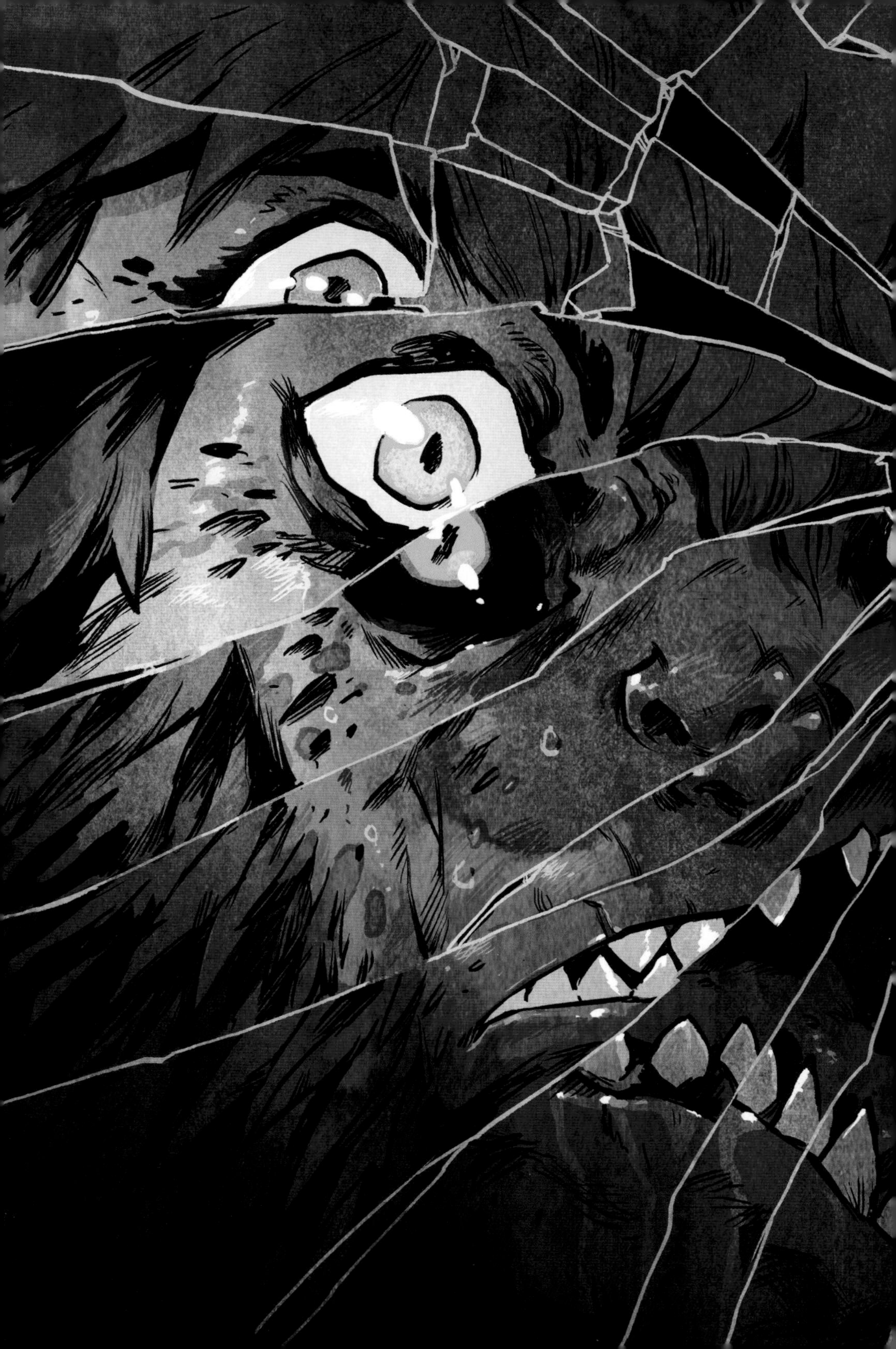

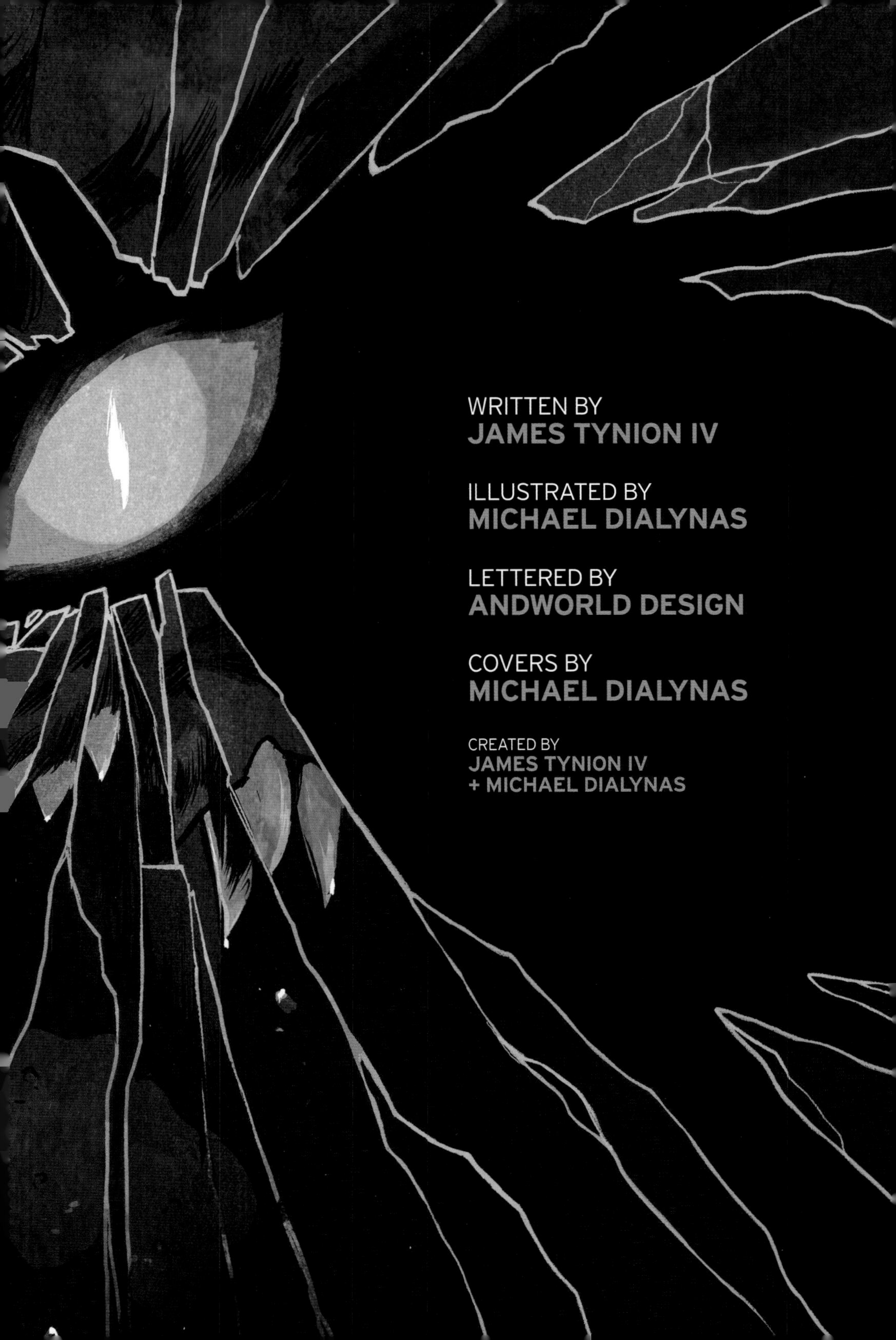

WRITTEN BY
JAMES TYNION IV

ILLUSTRATED BY
MICHAEL DIALYNAS

LETTERED BY
ANDWORLD DESIGN

COVERS BY
MICHAEL DIALYNAS

CREATED BY
JAMES TYNION IV
+ MICHAEL DIALYNAS

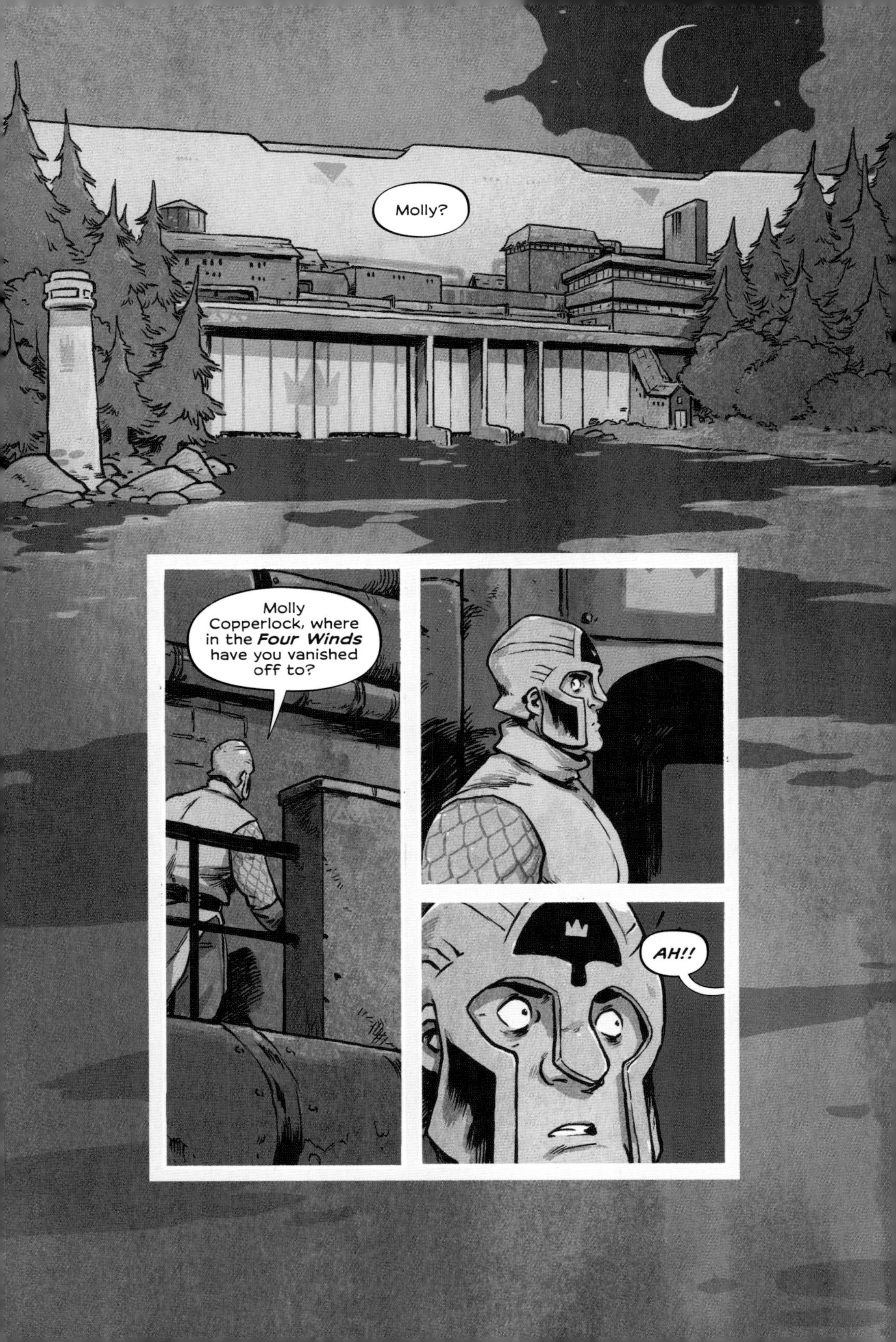
Molly?
Molly Copperlock, where in the *Four Winds* have you vanished off to?
AH!!

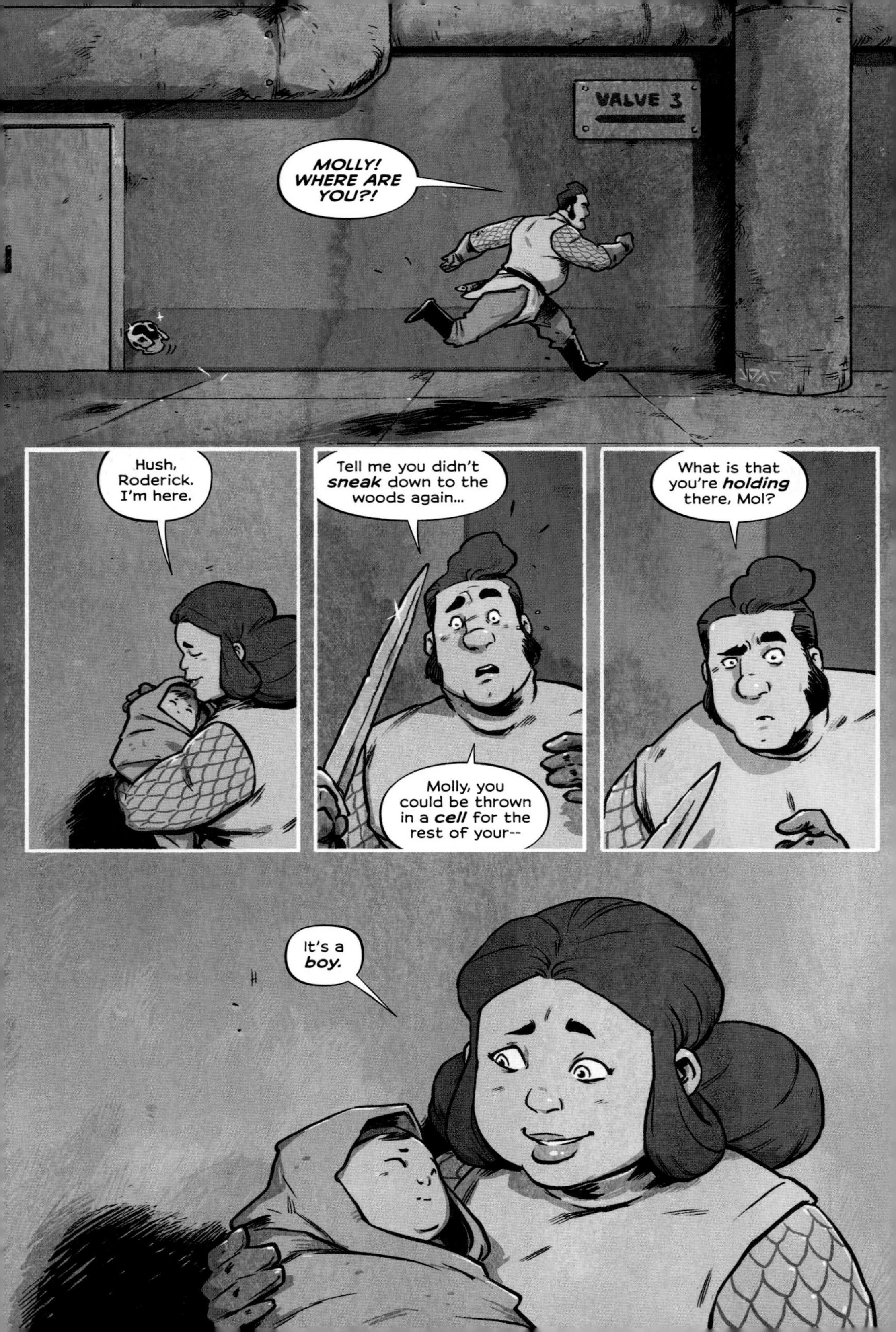
VALVE 3
MOLLY! WHERE ARE YOU?!
Hush, Roderick. I'm here.
Tell me you didn't *sneak* down to the woods again...
Molly, you could be thrown in a *cell* for the rest of your--
What is that you're *holding* there, Mol?
It's a *boy.*

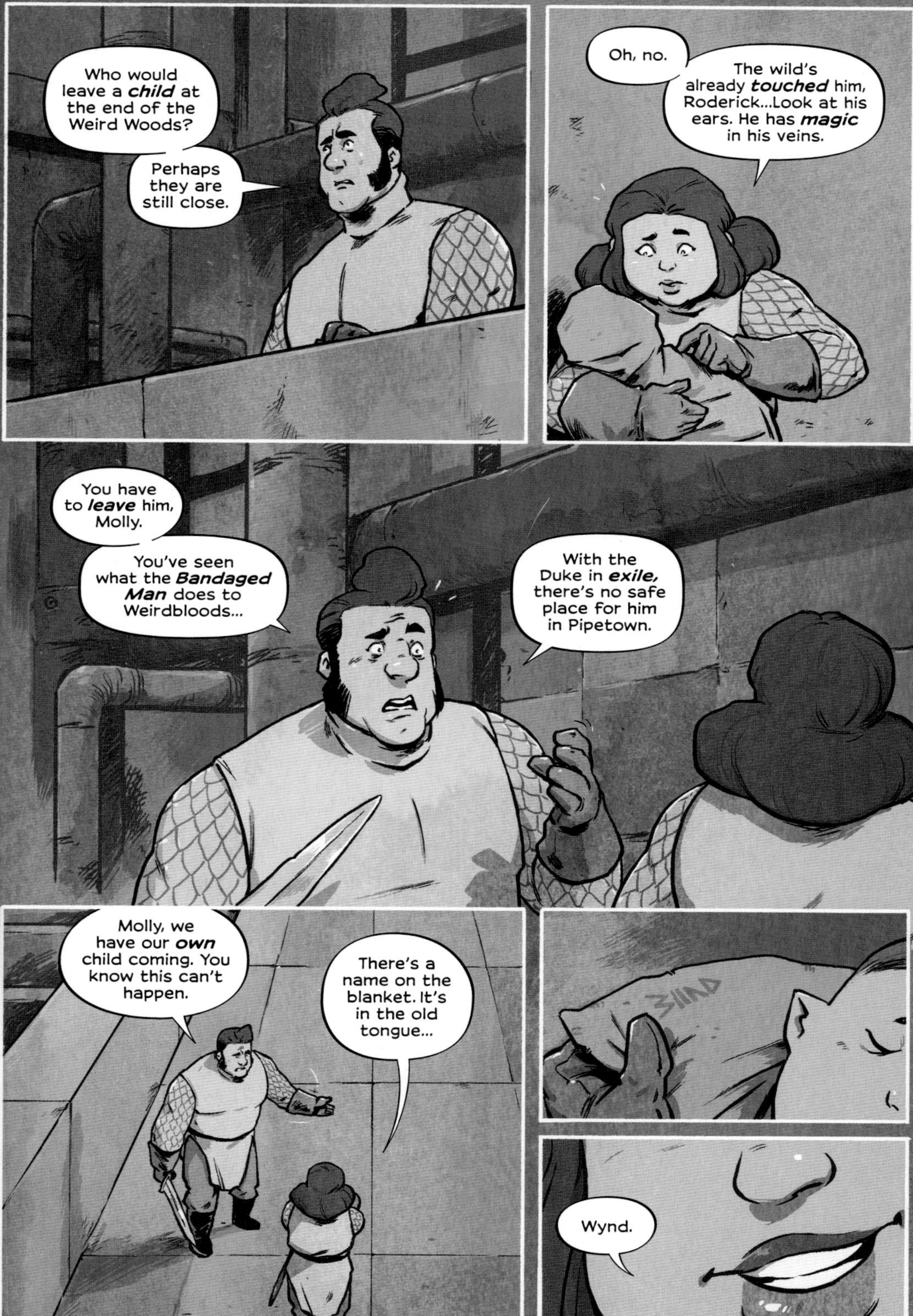
Who would leave a *child* at the end of the Weird Woods?
Perhaps they are still close.
Oh, no.
The wild's already *touched* him, Roderick...Look at his ears. He has *magic* in his veins.
You have to *leave* him, Molly.
You've seen what the *Bandaged Man* does to Weirdbloods...
With the Duke in *exile,* there's no safe place for him in Pipetown.
Molly, we have our *own* child coming. You know this can't happen.
There's a name on the blanket. It's in the old tongue...
Wynd.

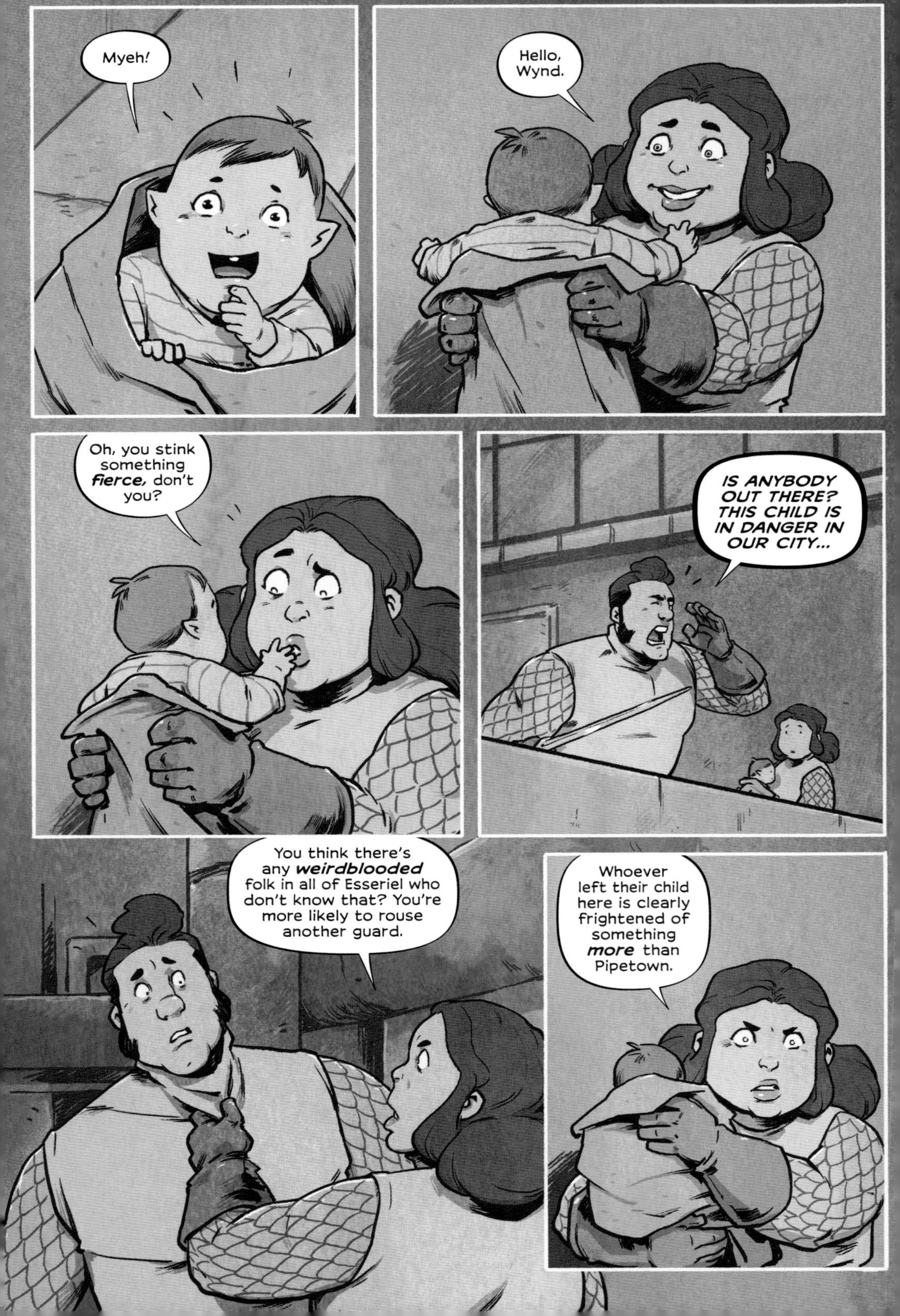
Myeh!
Hello, Wynd.
Oh, you stink something *fierce,* don't you?
IS ANYBODY OUT THERE? THIS CHILD IS IN DANGER IN OUR CITY...
You think there's any ***weirdblooded*** folk in all of Esseriel who don't know that? You're more likely to rouse another guard.
Whoever left their child here is clearly frightened of something ***more*** than Pipetown.

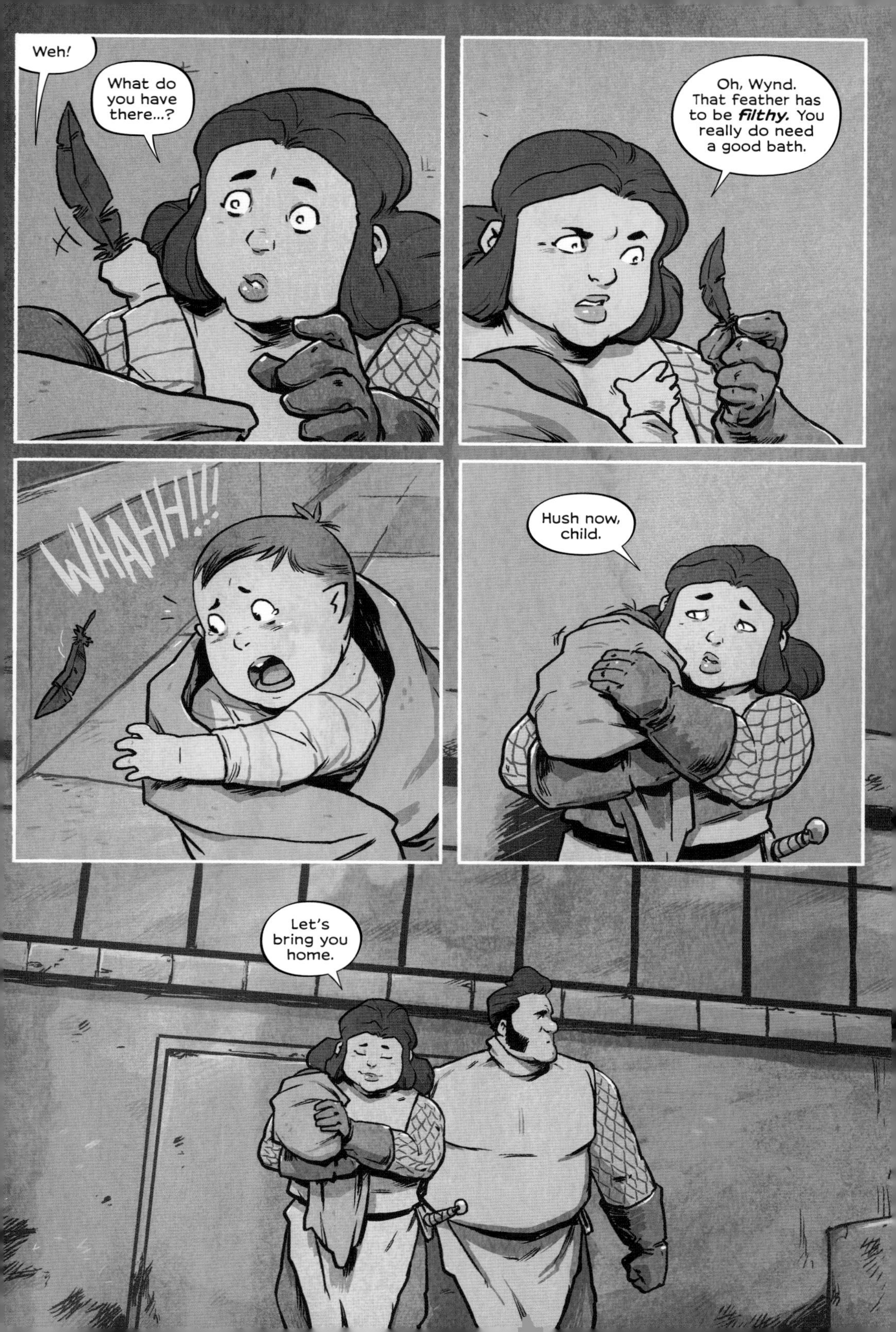

Weh!
What do you have there...?
Oh, Wynd. That feather has to be ***Filthy.*** You really do need a good bath.
WAAHH!!!
Hush now, child.
Let's bring you home.

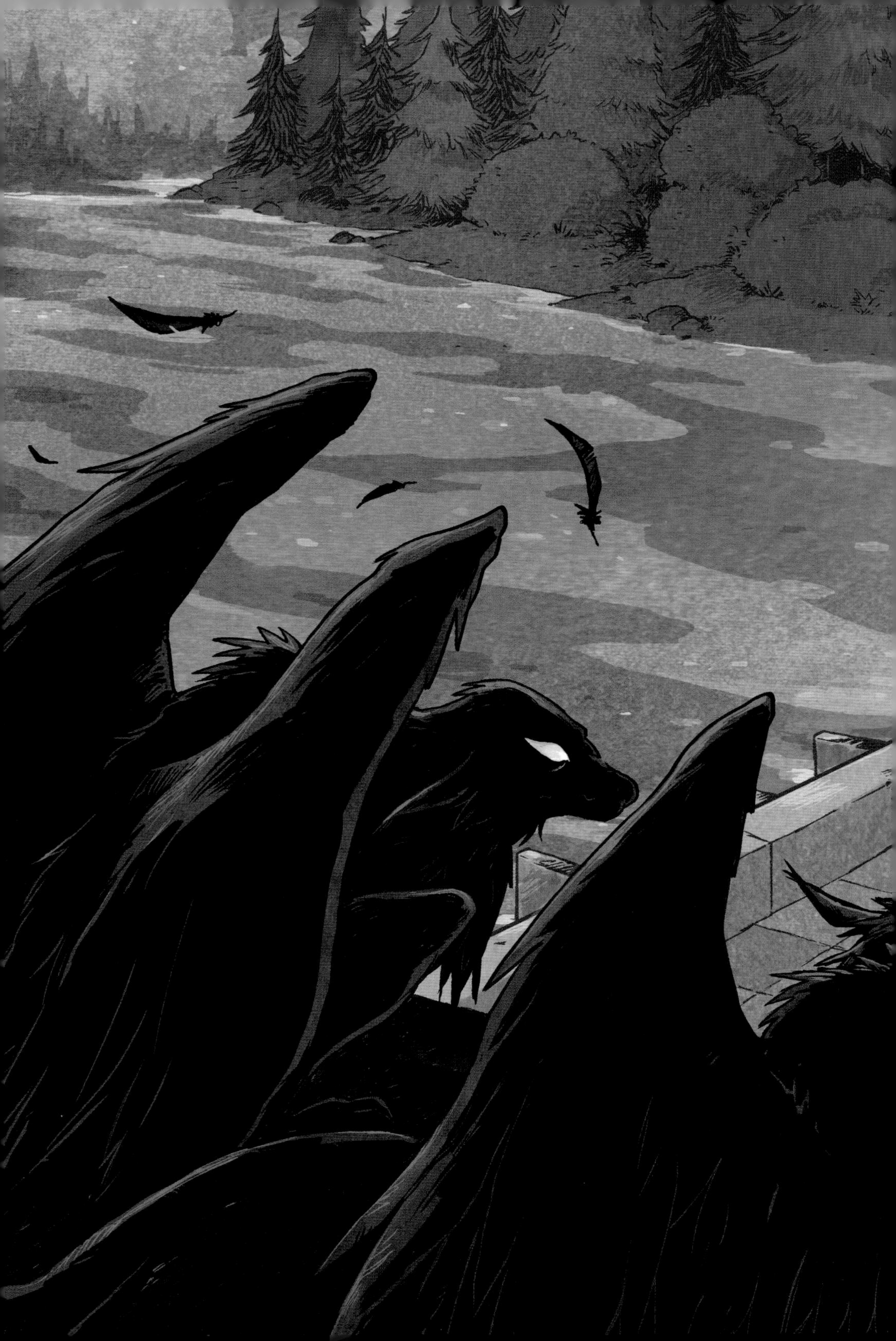

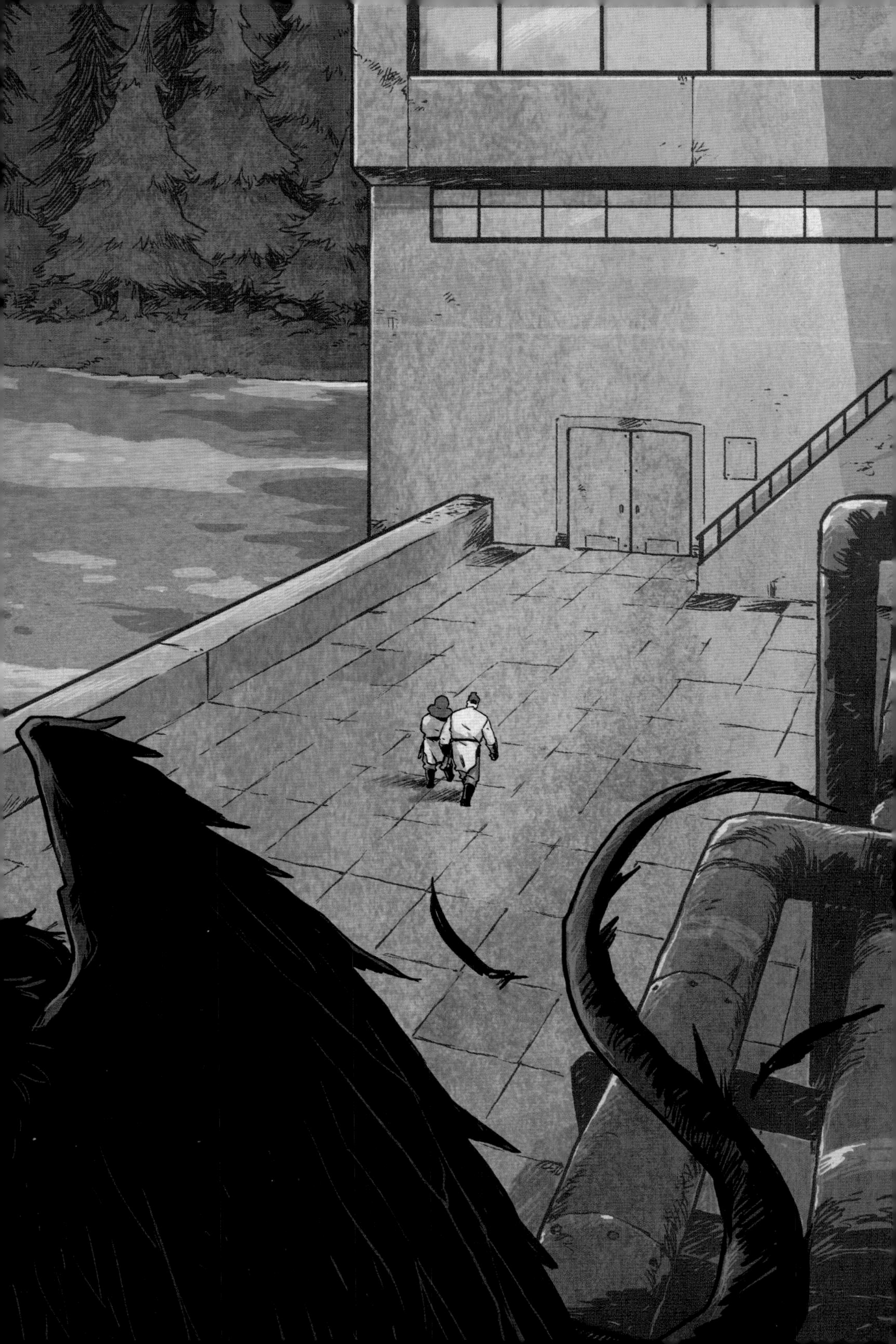

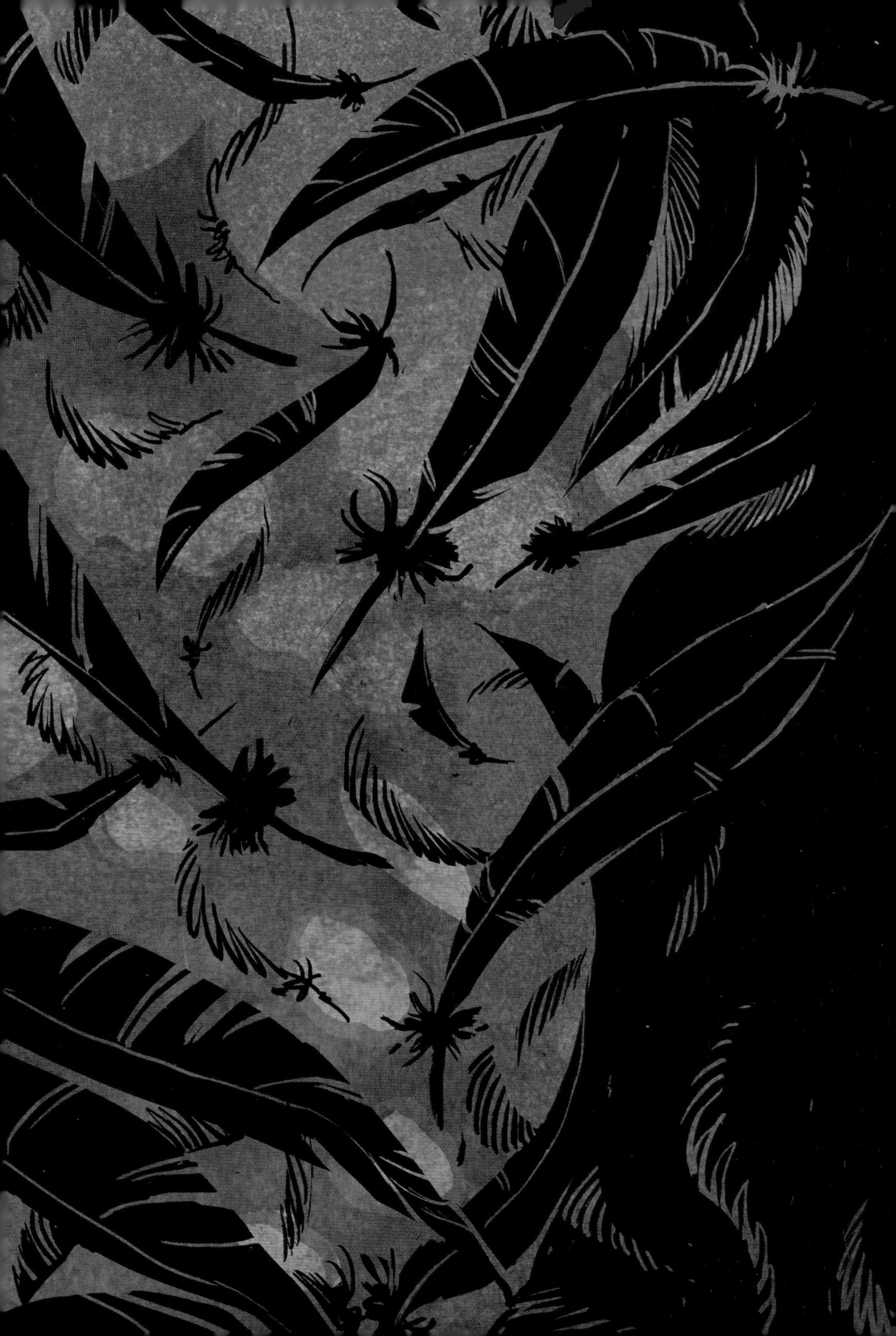

WYND

BOOK TWO:
THE SECRET OF THE WINGS

BY JAMES TYNION IV + MICHAEL DIALYNAS
WITH ANDWORLD DESIGN

CHAPTER ONE
THE BLACK SHIPS

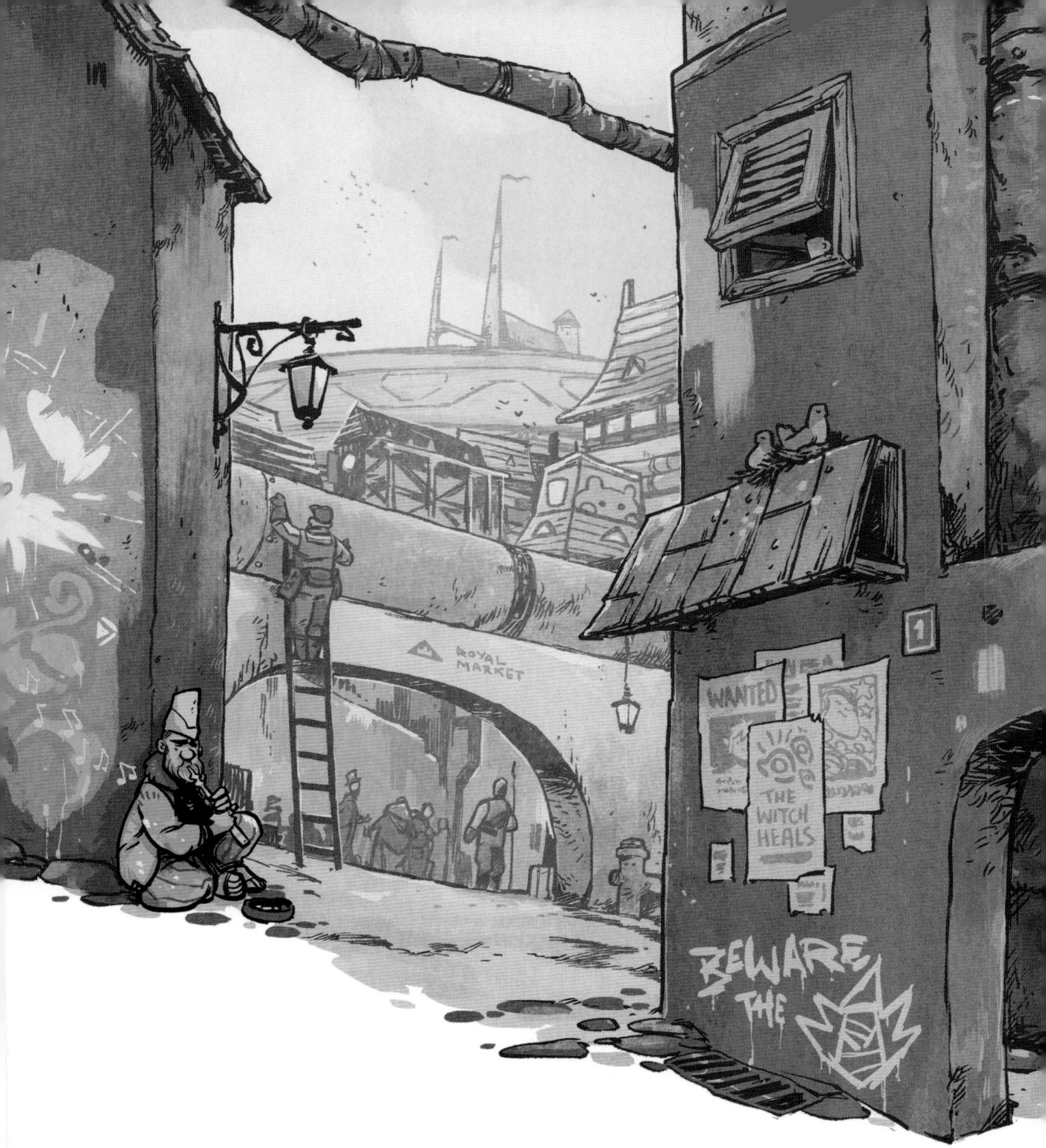
ROYAL MARKET
1
WANTED
THE WITCH HEALS
BEWARE THE

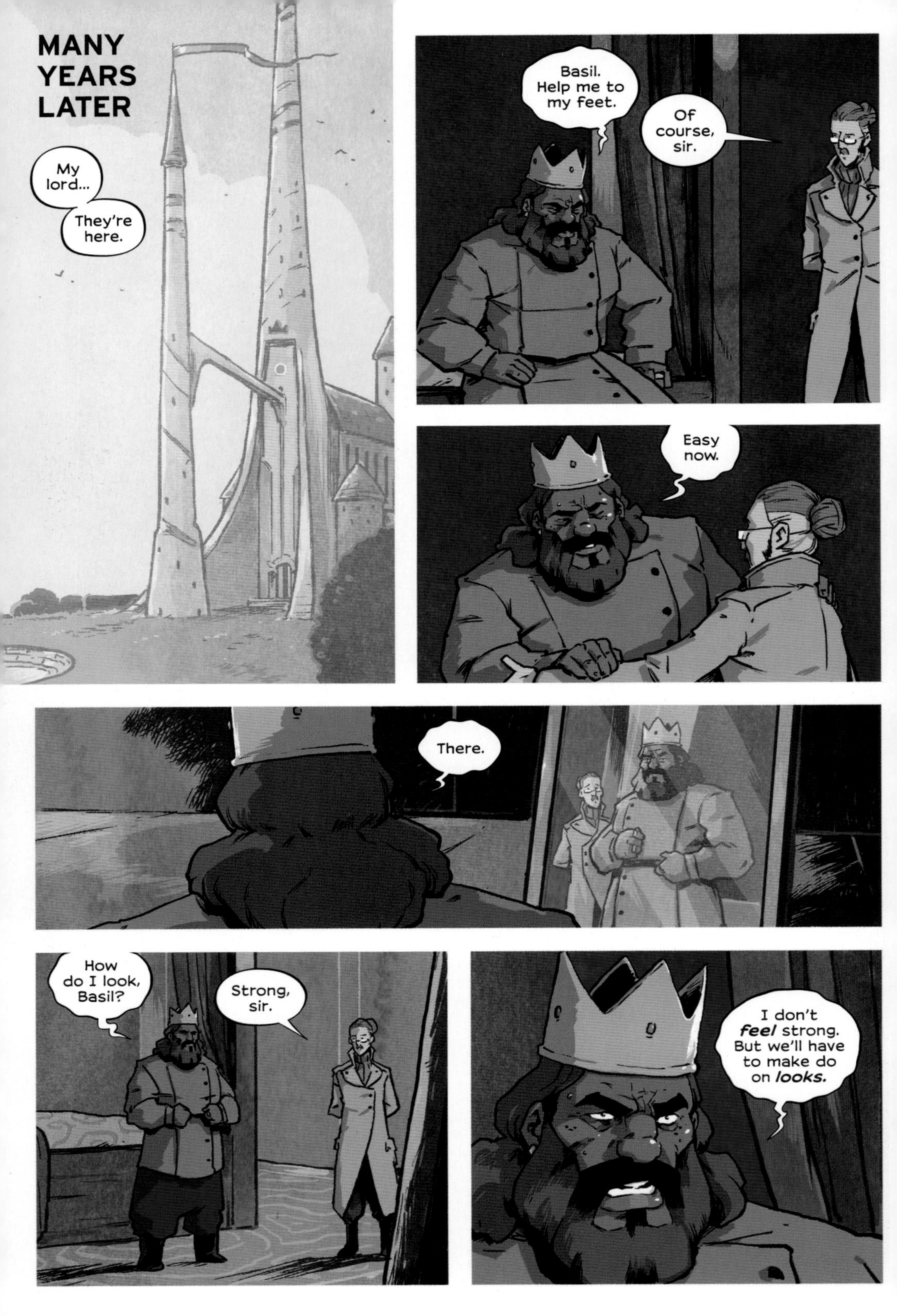
MANY YEARS LATER
My lord...
They're here.
Basil. Help me to my feet.
Of course, sir.
Easy now.
There.
How do I look, Basil?
Strong, sir.
I don't *feel* strong. But we'll have to make do on *looks.*

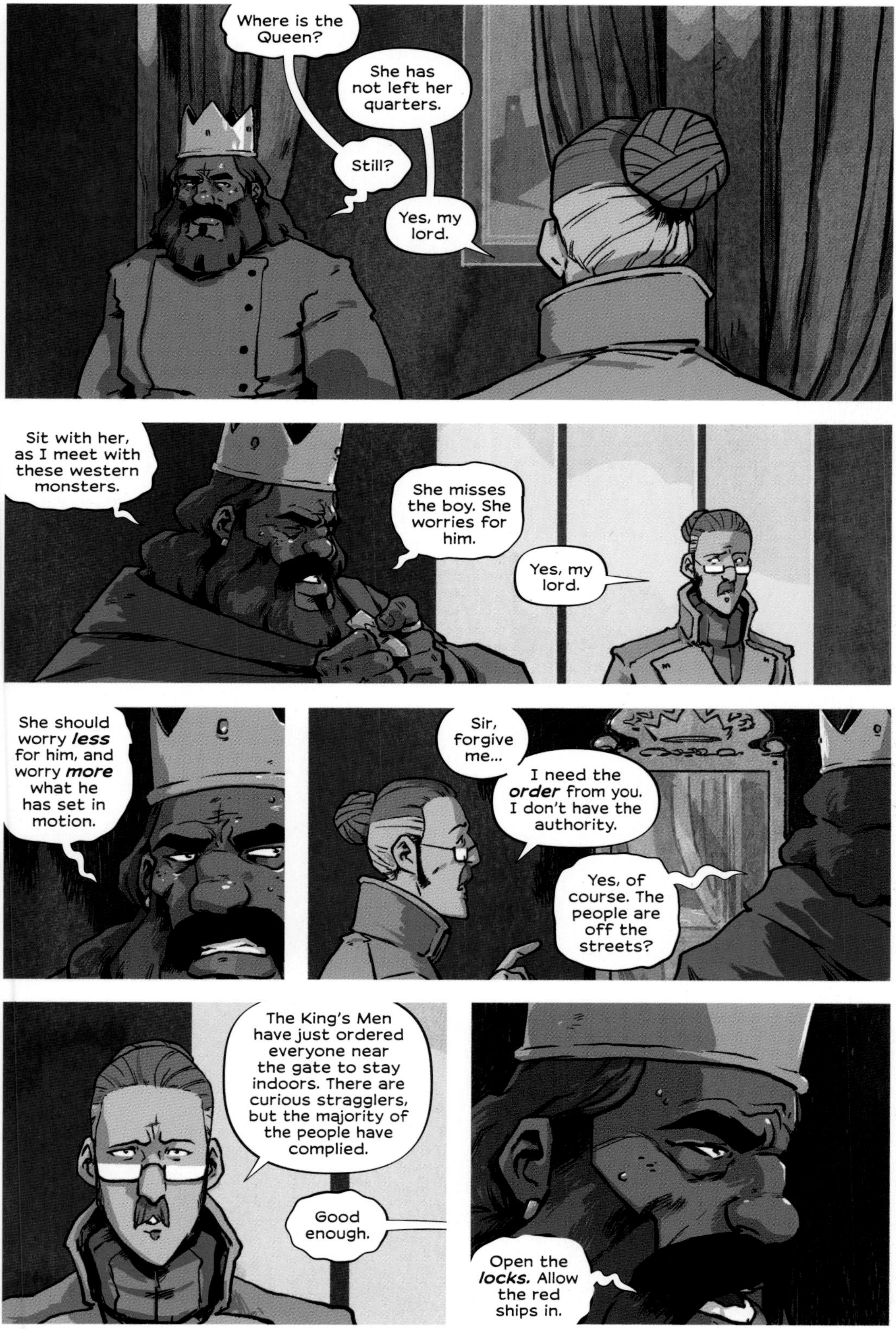

Where is the Queen?
She has not left her quarters.
Still?
Yes, my lord.
Sit with her, as I meet with these western monsters.
She misses the boy. She worries for him.
Yes, my lord.
She should worry *less* for him, and worry *more* what he has set in motion.
Sir, forgive me...
I need the *order* from you. I don't have the authority.
Yes, of course. The people are off the streets?
The King's Men have just ordered everyone near the gate to stay indoors. There are curious stragglers, but the majority of the people have complied.
Good enough.
Open the *locks.* Allow the red ships in.

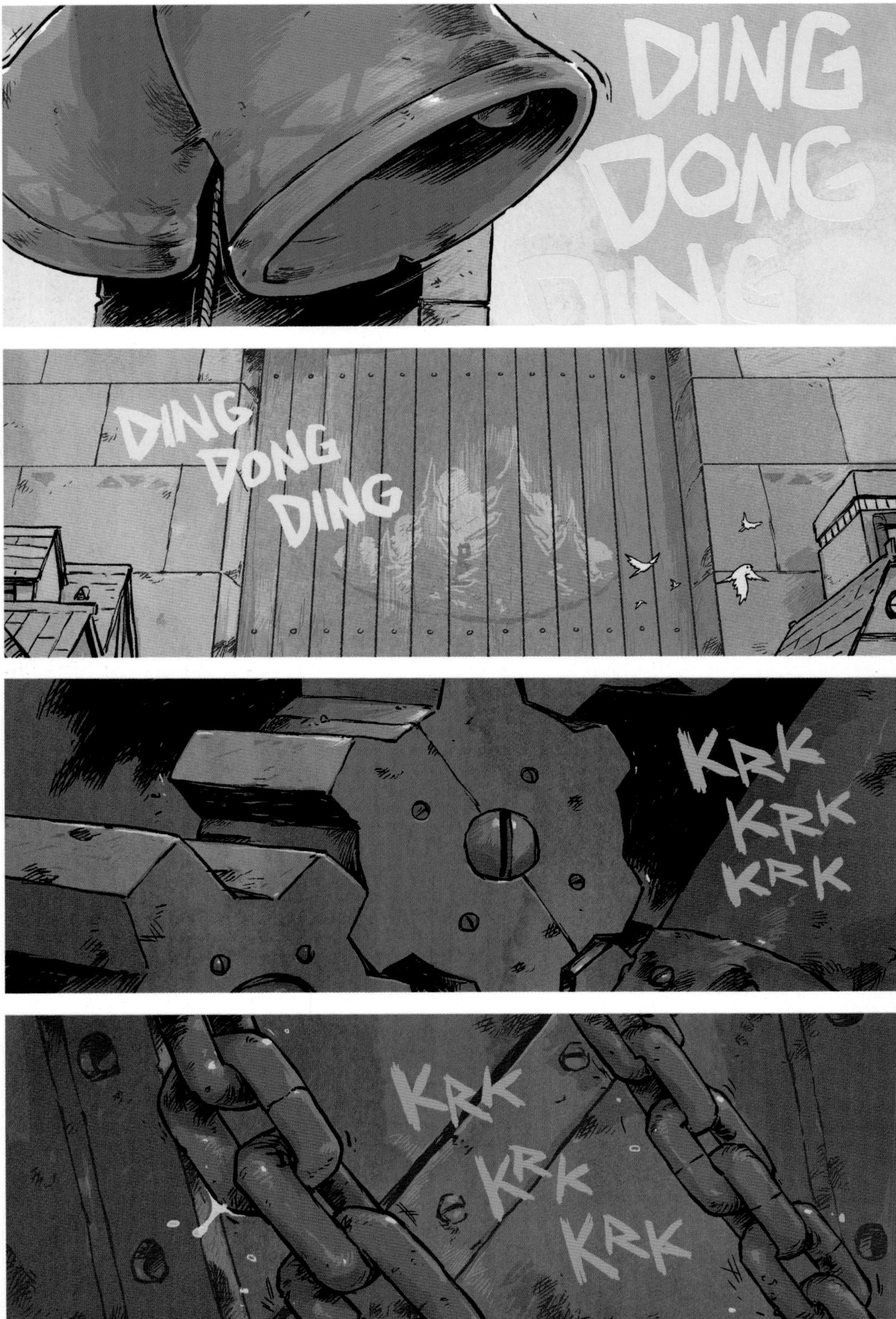
DING
DONG
DING
DONG
DING
KRK
KRK
KRK
KRK
KRK
KRK

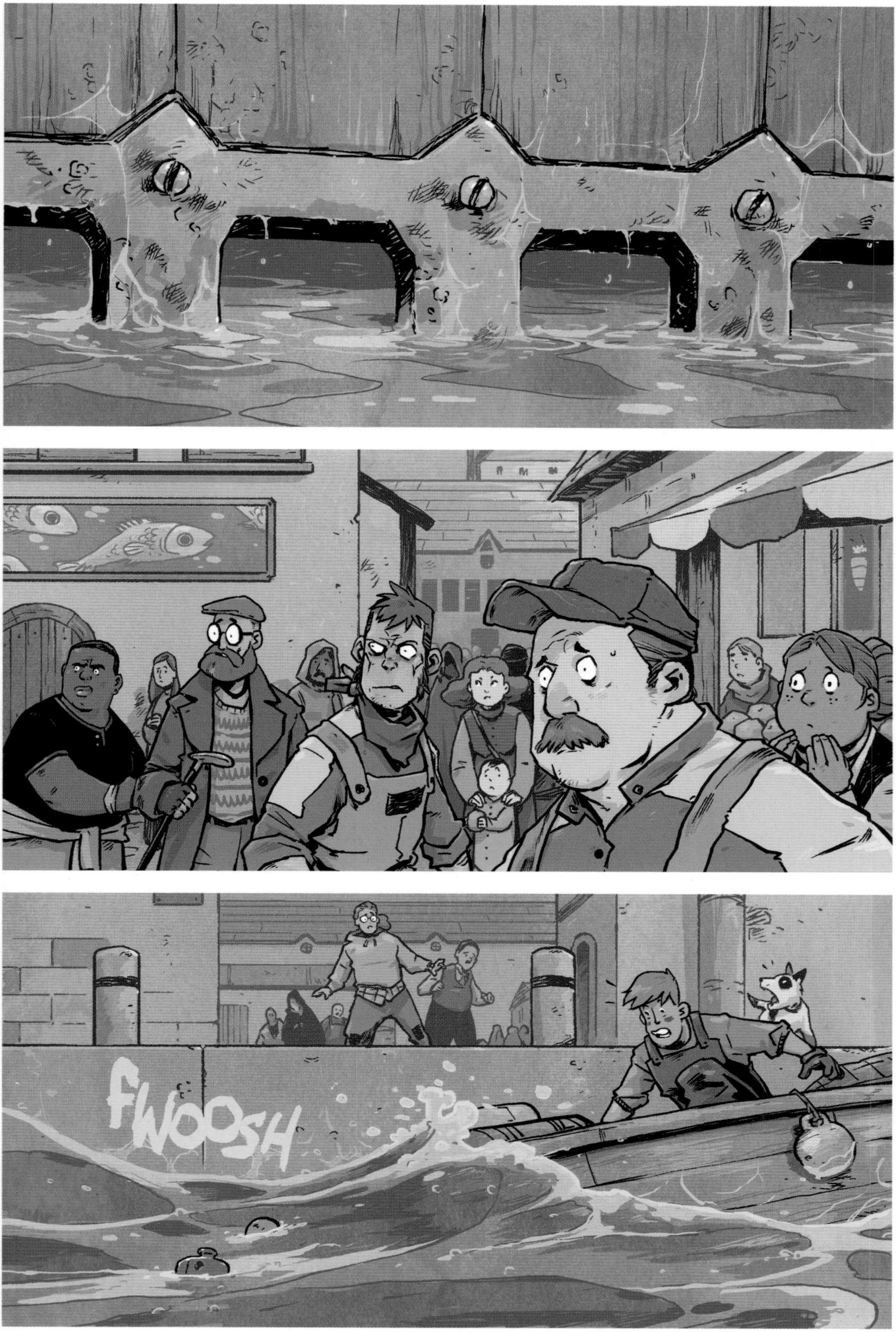
FWOOSH

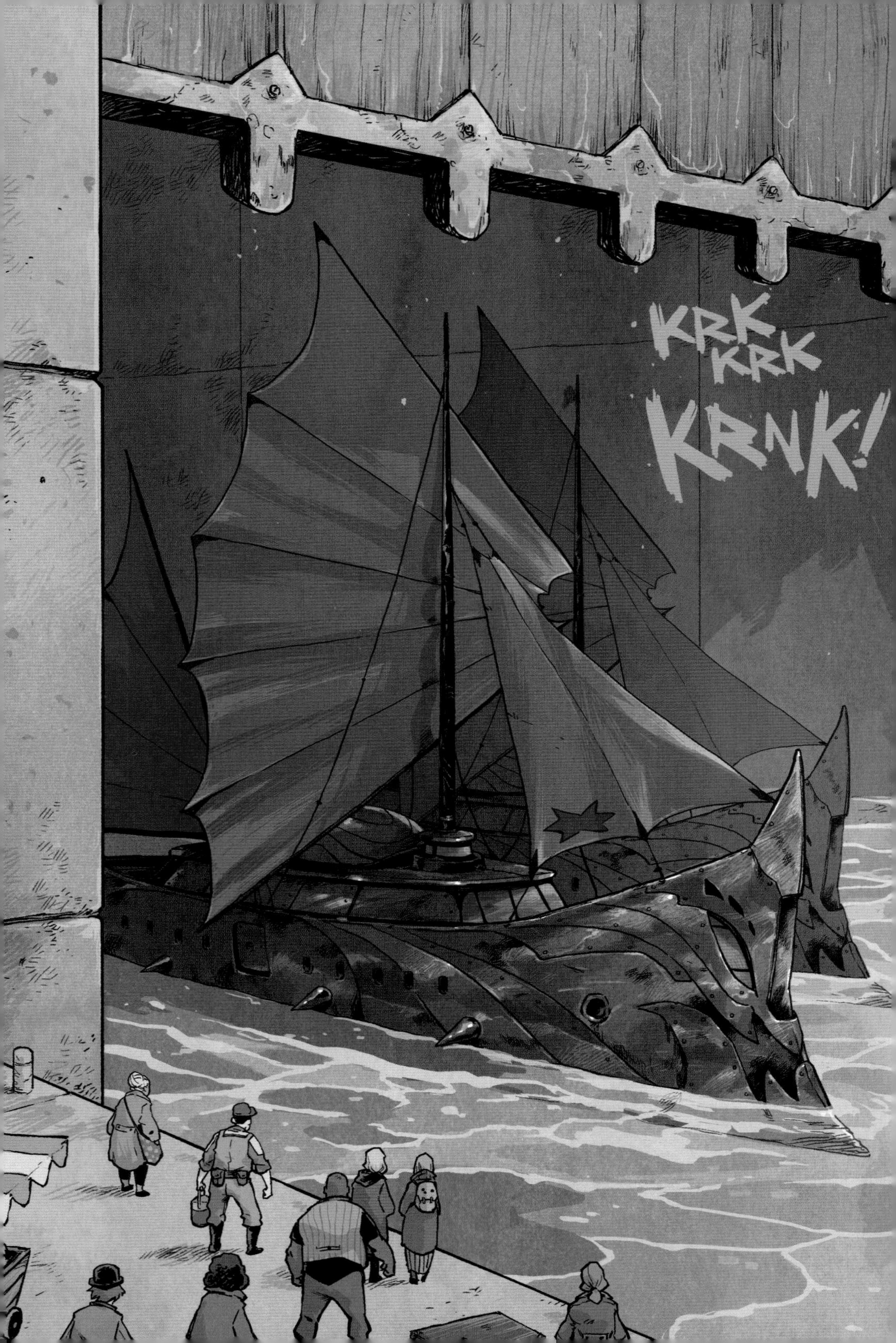
KRK
KRK
KRNK!

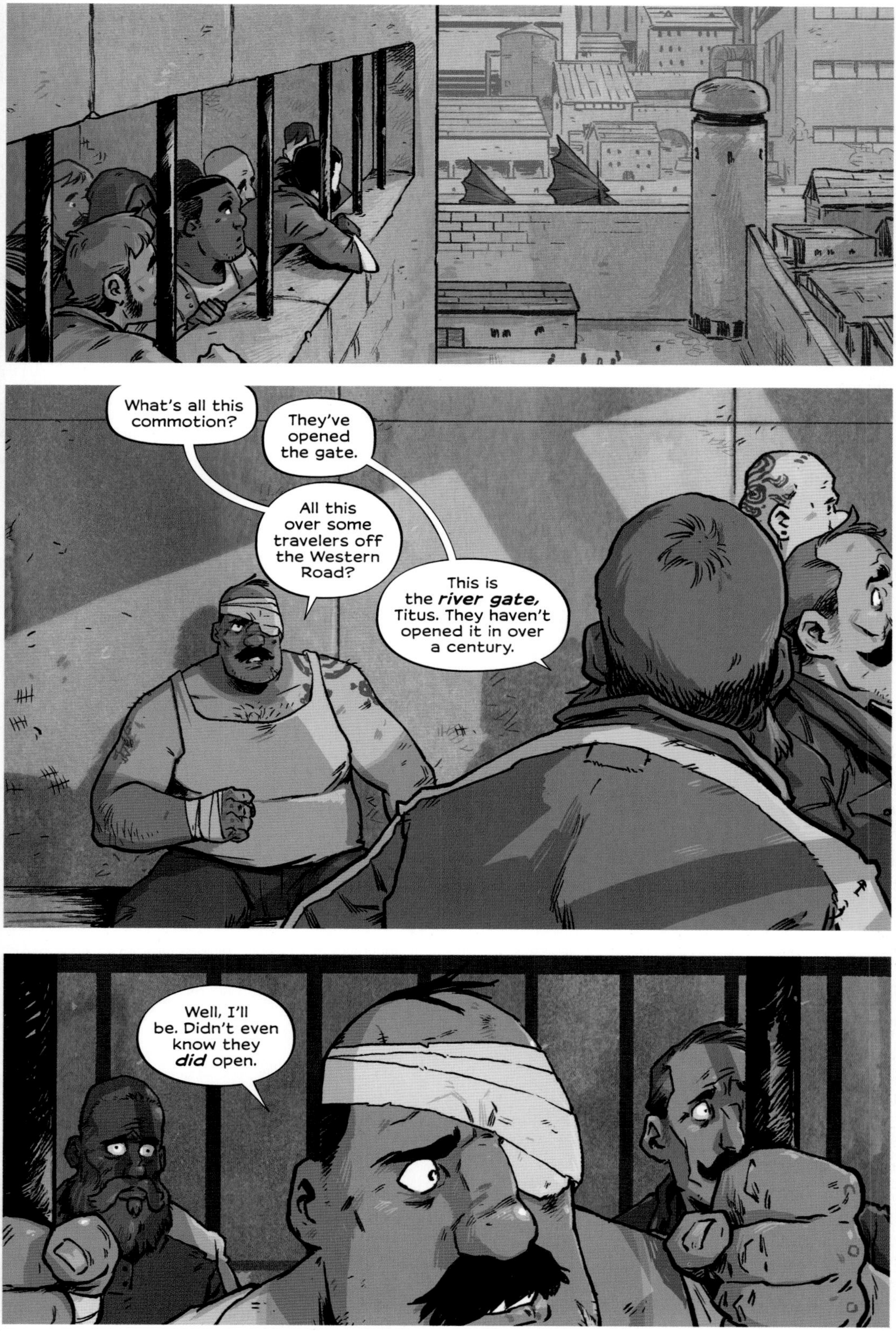

What's all this commotion?
They've opened the gate.
All this over some travelers off the Western Road?
This is the ***river gate,*** Titus. They haven't opened it in over a century.
Well, I'll be. Didn't even know they ***did*** open.

KLANG
KLANG

Get away from the walls!

Everyone, back in your cells.

Have to *trample* on every little bit of joy, don't you?

I serve at the pleasure of the King.

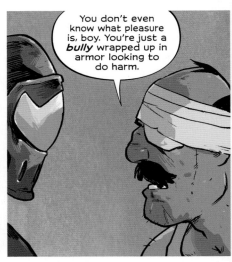

You don't even know what pleasure is, boy. You're just a *bully* wrapped up in armor looking to do harm.

Another word, prisoner, and I'll *gut* you.

I'm movin', I'm movin'.

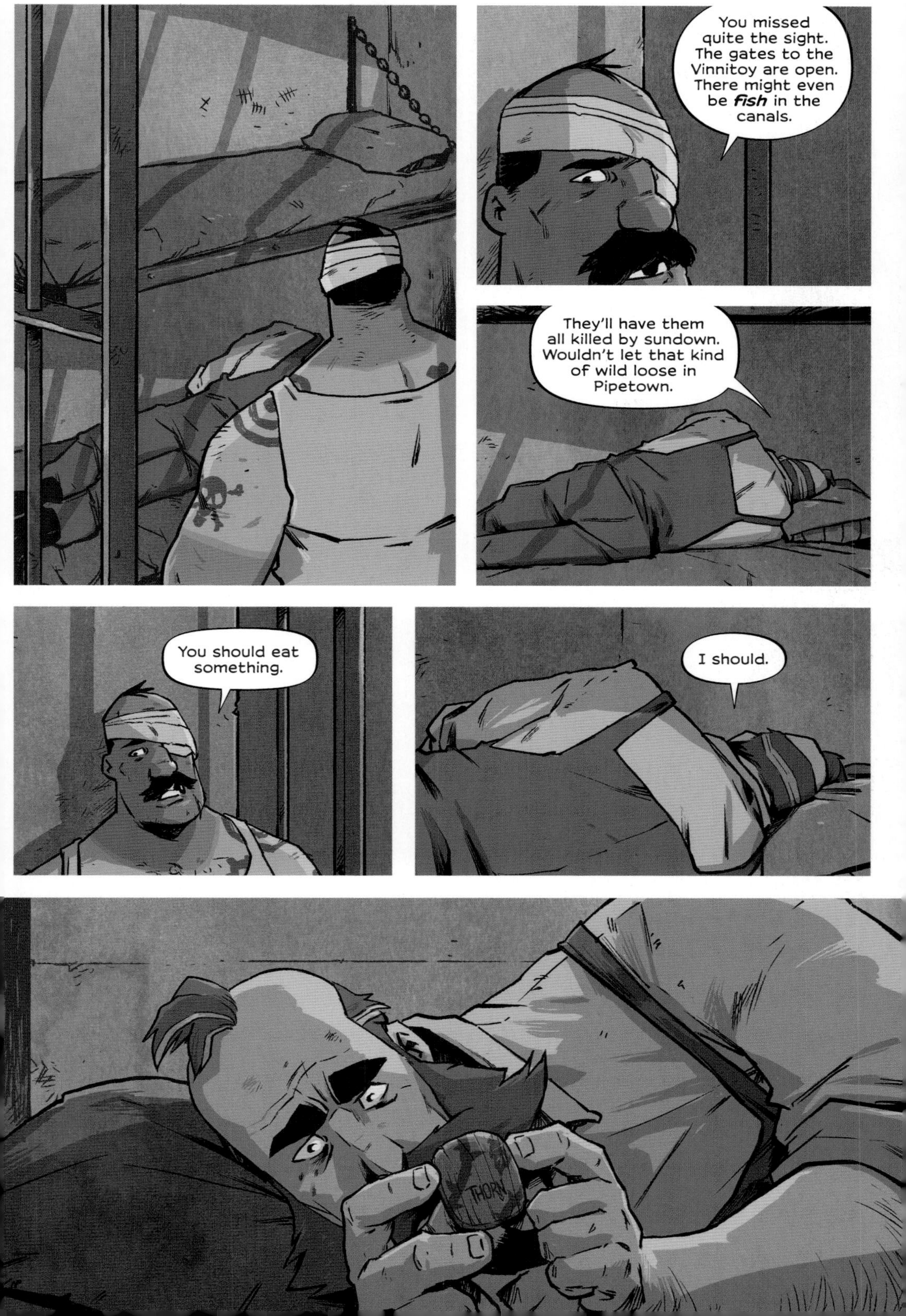
You missed quite the sight. The gates to the Vinnitoy are open. There might even be **fish** in the canals.
They'll have them all killed by sundown. Wouldn't let that kind of wild loose in Pipetown.
You should eat something.
I should.
THORN

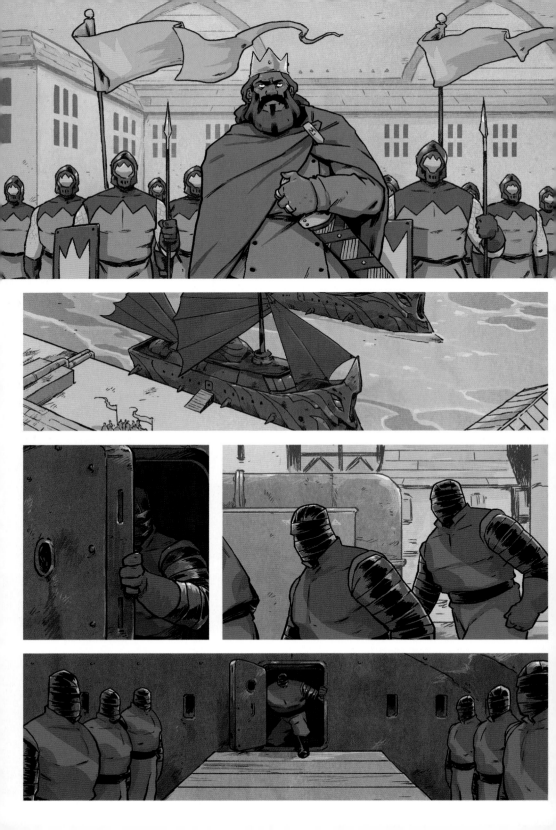

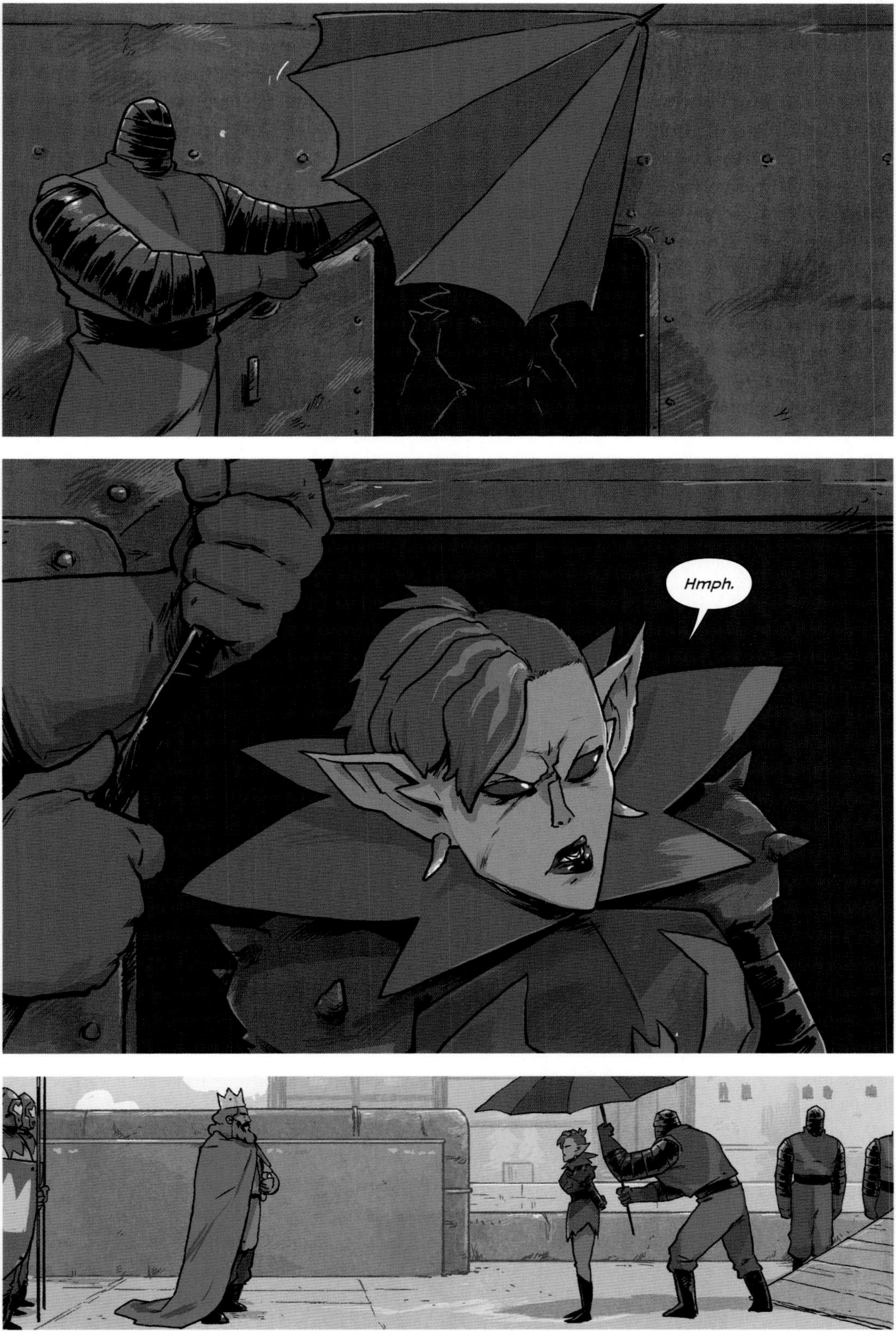
Hmph.

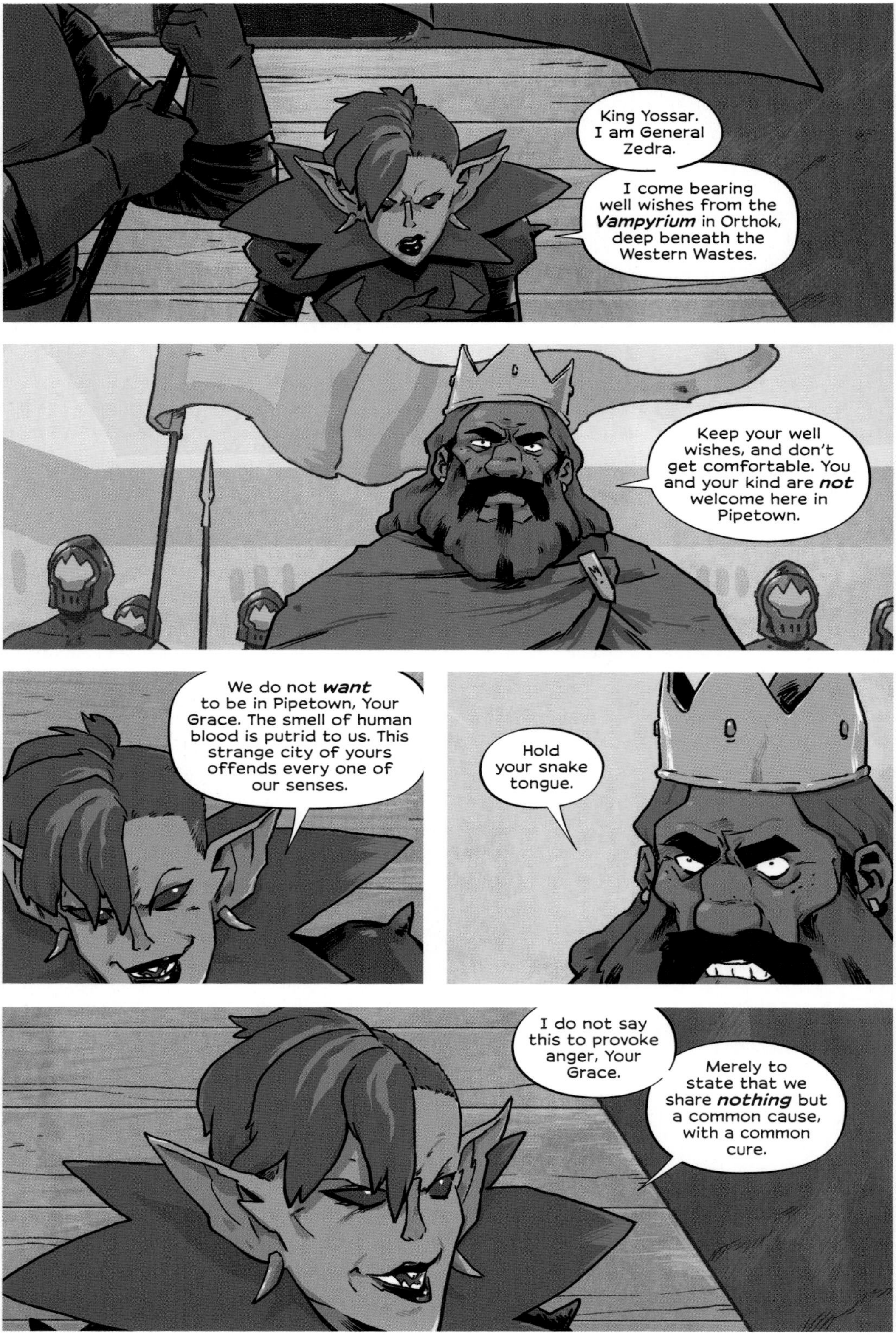
King Yossar. I am General Zedra.
I come bearing well wishes from the ***Vampyrium*** in Orthok, deep beneath the Western Wastes.
Keep your well wishes, and don't get comfortable. You and your kind are ***not*** welcome here in Pipetown.
We do not ***want*** to be in Pipetown, Your Grace. The smell of human blood is putrid to us. This strange city of yours offends every one of our senses.
Hold your snake tongue.
I do not say this to provoke anger, Your Grace.
Merely to state that we share ***nothing*** but a common cause, with a common cure.

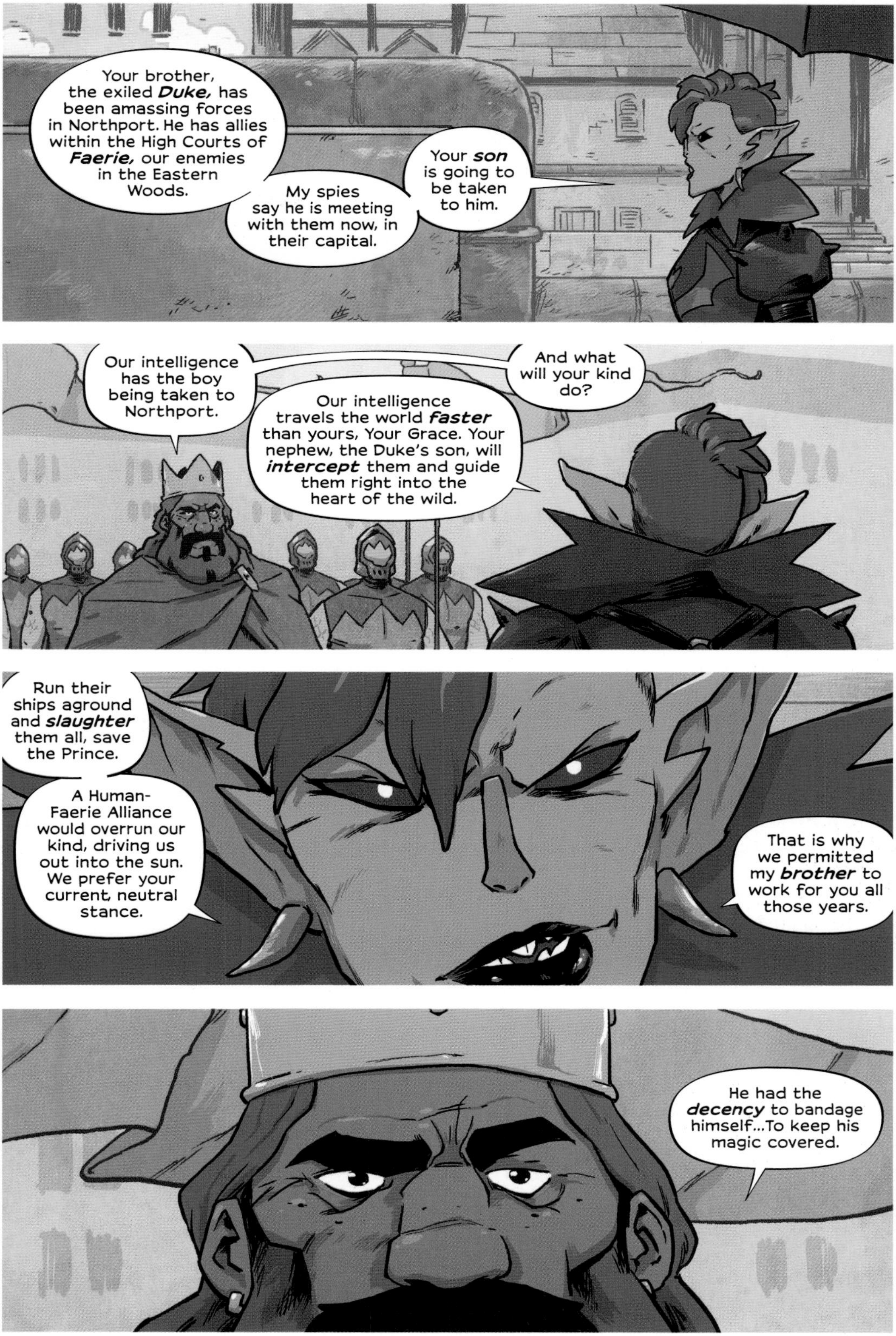
Your brother, the exiled *Duke,* has been amassing forces in Northport. He has allies within the High Courts of *Faerie,* our enemies in the Eastern Woods.
My spies say he is meeting with them now, in their capital.
Your *son* is going to be taken to him.
Our intelligence has the boy being taken to Northport.
And what will your kind do?
Our intelligence travels the world *faster* than yours, Your Grace. Your nephew, the Duke's son, will *intercept* them and guide them right into the heart of the wild.
Run their ships aground and *slaughter* them all, save the Prince.
A Human-Faerie Alliance would overrun our kind, driving us out into the sun. We prefer your current, neutral stance.
That is why we permitted my *brother* to work for you all those years.
He had the *decency* to bandage himself...To keep his magic covered.

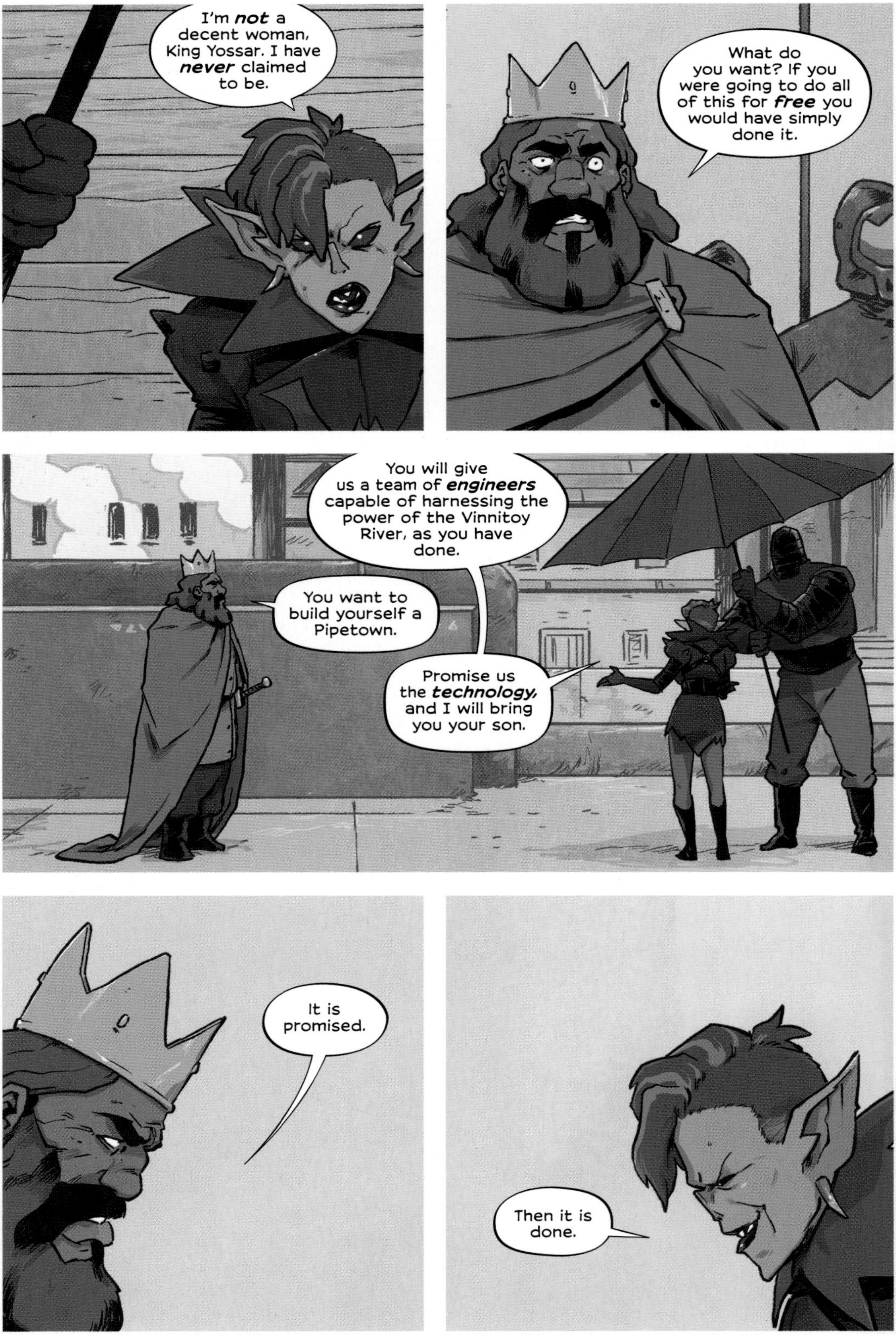
I'm *not* a decent woman, King Yossar. I have *never* claimed to be.
What do you want? If you were going to do all of this for *free* you would have simply done it.
You want to build yourself a Pipetown.
You will give us a team of *engineers* capable of harnessing the power of the Vinnitoy River, as you have done.
Promise us the *technology,* and I will bring you your son.
It is promised.
Then it is done.

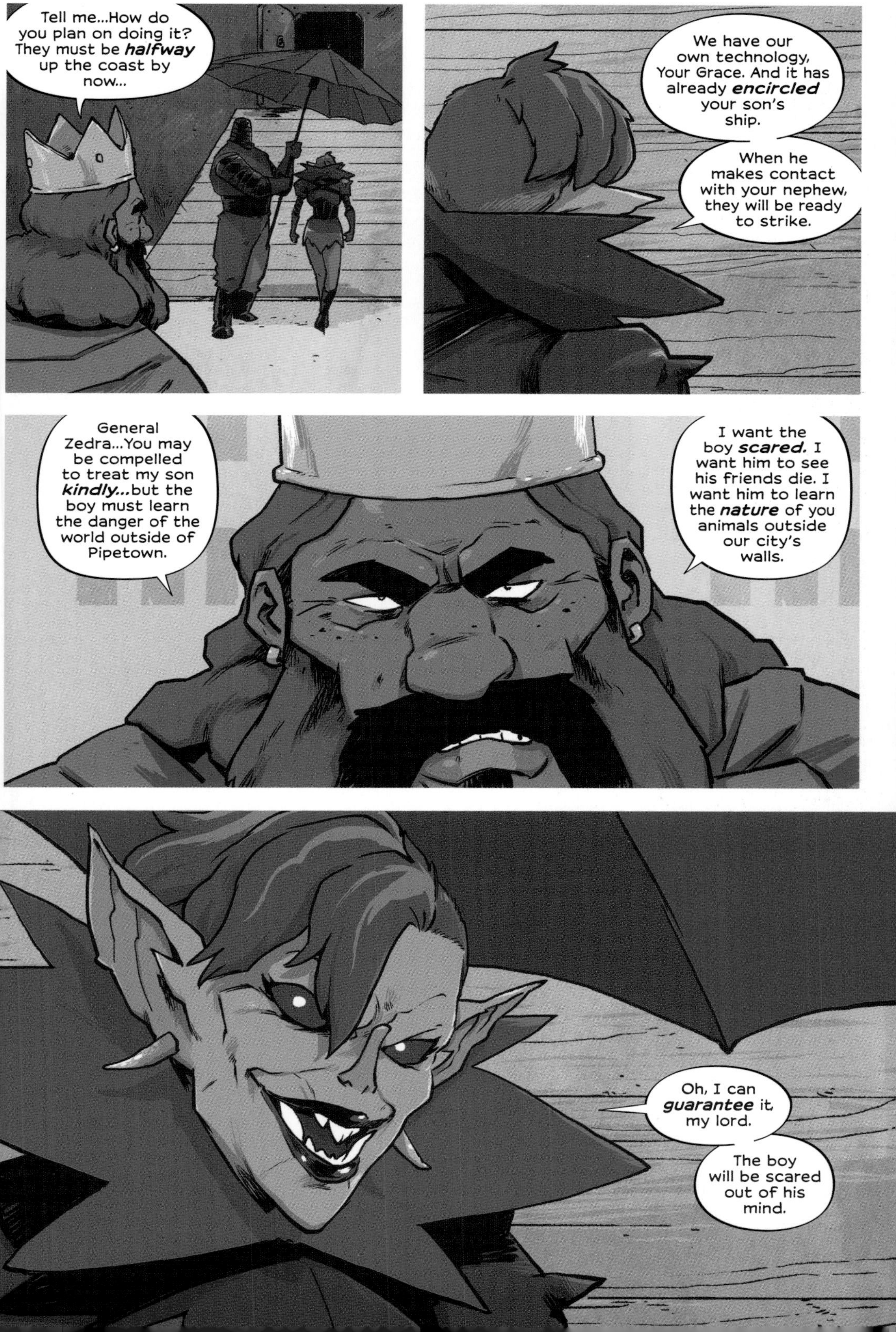

Tell me...How do you plan on doing it? They must be *halfway* up the coast by now...
We have our own technology, Your Grace. And it has already *encircled* your son's ship.
When he makes contact with your nephew, they will be ready to strike.
General Zedra...You may be compelled to treat my son *kindly...*but the boy must learn the danger of the world outside of Pipetown.
I want the boy *scared.* I want him to see his friends die. I want him to learn the *nature* of you animals outside our city's walls.
Oh, I can *guarantee* it, my lord.
The boy will be scared out of his mind.

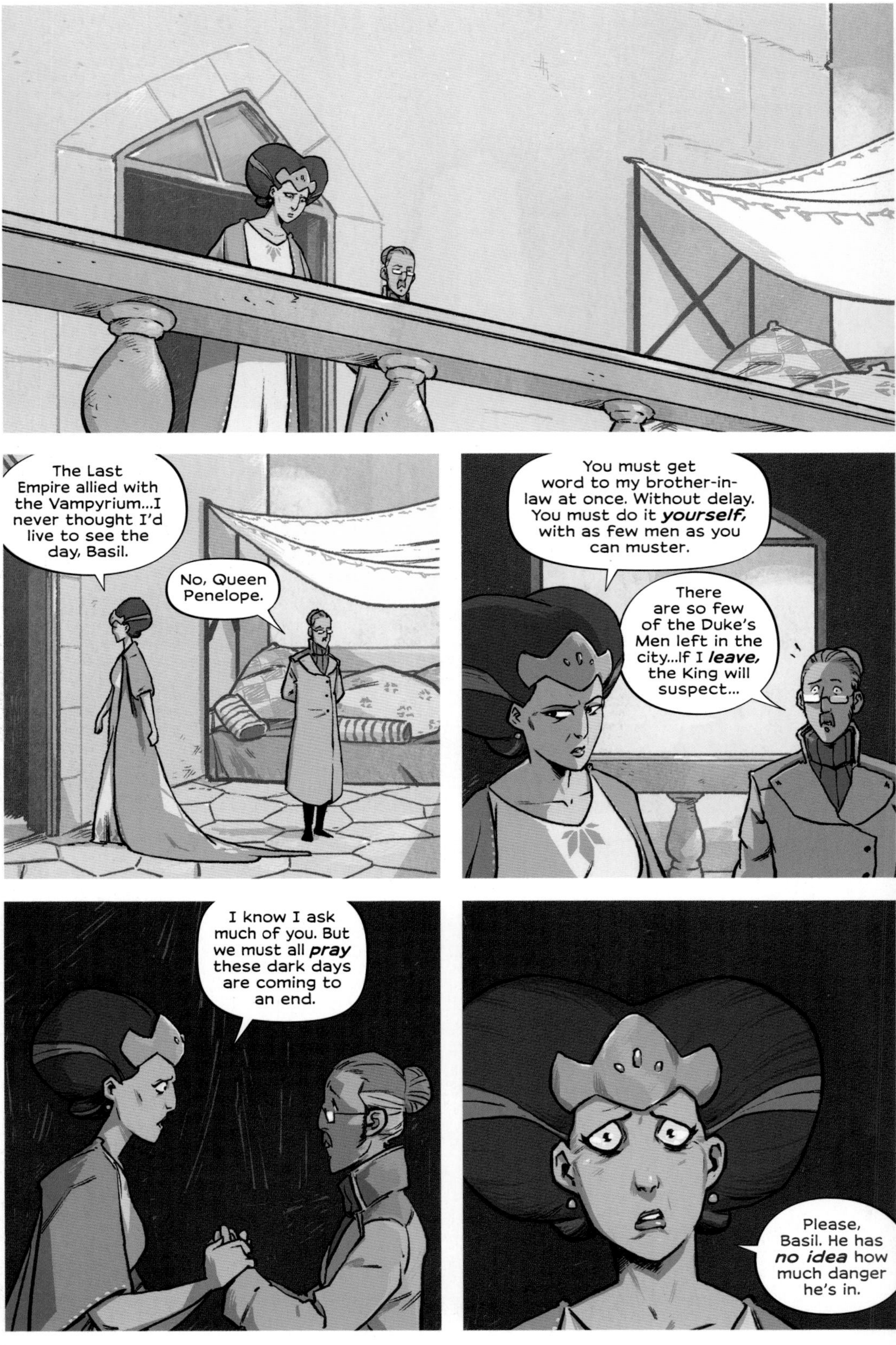
The Last Empire allied with the Vampyrium...I never thought I'd live to see the day, Basil.
No, Queen Penelope.
You must get word to my brother-in-law at once. Without delay. You must do it *yourself,* with as few men as you can muster.
There are so few of the Duke's Men left in the city...If I *leave,* the King will suspect...
I know I ask much of you. But we must all *pray* these dark days are coming to an end.
Please, Basil. He has *no idea* how much danger he's in.

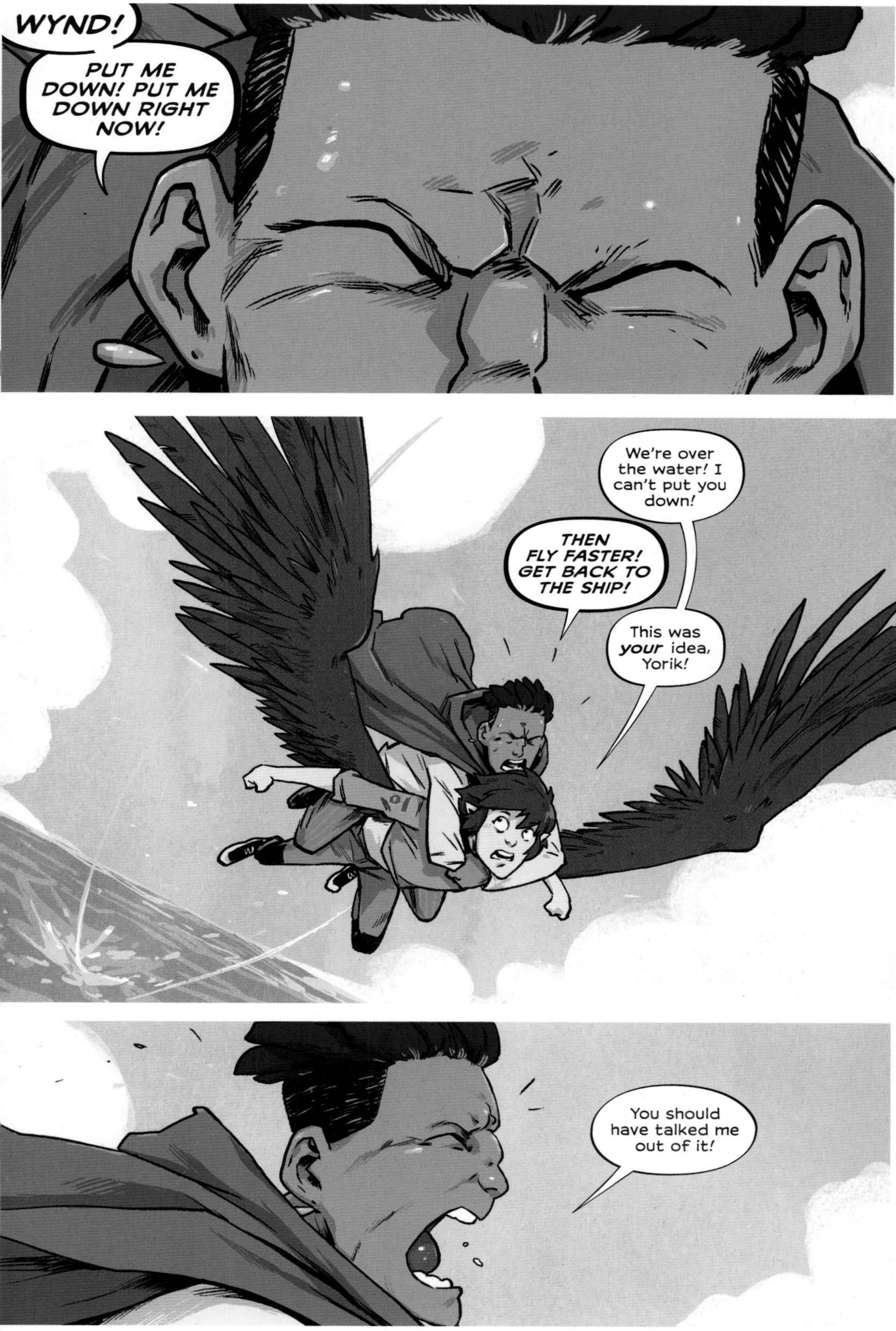
WYND!
PUT ME DOWN! PUT ME DOWN RIGHT NOW!
We're over the water! I can't put you down!
THEN FLY FASTER! GET BACK TO THE SHIP!
This was *your* idea, Yorik!
You should have talked me out of it!

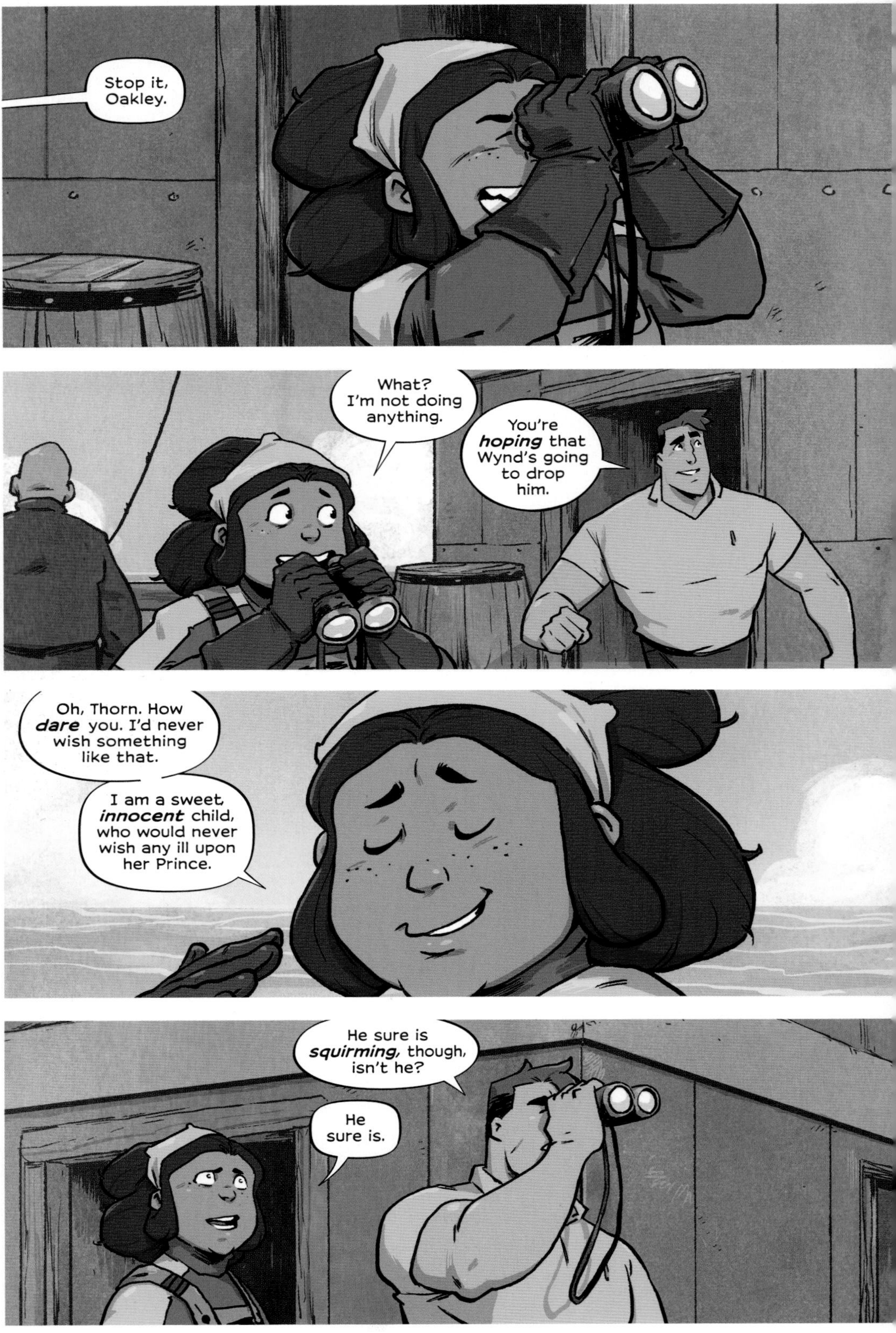
Stop it, Oakley.
What? I'm not doing anything.
You're *hoping* that Wynd's going to drop him.
Oh, Thorn. How *dare* you. I'd never wish something like that.
I am a sweet, *innocent* child, who would never wish any ill upon her Prince.
He sure is *squirming,* though, isn't he?
He sure is.

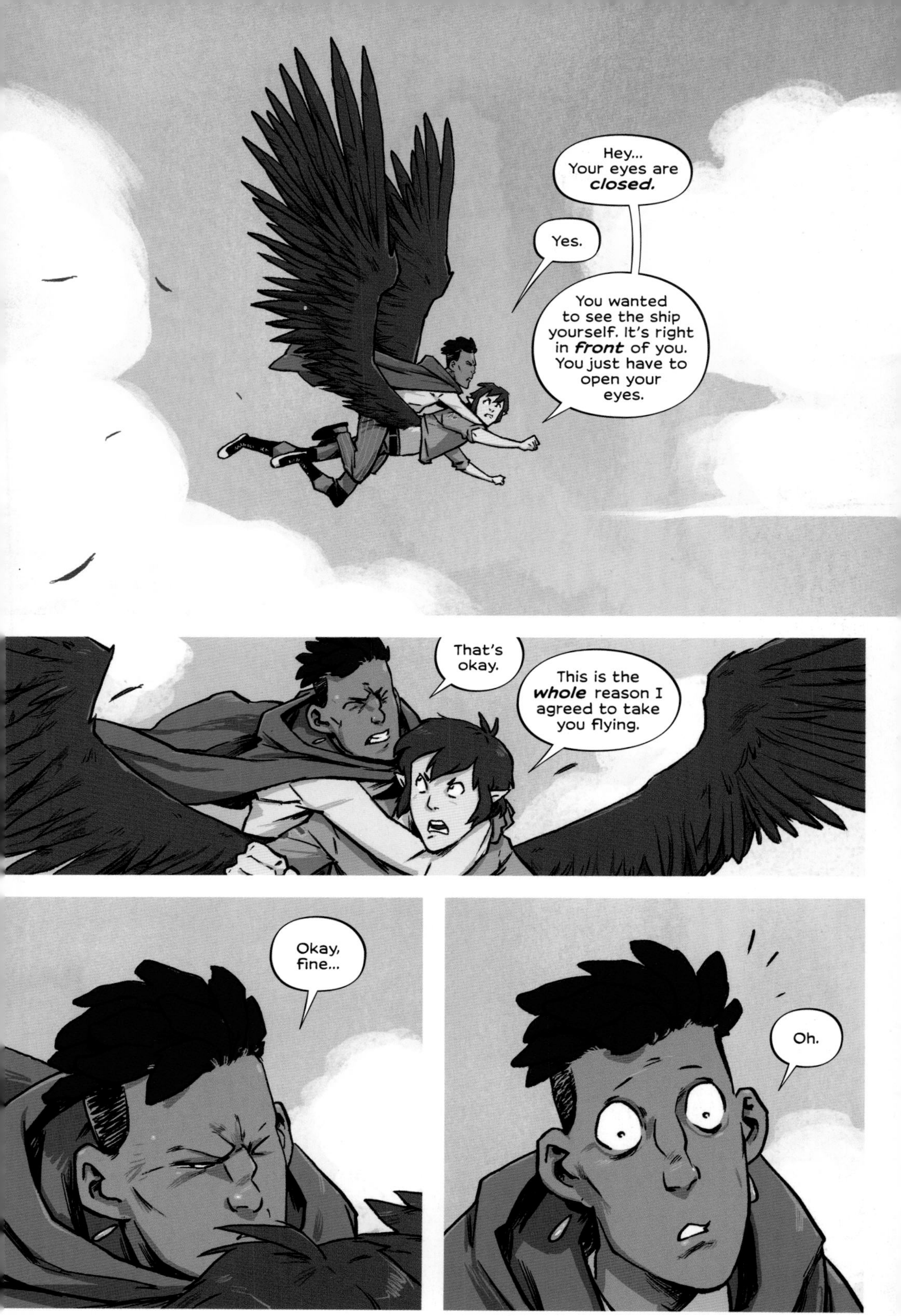
Hey...
Your eyes are
closed.
Yes.
You wanted to see the ship yourself. It's right in *front* of you. You just have to open your eyes.
That's okay.
This is the *whole* reason I agreed to take you flying.
Okay, fine...
Oh.

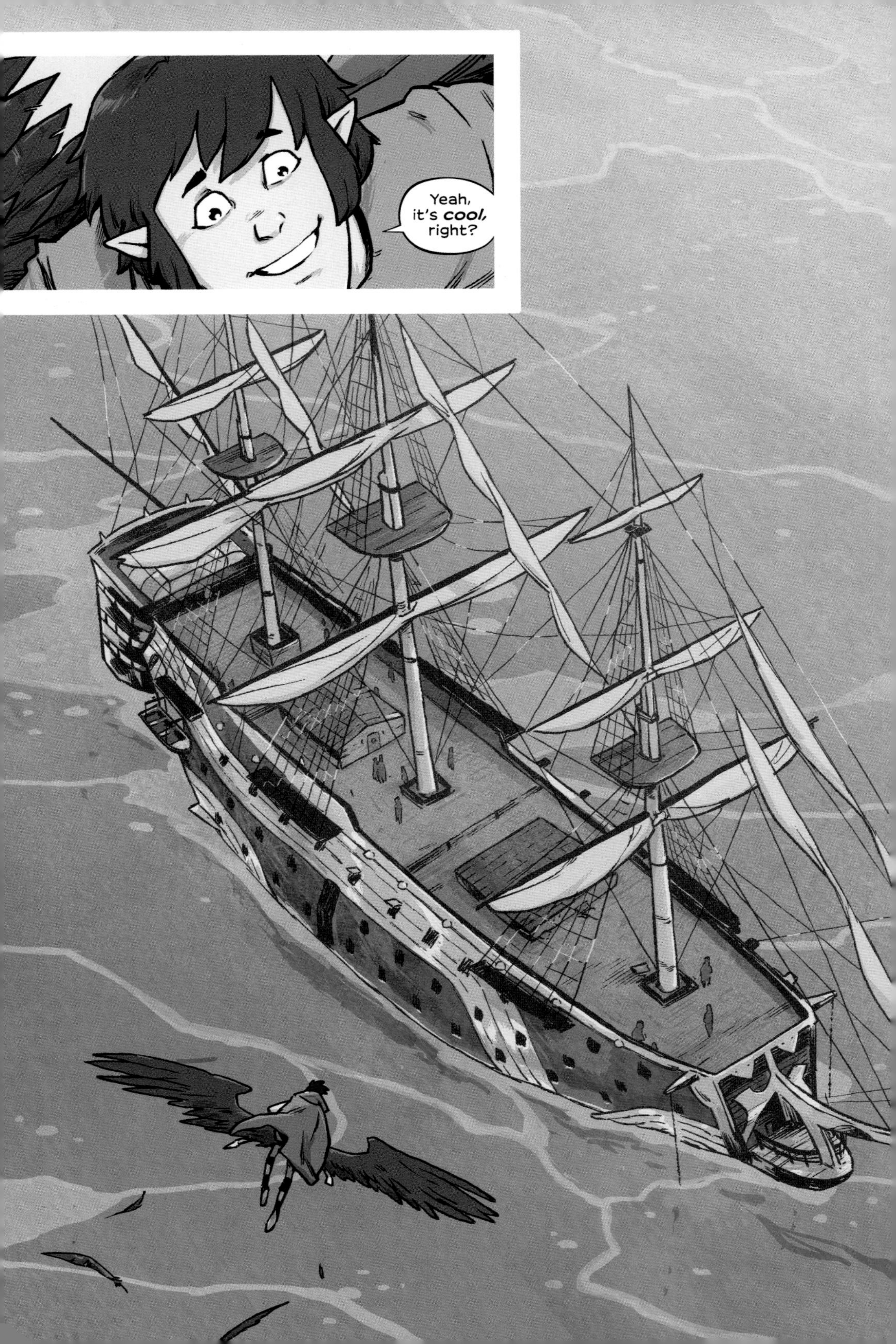
Yeah, it's cool, right?

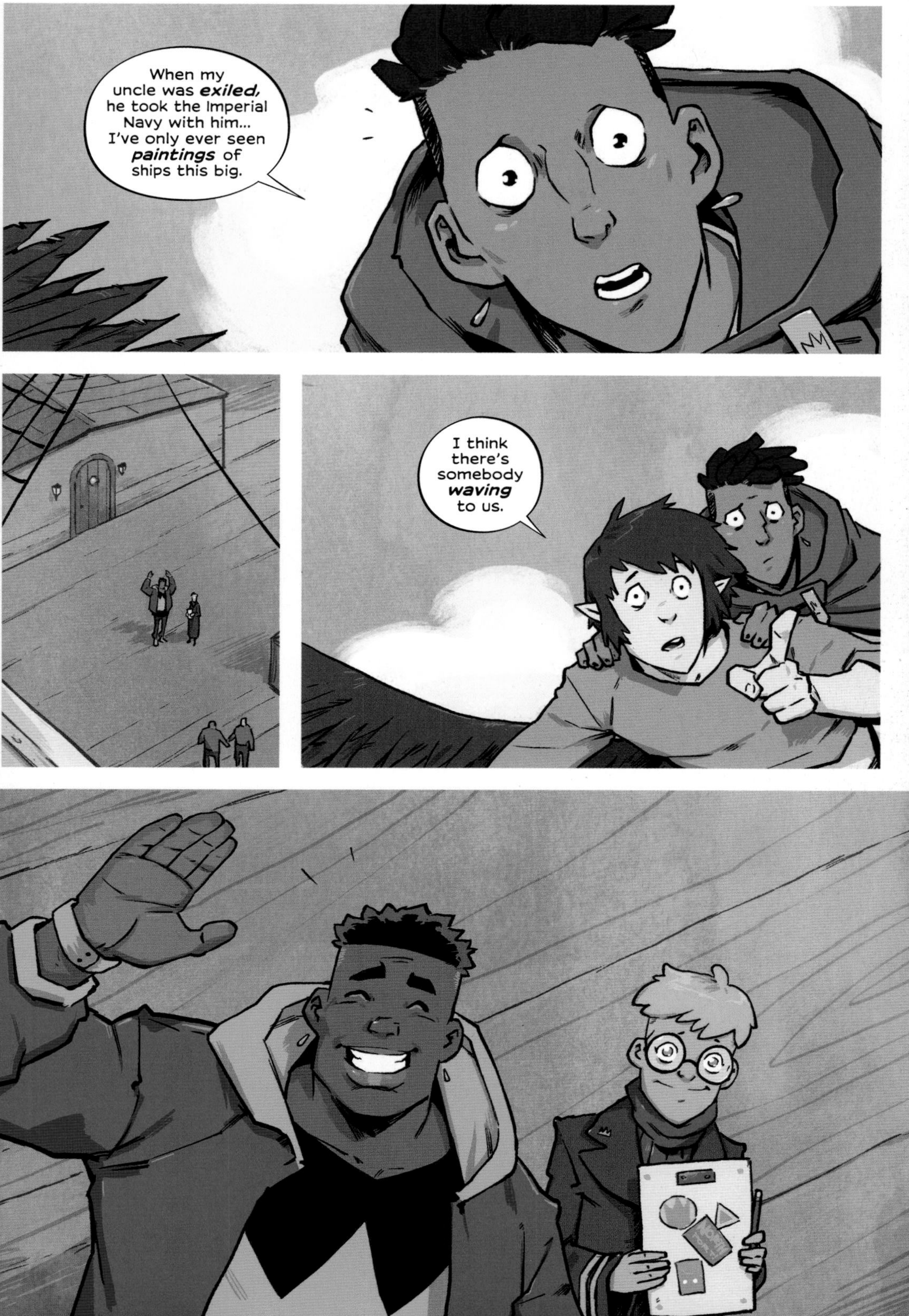
When my uncle was ***exiled,*** he took the Imperial Navy with him... I've only ever seen ***paintings*** of ships this big.
I think there's somebody ***waving*** to us.

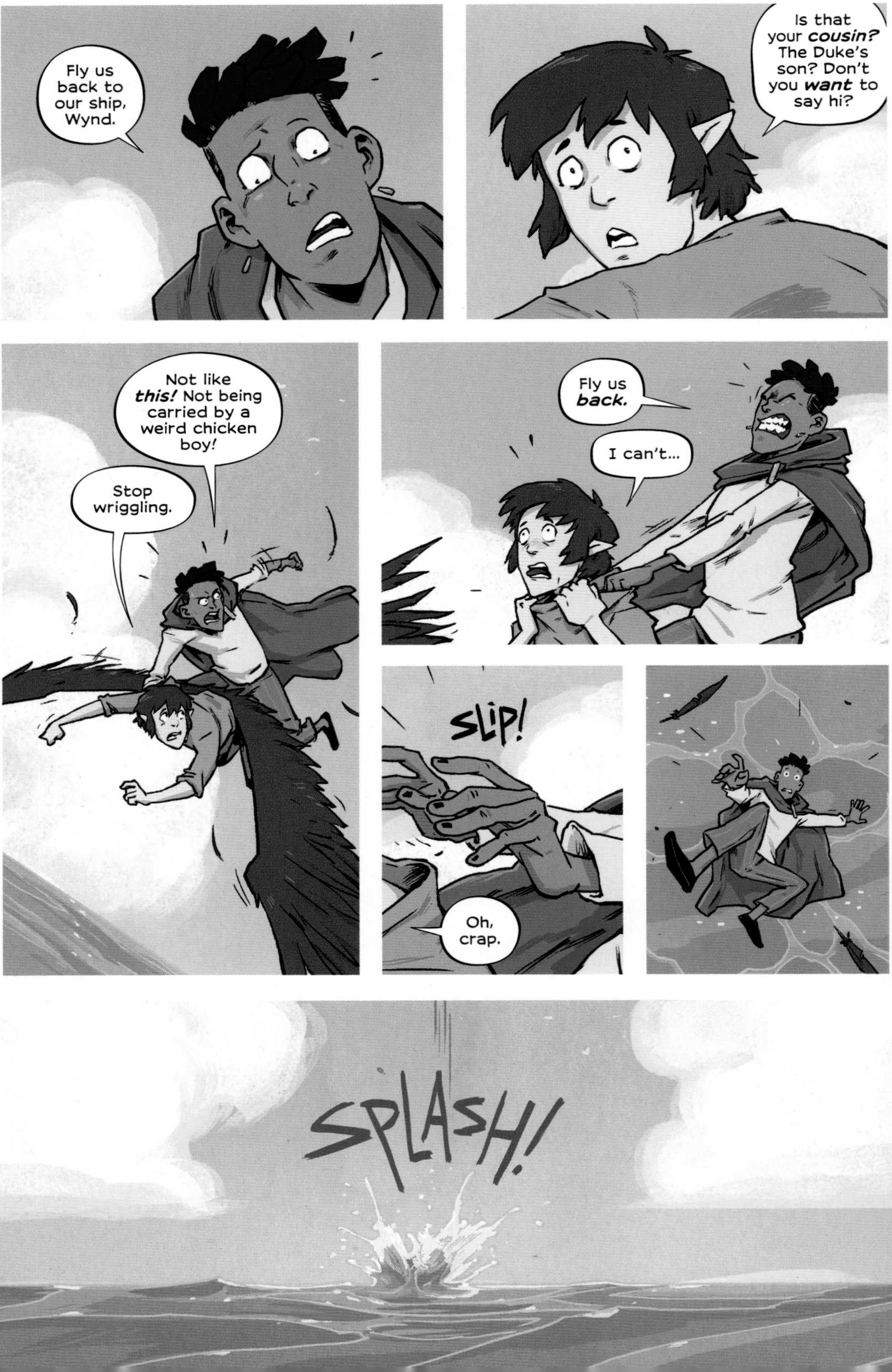
Fly us back to our ship, Wynd.
Is that your *cousin?* The Duke's son? Don't you *want* to say hi?
Not like *this!* Not being carried by a weird chicken boy!
Stop wriggling.
Fly us *back.*
I can't...
SLIP!
Oh, crap.
SPLASH!

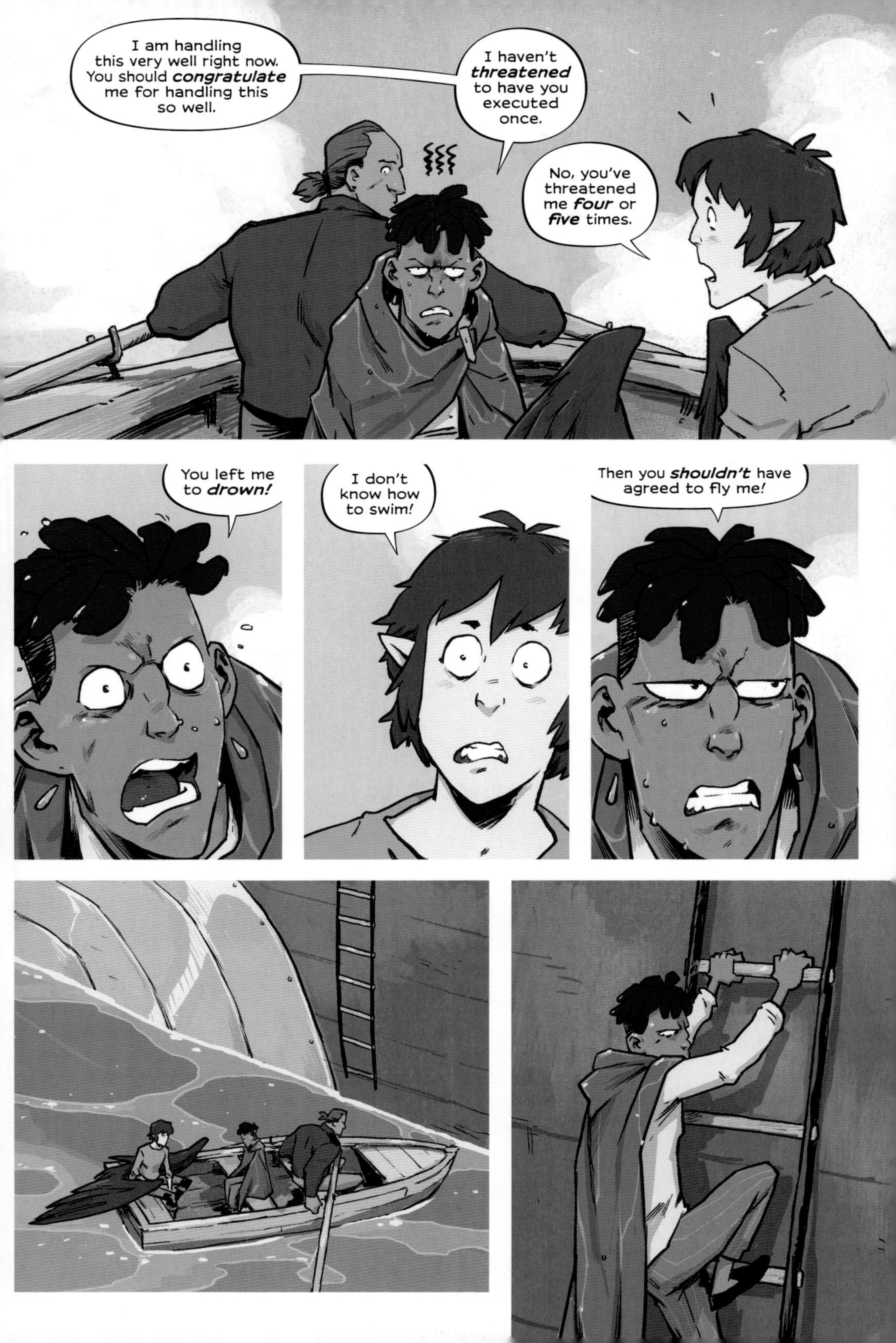
I am handling this very well right now. You should *congratulate* me for handling this so well.
I haven't *threatened* to have you executed once.
No, you've threatened me *four* or *five* times.
You left me to *drown!*
I don't know how to swim!
Then you *shouldn't* have agreed to fly me!

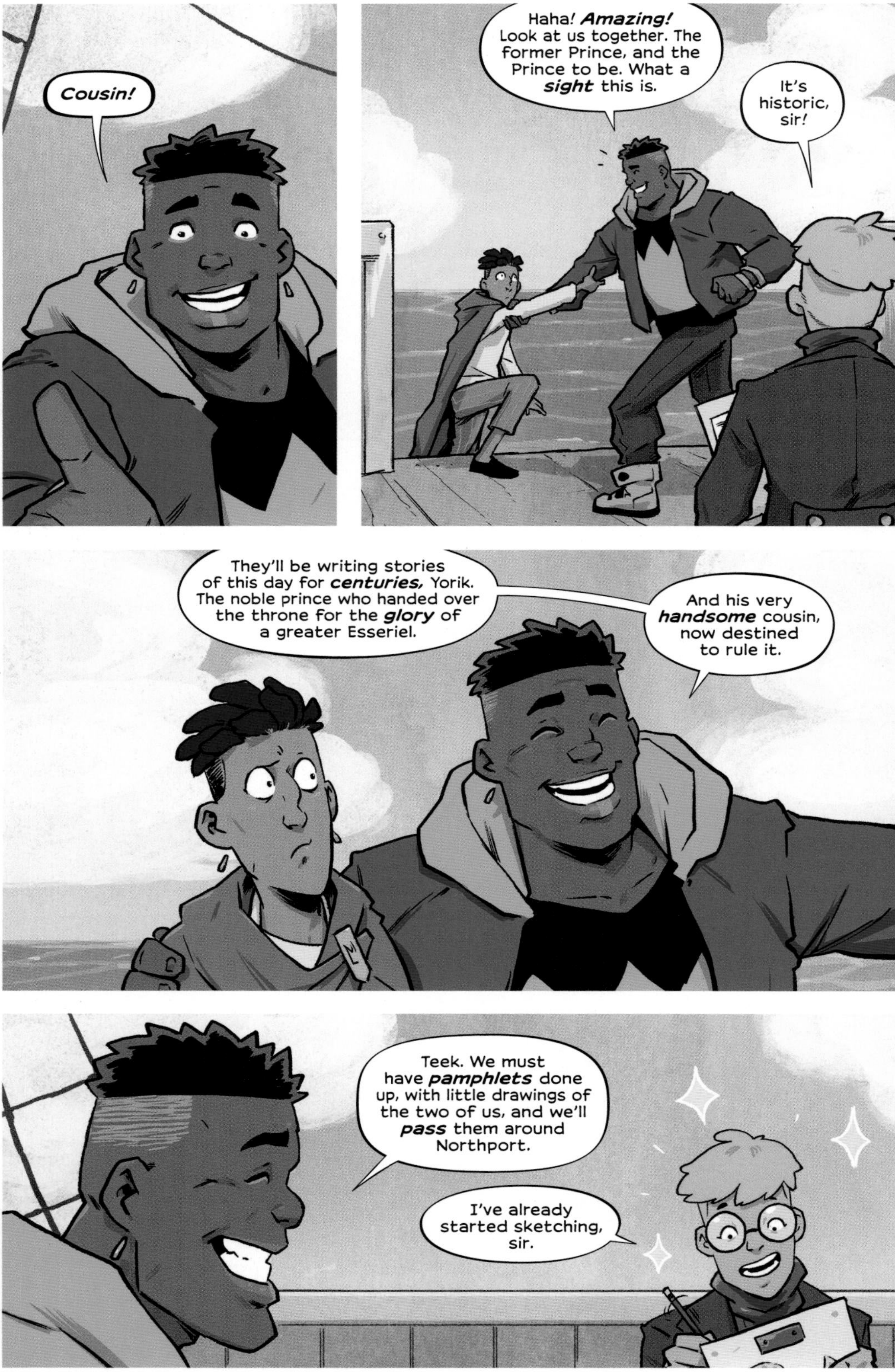
Cousin!
Haha! Amazing! Look at us together. The former Prince, and the Prince to be. What a sight this is.
It's historic, sir!
They'll be writing stories of this day for centuries, Yorik. The noble prince who handed over the throne for the glory of a greater Esseriel.
And his very handsome cousin, now destined to rule it.
Teek. We must have pamphlets done up, with little drawings of the two of us, and we'll pass them around Northport.
I've already started sketching, sir.

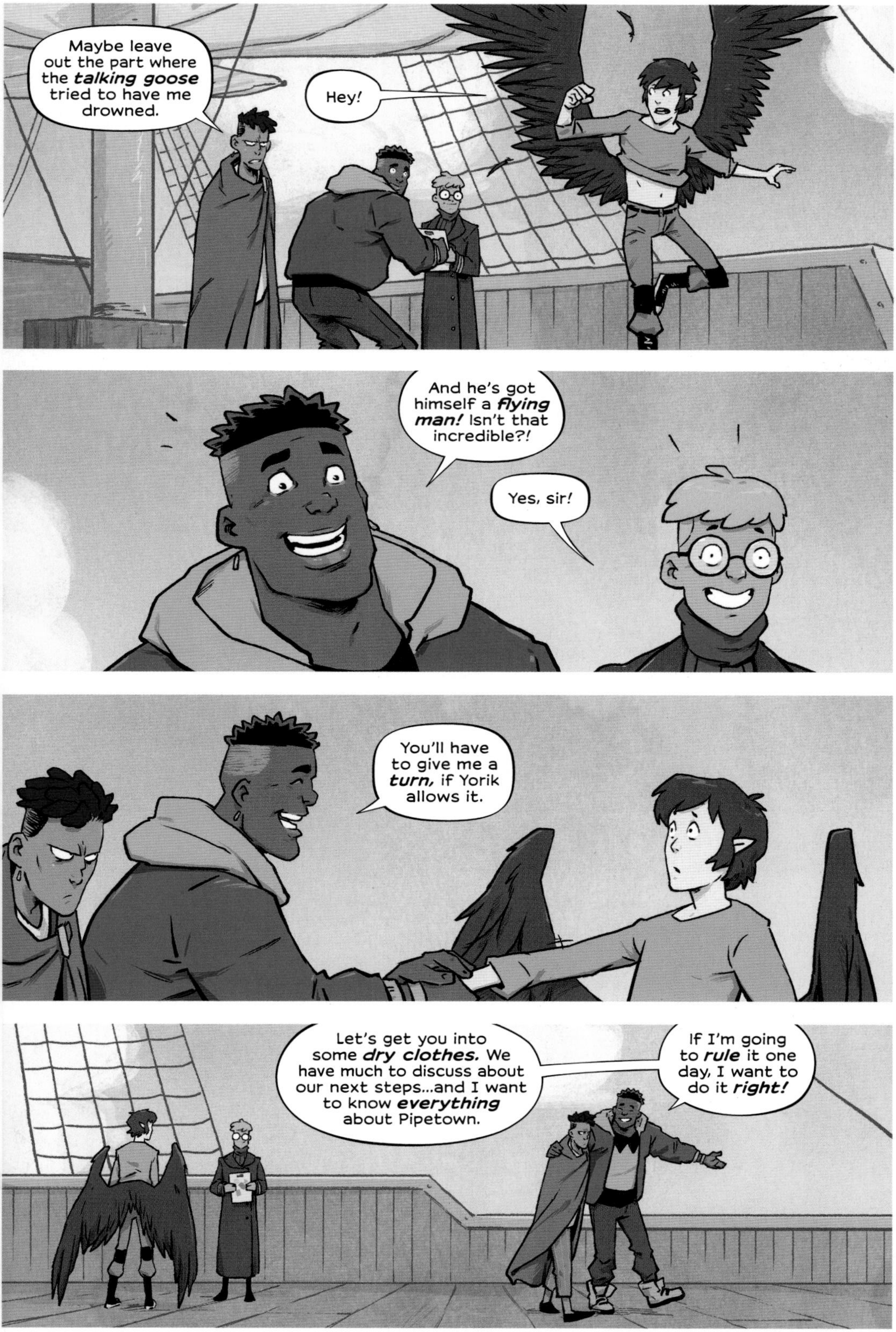
Maybe leave out the part where the *talking goose* tried to have me drowned.
Hey!
And he's got himself a *flying man!* Isn't that incredible?!
Yes, sir!
You'll have to give me a *turn,* if Yorik allows it.
Let's get you into some *dry clothes.* We have much to discuss about our next steps...and I want to know *everything* about Pipetown.
If I'm going to *rule* it one day, I want to do it *right!*

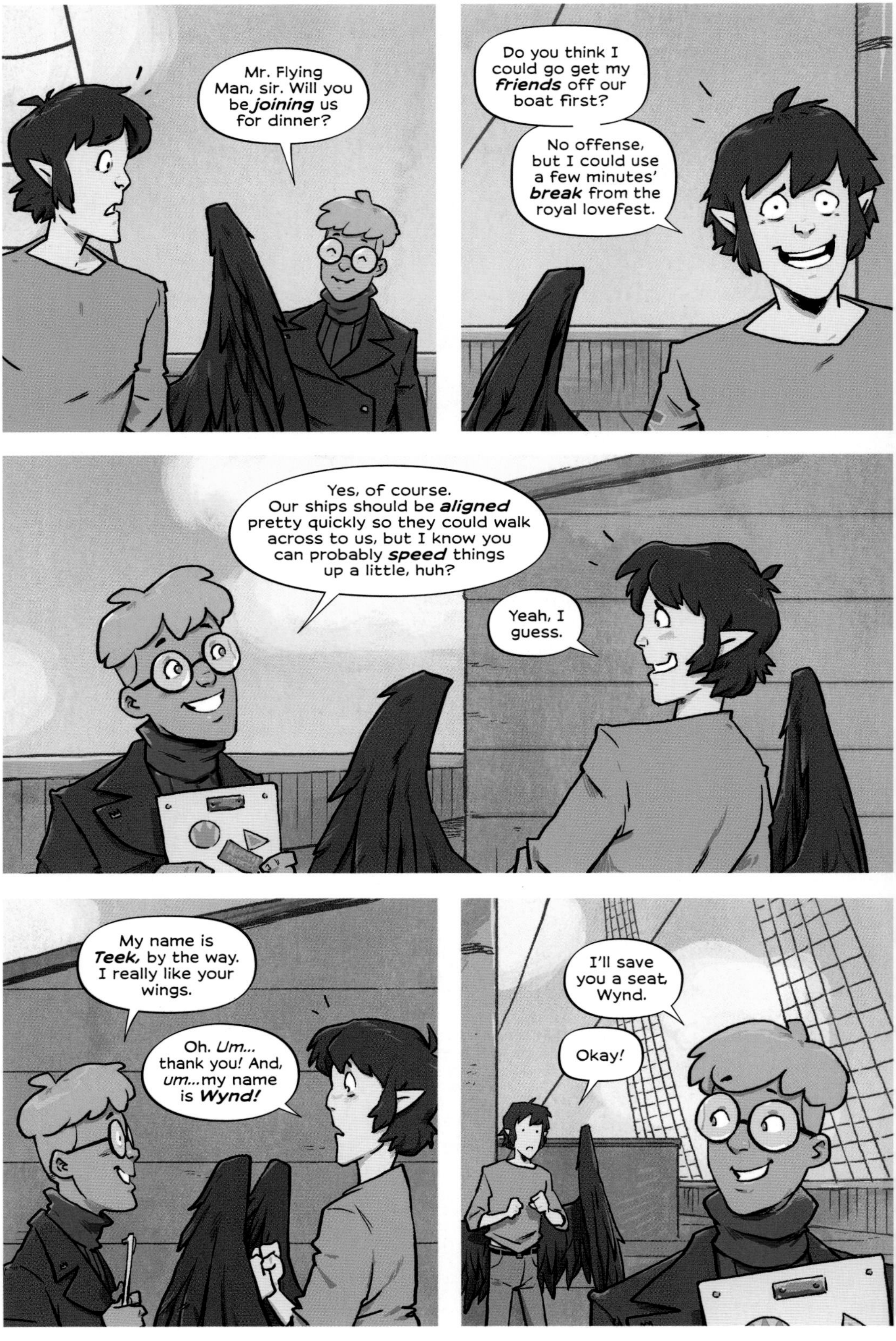
Mr. Flying Man, sir. Will you be *joining* us for dinner?
Do you think I could go get my *friends* off our boat first?
No offense, but I could use a few minutes' *break* from the royal lovefest.
Yes, of course. Our ships should be *aligned* pretty quickly so they could walk across to us, but I know you can probably *speed* things up a little, huh?
Yeah, I guess.
My name is *Teek,* by the way. I really like your wings.
Oh. *Um...* thank you! And, *um...*my name is *Wynd!*
I'll save you a seat, Wynd.
Okay!

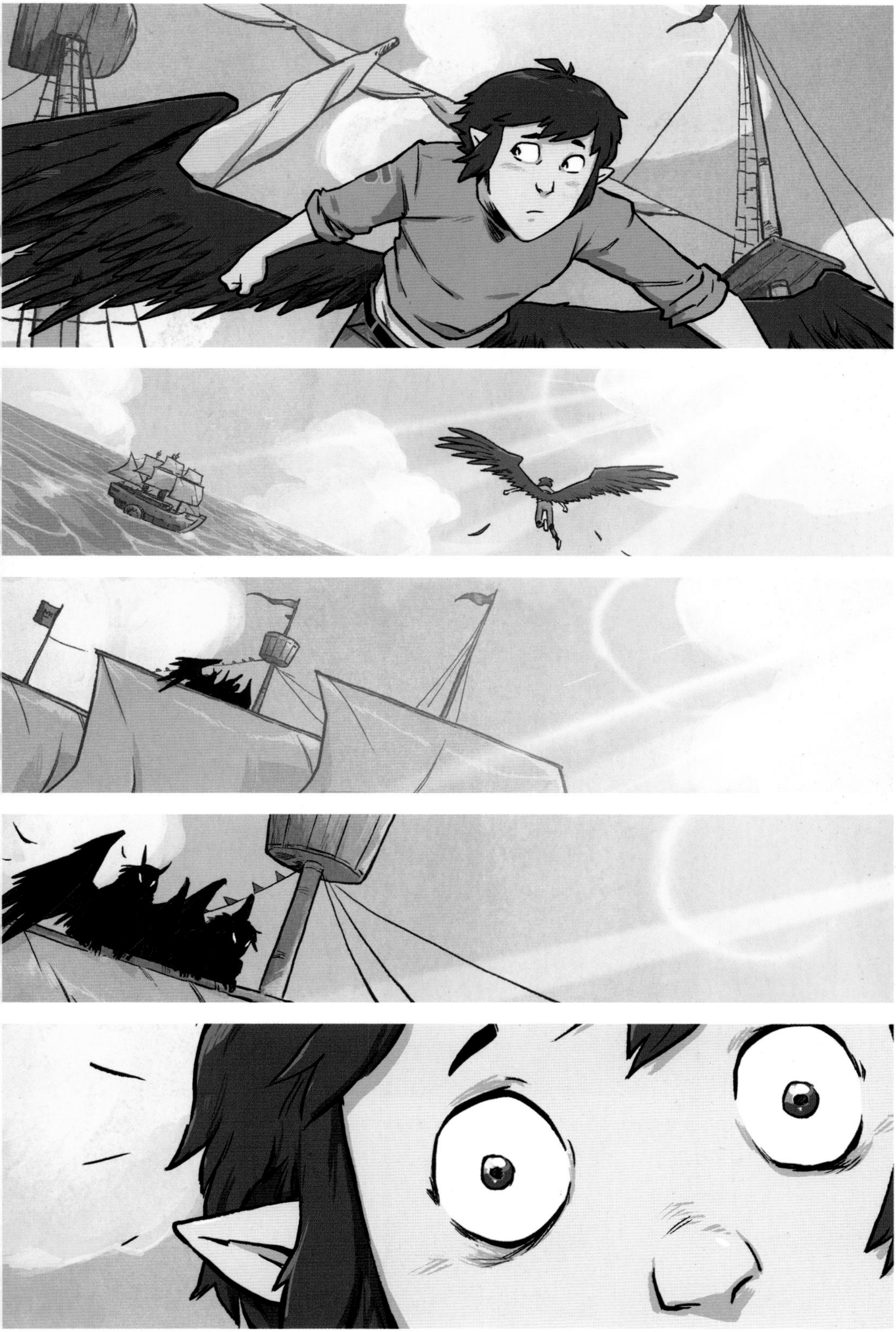

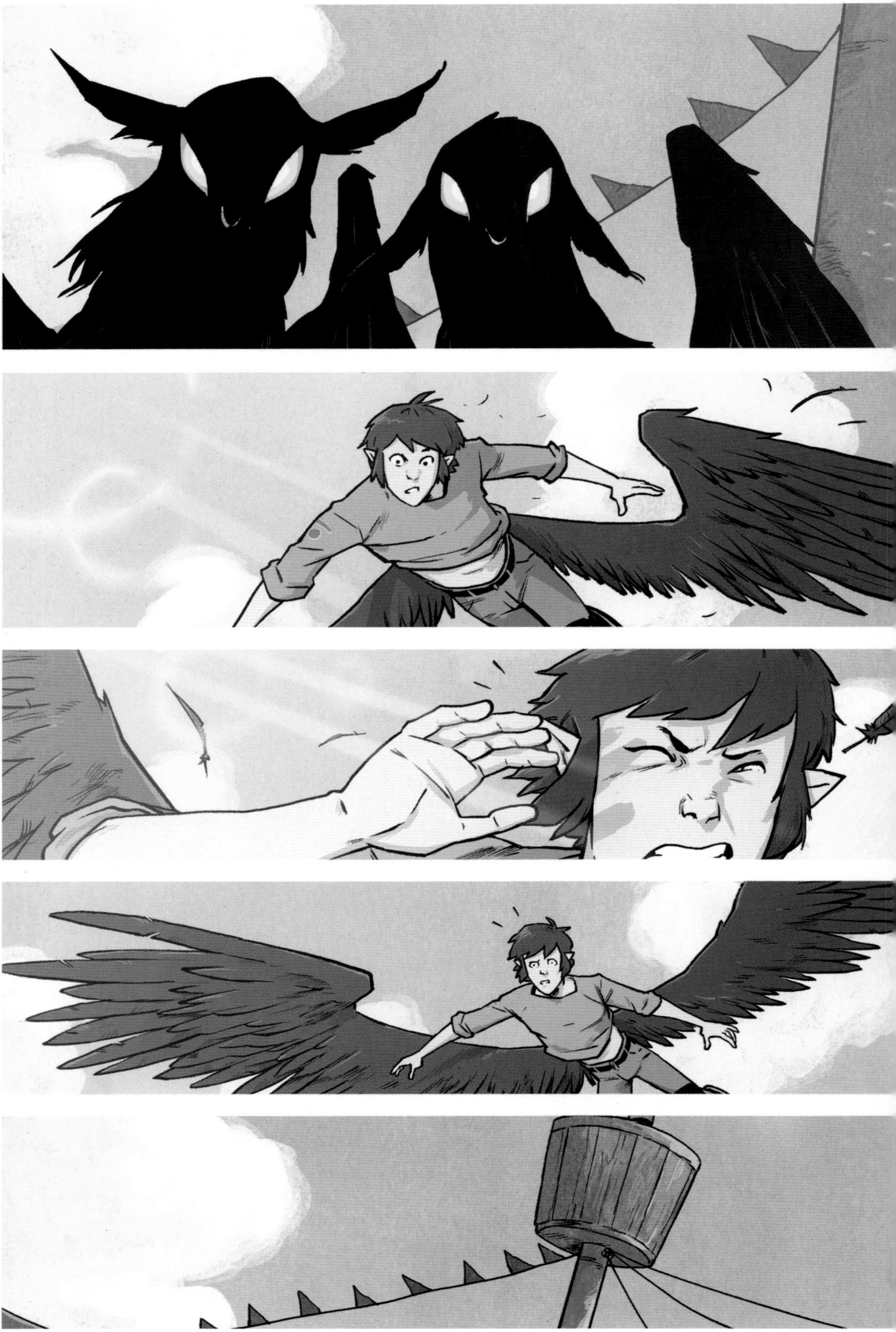

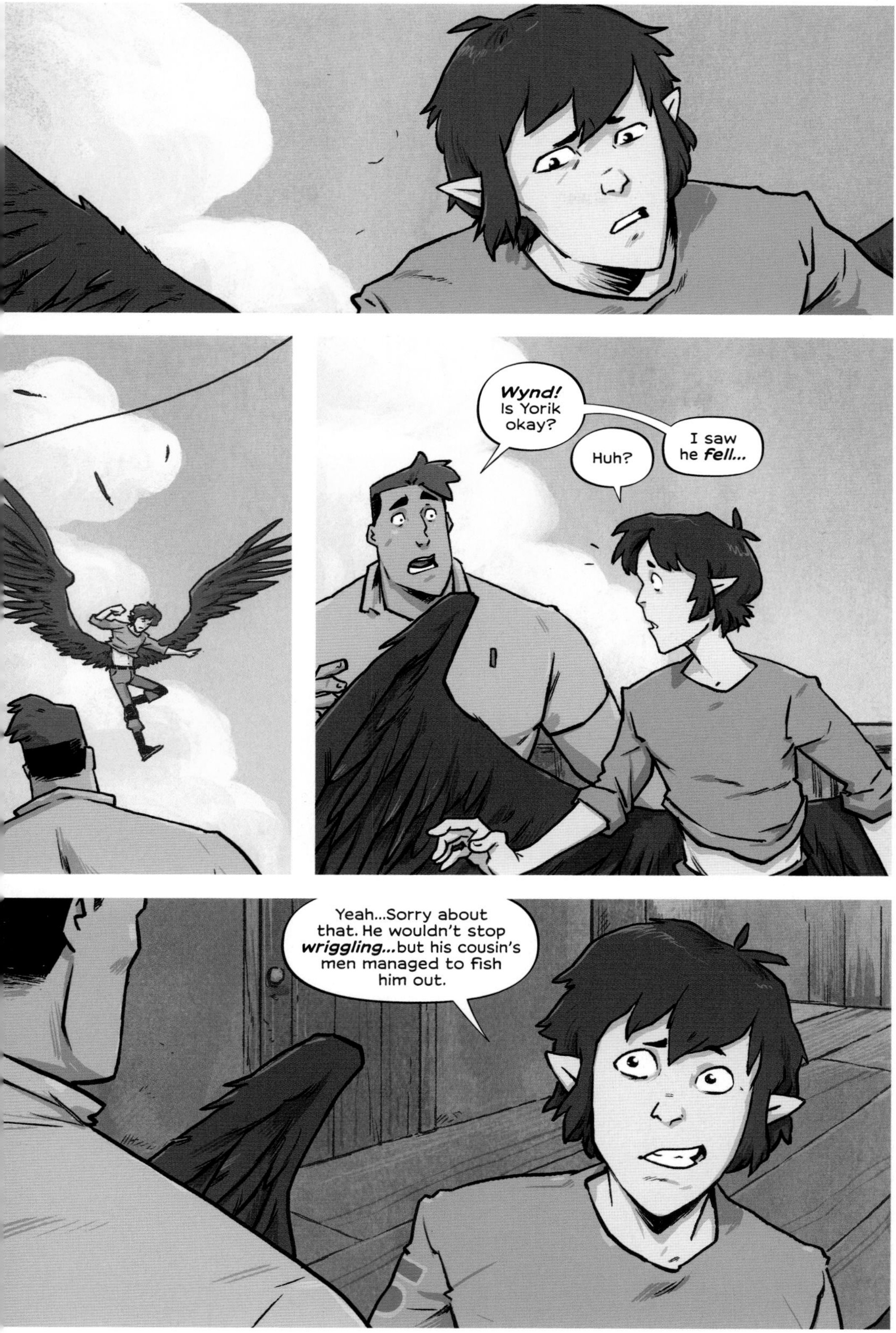

Wynd! Is Yorik okay?
Huh?
I saw he fell...
Yeah...Sorry about that. He wouldn't stop wriggling...but his cousin's men managed to fish him out.

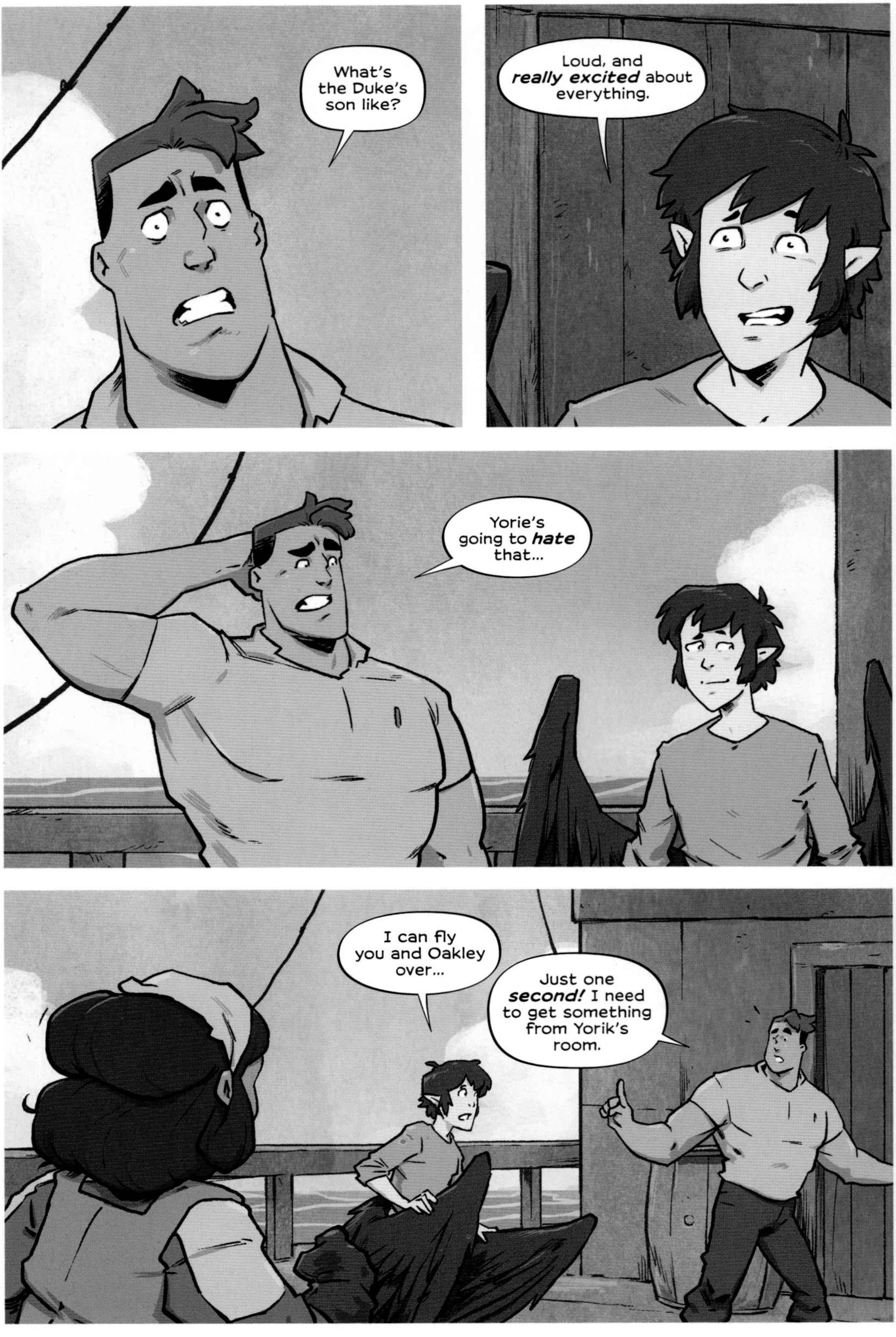
What's the Duke's son like?
Loud, and ***really excited*** about everything.
Yorie's going to ***hate*** that...
I can fly you and Oakley over...
Just one ***second!*** I need to get something from Yorik's room.

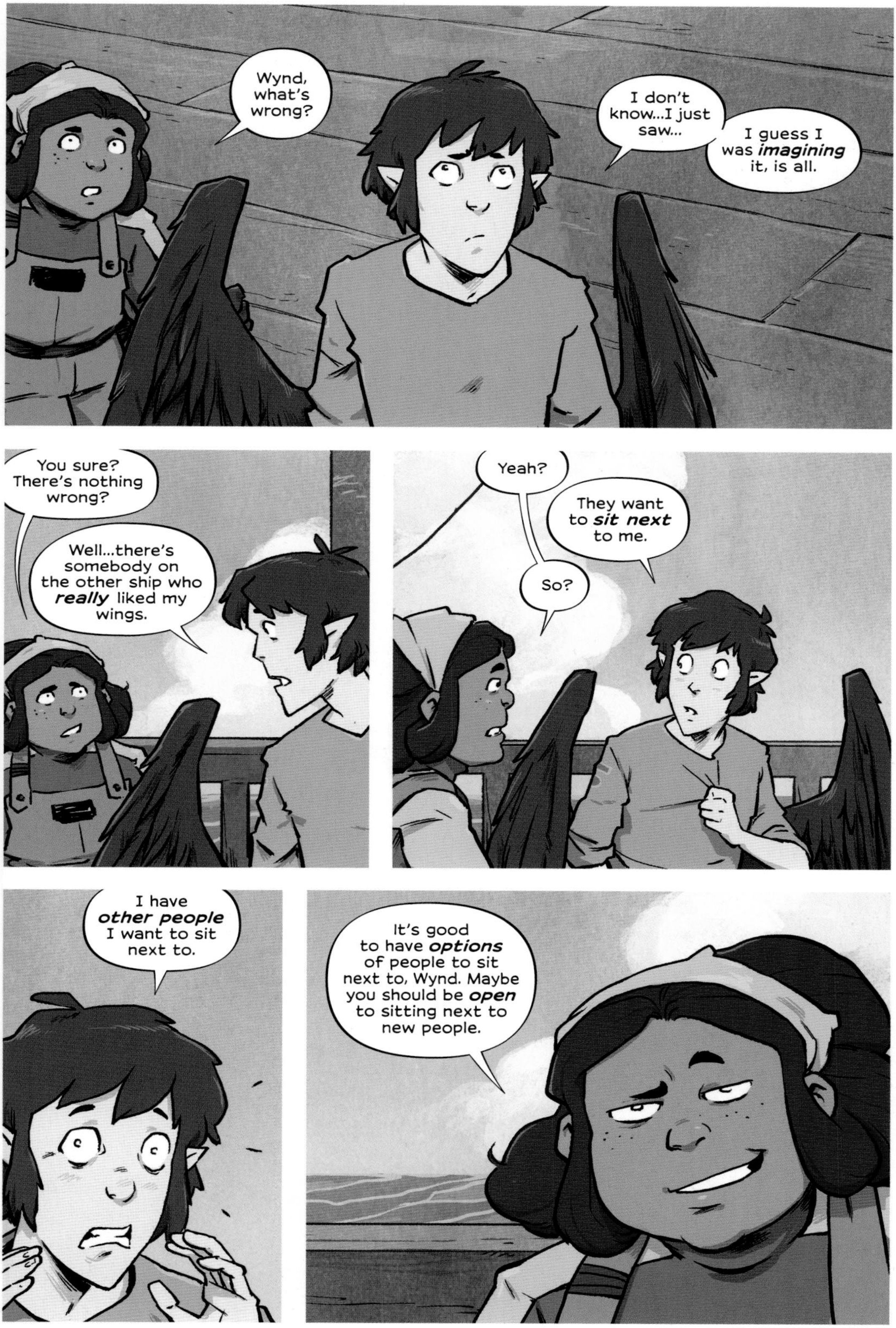
Wynd, what's wrong?
I don't know...I just saw...
I guess I was *imagining* it, is all.
You sure? There's nothing wrong?
Well...there's somebody on the other ship who *really* liked my wings.
Yeah?
They want to *sit next* to me.
So?
I have *other people* I want to sit next to.
It's good to have *options* of people to sit next to, Wynd. Maybe you should be *open* to sitting next to new people.

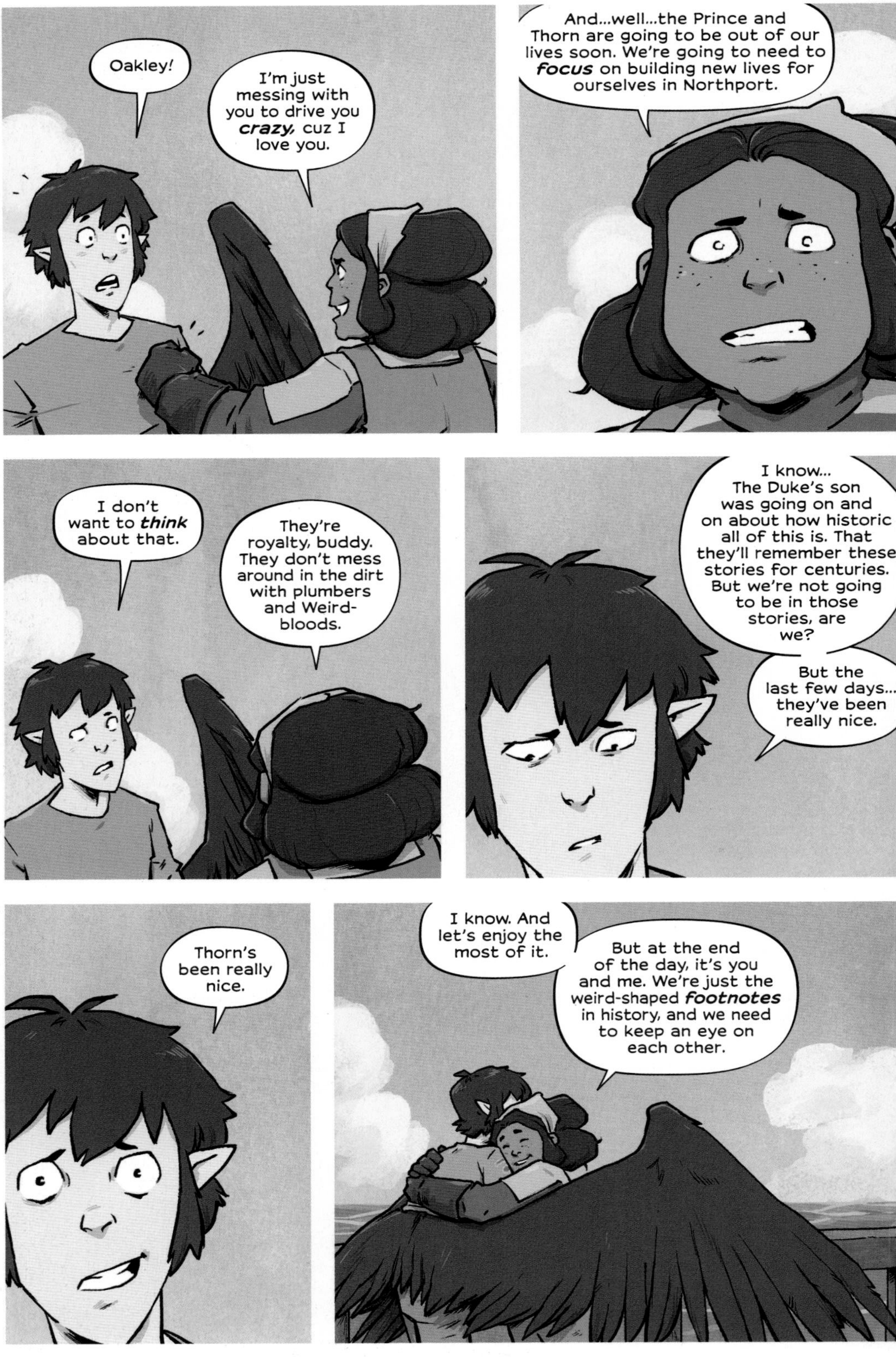
Oakley!
I'm just messing with you to drive you *crazy,* cuz I love you.
And...well...the Prince and Thorn are going to be out of our lives soon. We're going to need to *focus* on building new lives for ourselves in Northport.
I don't want to *think* about that.
They're royalty, buddy. They don't mess around in the dirt with plumbers and Weird-bloods.
I know... The Duke's son was going on and on about how historic all of this is. That they'll remember these stories for centuries. But we're not going to be in those stories, are we?
But the last few days... they've been really nice.
Thorn's been really nice.
I know. And let's enjoy the most of it.
But at the end of the day, it's you and me. We're just the weird-shaped *footnotes* in history, and we need to keep an eye on each other.

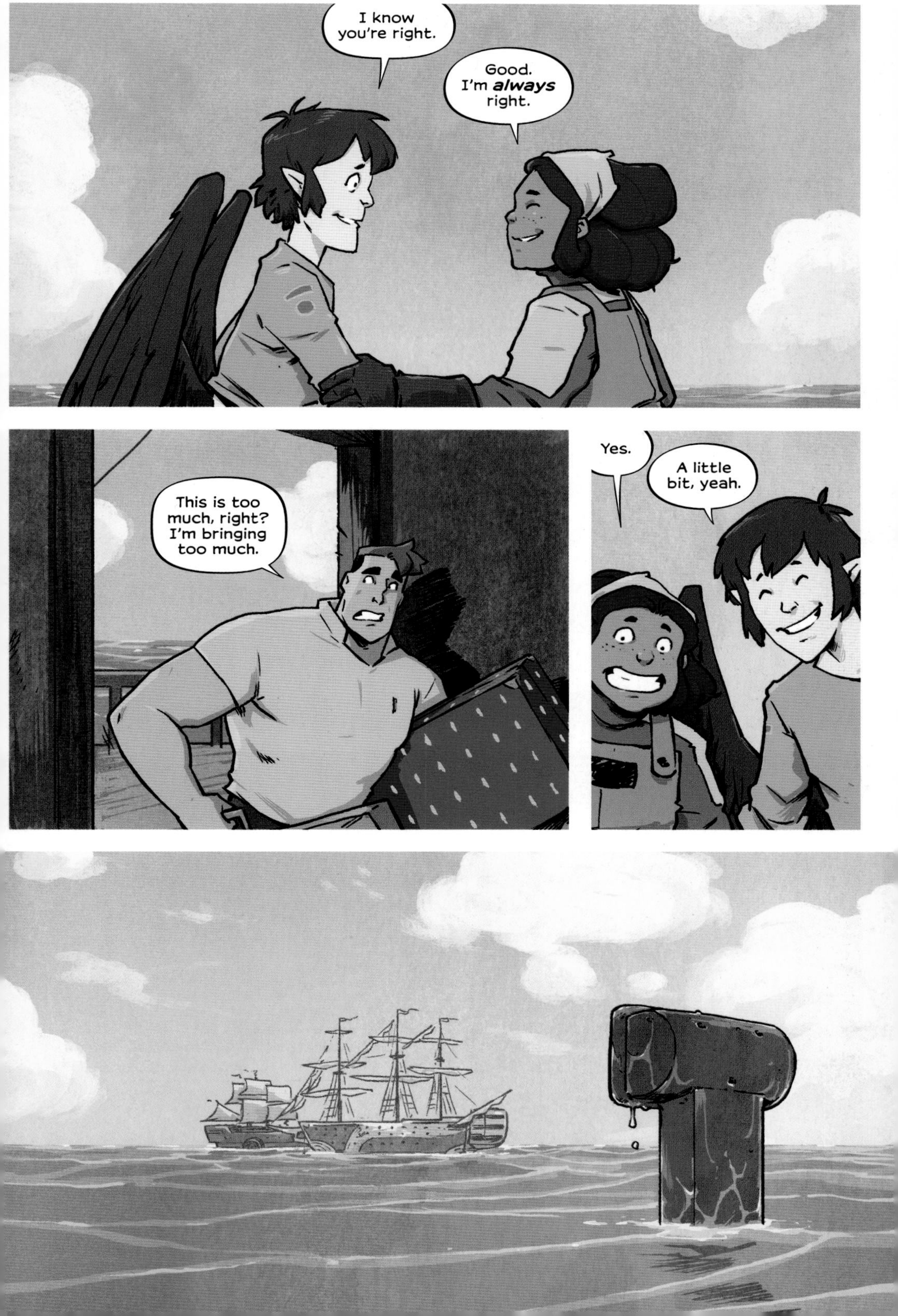

I know you're right.
Good. I'm ***always*** right.
This is too much, right? I'm bringing too much.
Yes.
A little bit, yeah.

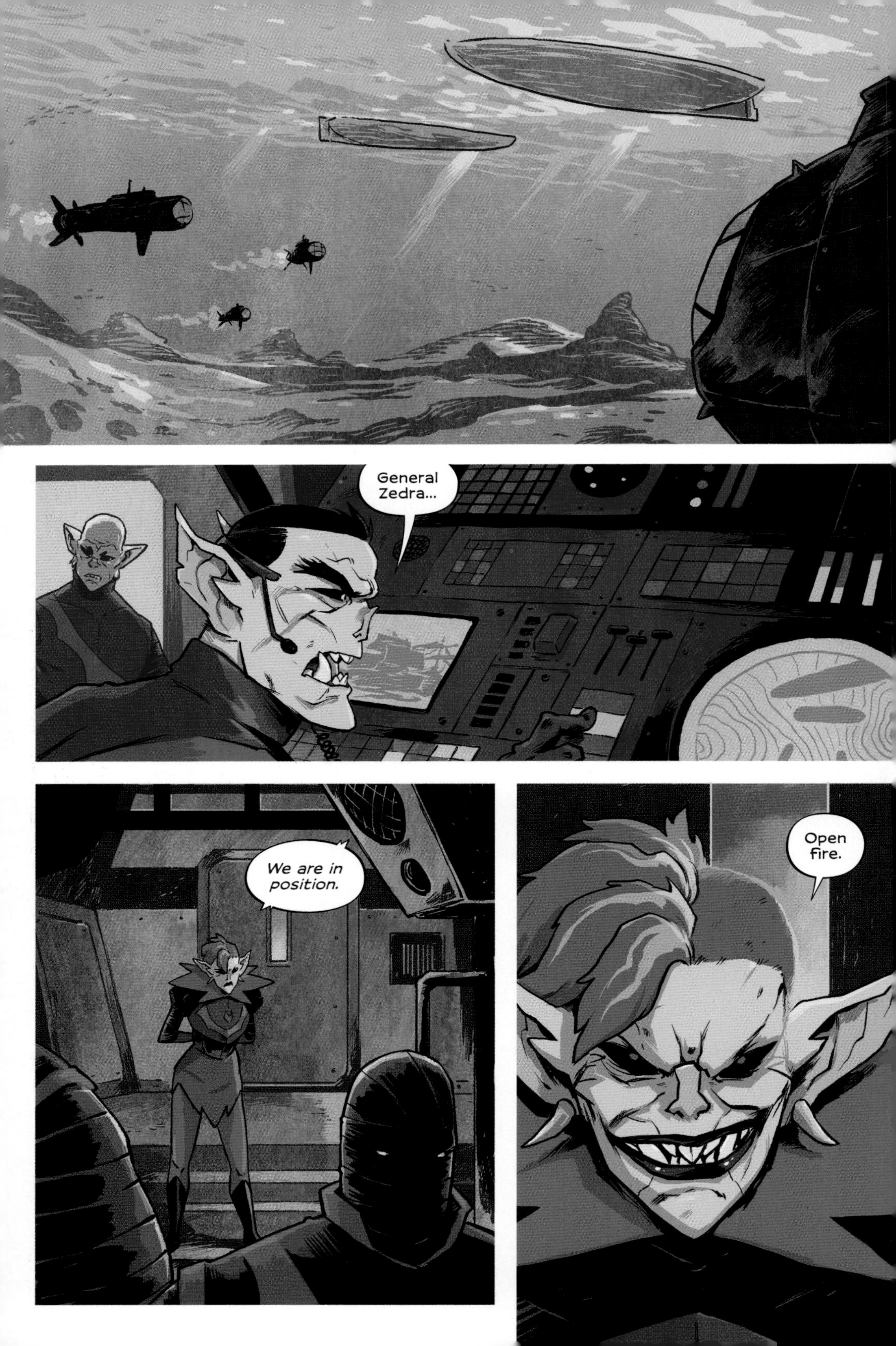
General Zedra...
We are in position.
Open fire.

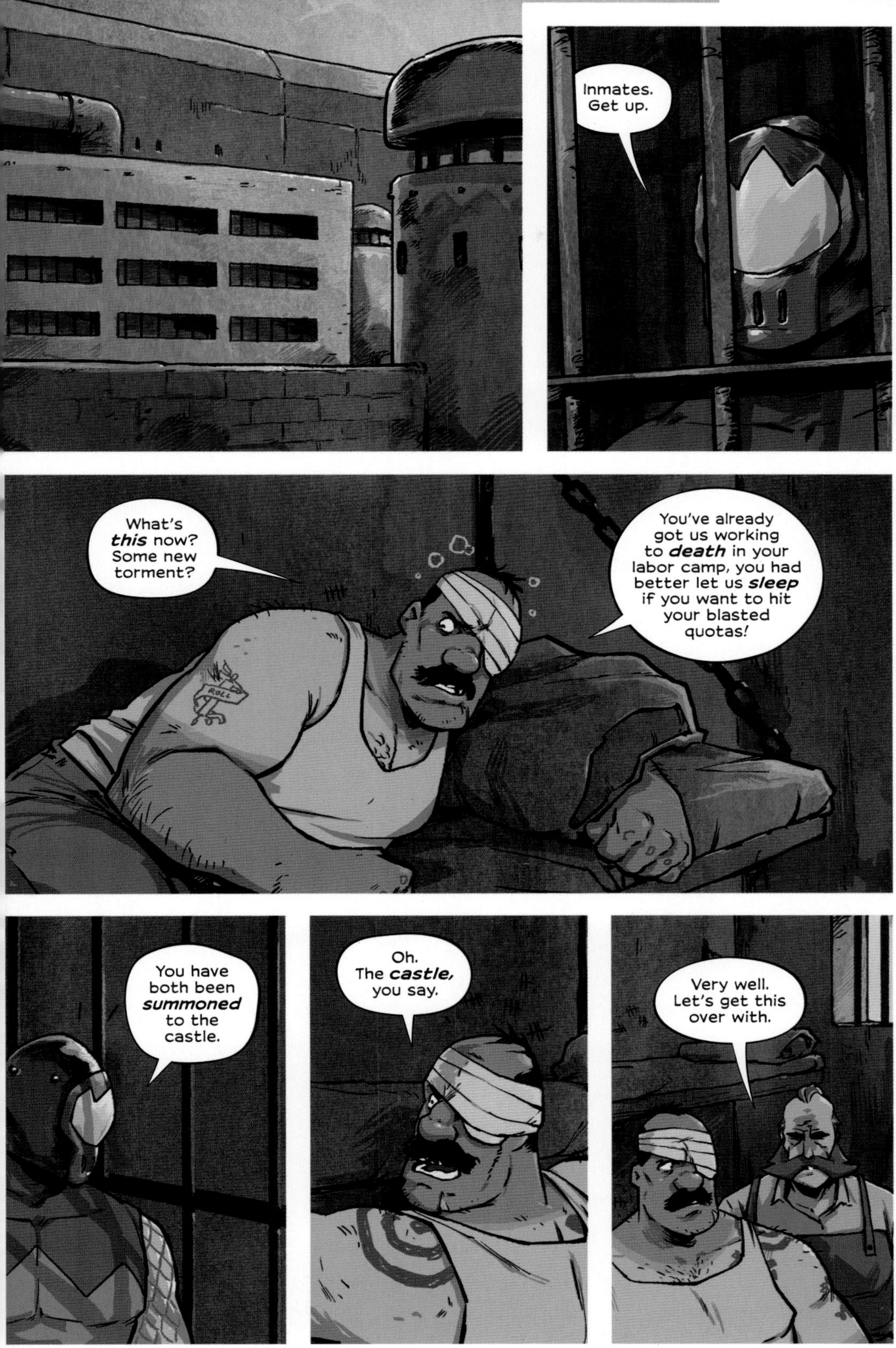
Inmates. Get up.
What's *this* now? Some new torment?
You've already got us working to *death* in your labor camp, you had better let us *sleep* if you want to hit your blasted quotas!
ROLL
You have both been *summoned* to the castle.
Oh. The *castle,* you say.
Very well. Let's get this over with.

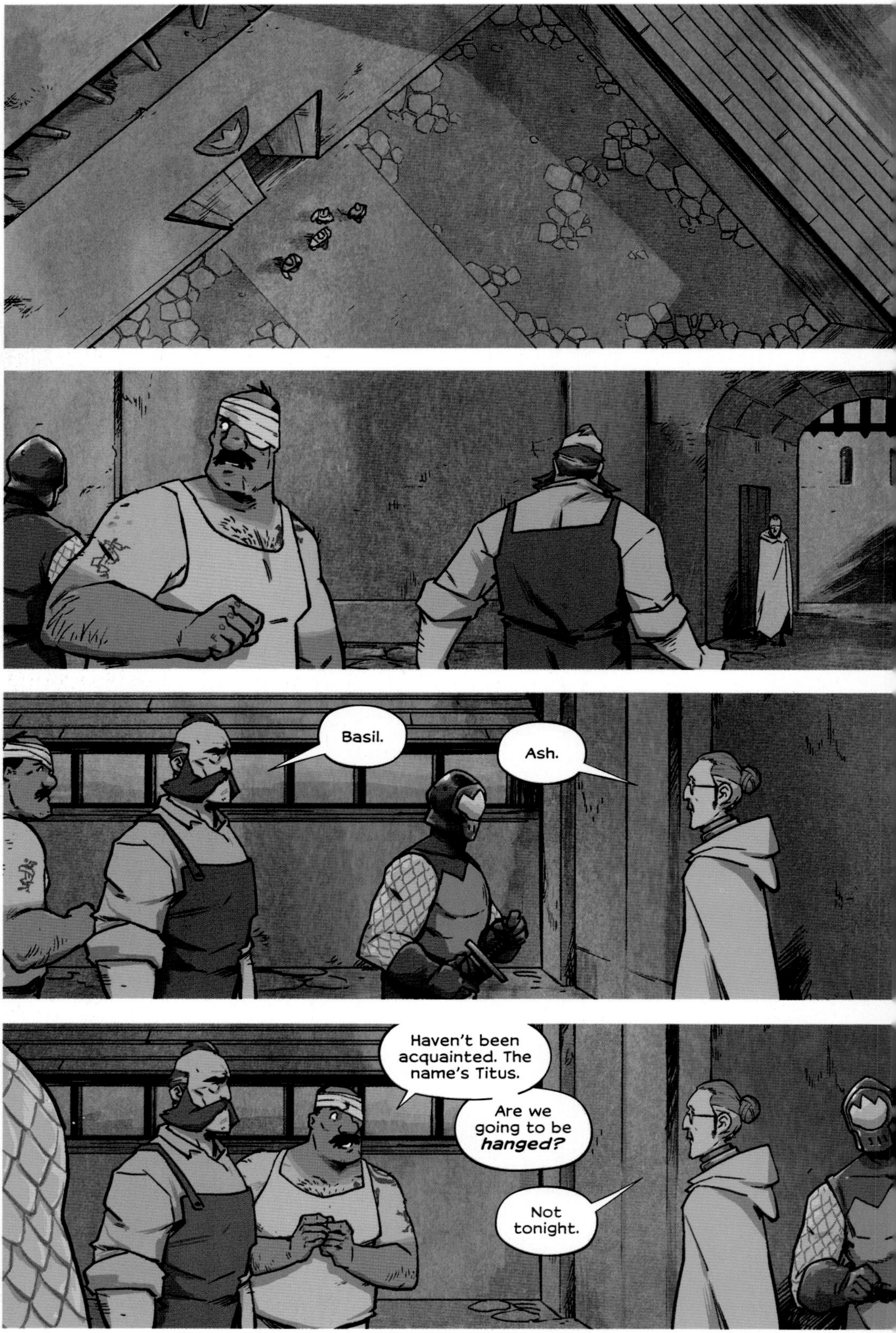
Basil.
Ash.
Haven't been acquainted. The name's Titus.
Are we going to be ***hanged?***
Not tonight.

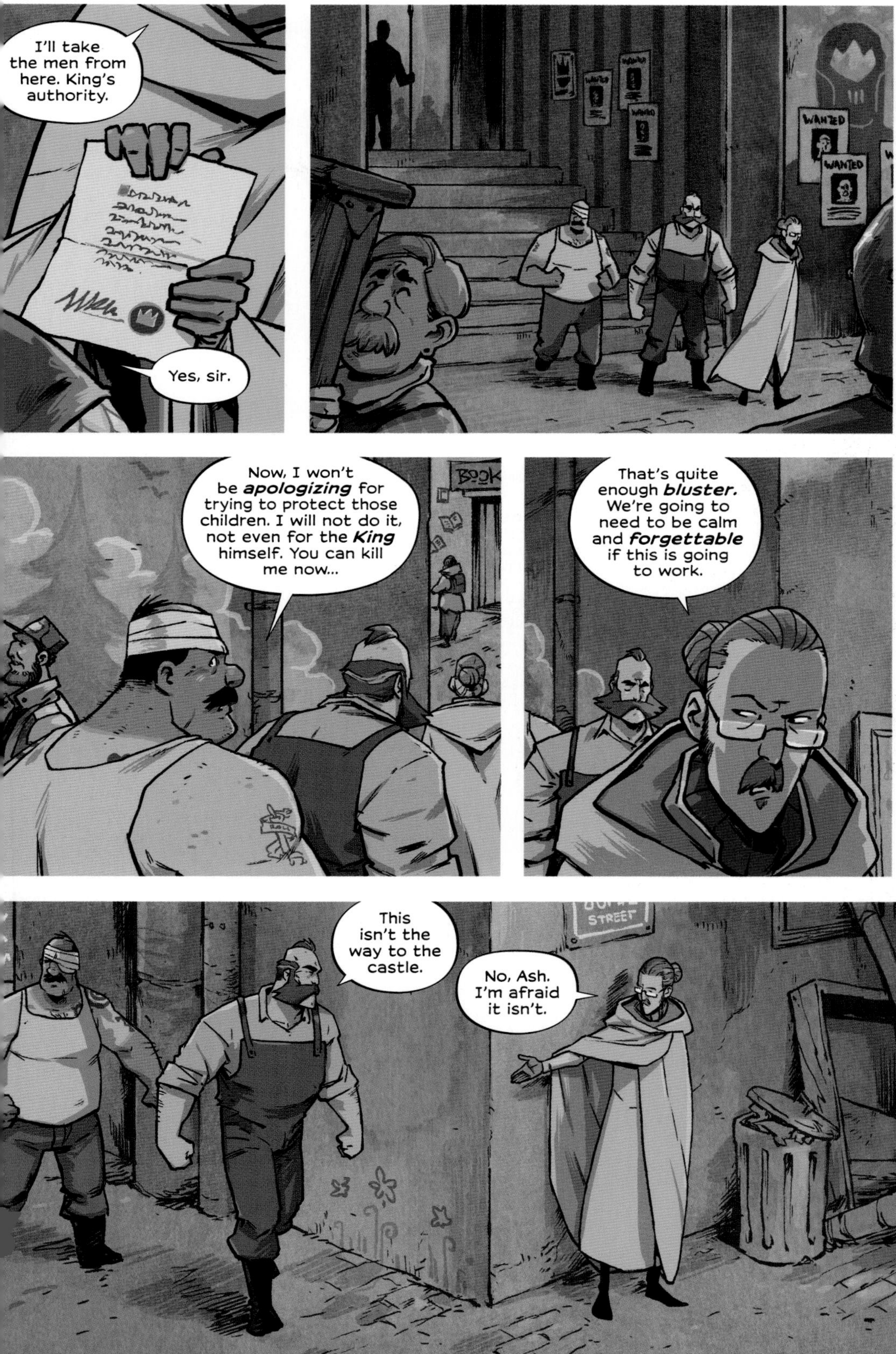
I'll take the men from here. King's authority.
Yes, sir.
WANTED
WANTED
WANTED
WANTED
WANTED
BOOK
Now, I won't be *apologizing* for trying to protect those children. I will not do it, not even for the *King* himself. You can kill me now...
That's quite enough *bluster.* We're going to need to be calm and *forgettable* if this is going to work.
STREET
This isn't the way to the castle.
No, Ash. I'm afraid it isn't.

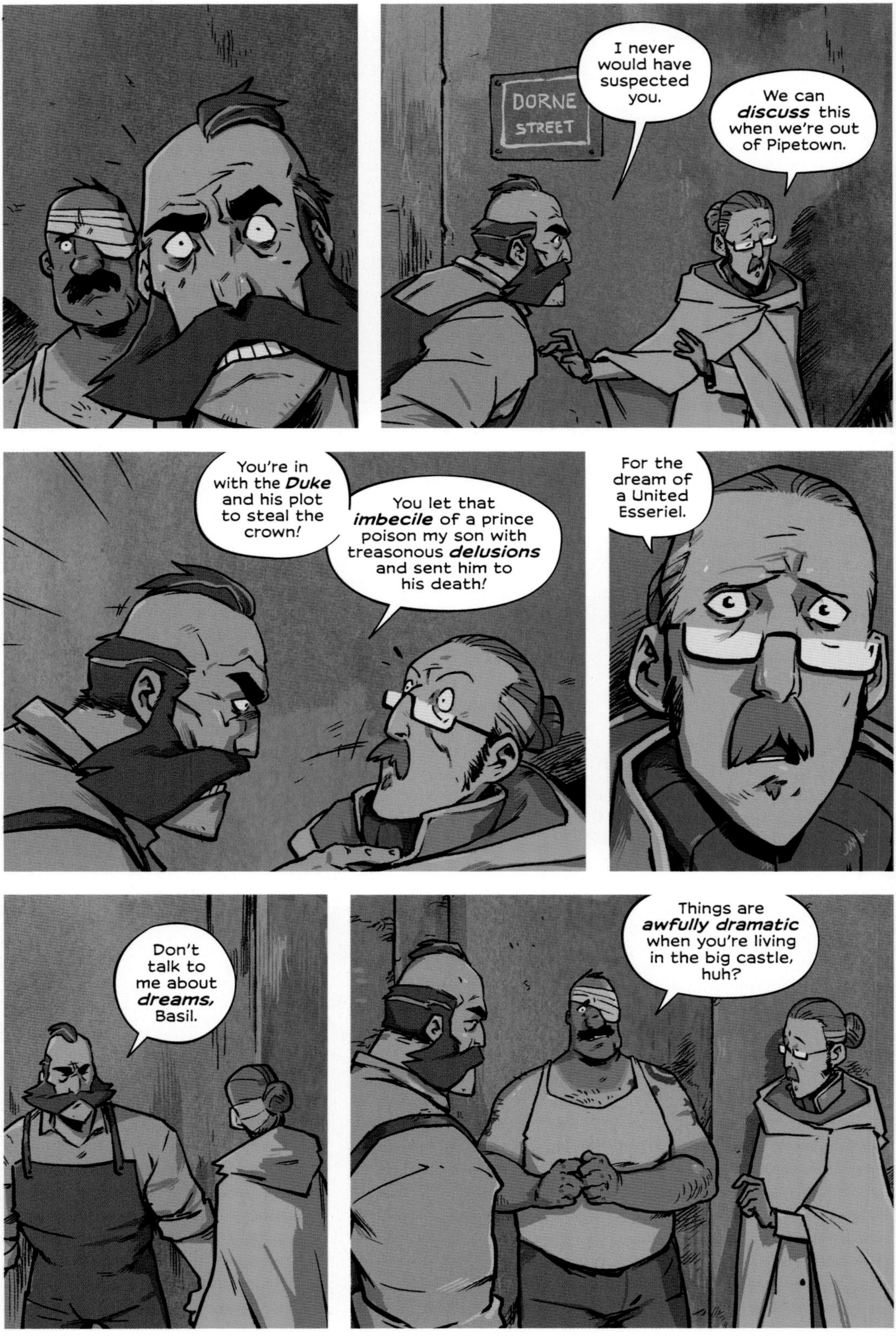
DORNE STREET
I never would have suspected you.
We can *discuss* this when we're out of Pipetown.
You're in with the *Duke* and his plot to steal the crown!
You let that *imbecile* of a prince poison my son with treasonous *delusions* and sent him to his death!
For the dream of a United Esseriel.
Don't talk to me about *dreams,* Basil.
Things are *awfully dramatic* when you're living in the big castle, huh?

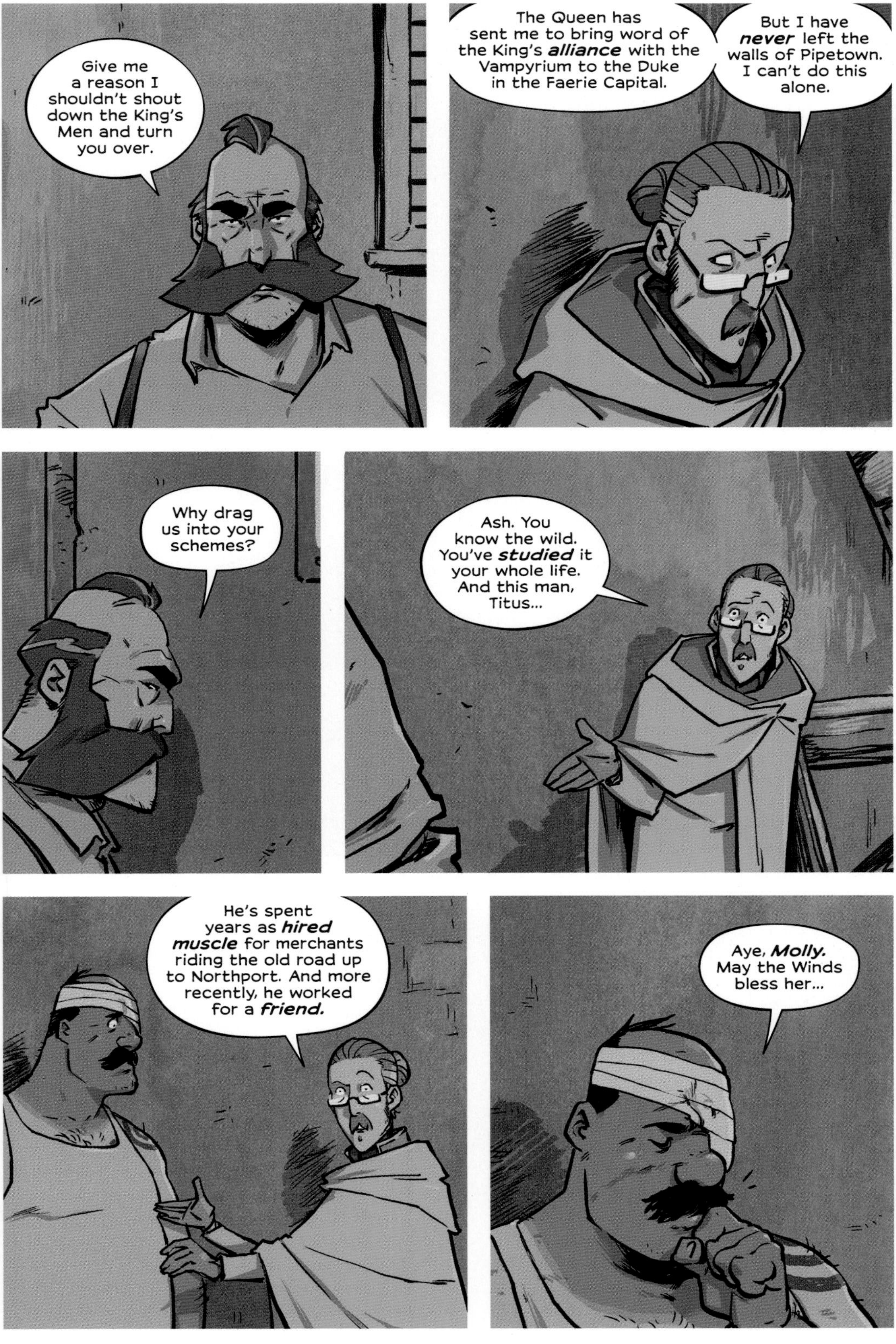
Give me a reason I shouldn't shout down the King's Men and turn you over.
The Queen has sent me to bring word of the King's ***alliance*** with the Vampyrium to the Duke in the Faerie Capital.
But I have ***never*** left the walls of Pipetown. I can't do this alone.
Why drag us into your schemes?
Ash. You know the wild. You've ***studied*** it your whole life. And this man, Titus...
He's spent years as ***hired muscle*** for merchants riding the old road up to Northport. And more recently, he worked for a ***friend.***
Aye, ***Molly.*** May the Winds bless her...

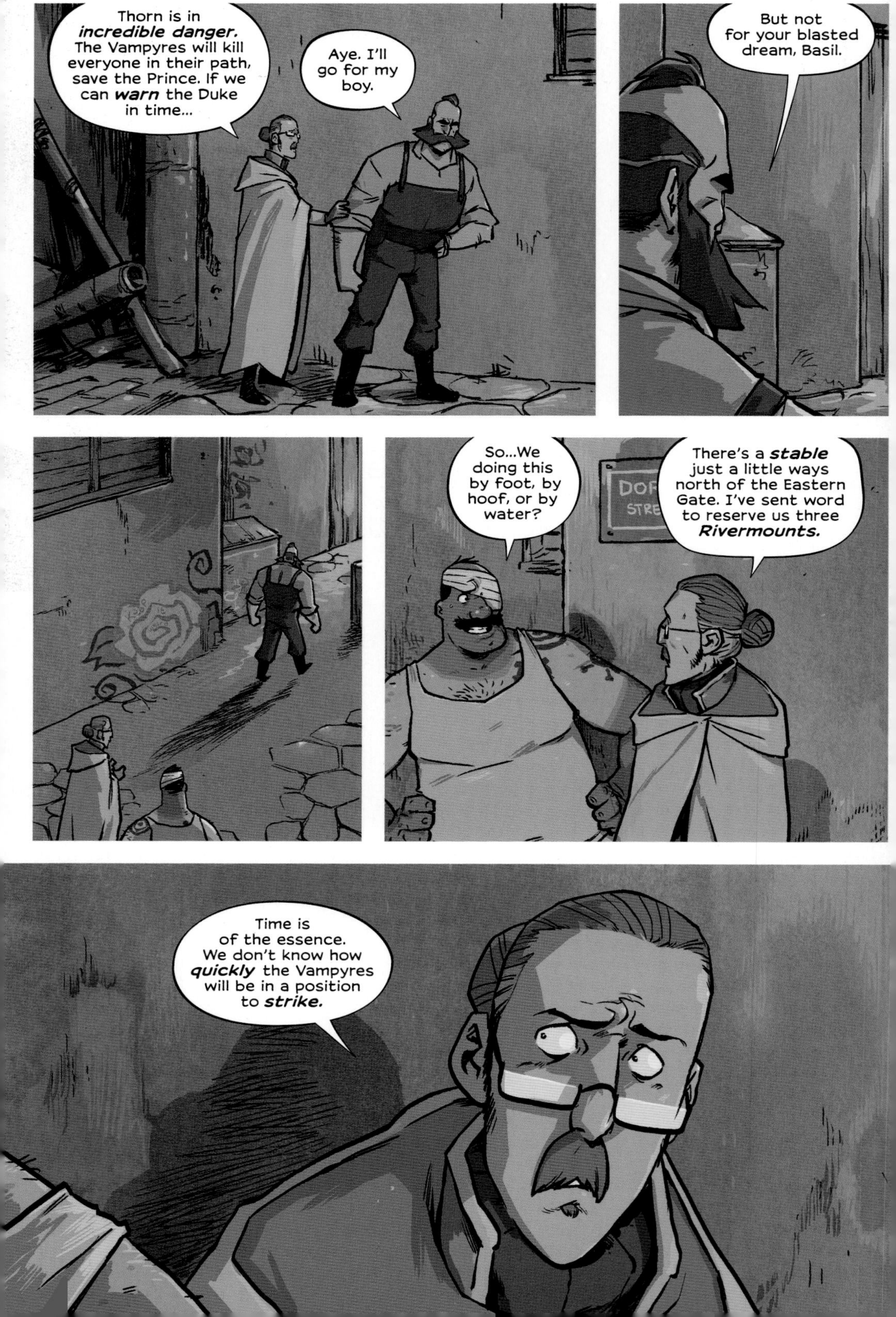
Thorn is in *incredible danger.* The Vampyres will kill everyone in their path, save the Prince. If we can *warn* the Duke in time...
Aye. I'll go for my boy.
But not for your blasted dream, Basil.
So...We doing this by foot, by hoof, or by water?
DOR STRE
There's a *stable* just a little ways north of the Eastern Gate. I've sent word to reserve us three *Rivermounts.*
Time is of the essence. We don't know how *quickly* the Vampyres will be in a position to *strike.*

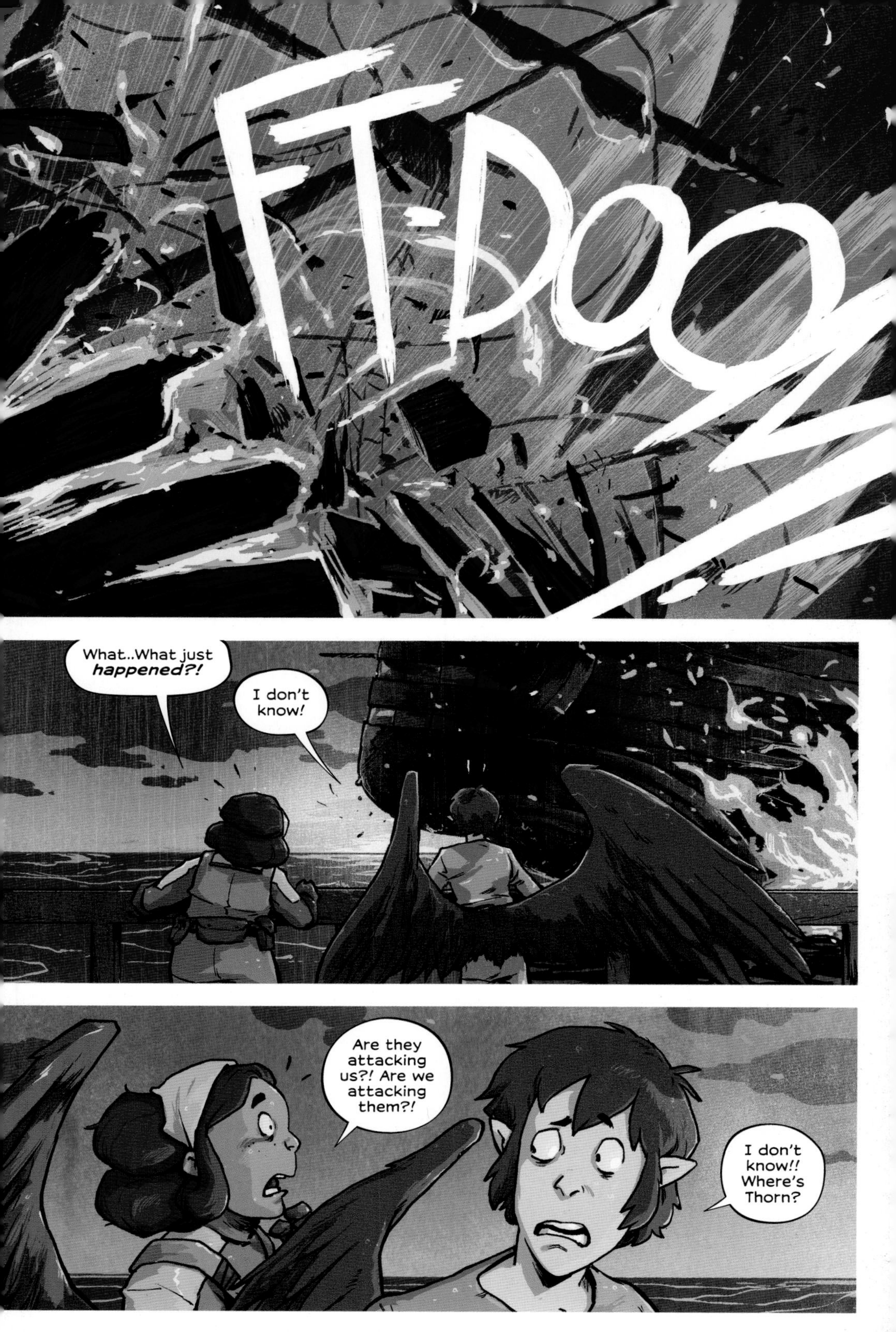
FT-DOOM
What..What just *happened?!*
I don't know!
Are they attacking us?! Are we attacking them?!
I don't know!! Where's Thorn?

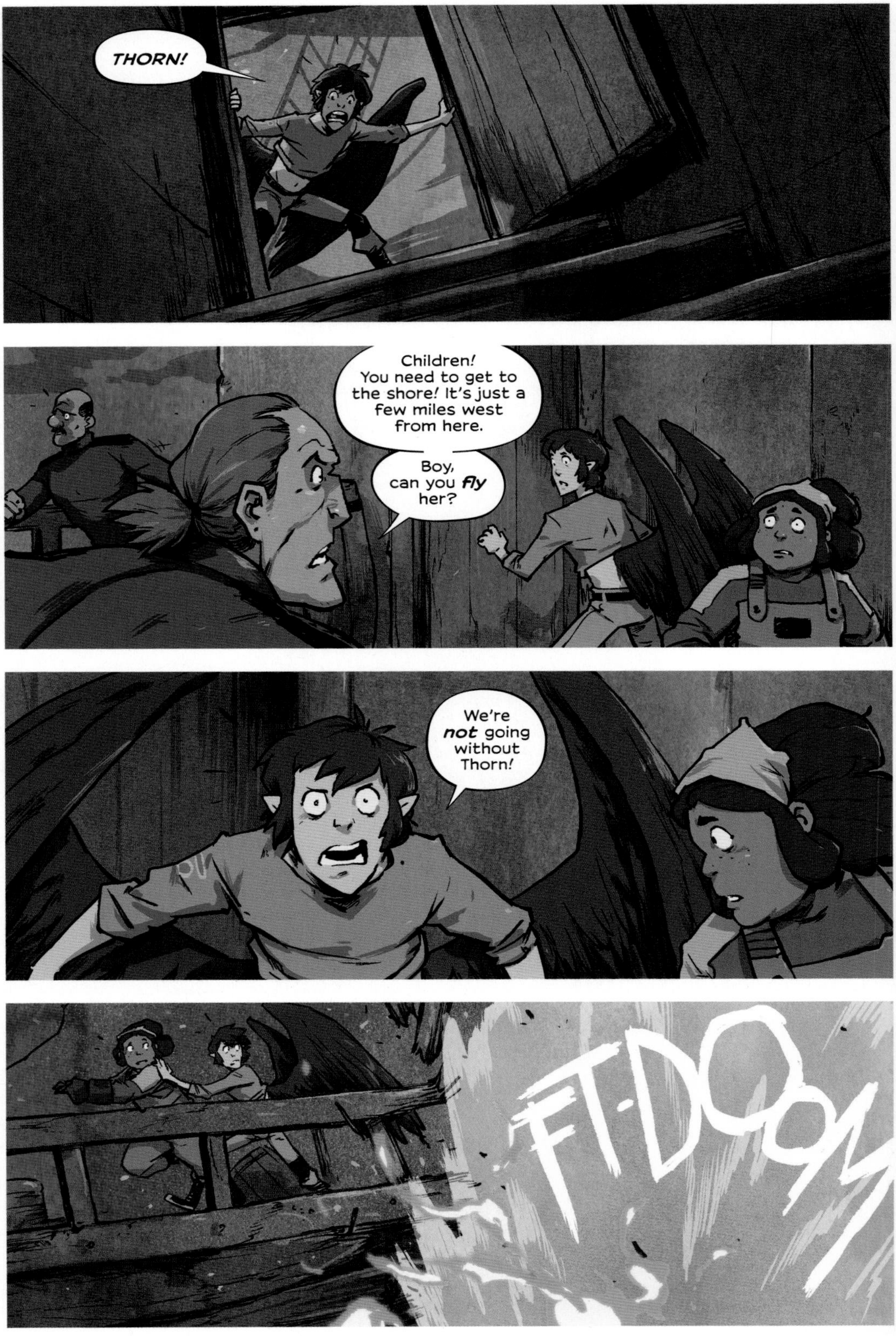
THORN!
Children! You need to get to the shore! It's just a few miles west from here.
Boy, can you fly her?
We're not going without Thorn!
FT-DOOM

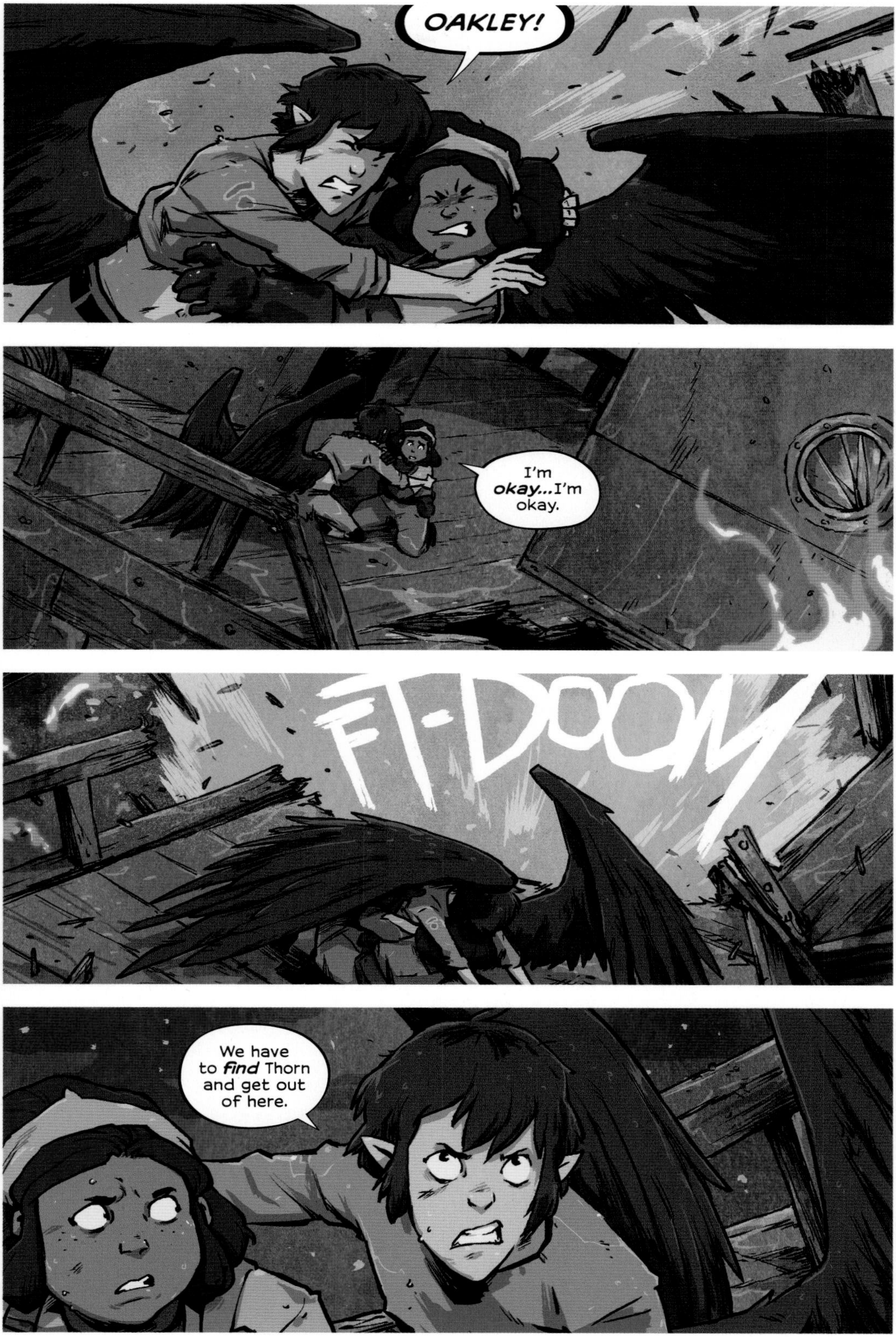
OAKLEY!
I'm *okay...* I'm okay.
FT-DOOM
We have to *find* Thorn and get out of here.

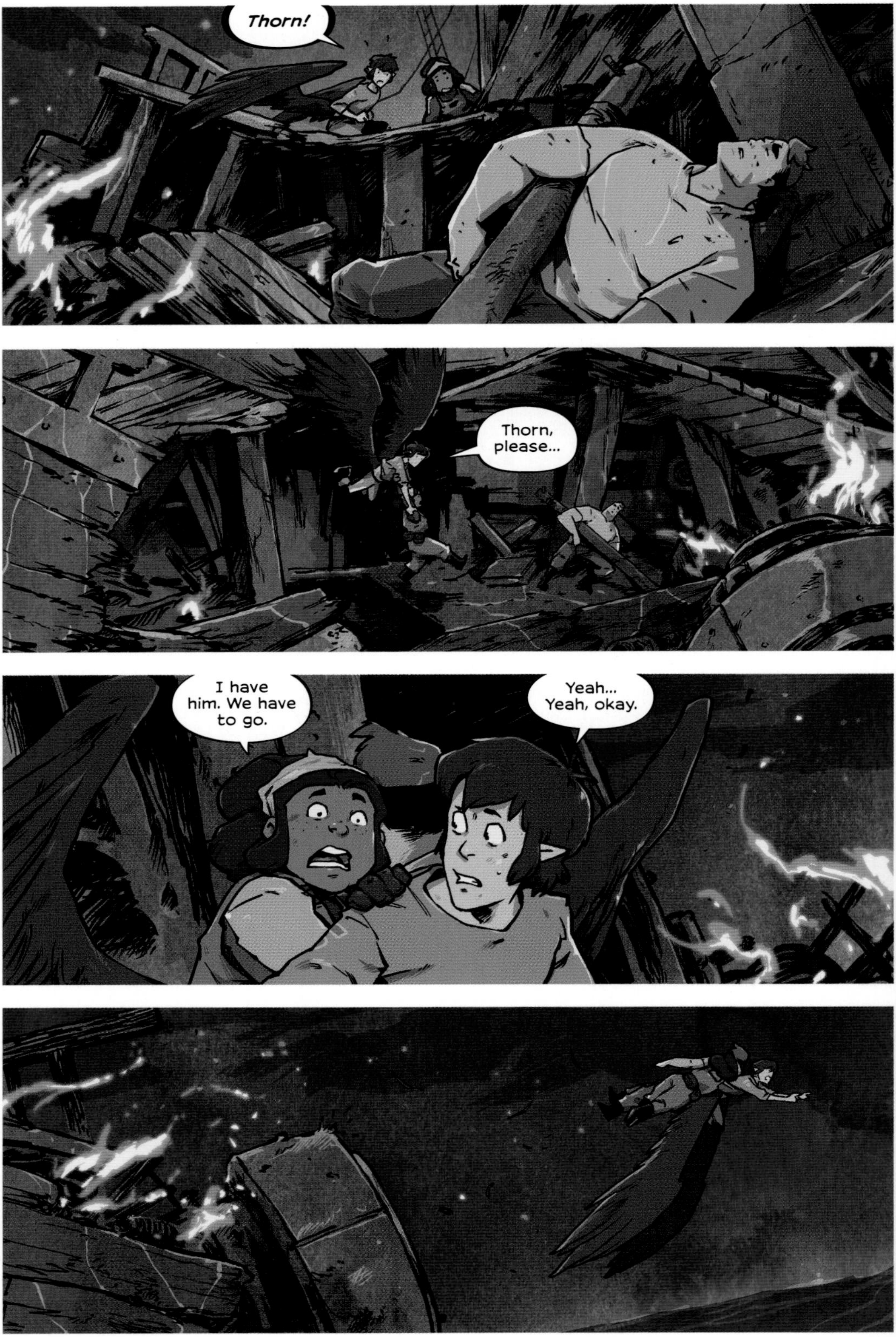
Thorn!
Thorn, please...
I have him. We have to go.
Yeah... Yeah, okay.

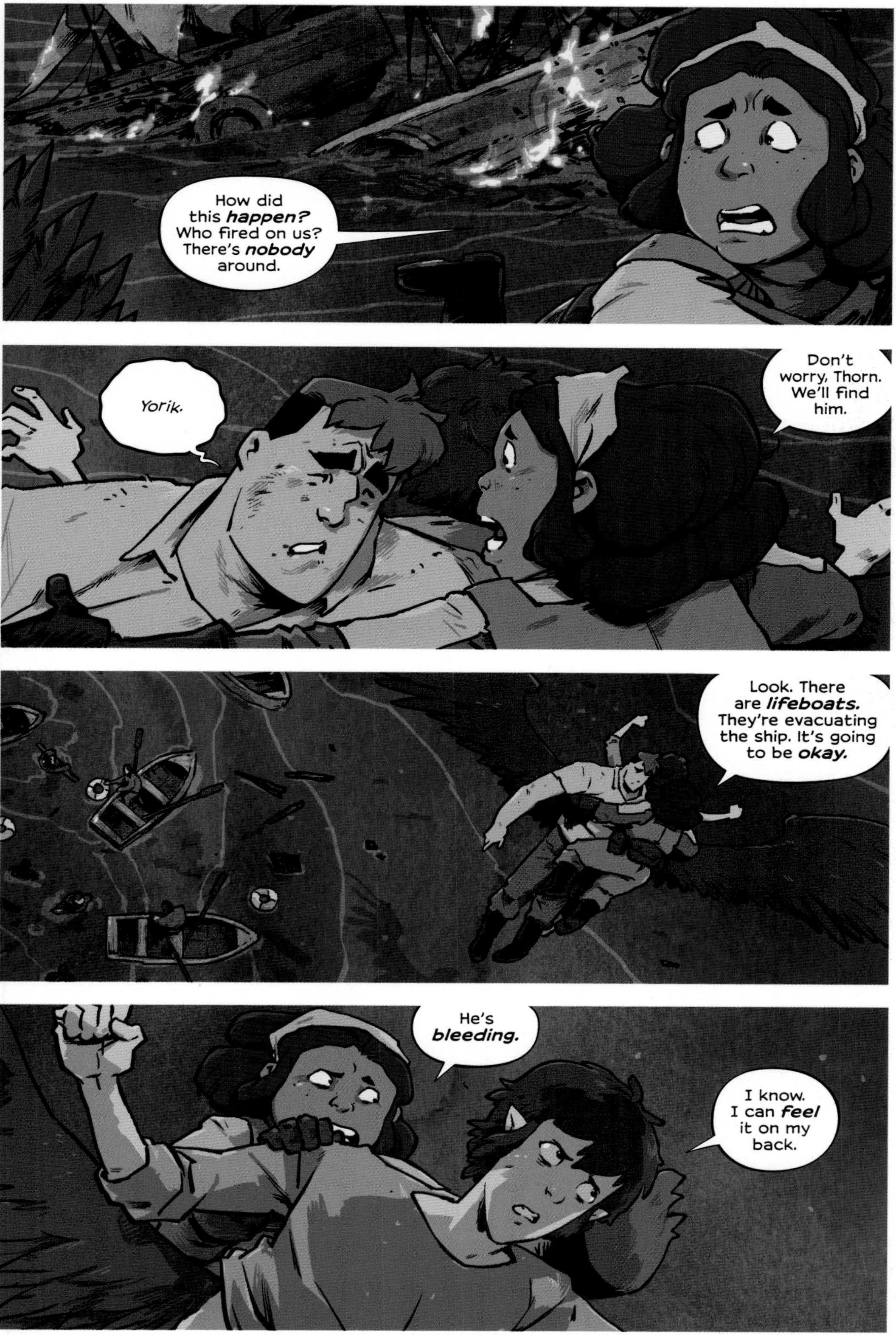
How did this *happen?* Who fired on us? There's *nobody* around.
Yorik.
Don't worry, Thorn. We'll find him.
Look. There are *lifeboats.* They're evacuating the ship. It's going to be *okay.*
He's *bleeding.*
I know. I can *feel* it on my back.

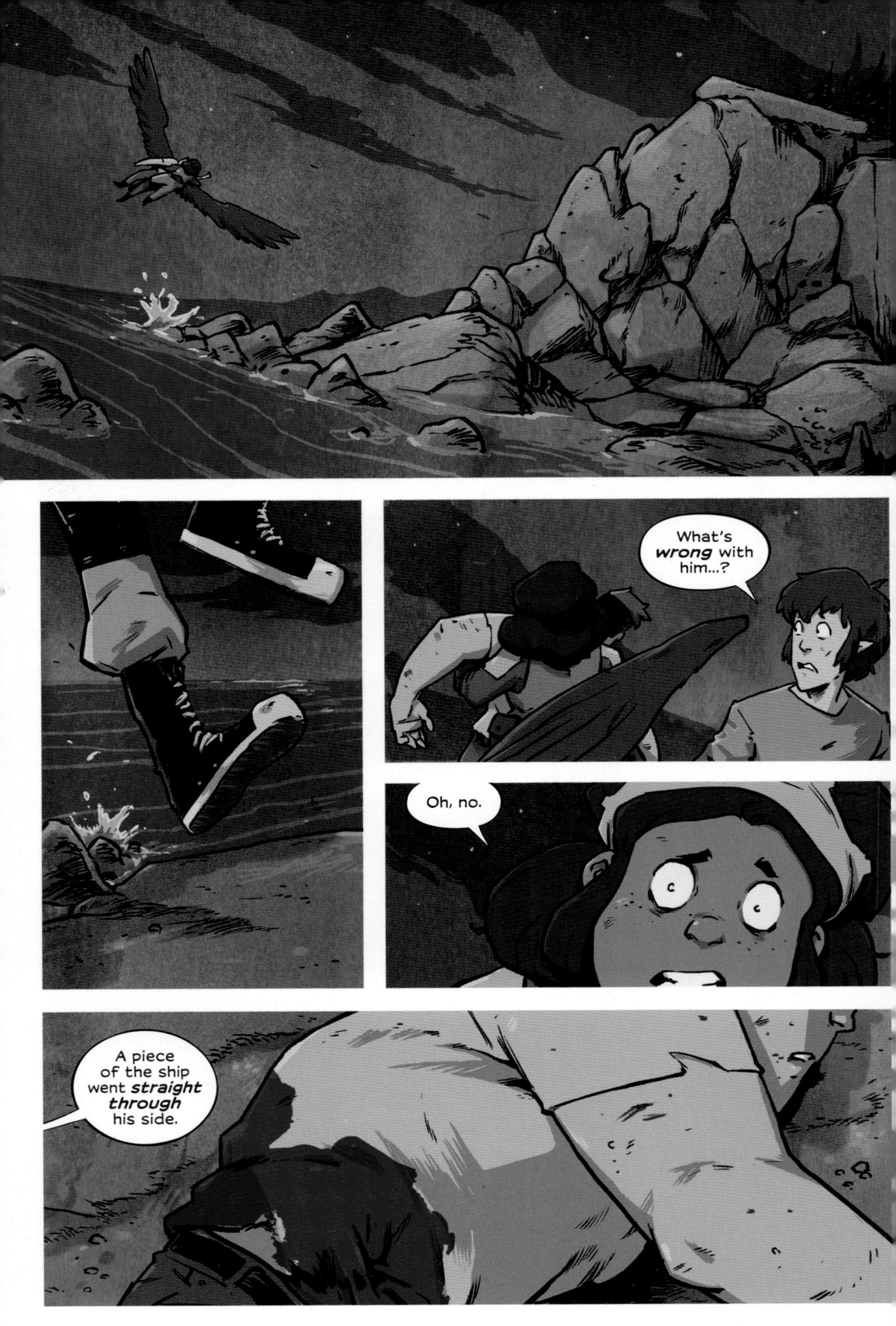

What's **wrong** with him...?
Oh, no.
A piece of the ship went **straight through** his side.

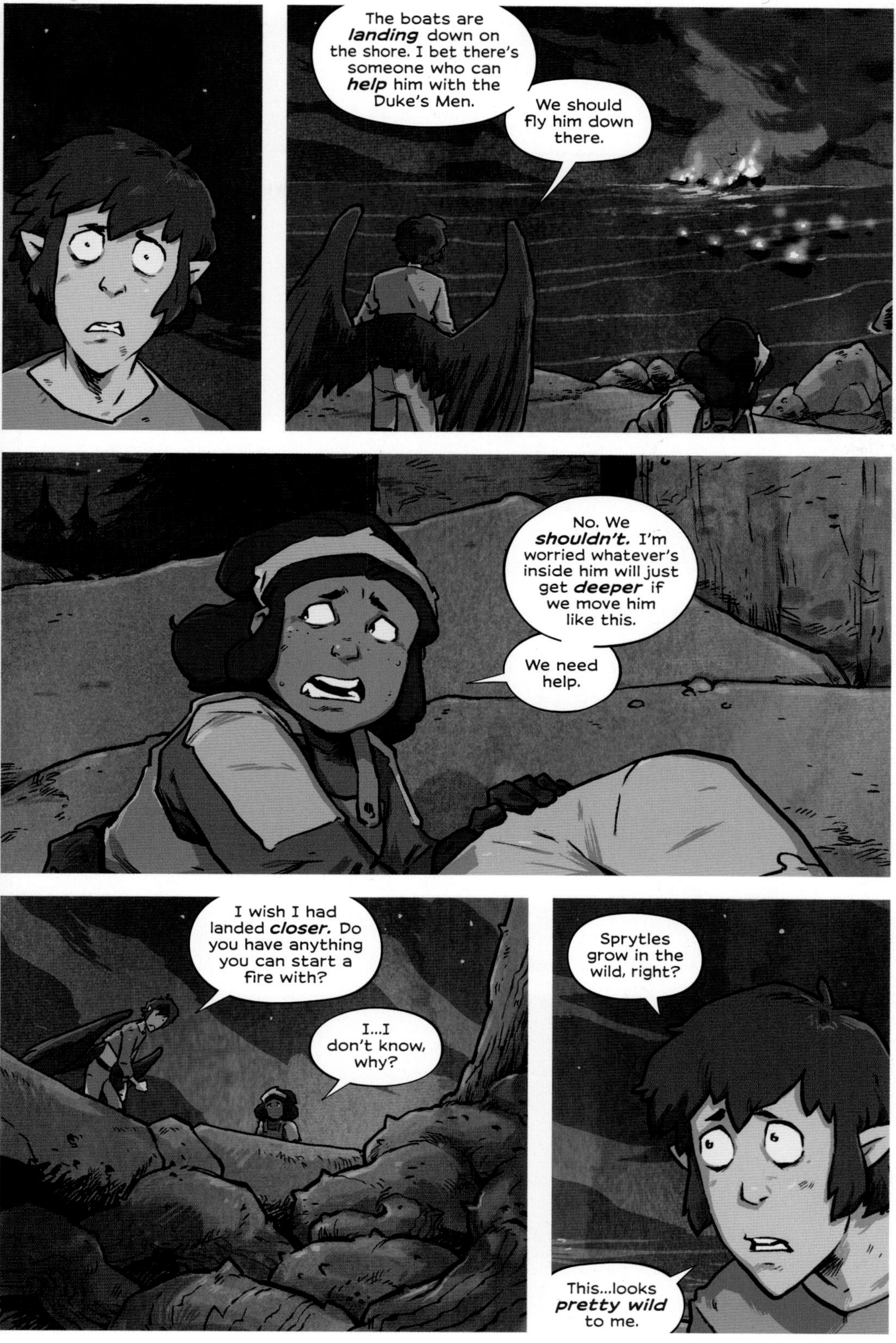
The boats are *landing* down on the shore. I bet there's someone who can *help* him with the Duke's Men.
We should fly him down there.
No. We *shouldn't.* I'm worried whatever's inside him will just get *deeper* if we move him like this.
We need help.
I wish I had landed *closer.* Do you have anything you can start a fire with?
I...I don't know, why?
Sprytles grow in the wild, right?
This...looks *pretty wild* to me.

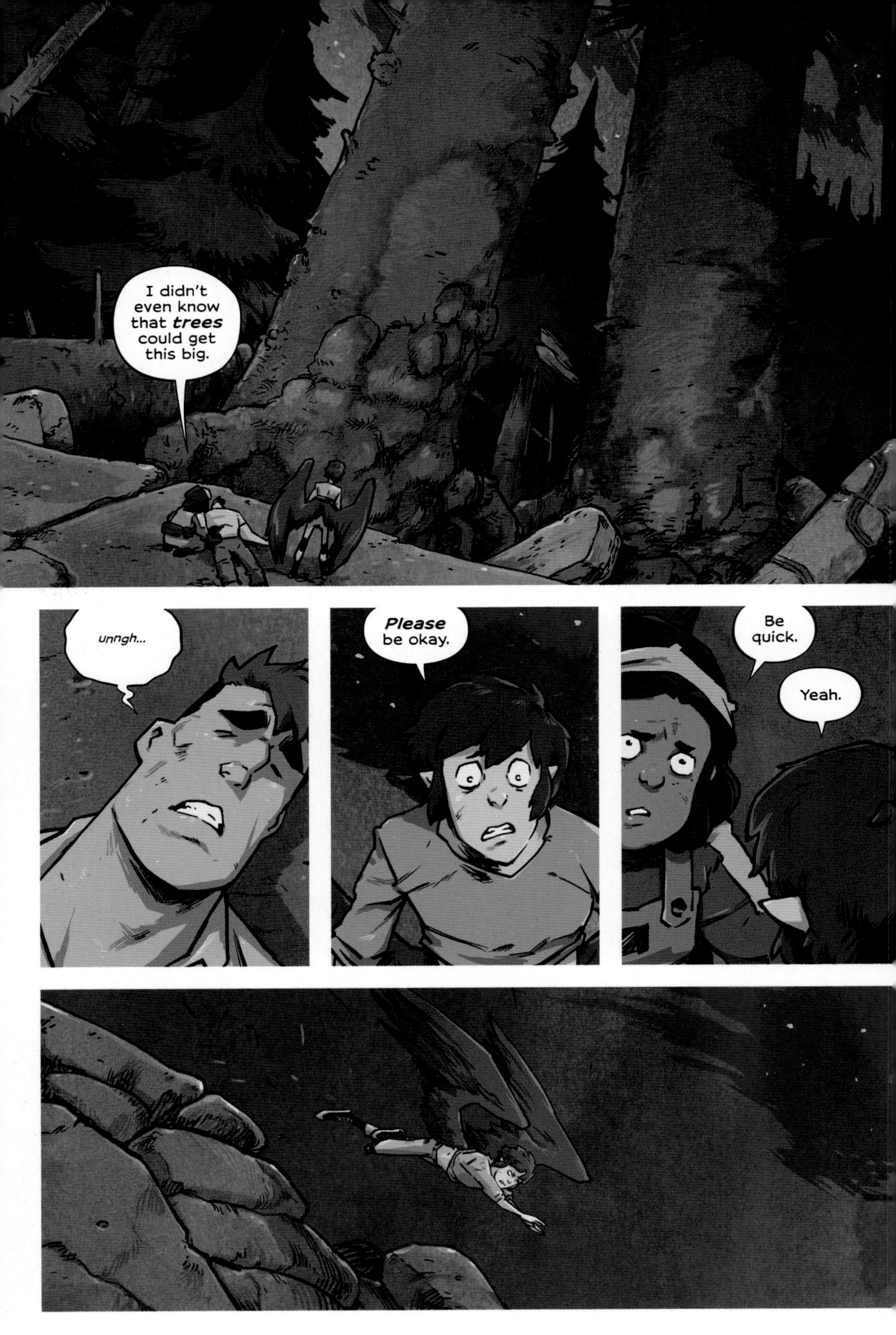

I didn't even know that ***trees*** could get this big.
unngh...
Please be okay.
Be quick.
Yeah.

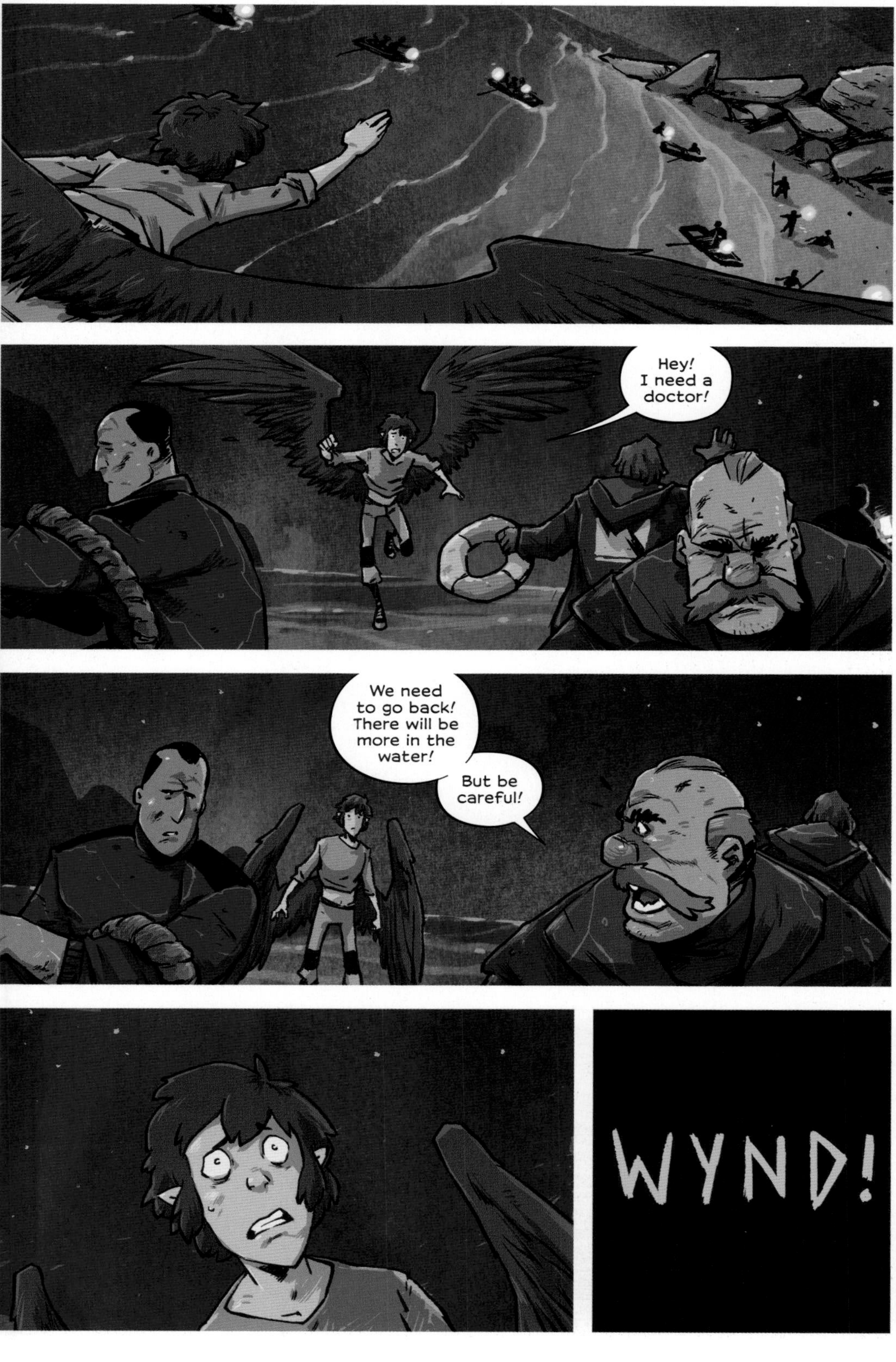
Hey! I need a doctor!
We need to go back! There will be more in the water!
But be careful!
WYND!

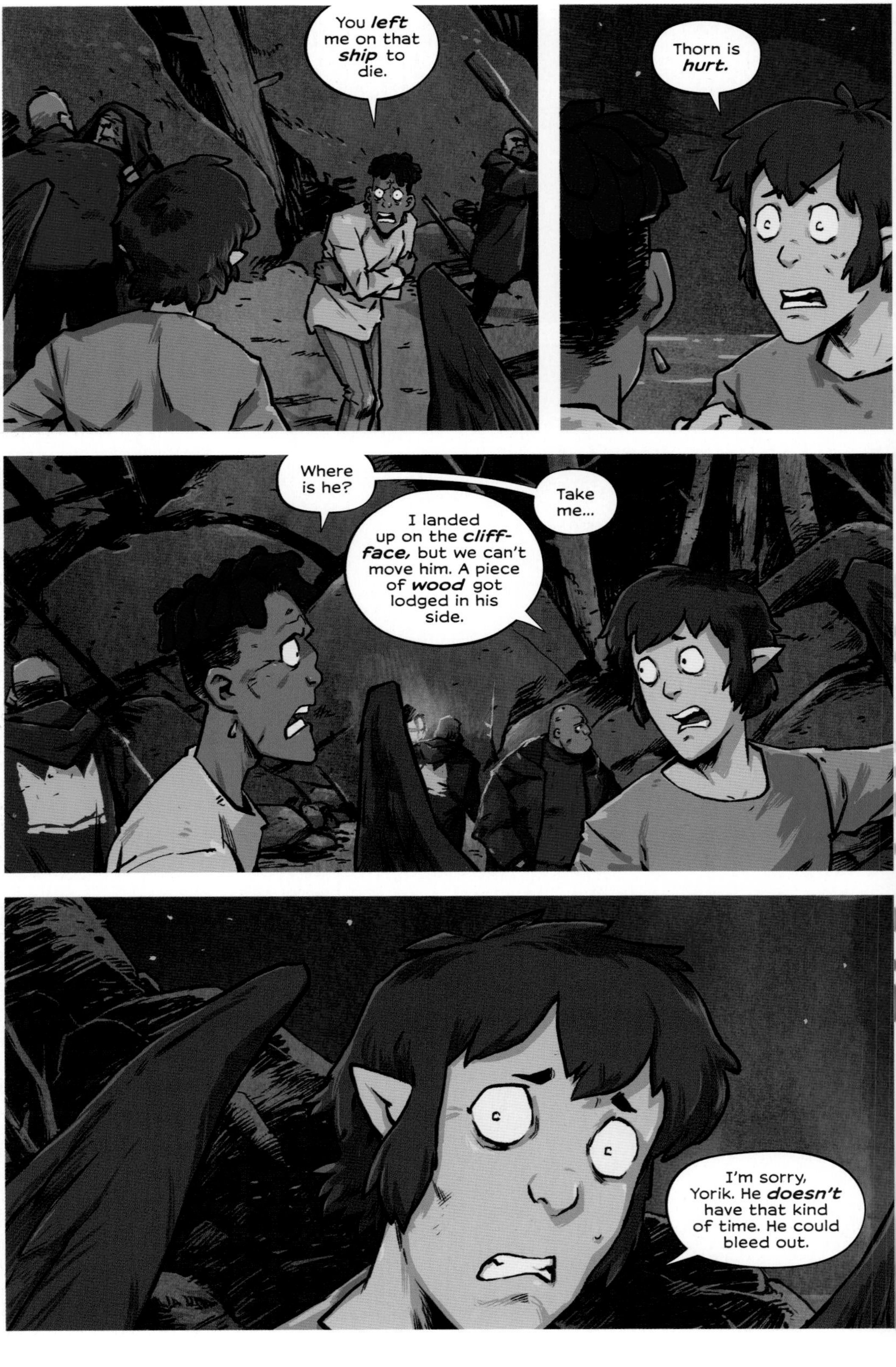
You *left* me on that *ship* to die.
Thorn is *hurt.*
Where is he?
Take me...
I landed up on the *cliff-face,* but we can't move him. A piece of *wood* got lodged in his side.
I'm sorry, Yorik. He *doesn't* have that kind of time. He could bleed out.

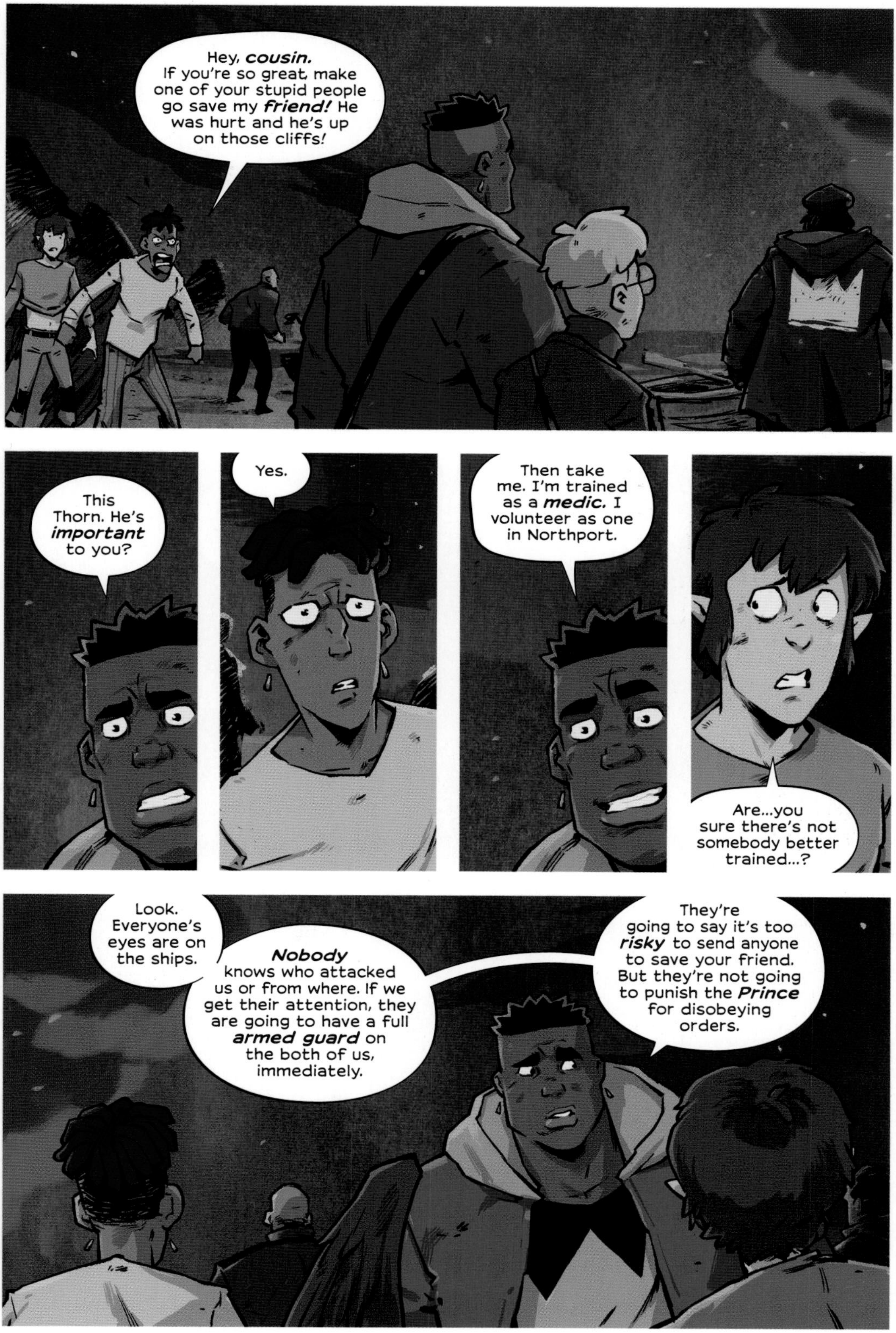
Hey, ***cousin.*** If you're so great, make one of your stupid people go save my ***friend!*** He was hurt and he's up on those cliffs!
This Thorn. He's ***important*** to you?
Yes.
Then take me. I'm trained as a ***medic.*** I volunteer as one in Northport.
Are...you sure there's not somebody better trained...?
Look. Everyone's eyes are on the ships.
Nobody knows who attacked us or from where. If we get their attention, they are going to have a full ***armed guard*** on the both of us, immediately.
They're going to say it's too ***risky*** to send anyone to save your friend. But they're not going to punish the ***Prince*** for disobeying orders.

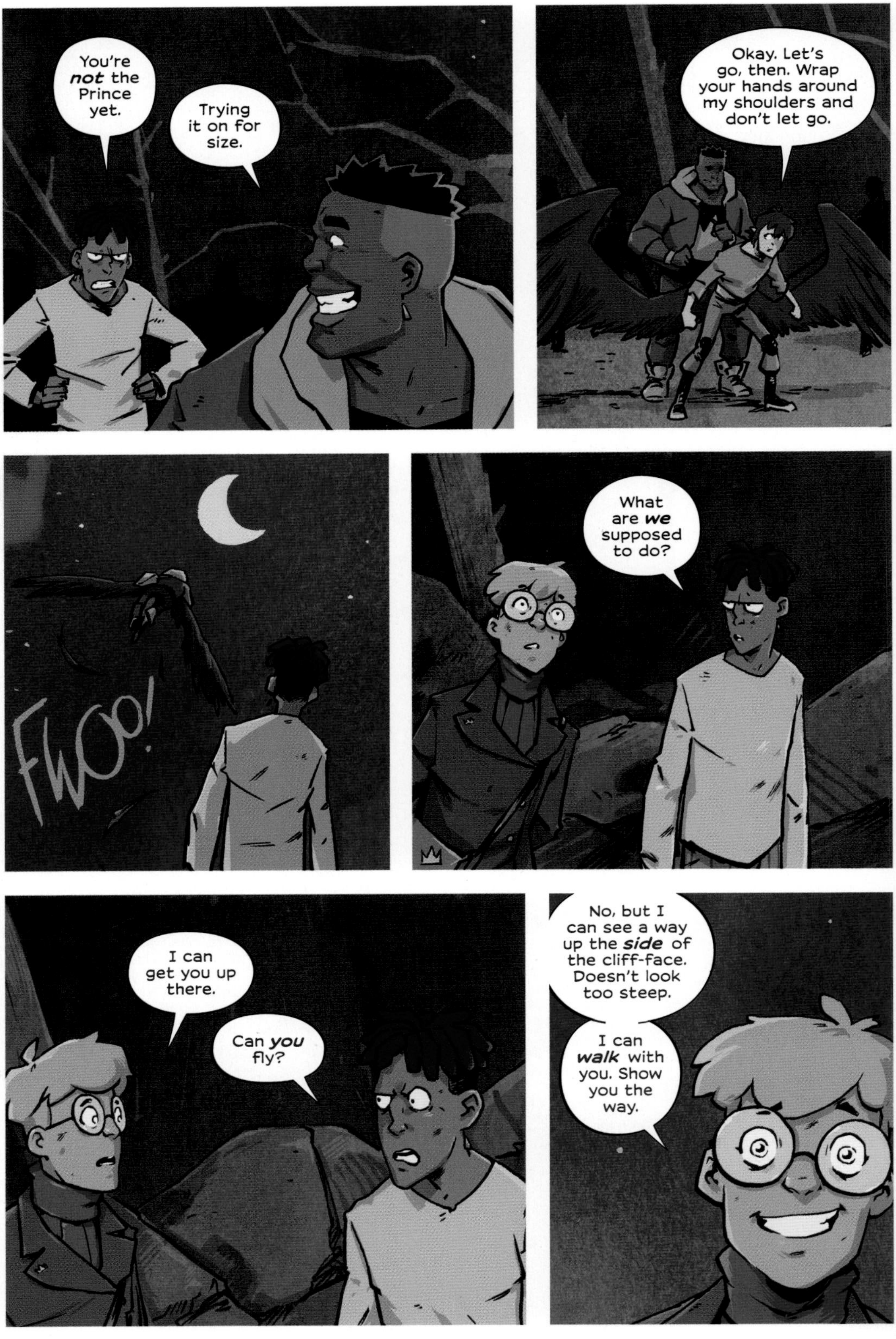
You're *not* the Prince yet.
Trying it on for size.
Okay. Let's go, then. Wrap your hands around my shoulders and don't let go.
FWOO!
What are *we* supposed to do?
I can get you up there.
Can *you* fly?
No, but I can see a way up the *side* of the cliff-face. Doesn't look too steep.
I can *walk* with you. Show you the way.

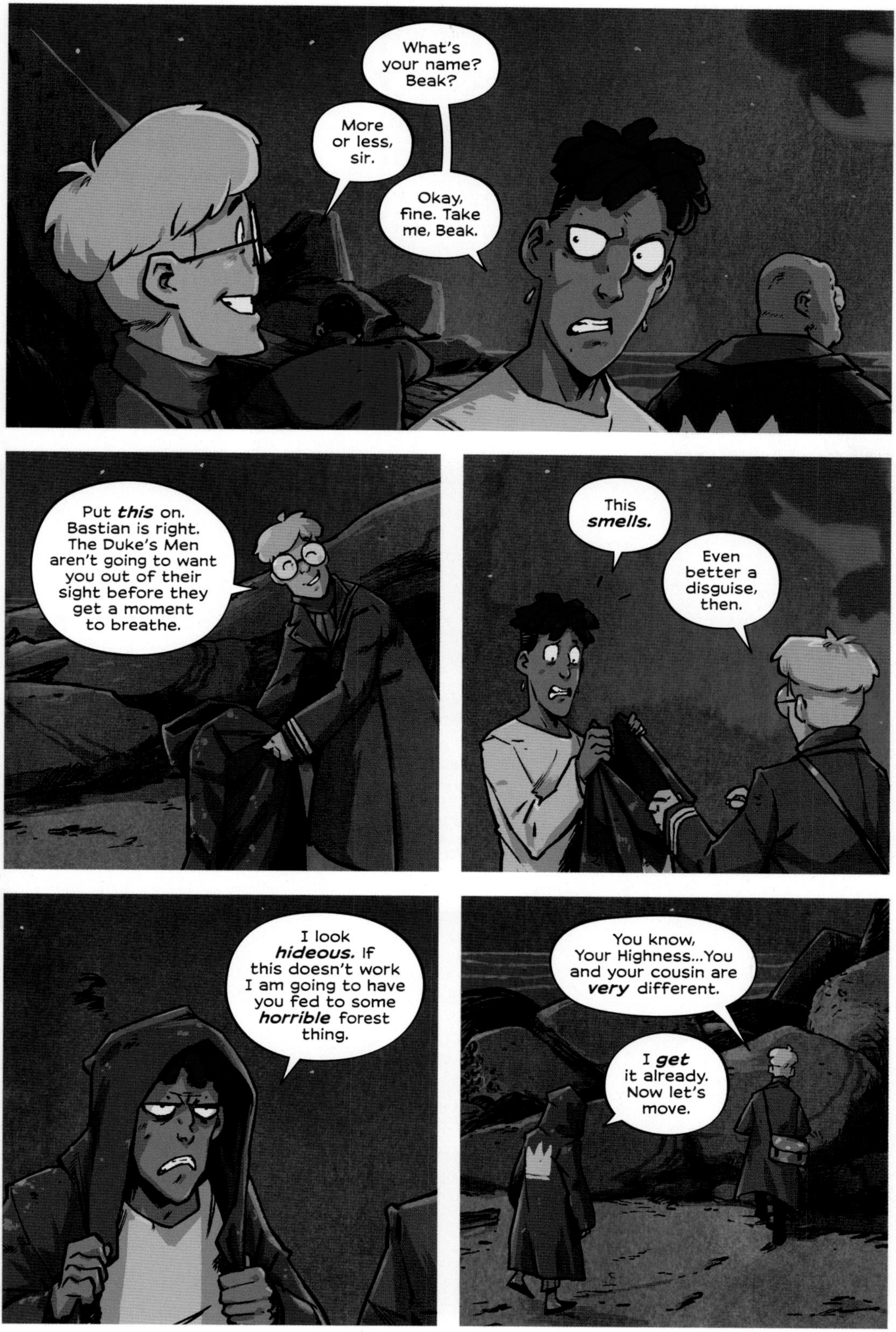
What's your name? Beak?
More or less, sir.
Okay, fine. Take me, Beak.
Put *this* on. Bastian is right. The Duke's Men aren't going to want you out of their sight before they get a moment to breathe.
This *smells.*
Even better a disguise, then.
I look *hideous.* If this doesn't work I am going to have you fed to some *horrible* forest thing.
You know, Your Highness...You and your cousin are *very* different.
I *get* it already. Now let's move.

Oh, he's a *big* fella. Look at those muscles.

Trust me, Wynd's looked.

Ho ho *ho!*

Oakley!

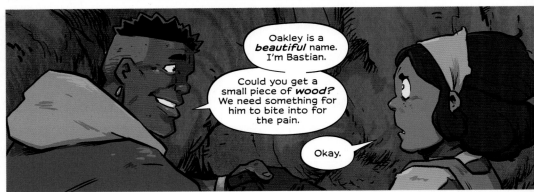

Oakley is a *beautiful* name. I'm Bastian.

Could you get a small piece of *wood?* We need something for him to bite into for the pain.

Okay.

Wynd. I want you to sit *here,* and hold his hand.

Hold his hand? Will that help?

Yeah. He needs to know his *people* are with him. Are *you* his people?

Yes.

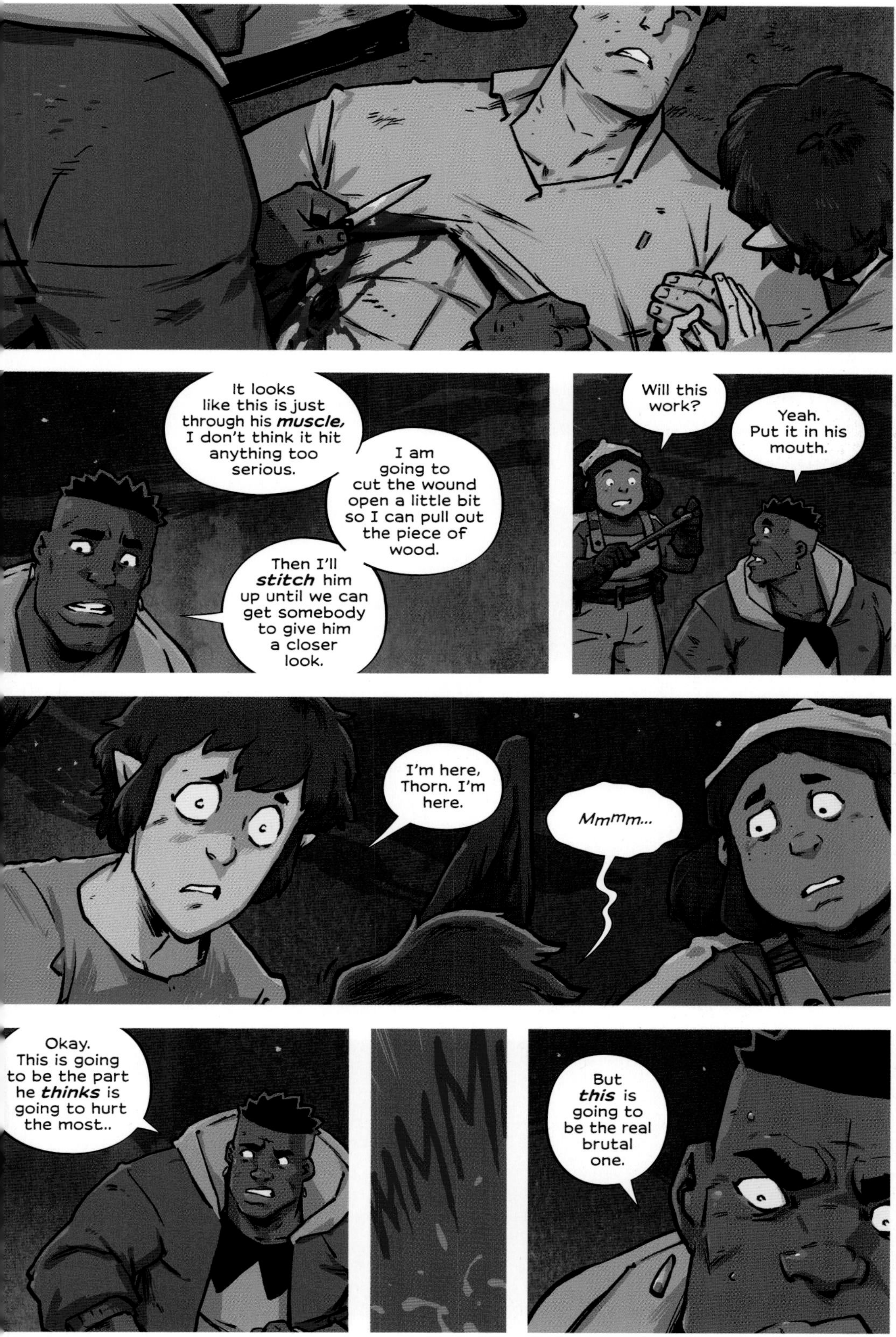
It looks like this is just through his *muscle,* I don't think it hit anything too serious.
I am going to cut the wound open a little bit so I can pull out the piece of wood.
Then I'll *stitch* him up until we can get somebody to give him a closer look.
Will this work?
Yeah. Put it in his mouth.
I'm here, Thorn. I'm here.
Mmmm...
Okay. This is going to be the part he *thinks* is going to hurt the most..
MMMM
But *this* is going to be the real brutal one.

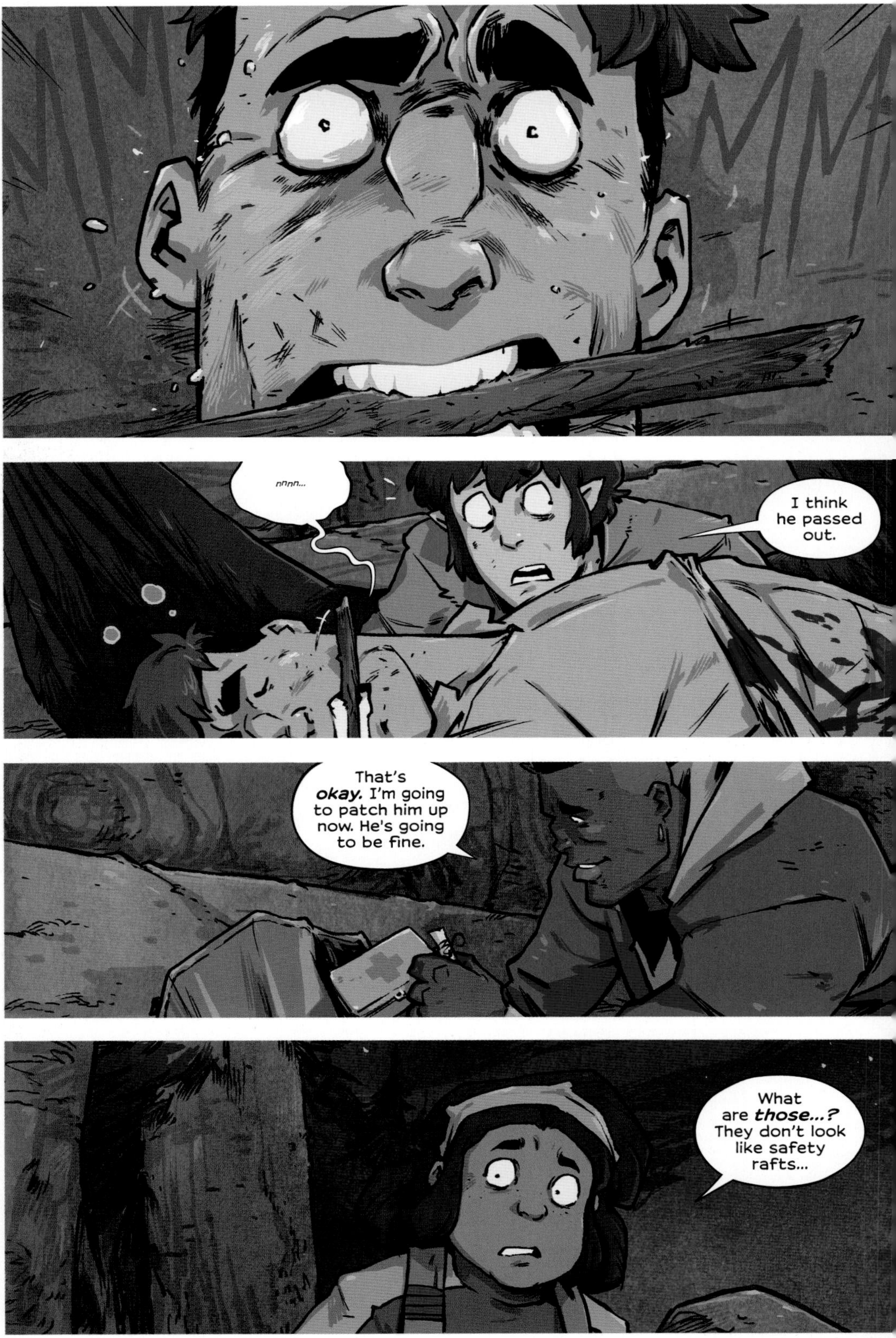
nnnn...
I think he passed out.
That's ***okay.*** I'm going to patch him up now. He's going to be fine.
What are ***those...?*** They don't look like safety rafts...

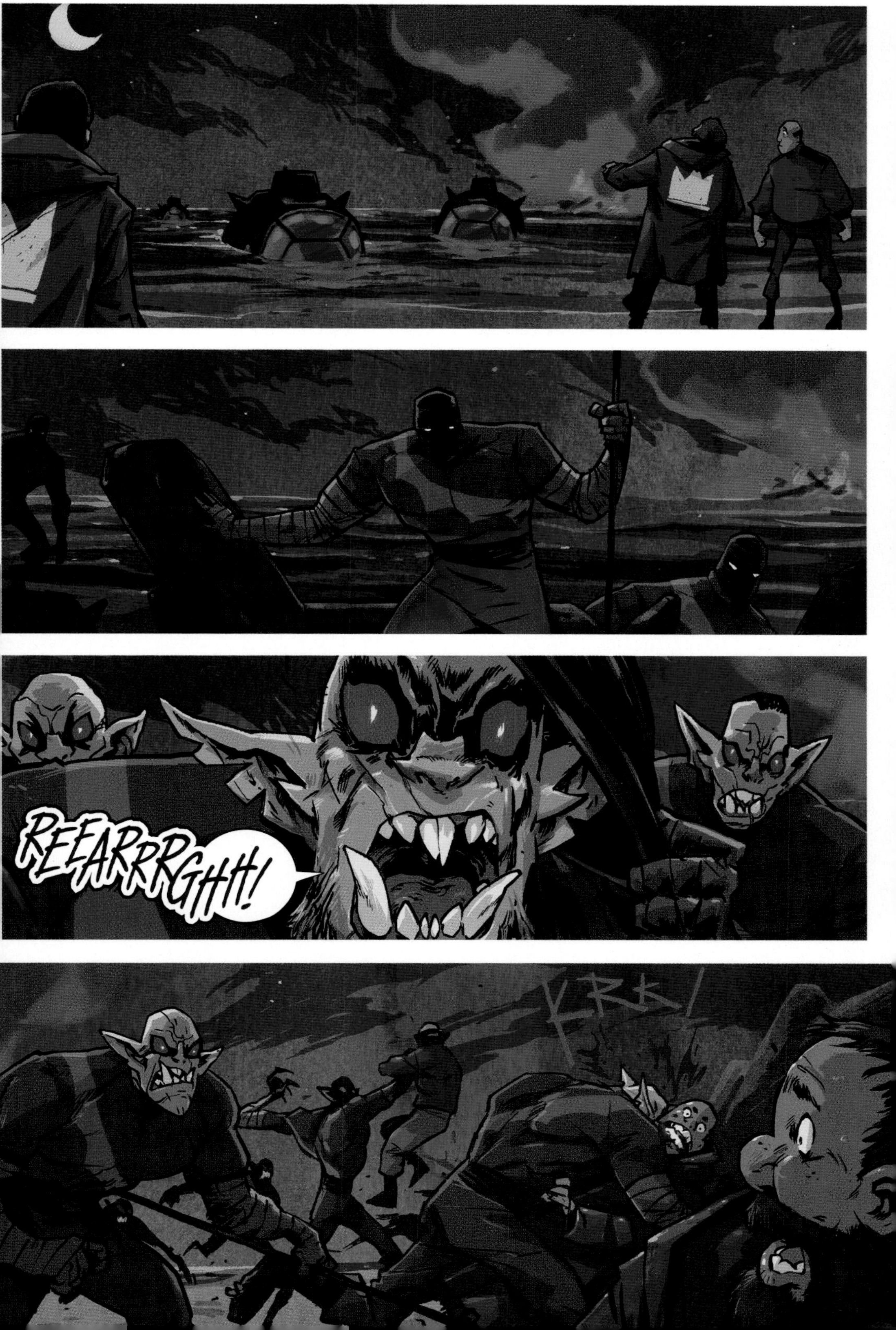
REEARRRGHH!
KRK!

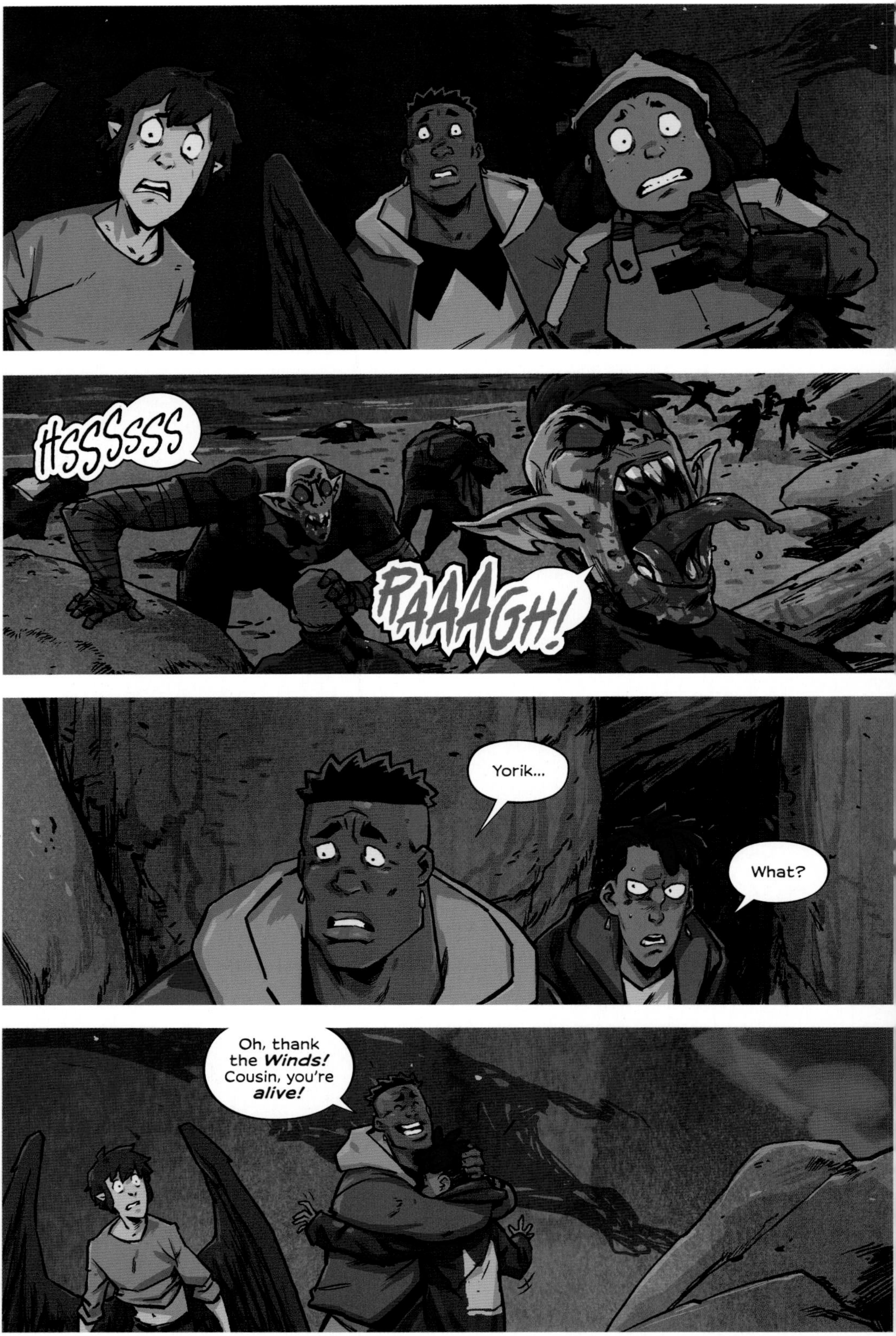
HSSSSSS
RAAAGH!
Yorik...
What?
Oh, thank the *Winds!* Cousin, you're *alive!*

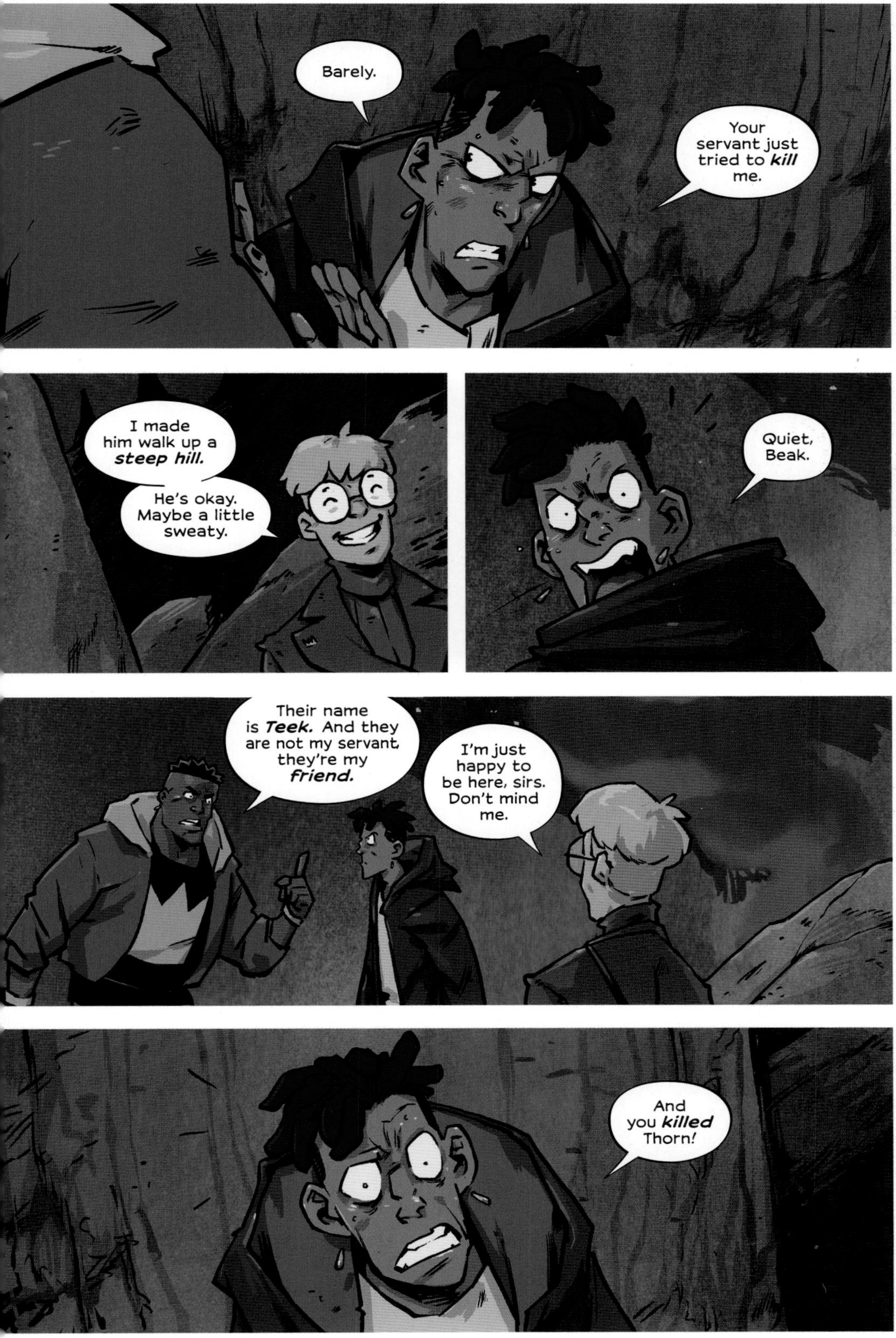
Barely.
Your servant just tried to kill me.
I made him walk up a steep hill.
He's okay. Maybe a little sweaty.
Quiet, Beak.
Their name is Teek. And they are not my servant, they're my friend.
I'm just happy to be here, sirs. Don't mind me.
And you killed Thorn!

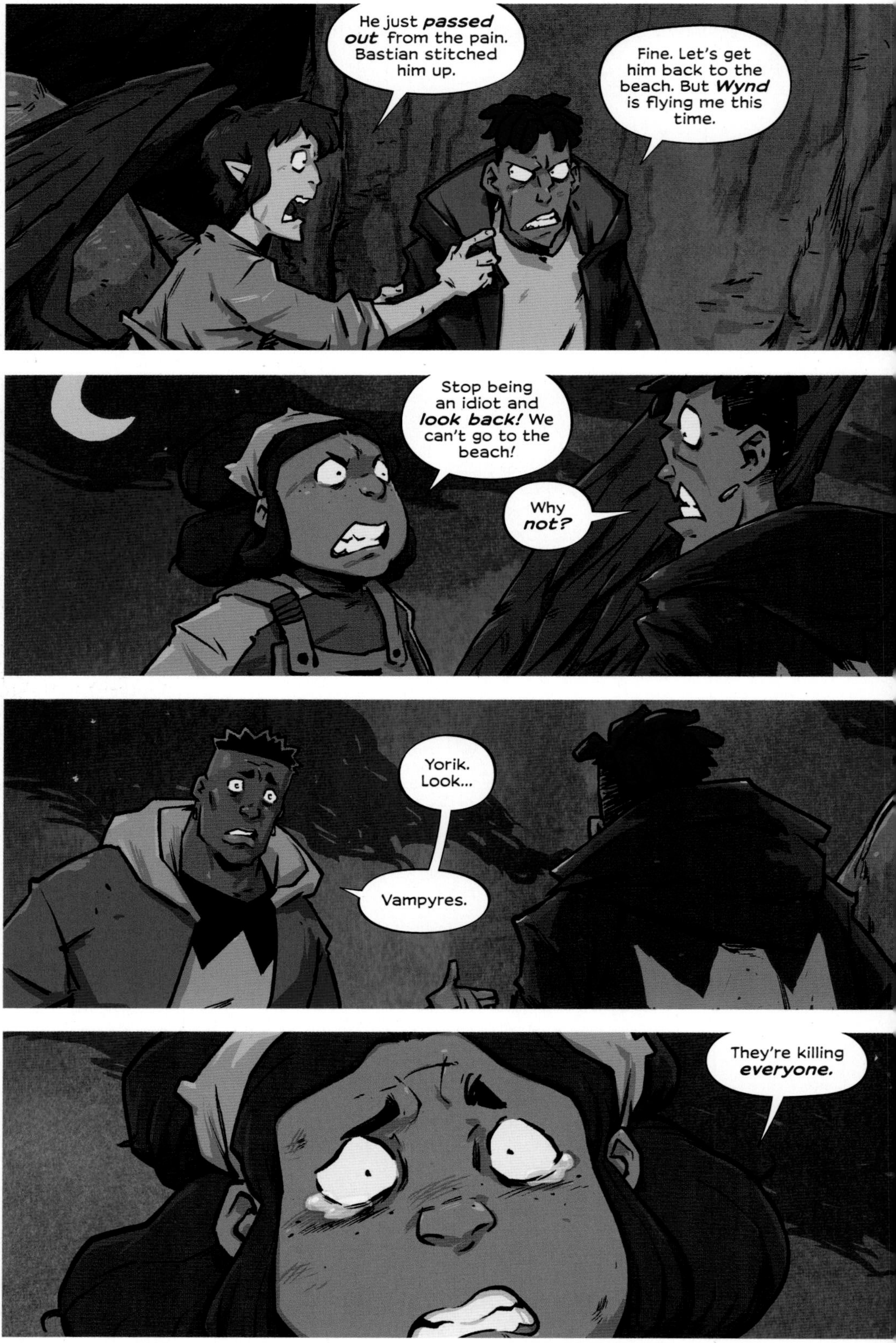
He just *passed out* from the pain. Bastian stitched him up.
Fine. Let's get him back to the beach. But *Wynd* is flying me this time.
Stop being an idiot and *look back!* We can't go to the beach!
Why *not?*
Yorik. Look...
Vampyres.
They're killing *everyone.*

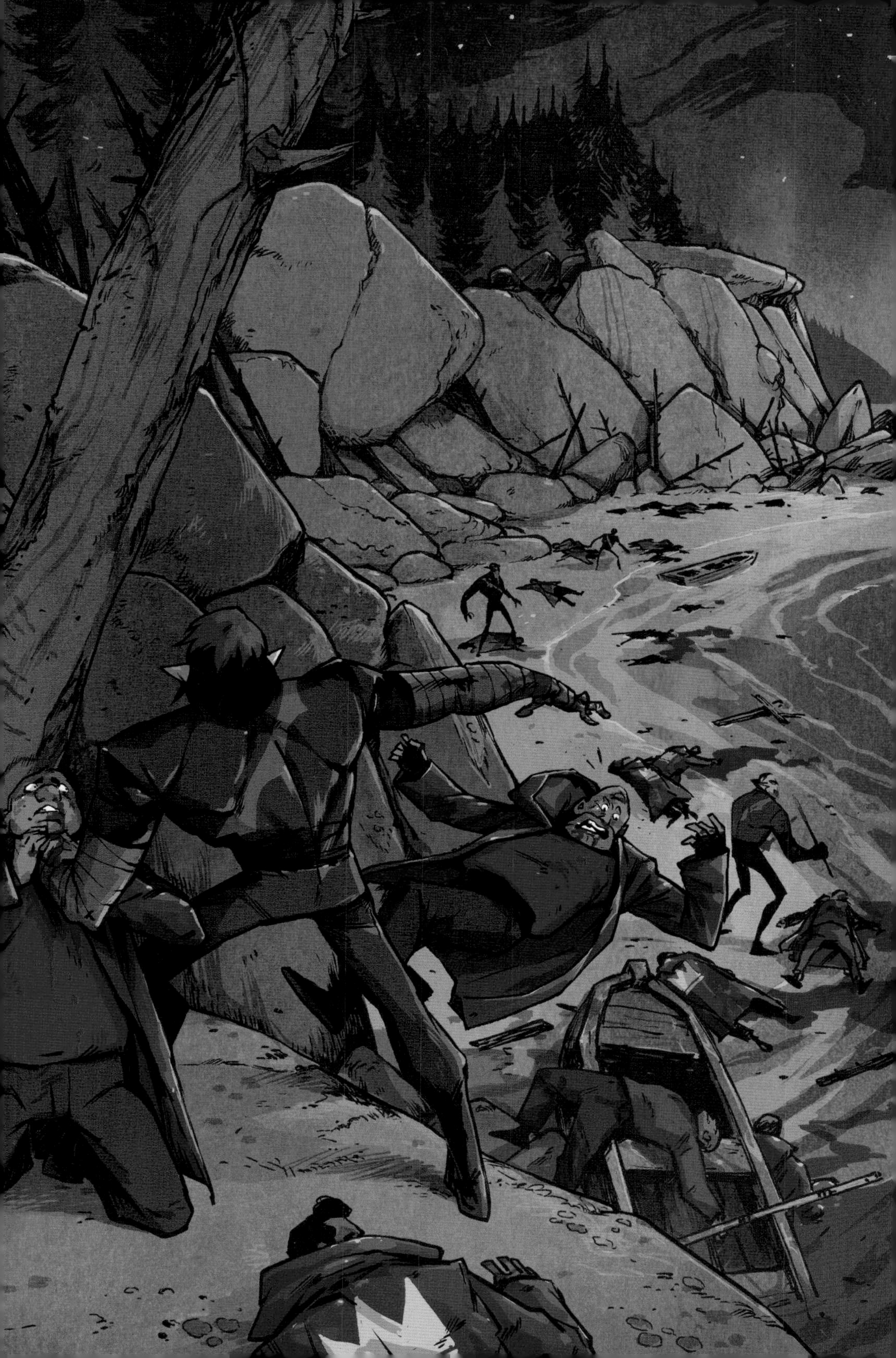

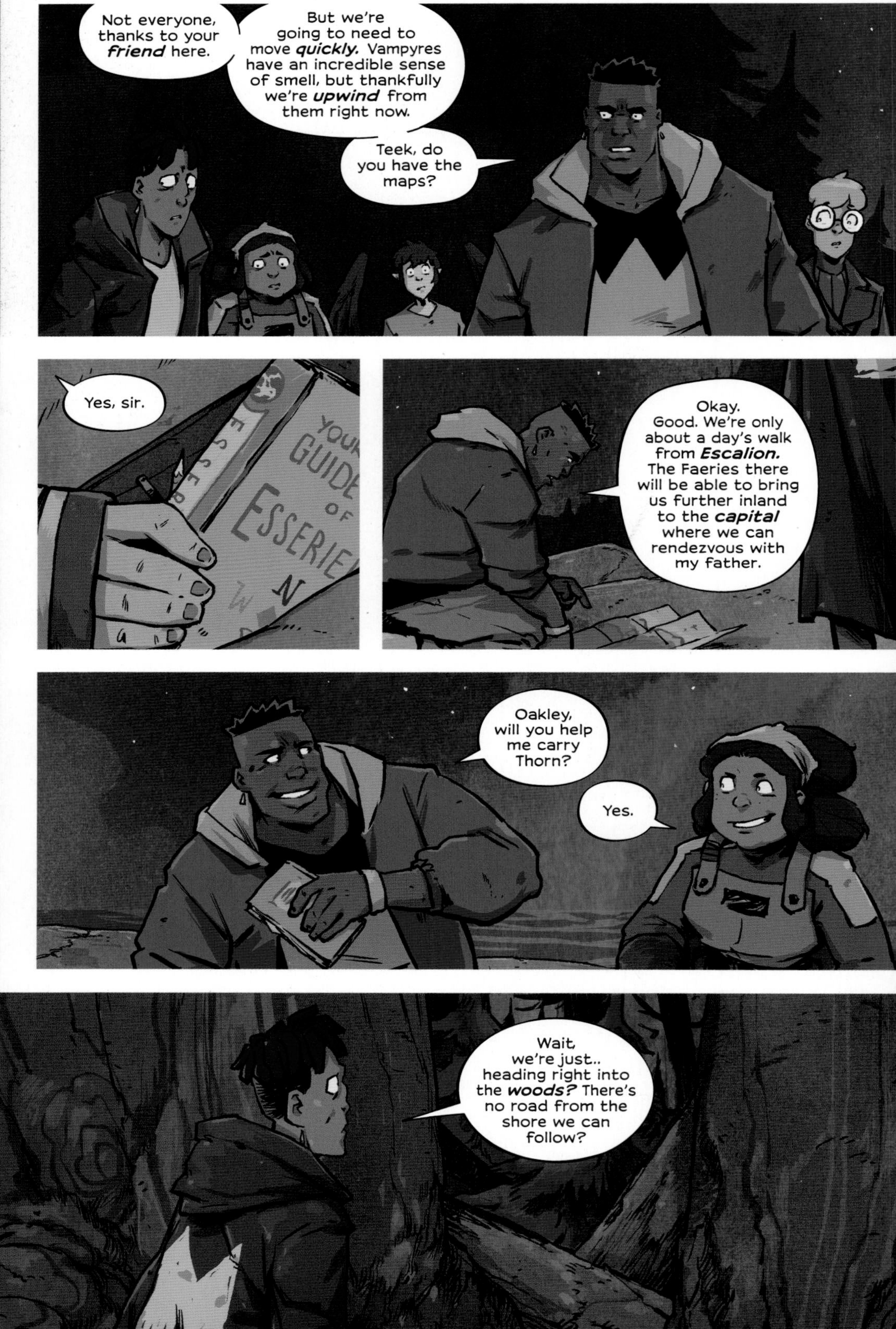

Not everyone, thanks to your *friend* here.
But we're going to need to move *quickly.* Vampyres have an incredible sense of smell, but thankfully we're *upwind* from them right now.
Teek, do you have the maps?
Yes, sir.
YOUR GUIDE OF ESSERIEL
ESSER
Okay. Good. We're only about a day's walk from *Escalion.* The Faeries there will be able to bring us further inland to the *capital* where we can rendezvous with my father.
Oakley, will you help me carry Thorn?
Yes.
Wait, we're just.. heading right into the *woods?* There's no road from the shore we can follow?

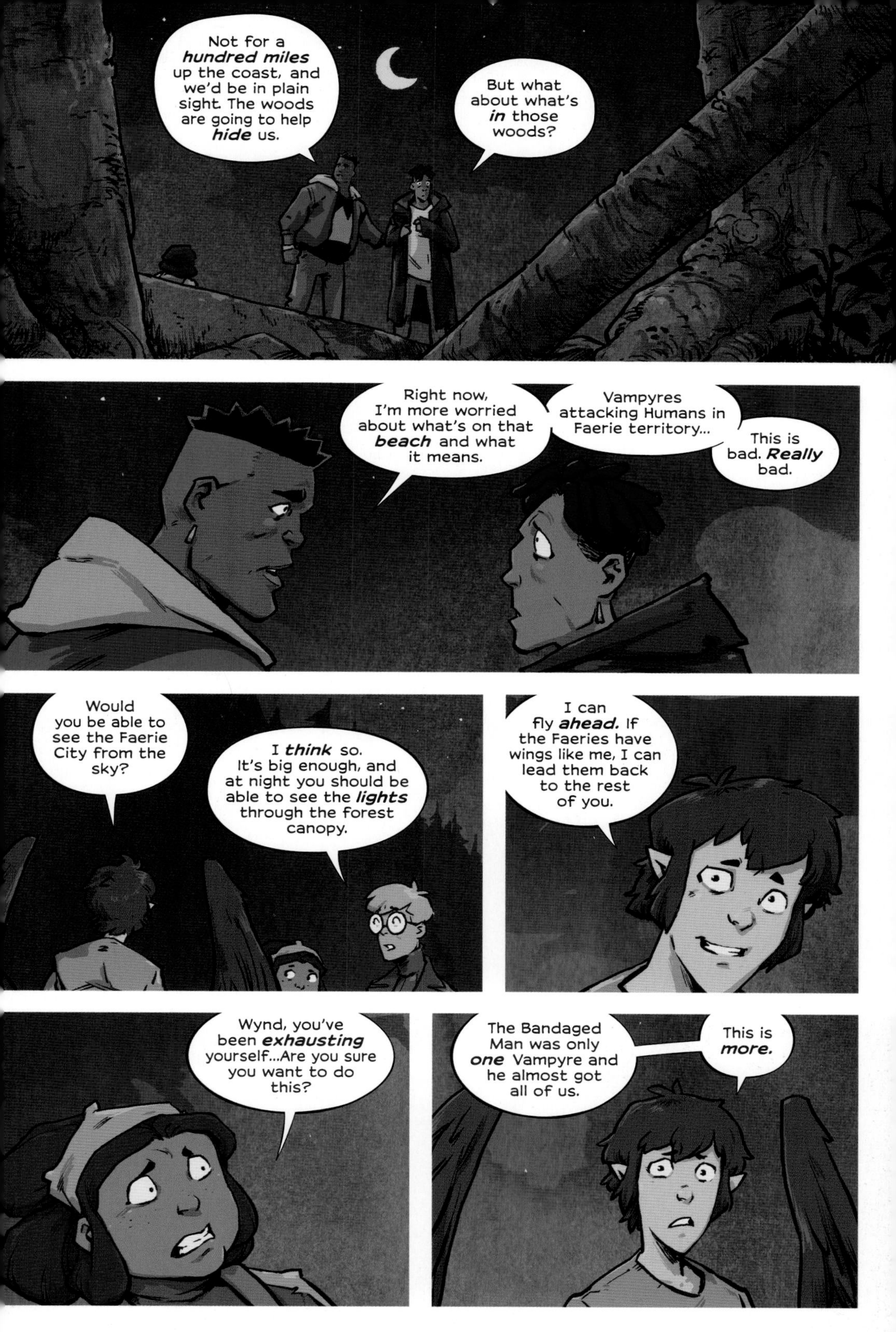
Not for a ***hundred miles*** up the coast, and we'd be in plain sight. The woods are going to help ***hide*** us.
But what about what's ***in*** those woods?
Right now, I'm more worried about what's on that ***beach*** and what it means.
Vampyres attacking Humans in Faerie territory...
This is bad. ***Really*** bad.
Would you be able to see the Faerie City from the sky?
I ***think*** so. It's big enough, and at night you should be able to see the ***lights*** through the forest canopy.
I can fly ***ahead.*** If the Faeries have wings like me, I can lead them back to the rest of you.
Wynd, you've been ***exhausting*** yourself...Are you sure you want to do this?
The Bandaged Man was only ***one*** Vampyre and he almost got all of us.
This is ***more.***

This is very **brave** of you.

Can you show me where I need to go?

It'll be hard to see at night, but you're flying straight toward the **Windshorn Peak.** The highest mountain in all of Esseriel. But right now...

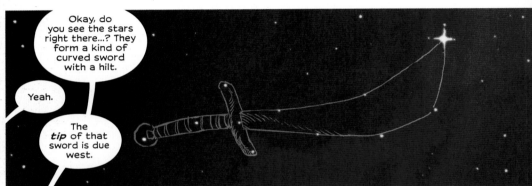

Okay, do you see the stars right there...? They form a kind of curved sword with a hilt.

Yeah.

The **tip** of that sword is due west.

Okay.

Be safe.

I will.

Keep Thorn **alive,** okay?

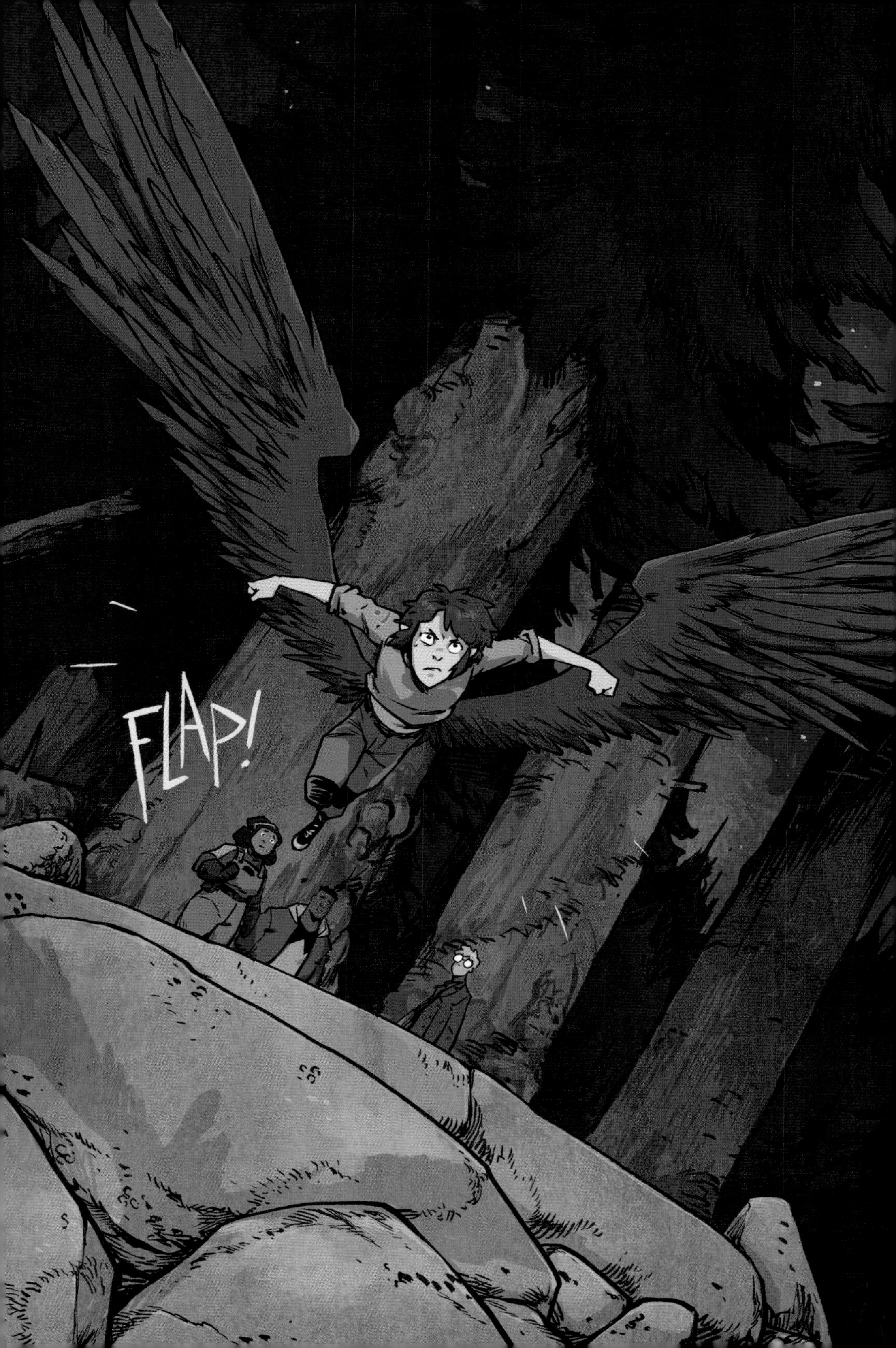
FLAP!

CHAPTER TWO
THE WEIRD WOODS

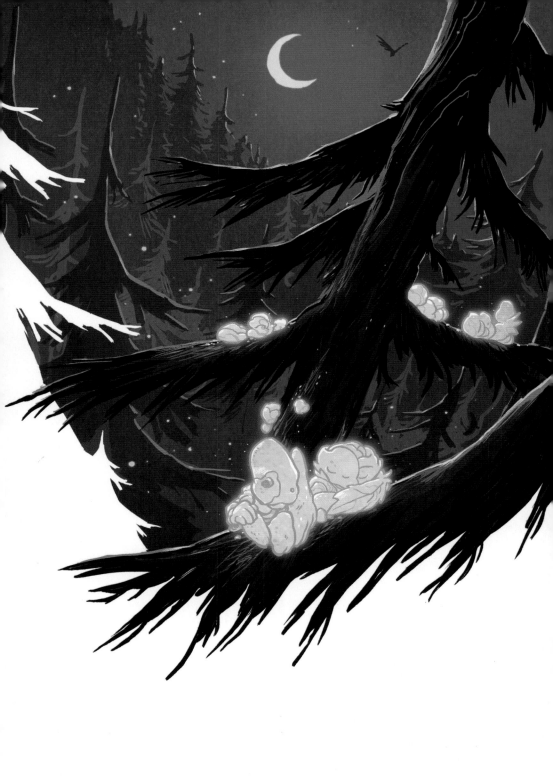

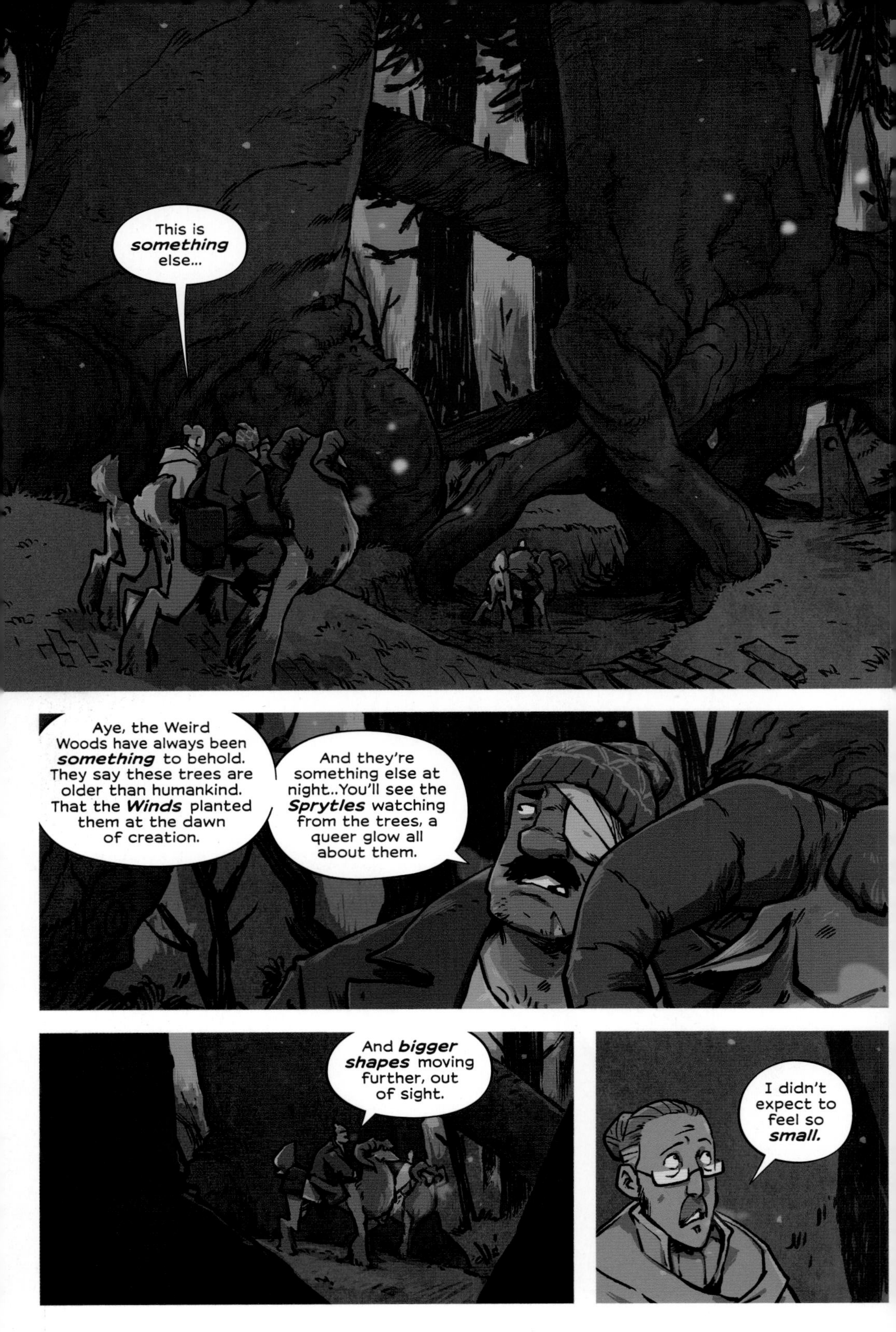
This is *something* else...
Aye, the Weird Woods have always been *something* to behold. They say these trees are older than humankind. That the *Winds* planted them at the dawn of creation.
And they're something else at night... You'll see the *Sprytles* watching from the trees, a queer glow all about them.
And *bigger shapes* moving further, out of sight.
I didn't expect to feel so *small.*

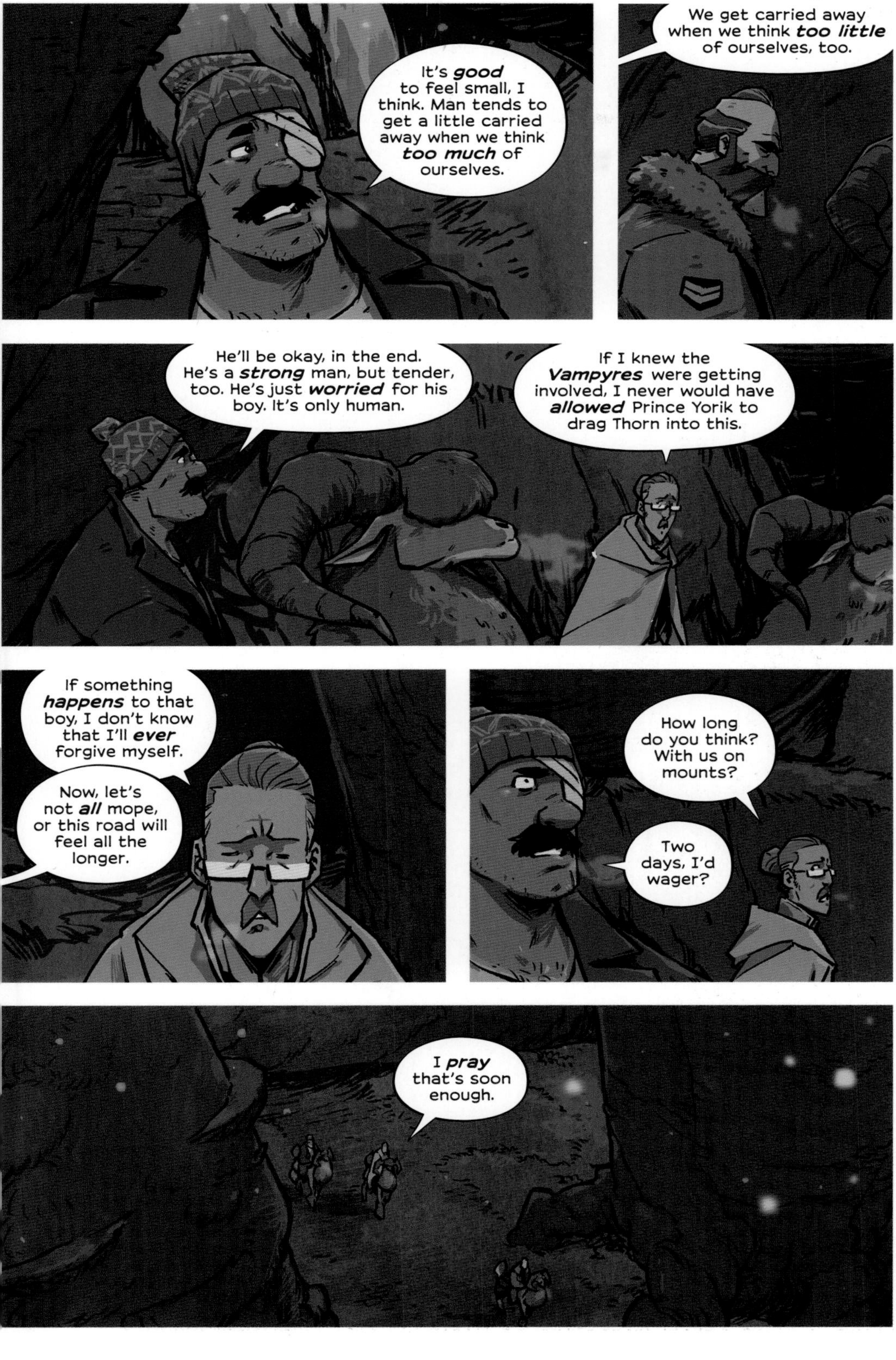

It's *good* to feel small, I think. Man tends to get a little carried away when we think *too much* of ourselves.
We get carried away when we think *too little* of ourselves, too.
He'll be okay, in the end. He's a *strong* man, but tender, too. He's just *worried* for his boy. It's only human.
If I knew the *Vampyres* were getting involved, I never would have *allowed* Prince Yorik to drag Thorn into this.
If something *happens* to that boy, I don't know that I'll *ever* forgive myself.
Now, let's not *all* mope, or this road will feel all the longer.
How long do you think? With us on mounts?
Two days, I'd wager?
I *pray* that's soon enough.

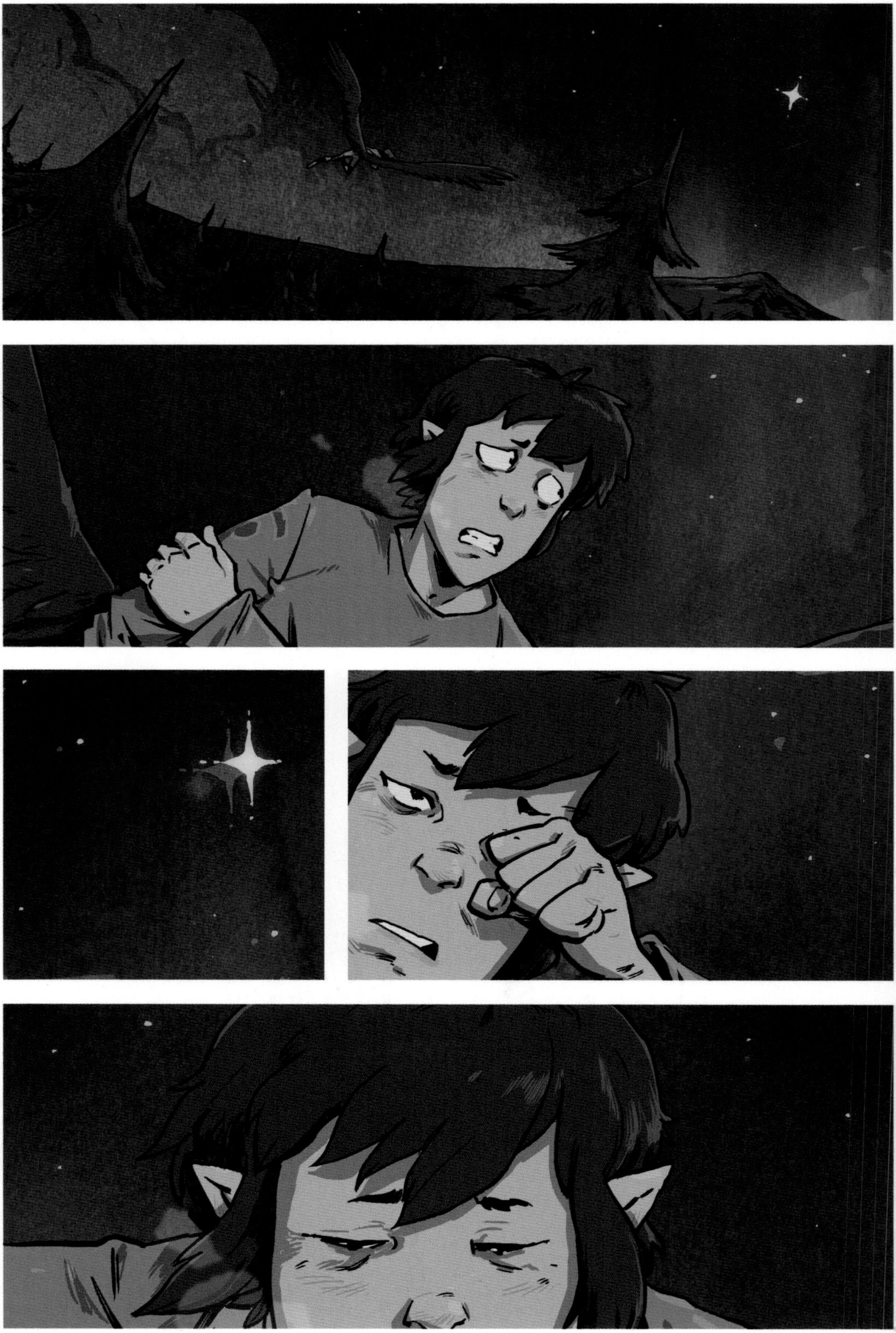

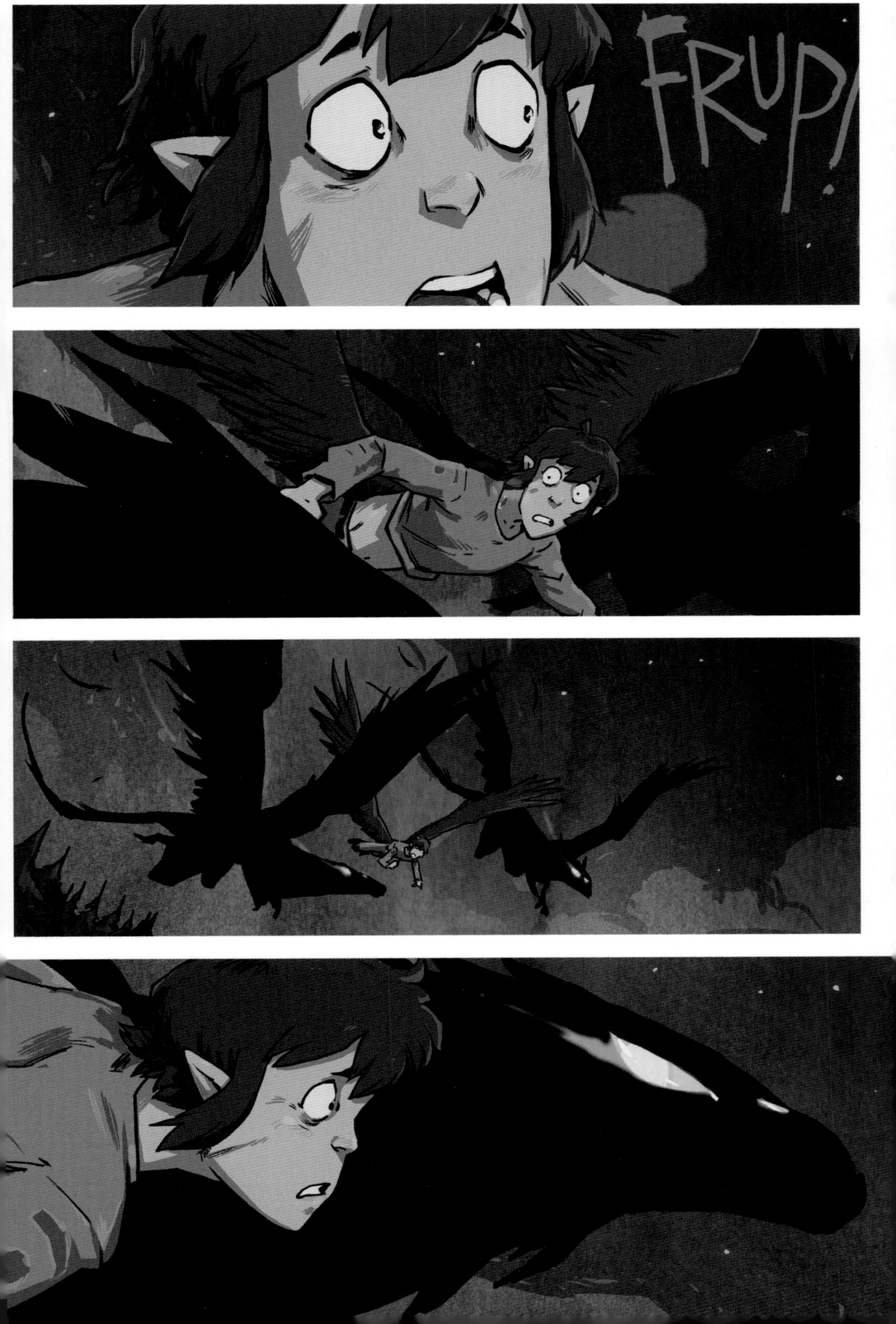
FRUP!

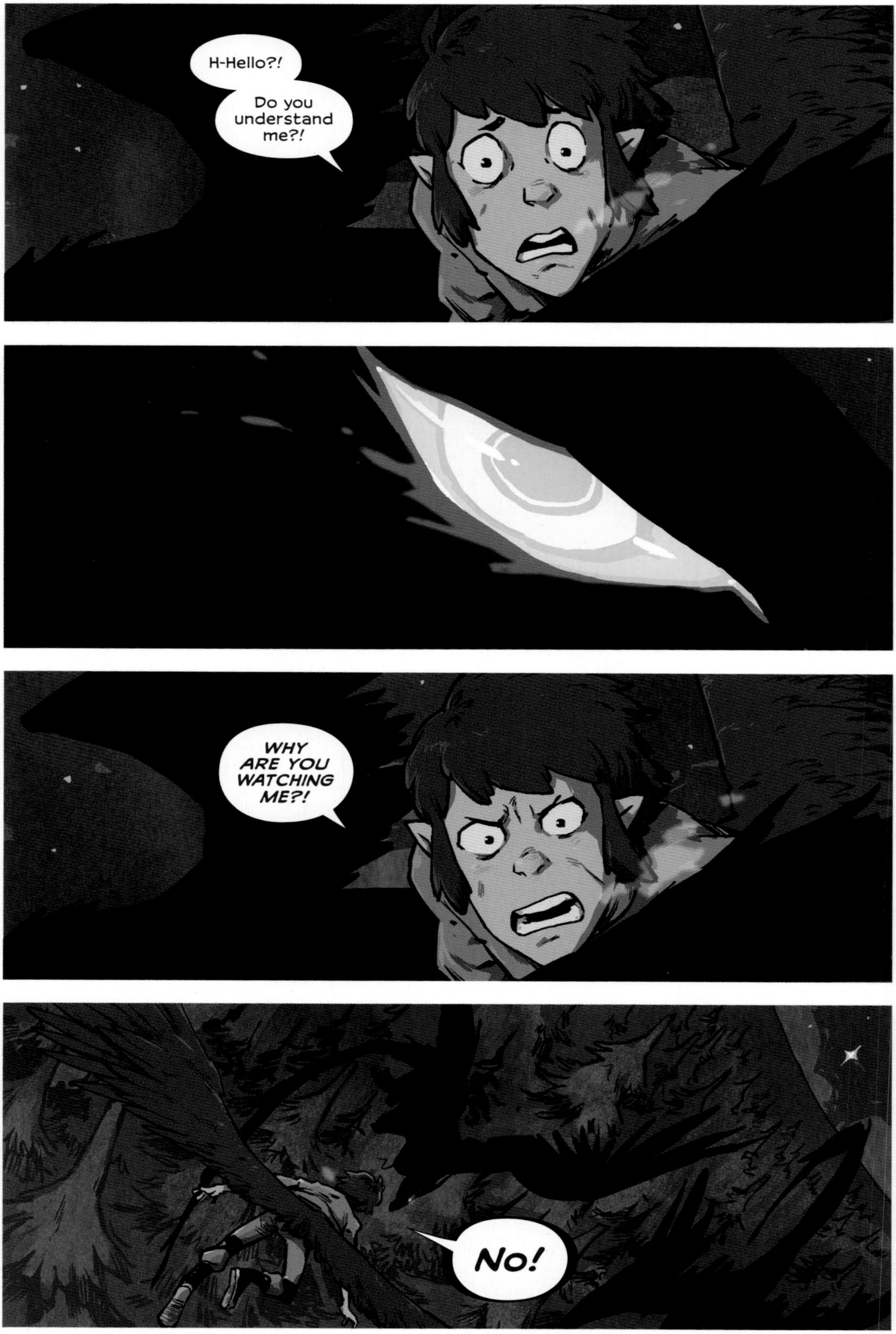
H-Hello?!
Do you understand me?!
WHY ARE YOU WATCHING ME?!
No!

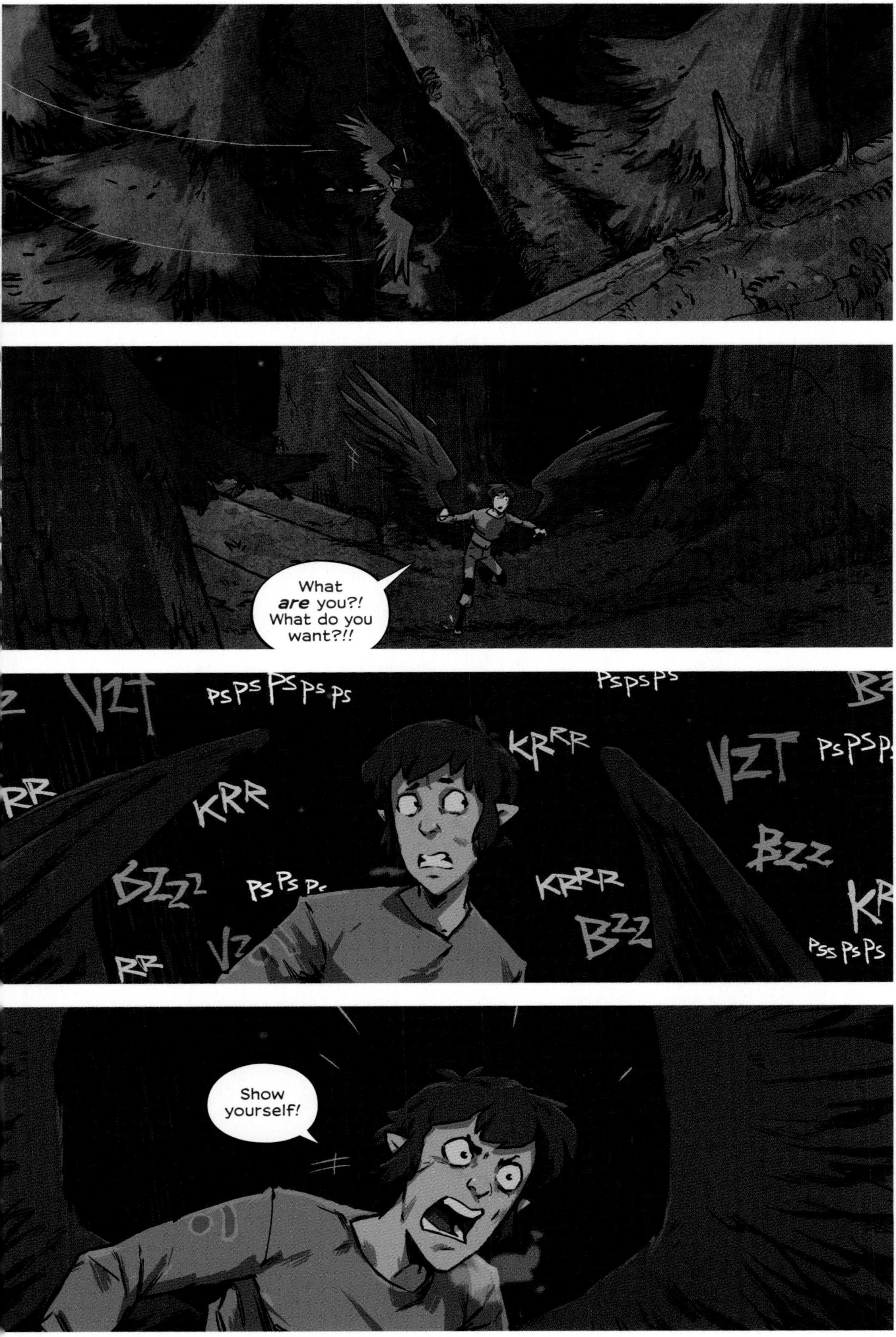
What *are* you?! What do you want?!!
VZT
KRRR
KRR
BZZZ
VZT
BZZ
Show yourself!

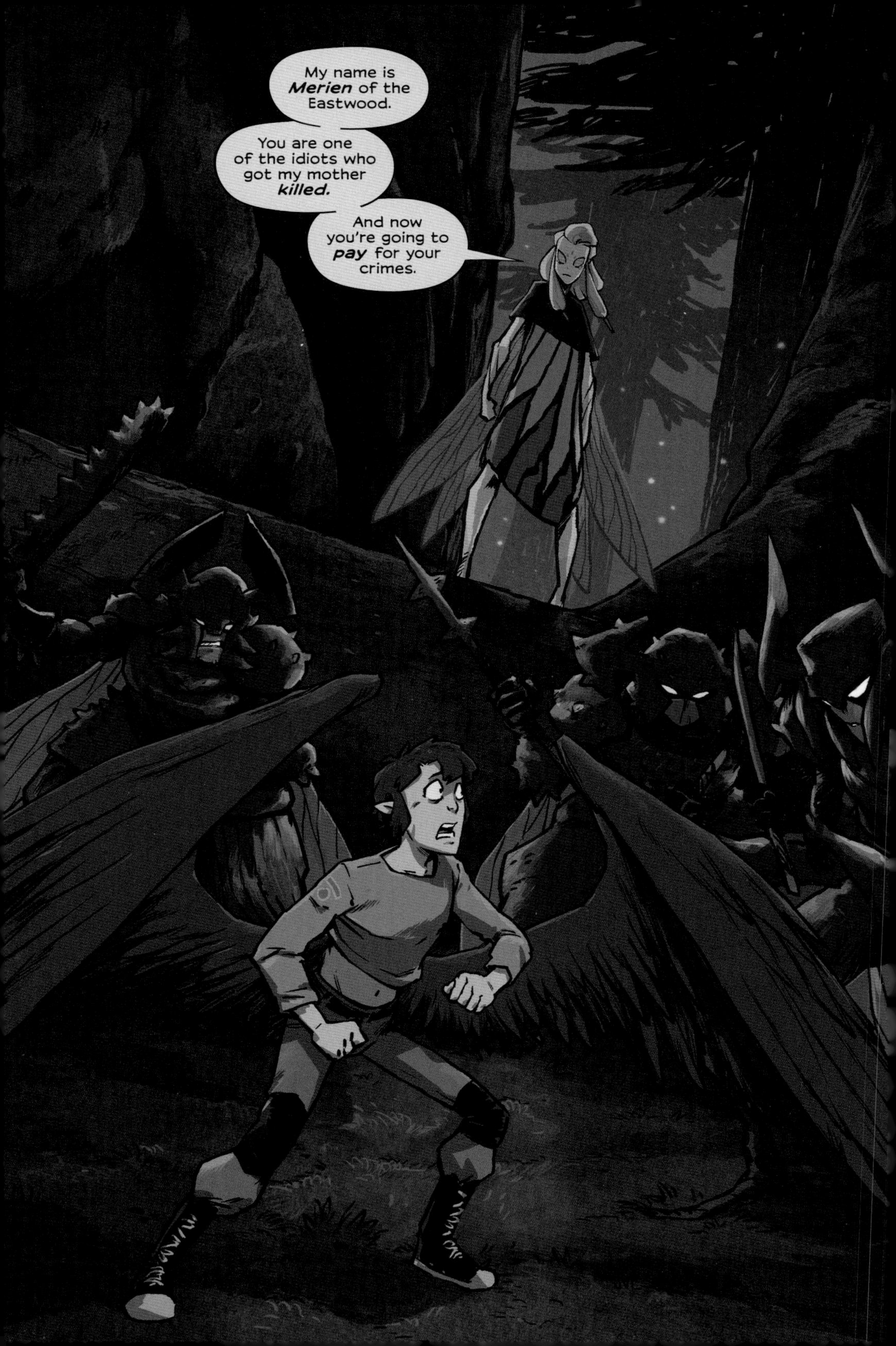
My name is *Merien* of the Eastwood.
You are one of the idiots who got my mother *killed.*
And now you're going to *pay* for your crimes.

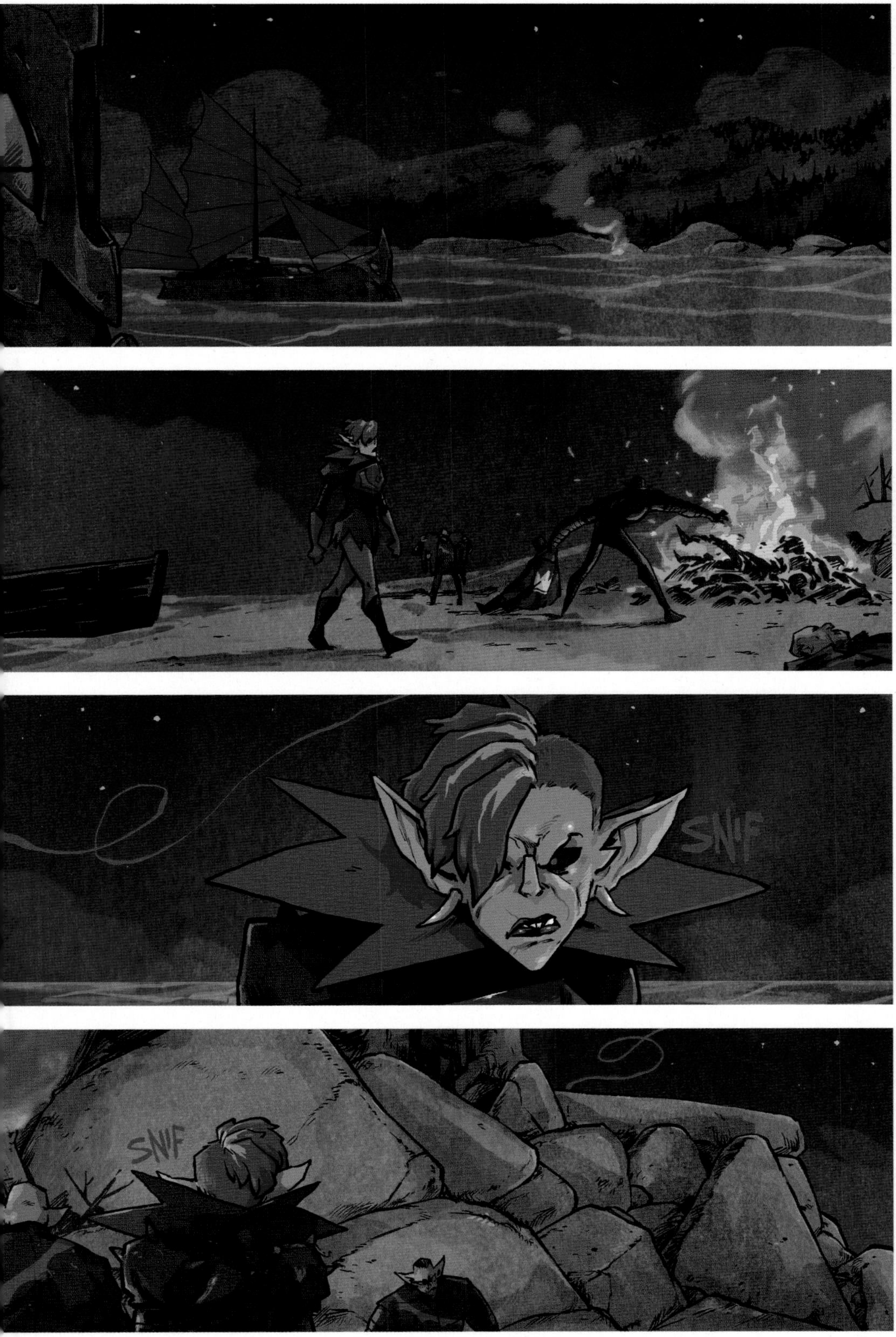
SNIF
SNIF

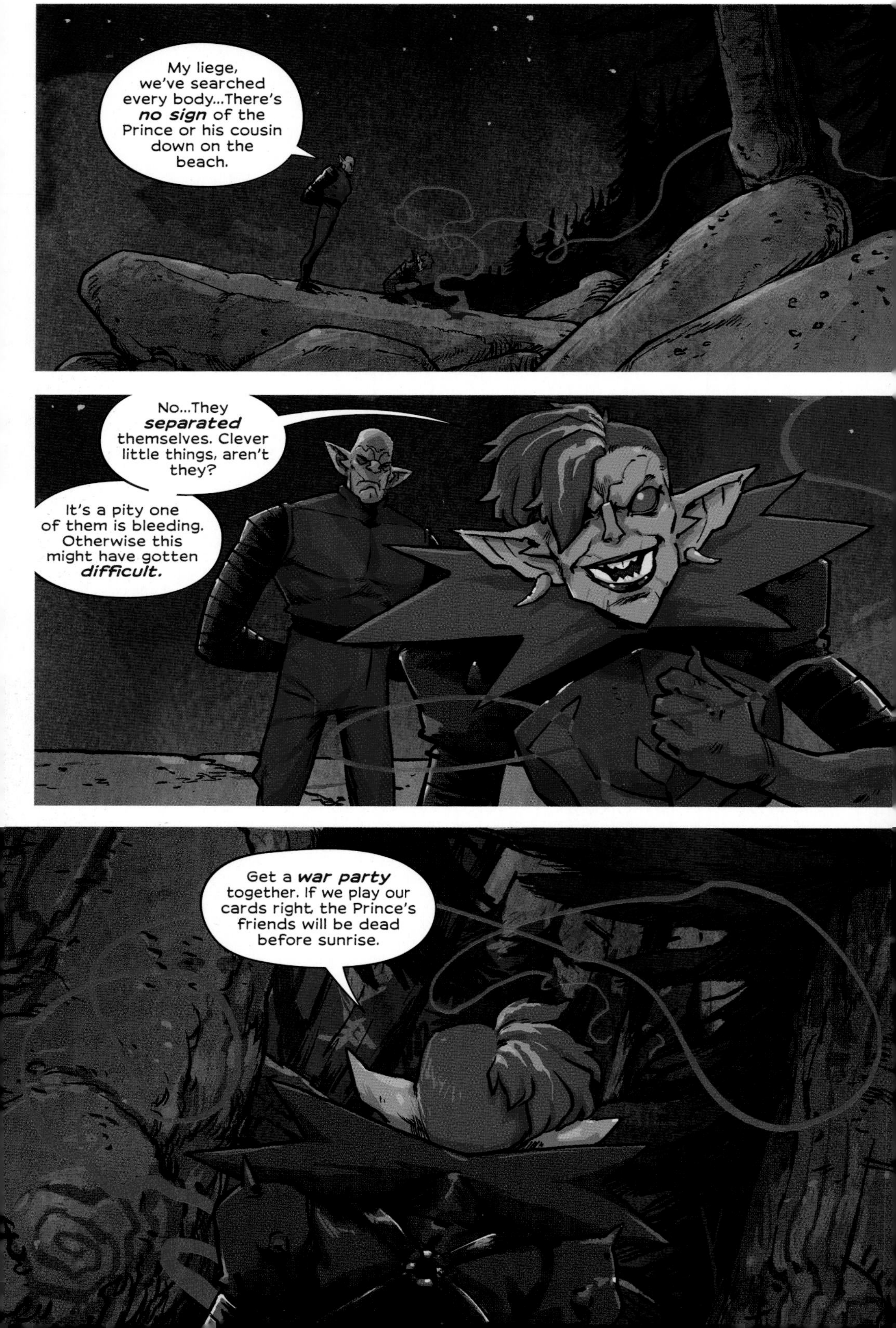
My liege, we've searched every body...There's ***no sign*** of the Prince or his cousin down on the beach.
No...They ***separated*** themselves. Clever little things, aren't they?
It's a pity one of them is bleeding. Otherwise this might have gotten ***difficult.***
Get a ***war party*** together. If we play our cards right, the Prince's friends will be dead before sunrise.

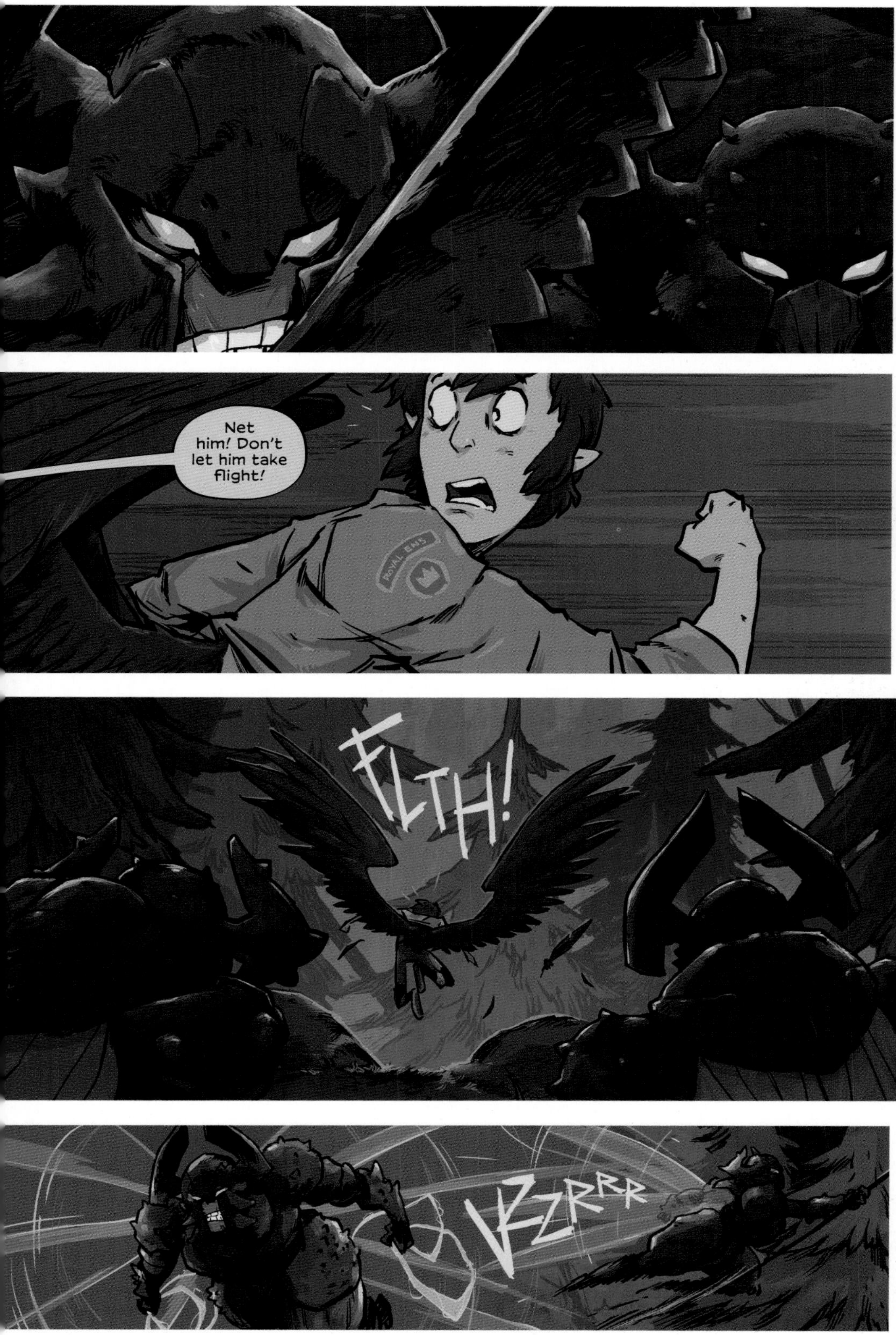
Net him! Don't let him take flight!
FLTH!
VZZRRR

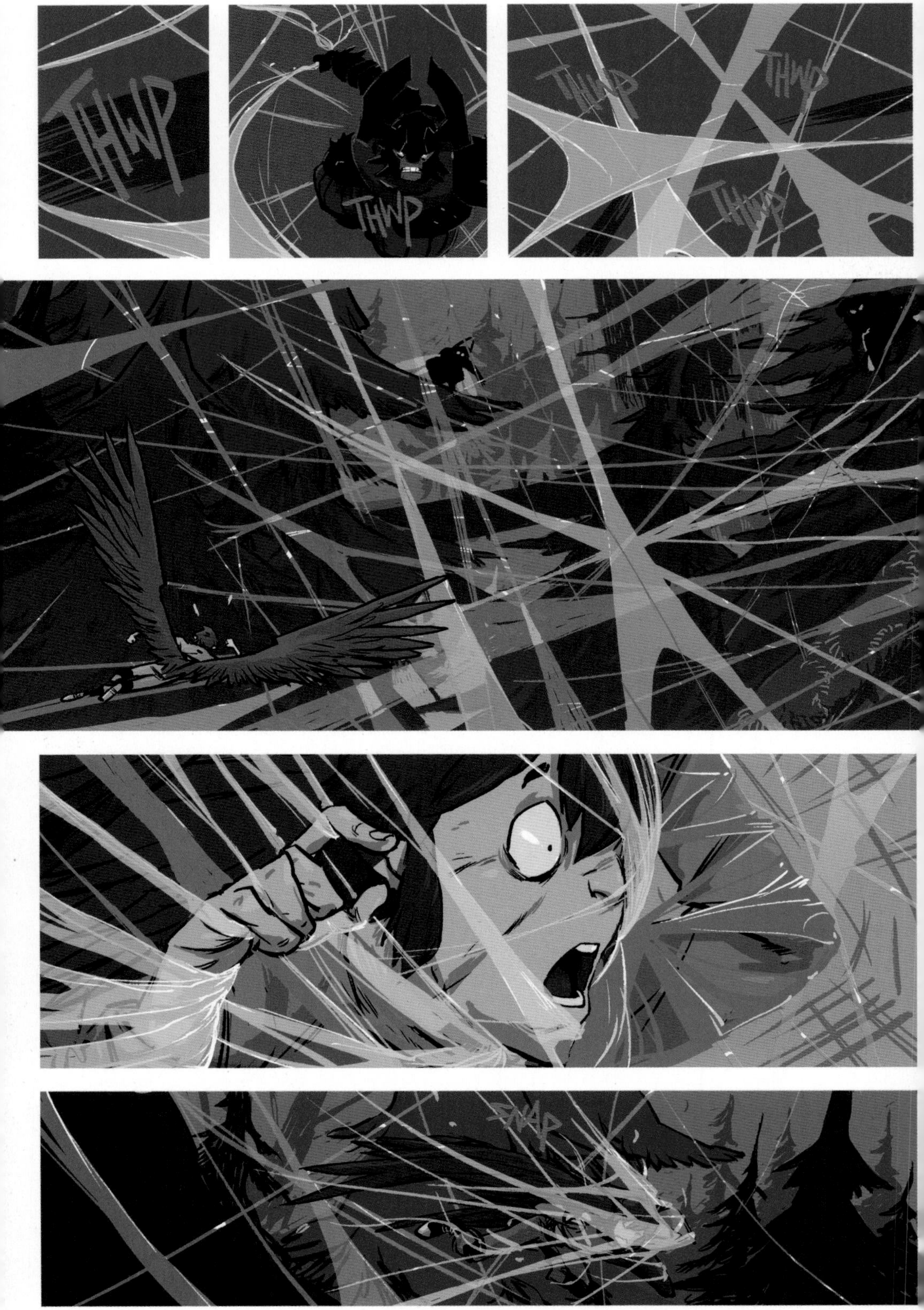
THWP
THWP
THWP
THWP
THWP
SNAP

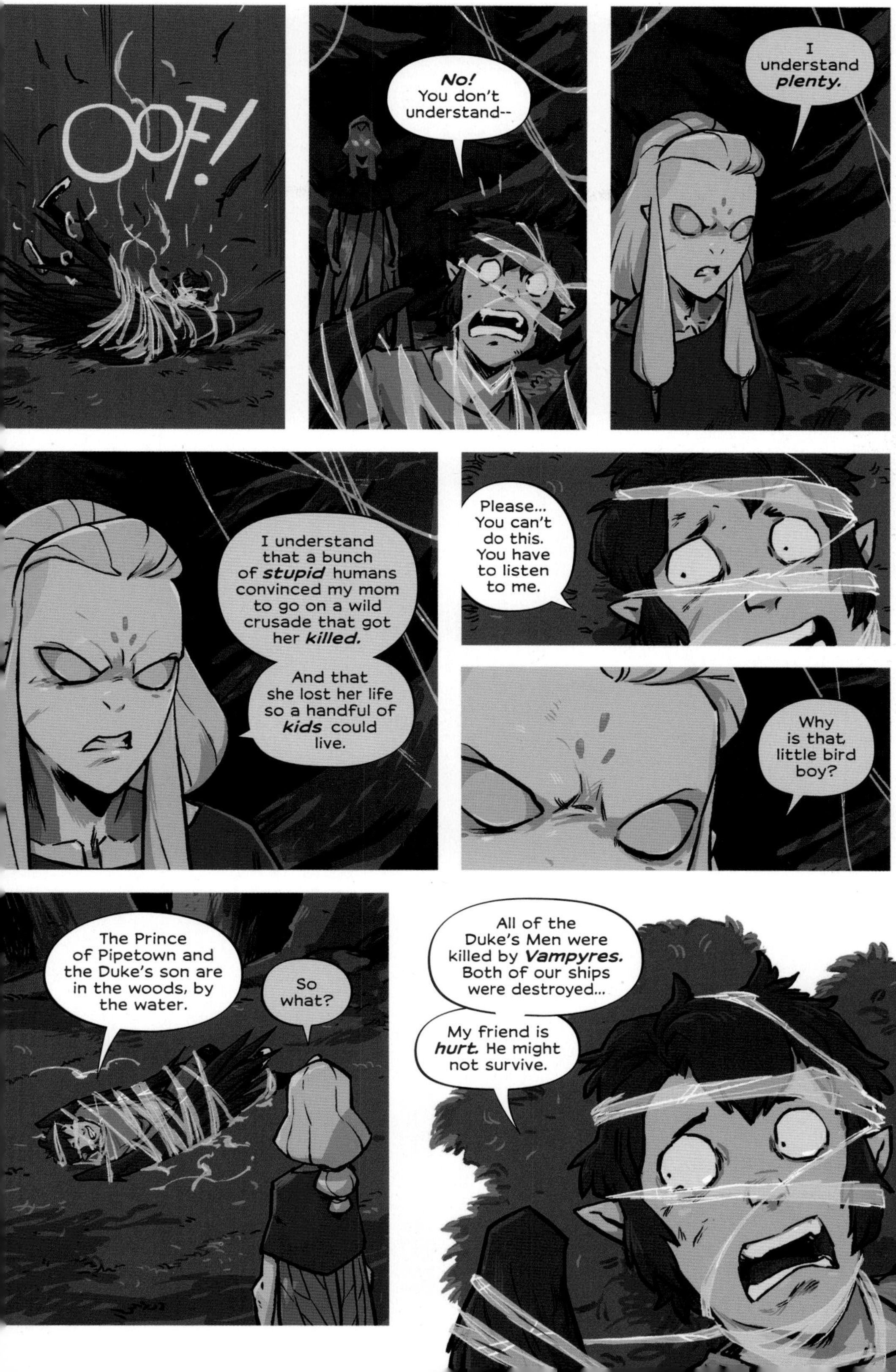
OOF!
No! You don't understand--
I understand plenty.
I understand that a bunch of stupid humans convinced my mom to go on a wild crusade that got her killed.
And that she lost her life so a handful of kids could live.
Please... You can't do this. You have to listen to me.
Why is that little bird boy?
The Prince of Pipetown and the Duke's son are in the woods, by the water.
So what?
All of the Duke's Men were killed by Vampyres. Both of our ships were destroyed...
My friend is hurt. He might not survive.

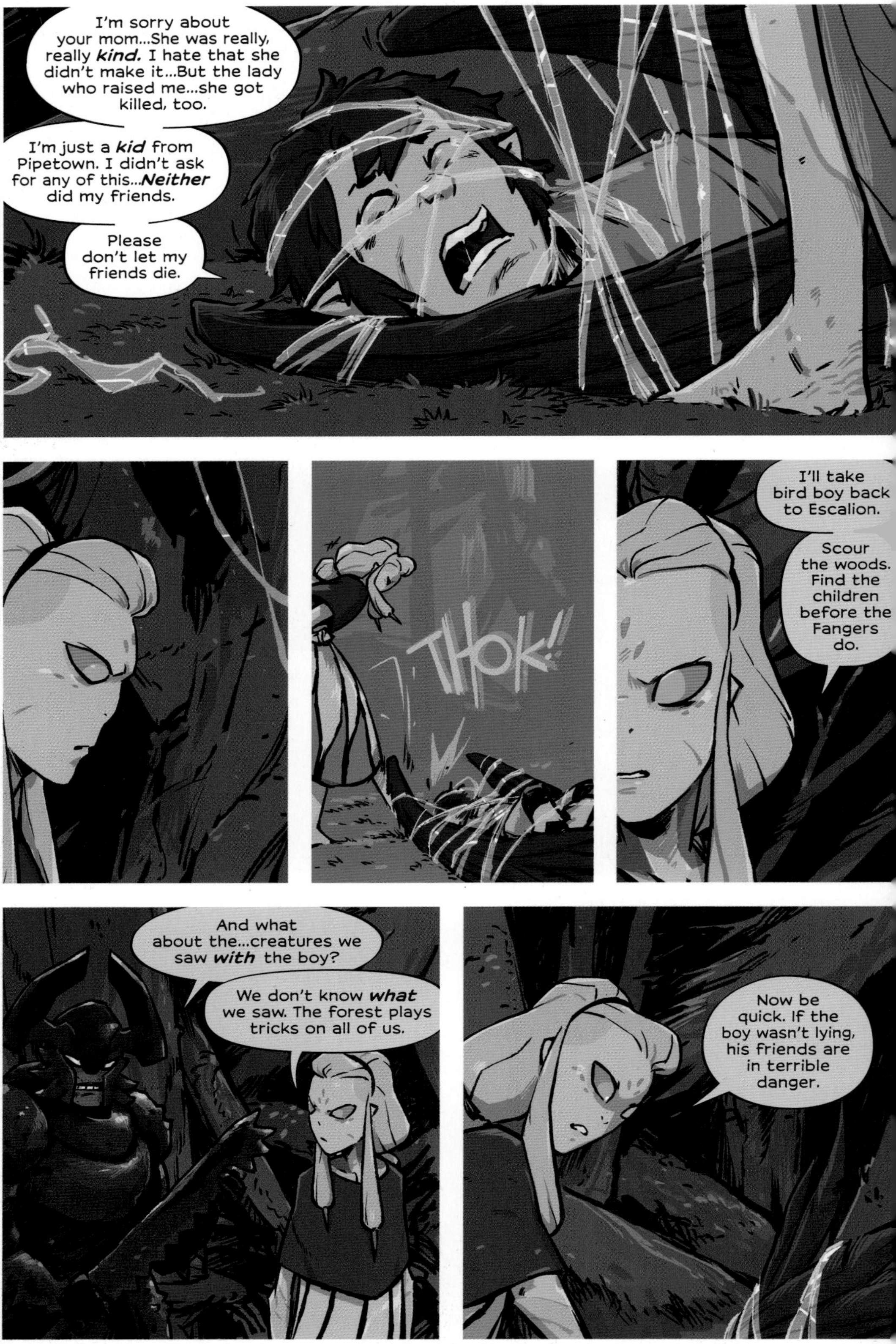
I'm sorry about your mom...She was really, really *kind.* I hate that she didn't make it...But the lady who raised me...she got killed, too.
I'm just a *kid* from Pipetown. I didn't ask for any of this...*Neither* did my friends.
Please don't let my friends die.
THOK!
I'll take bird boy back to Escalion.
Scour the woods. Find the children before the Fangers do.
And what about the...creatures we saw *with* the boy?
We don't know *what* we saw. The forest plays tricks on all of us.
Now be quick. If the boy wasn't lying, his friends are in terrible danger.

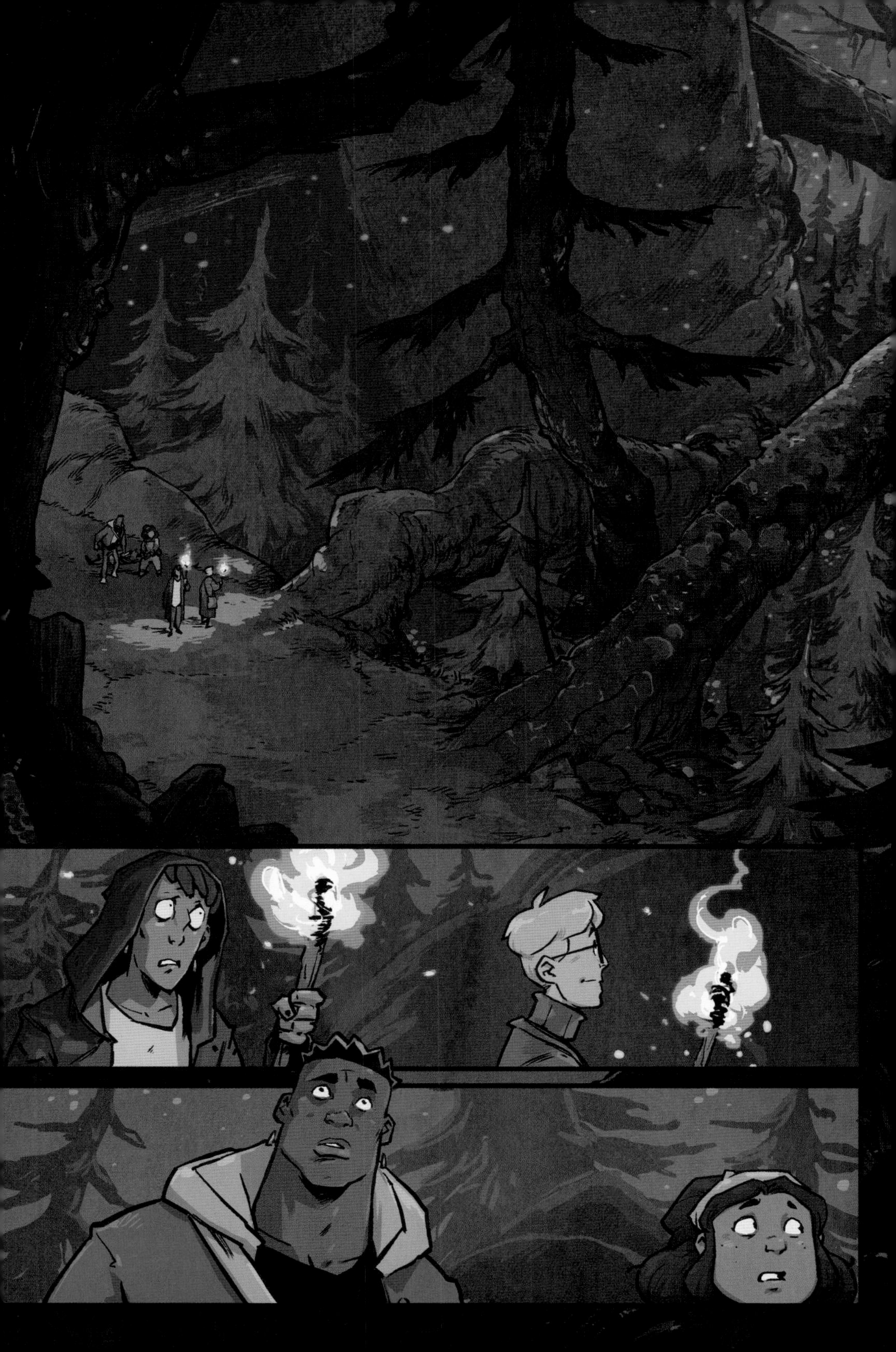

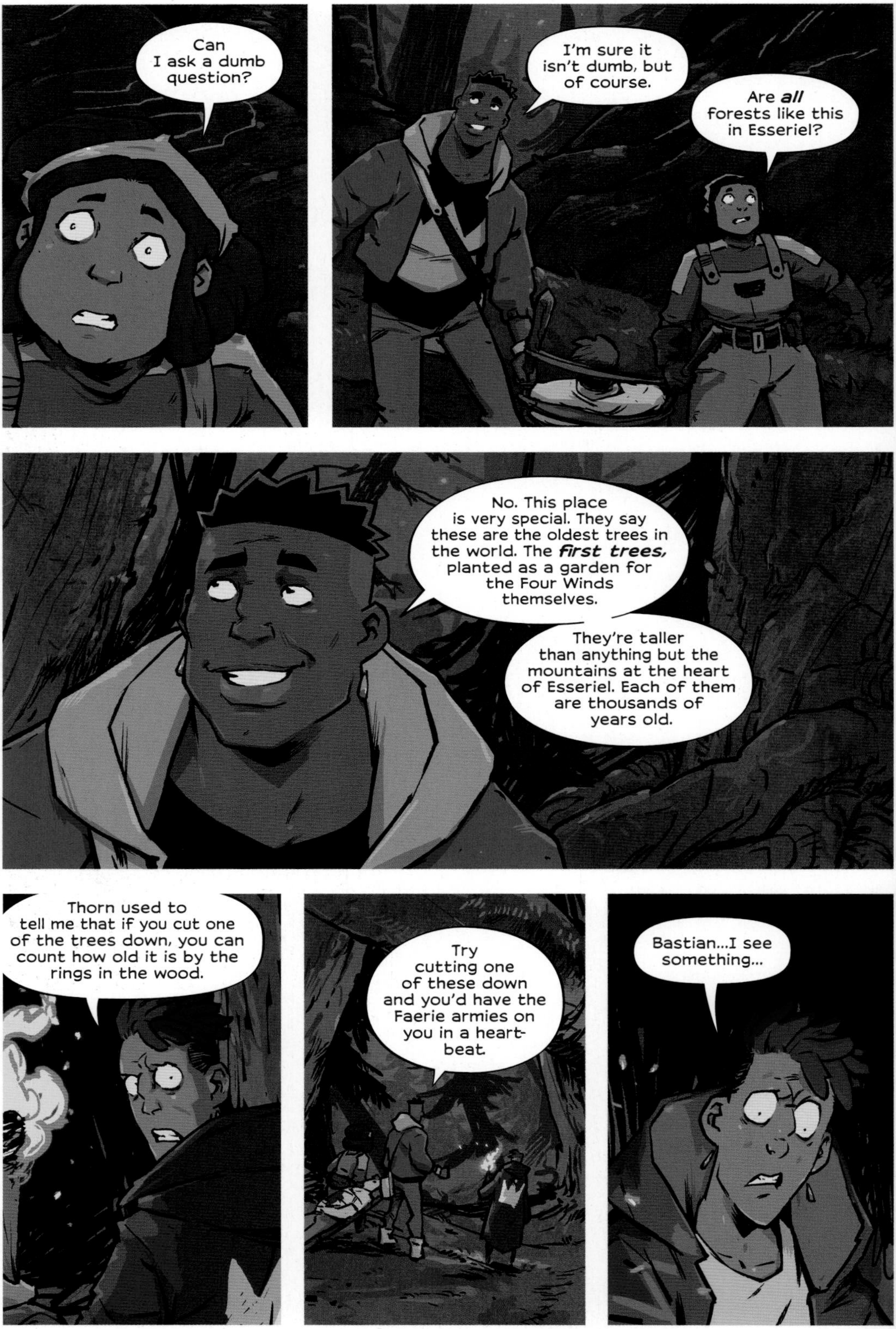
Can I ask a dumb question?
I'm sure it isn't dumb, but of course.
Are *all* forests like this in Esseriel?
No. This place is very special. They say these are the oldest trees in the world. The *first trees,* planted as a garden for the Four Winds themselves.
They're taller than anything but the mountains at the heart of Esseriel. Each of them are thousands of years old.
Thorn used to tell me that if you cut one of the trees down, you can count how old it is by the rings in the wood.
Try cutting one of these down and you'd have the Faerie armies on you in a heart-beat.
Bastian...I see something...

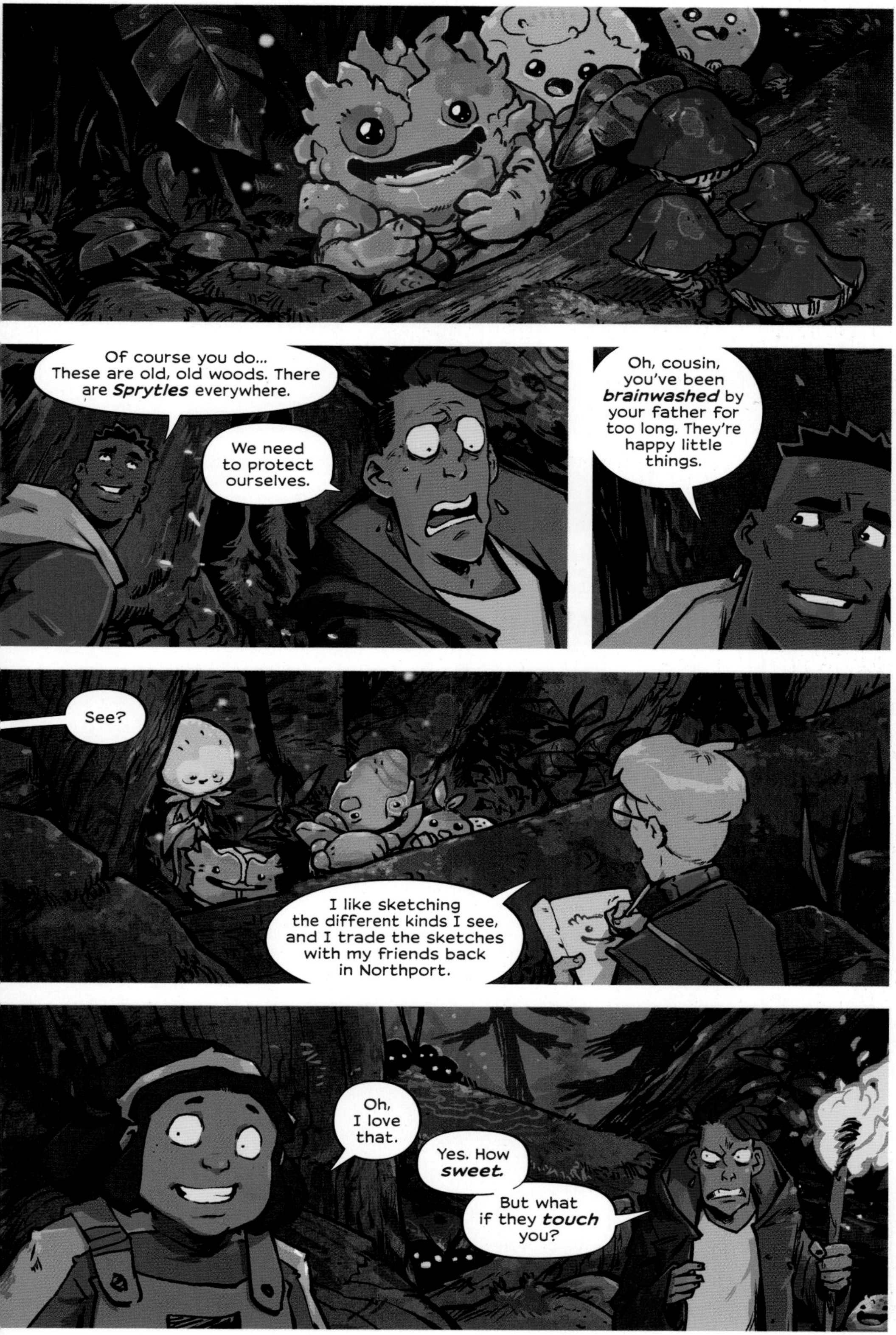
Of course you do... These are old, old woods. There are *Sprytles* everywhere.
We need to protect ourselves.
Oh, cousin, you've been ***brainwashed*** by your father for too long. They're happy little things.
See?
I like sketching the different kinds I see, and I trade the sketches with my friends back in Northport.
Oh, I love that.
Yes. How ***sweet.***
But what if they ***touch*** you?

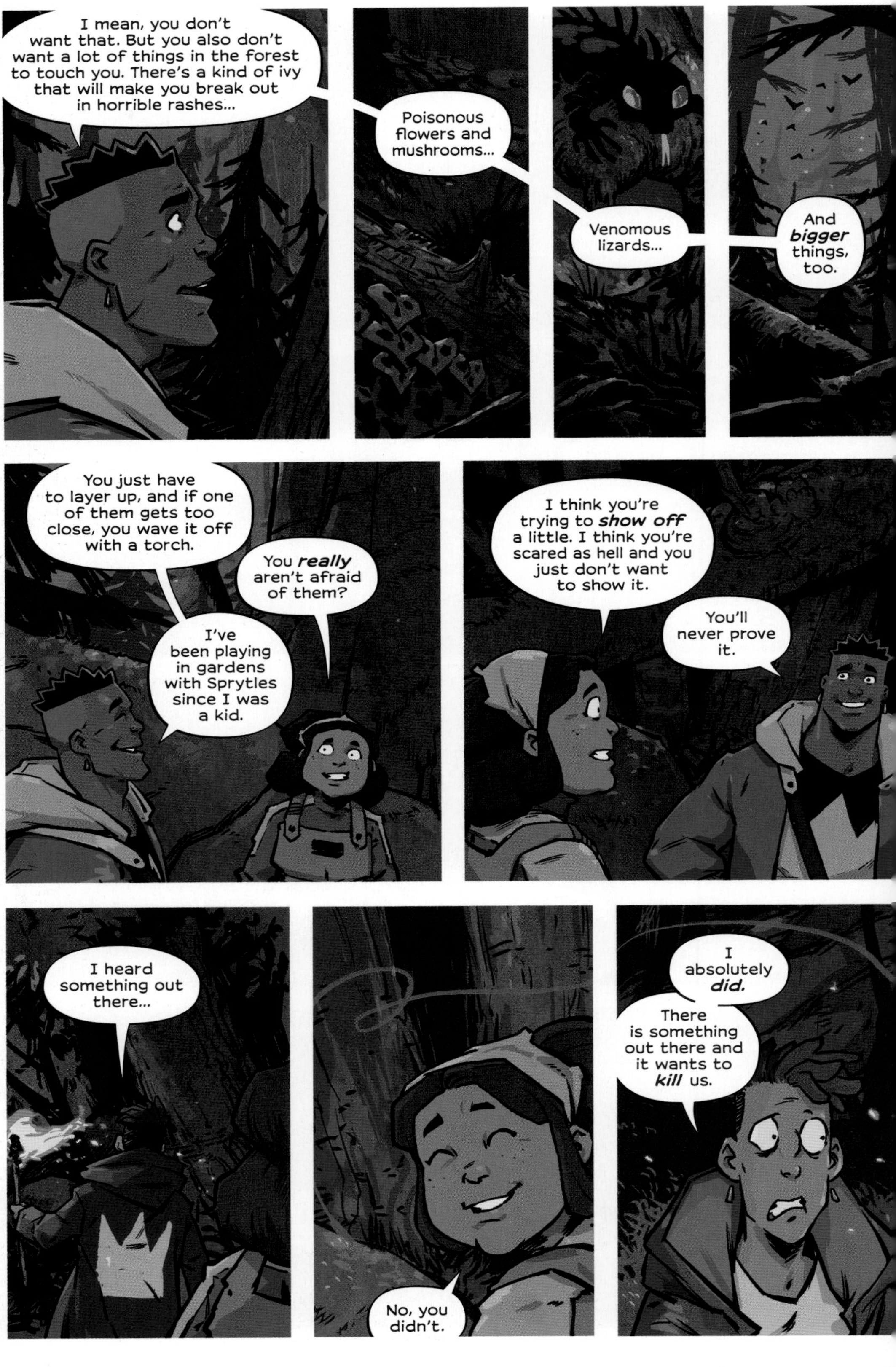
I mean, you don't want that. But you also don't want a lot of things in the forest to touch you. There's a kind of ivy that will make you break out in horrible rashes...
Poisonous flowers and mushrooms...
Venomous lizards...
And *bigger* things, too.
You just have to layer up, and if one of them gets too close, you wave it off with a torch.
You *really* aren't afraid of them?
I've been playing in gardens with Sprytles since I was a kid.
I think you're trying to *show off* a little. I think you're scared as hell and you just don't want to show it.
You'll never prove it.
I heard something out there...
No, you didn't.
I absolutely *did.*
There is something out there and it wants to *kill* us.

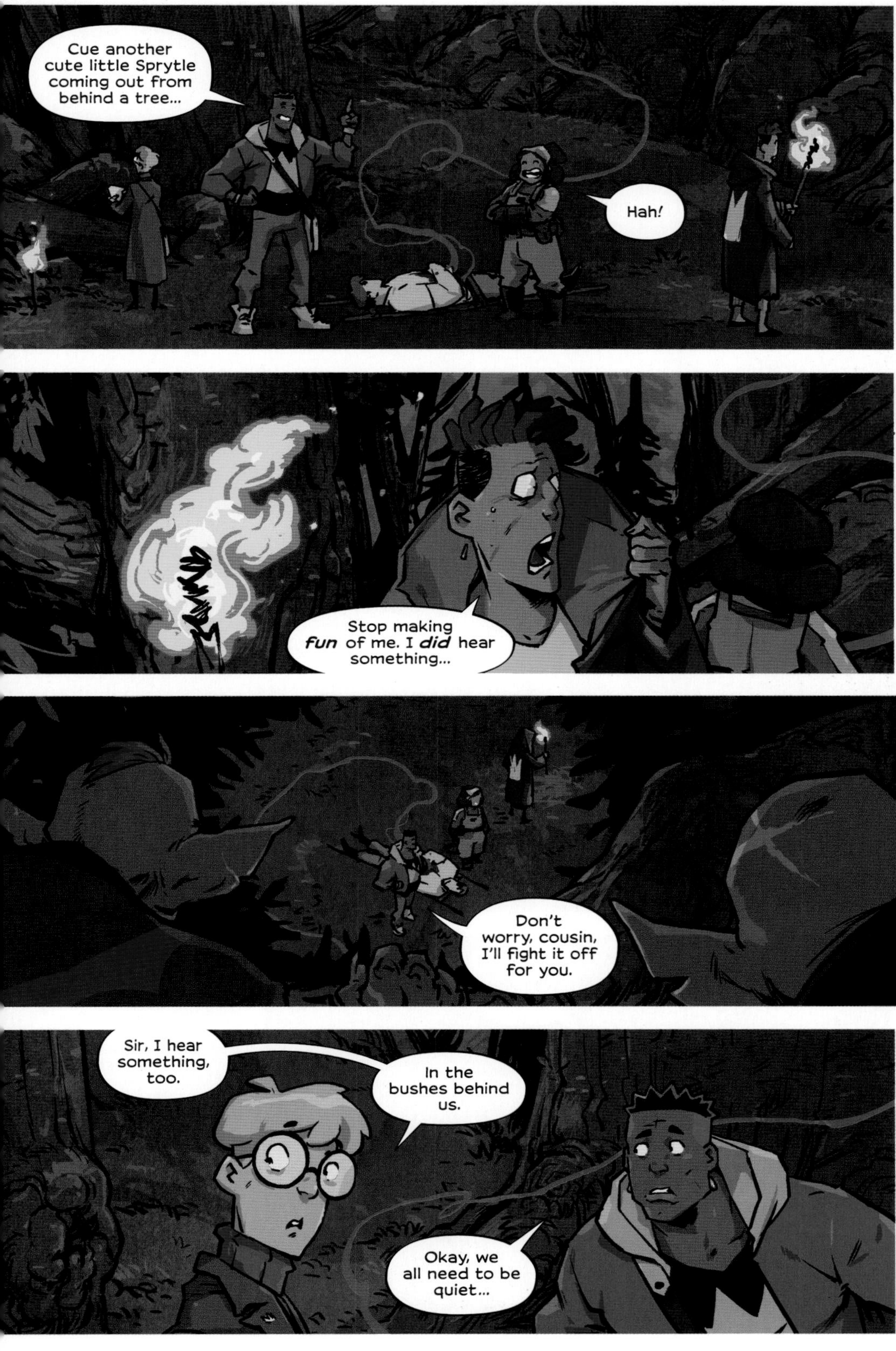
Cue another cute little Sprytle coming out from behind a tree...
Hah!
Stop making *fun* of me. I *did* hear something...
Don't worry, cousin, I'll fight it off for you.
Sir, I hear something, too.
In the bushes behind us.
Okay, we all need to be quiet...

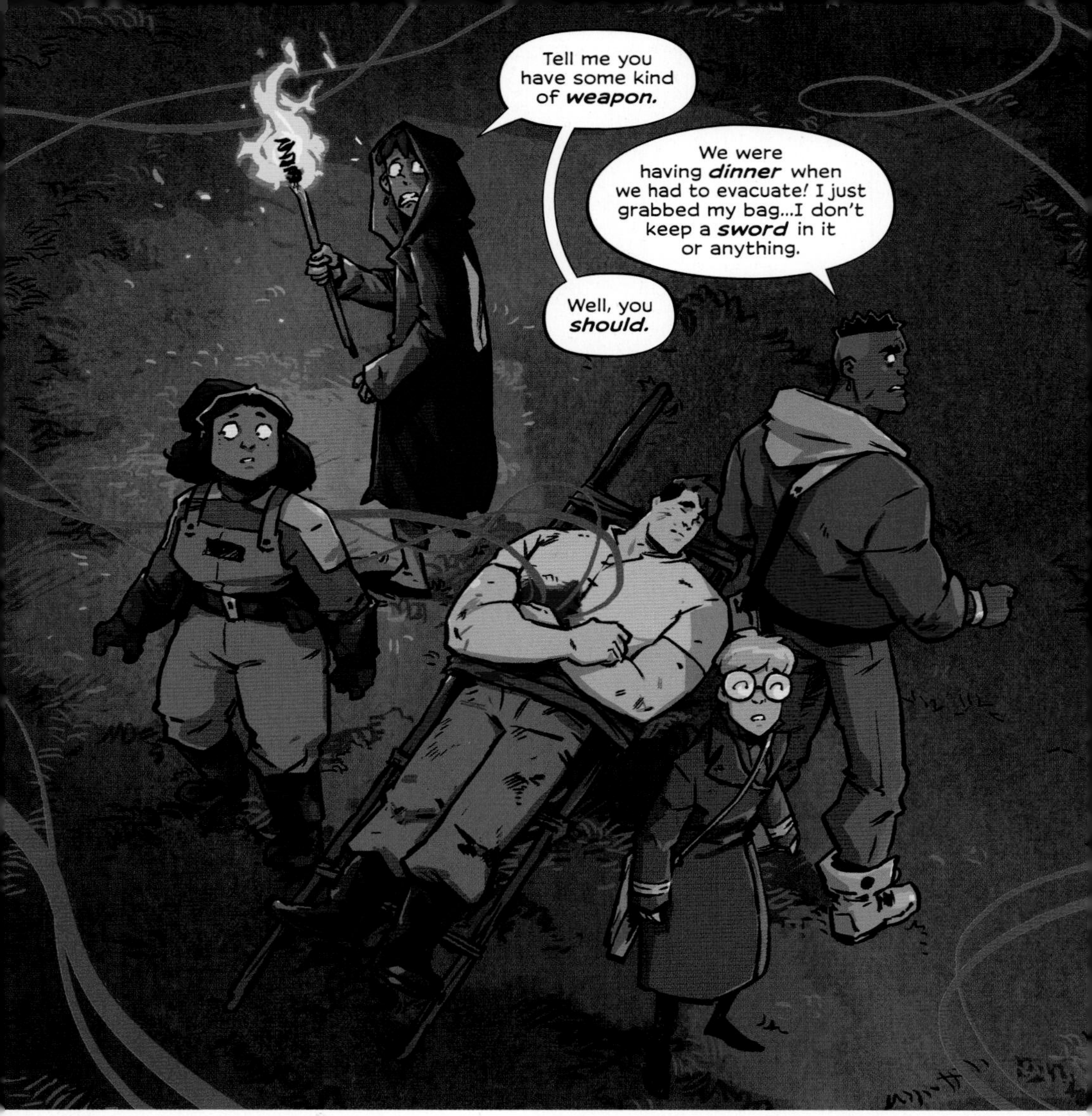
Tell me you have some kind of ***weapon.***
We were having ***dinner*** when we had to evacuate! I just grabbed my bag...I don't keep a ***sword*** in it or anything.
Well, you ***should.***

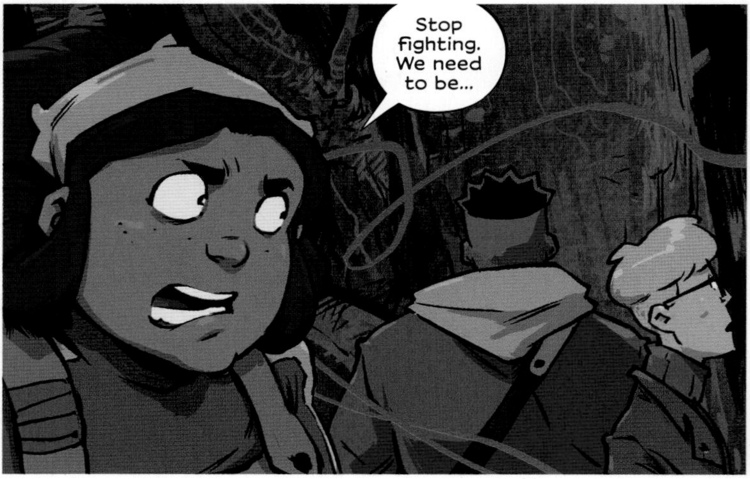
Stop fighting. We need to be...

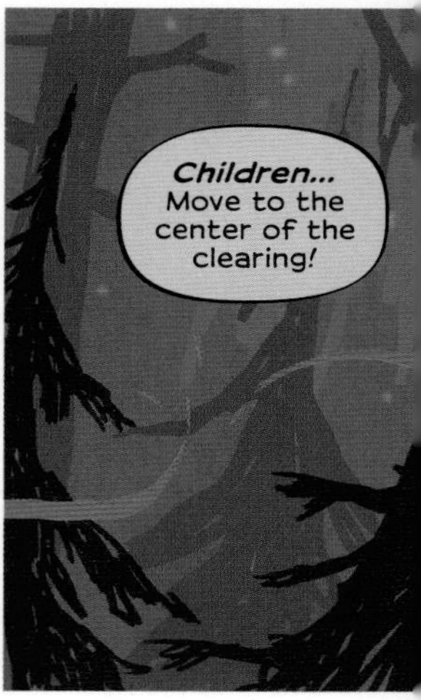
Children... Move to the center of the clearing!

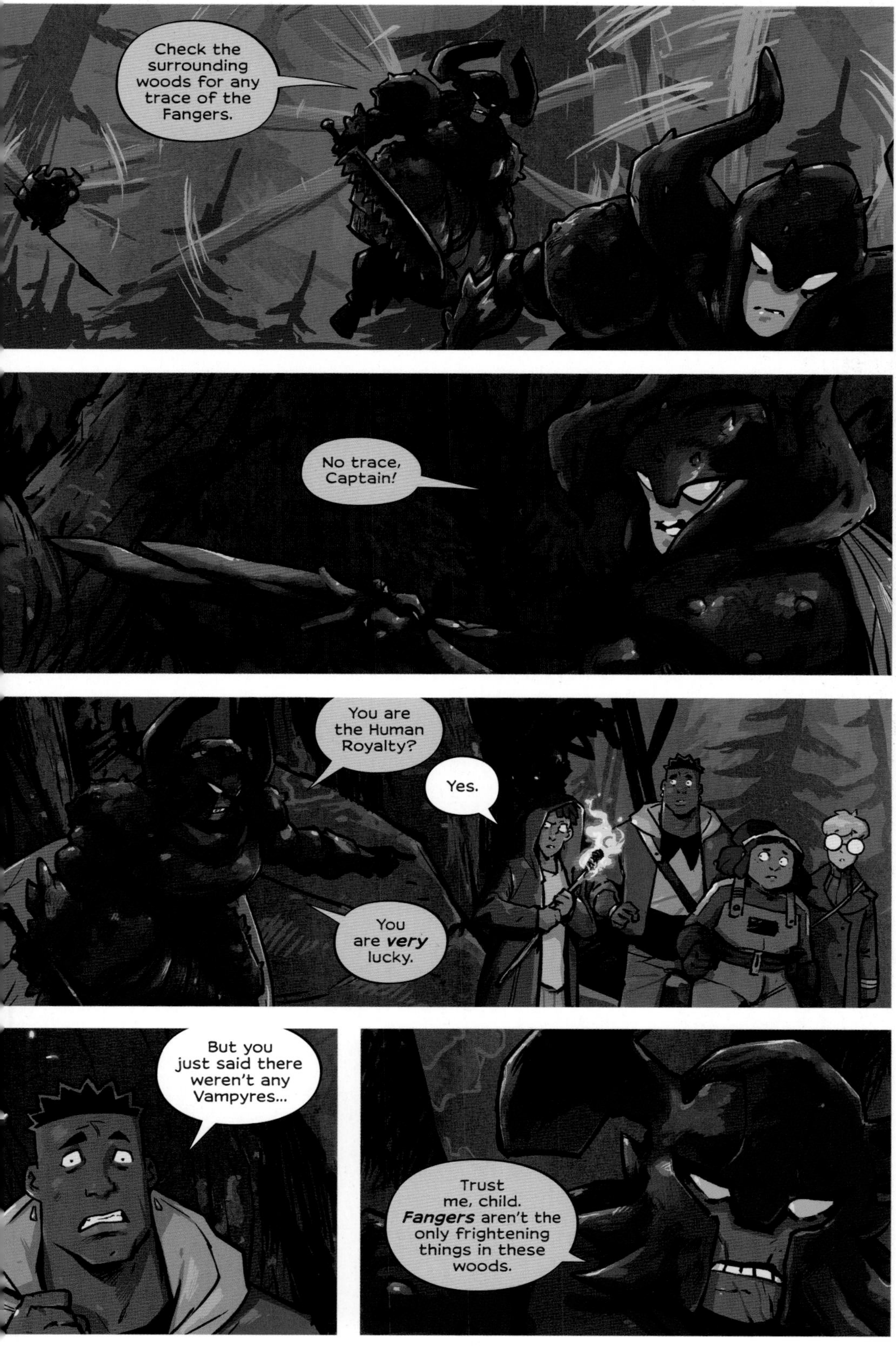
Check the surrounding woods for any trace of the Fangers.
No trace, Captain!
You are the Human Royalty?
Yes.
You are ***very*** lucky.
But you just said there weren't any Vampyres...
Trust me, child. ***Fangers*** aren't the only frightening things in these woods.

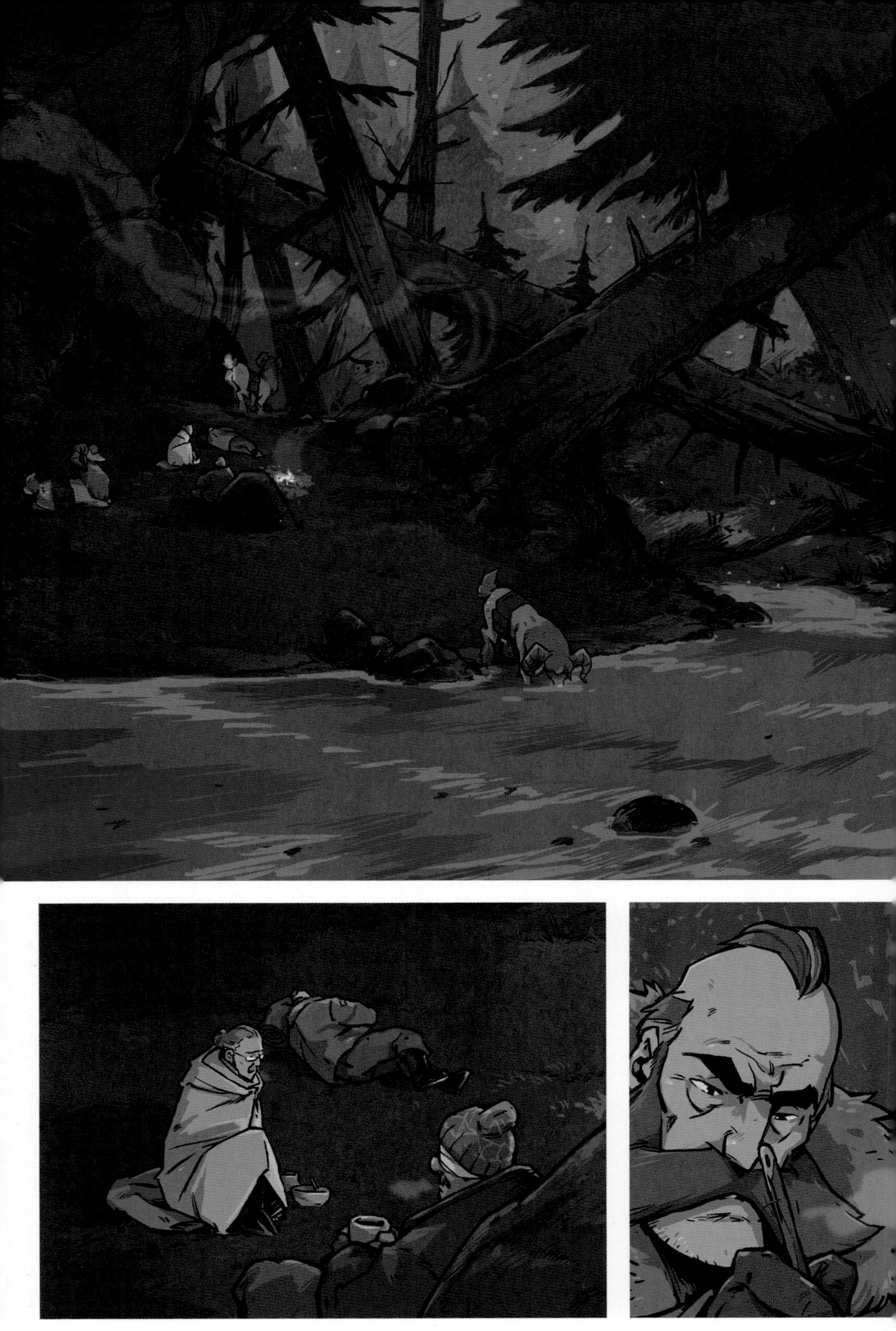

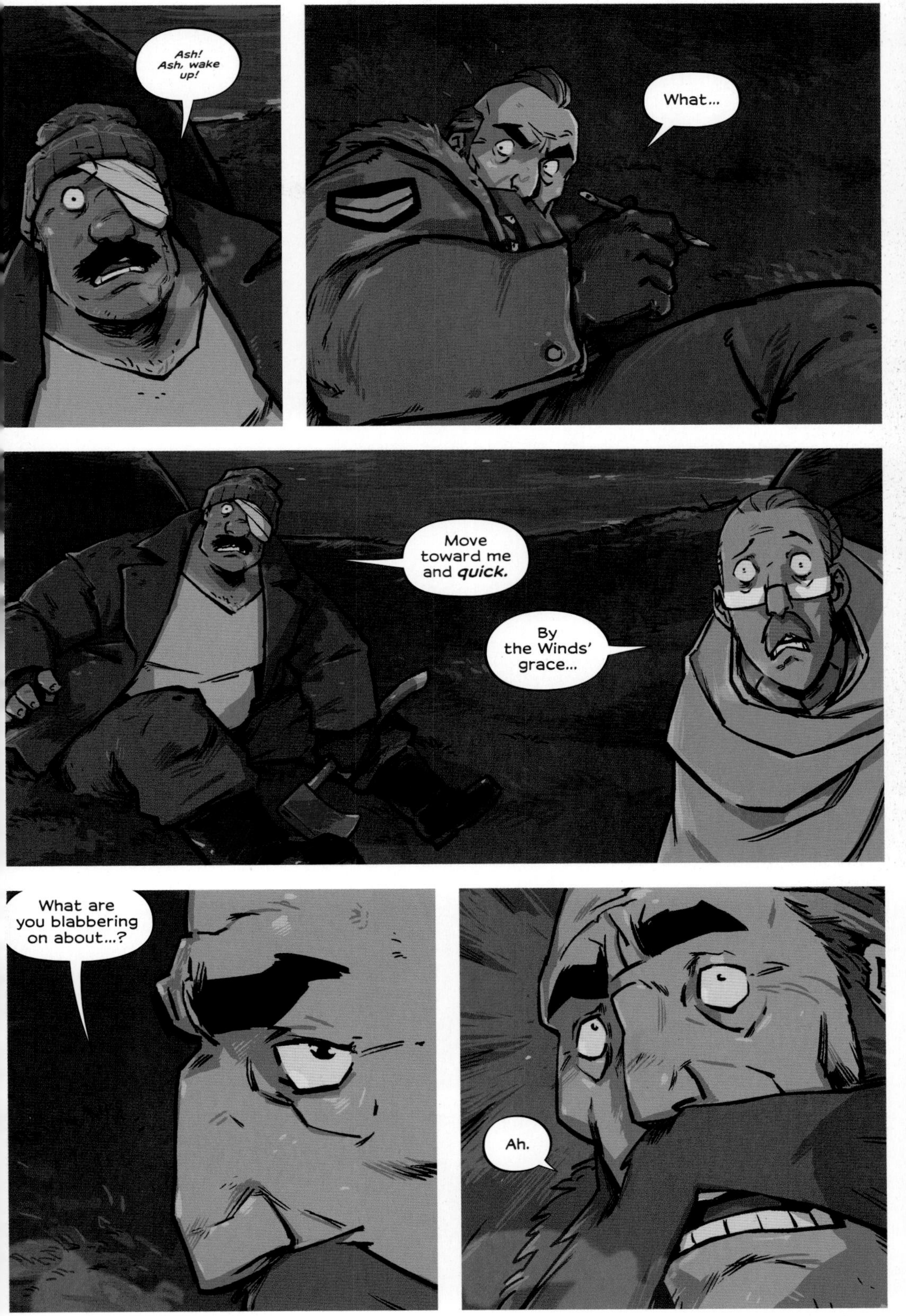
Ash! Ash, wake up!
What...
Move toward me and *quick.*
By the Winds' grace...
What are you blabbering on about...?
Ah.

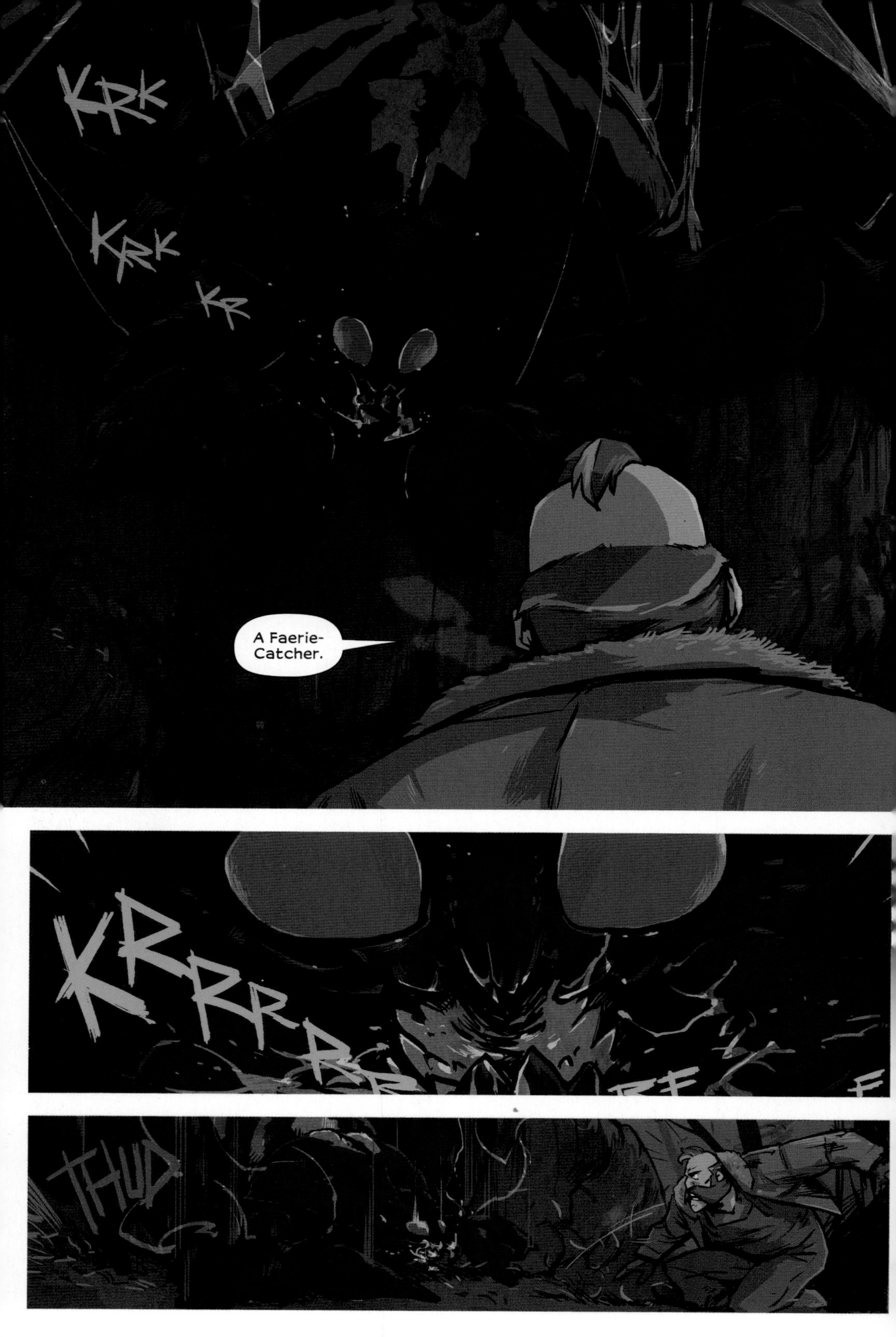
KRK
KRK
KR
A Faerie-Catcher.
KRRR
THUD

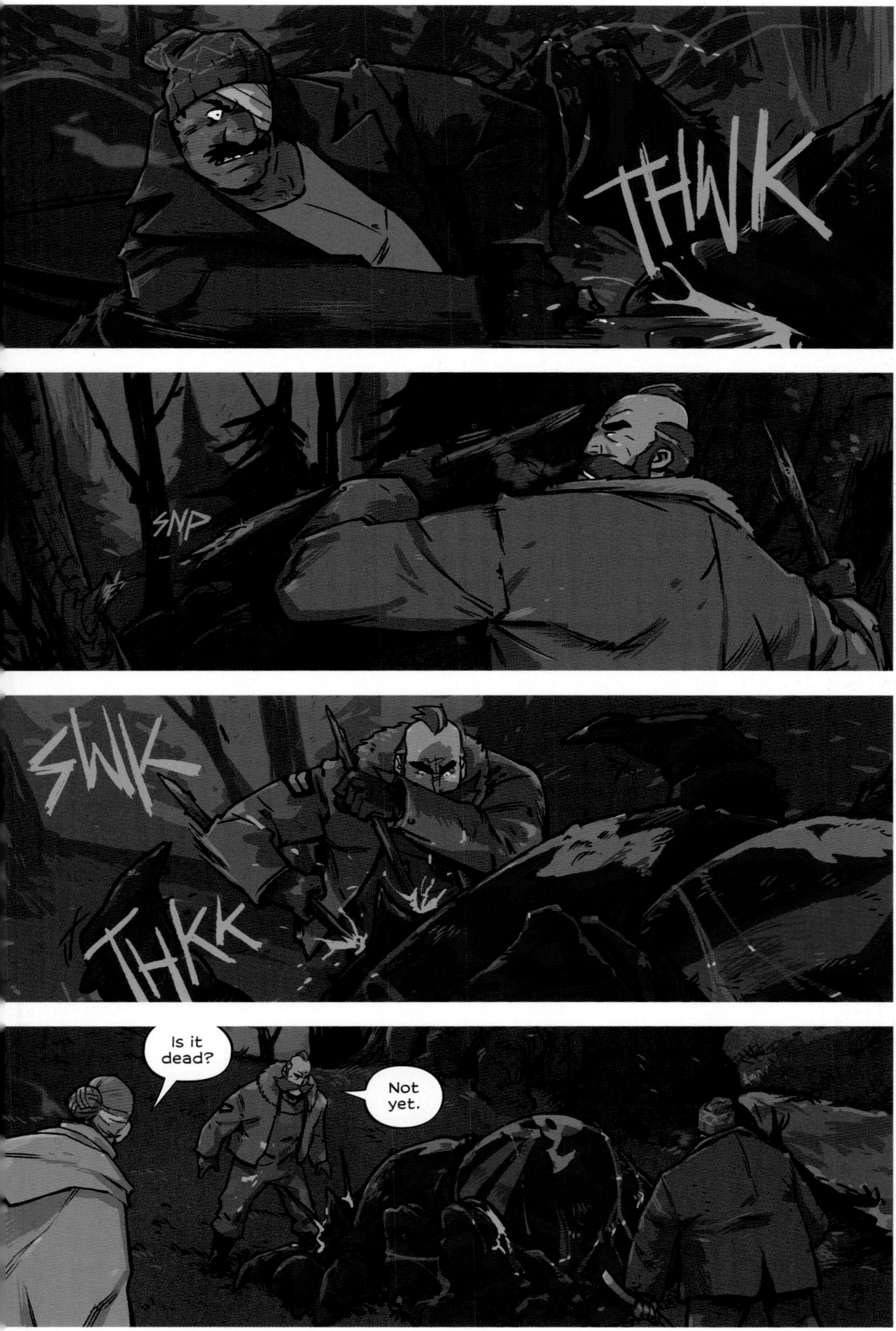
THWK
SNP
SWK
THKK
Is it dead?
Not yet.

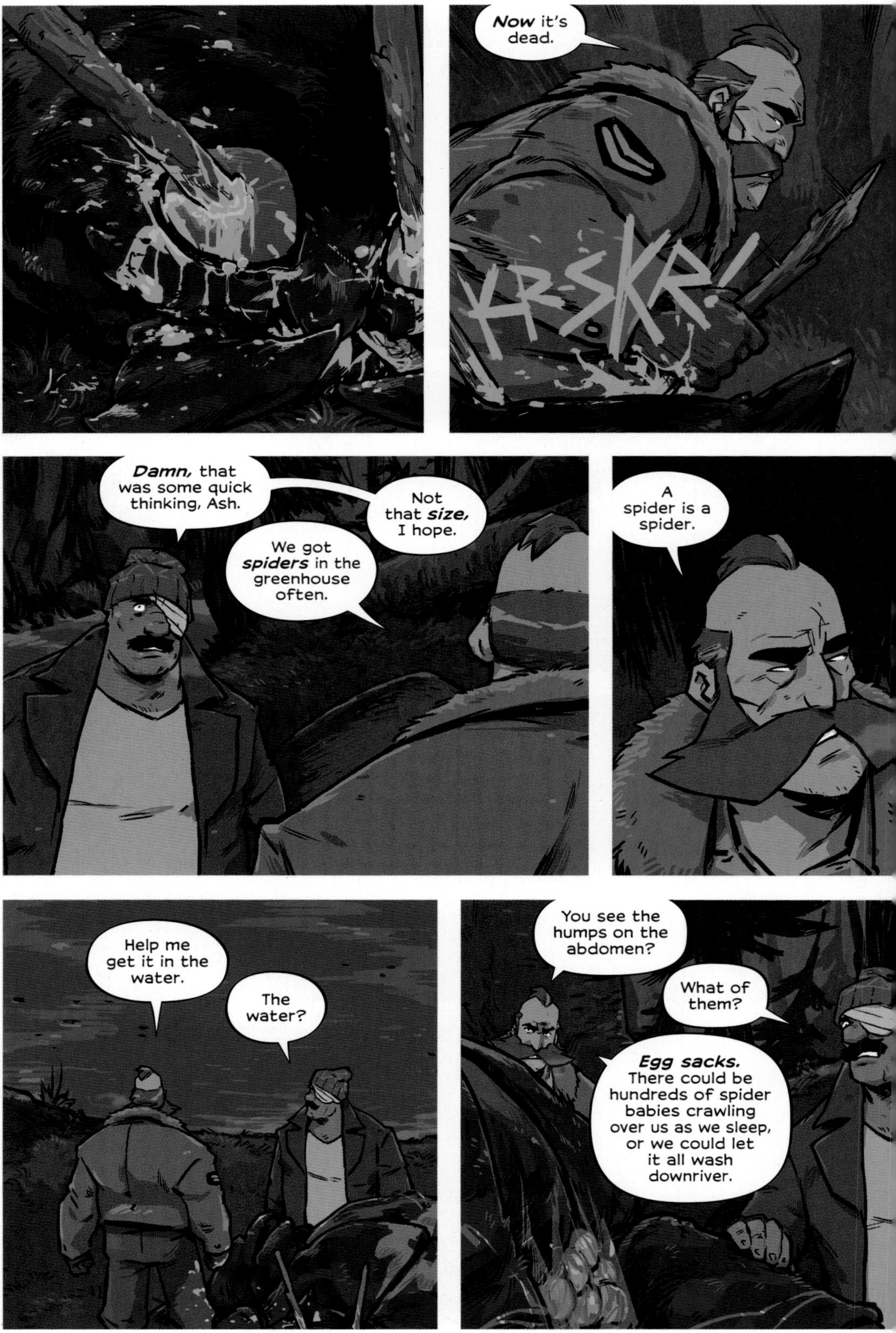
Now it's dead.
KRSKR!
Damn, that was some quick thinking, Ash.
We got *spiders* in the greenhouse often.
Not that *size,* I hope.
A spider is a spider.
Help me get it in the water.
The water?
You see the humps on the abdomen?
What of them?
Egg sacks. There could be hundreds of spider babies crawling over us as we sleep, or we could let it all wash downriver.

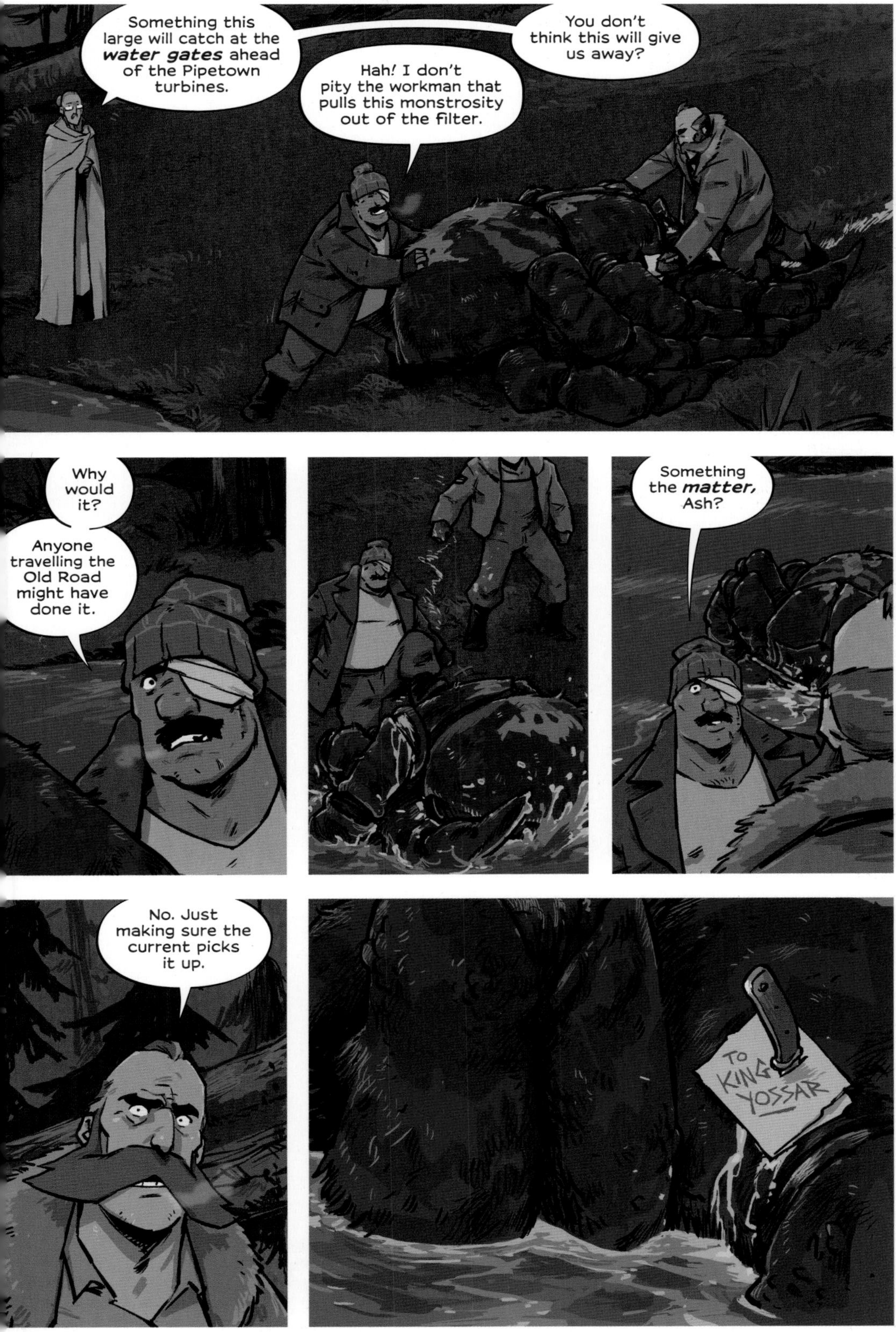

Something this large will catch at the *water gates* ahead of the Pipetown turbines.
You don't think this will give us away?
Hah! I don't pity the workman that pulls this monstrosity out of the filter.
Why would it?
Anyone travelling the Old Road might have done it.
Something the *matter,* Ash?
No. Just making sure the current picks it up.
TO KING YOSSAR

CHAPTER THREE
THE TWO SISTERS

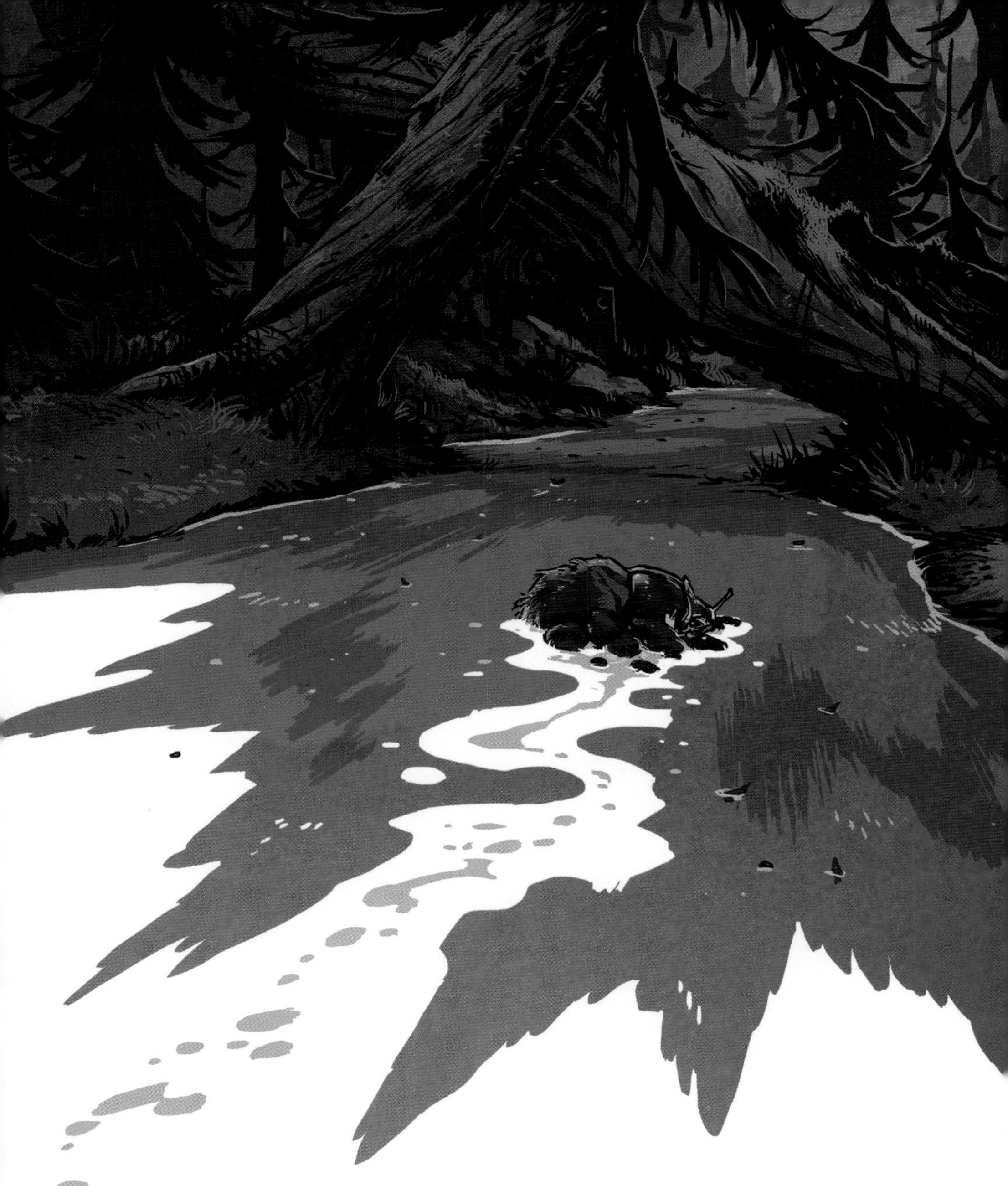

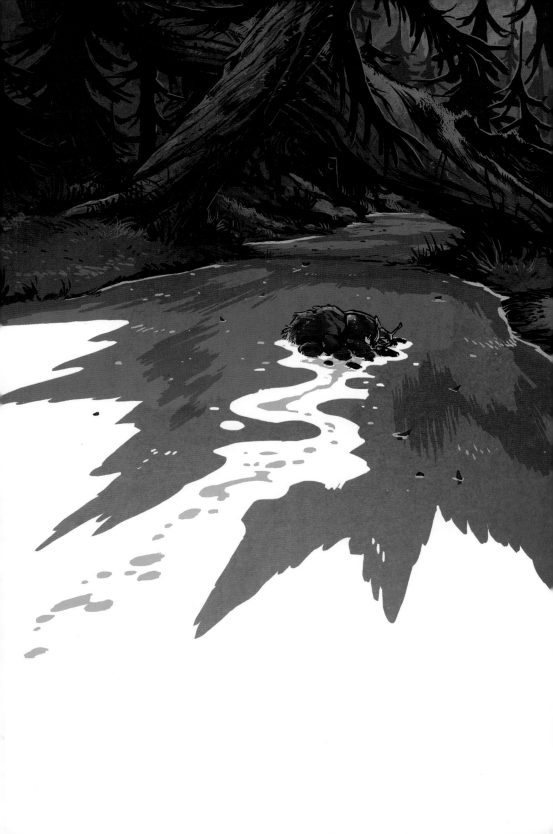

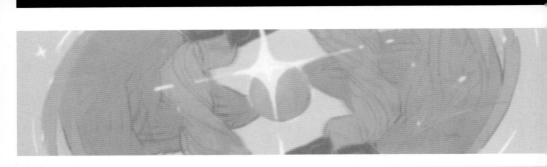

W-what am I looking at?

It's the story of the *two tribes.*

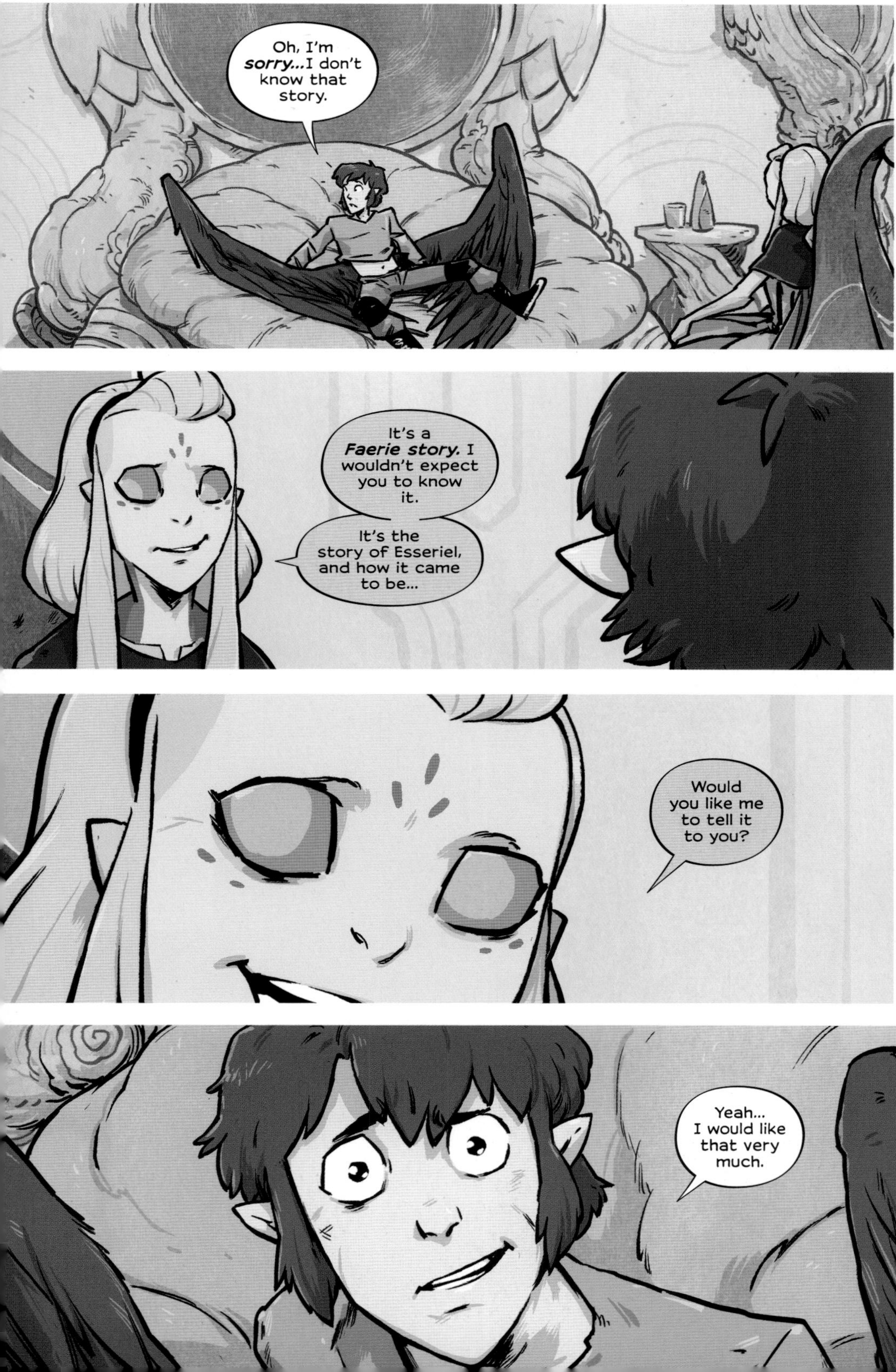
Oh, I'm *sorry...* I don't know that story.
It's a *Faerie story.* I wouldn't expect you to know it.
It's the story of Esseriel, and how it came to be...
Would you like me to tell it to you?
Yeah... I would like that very much.

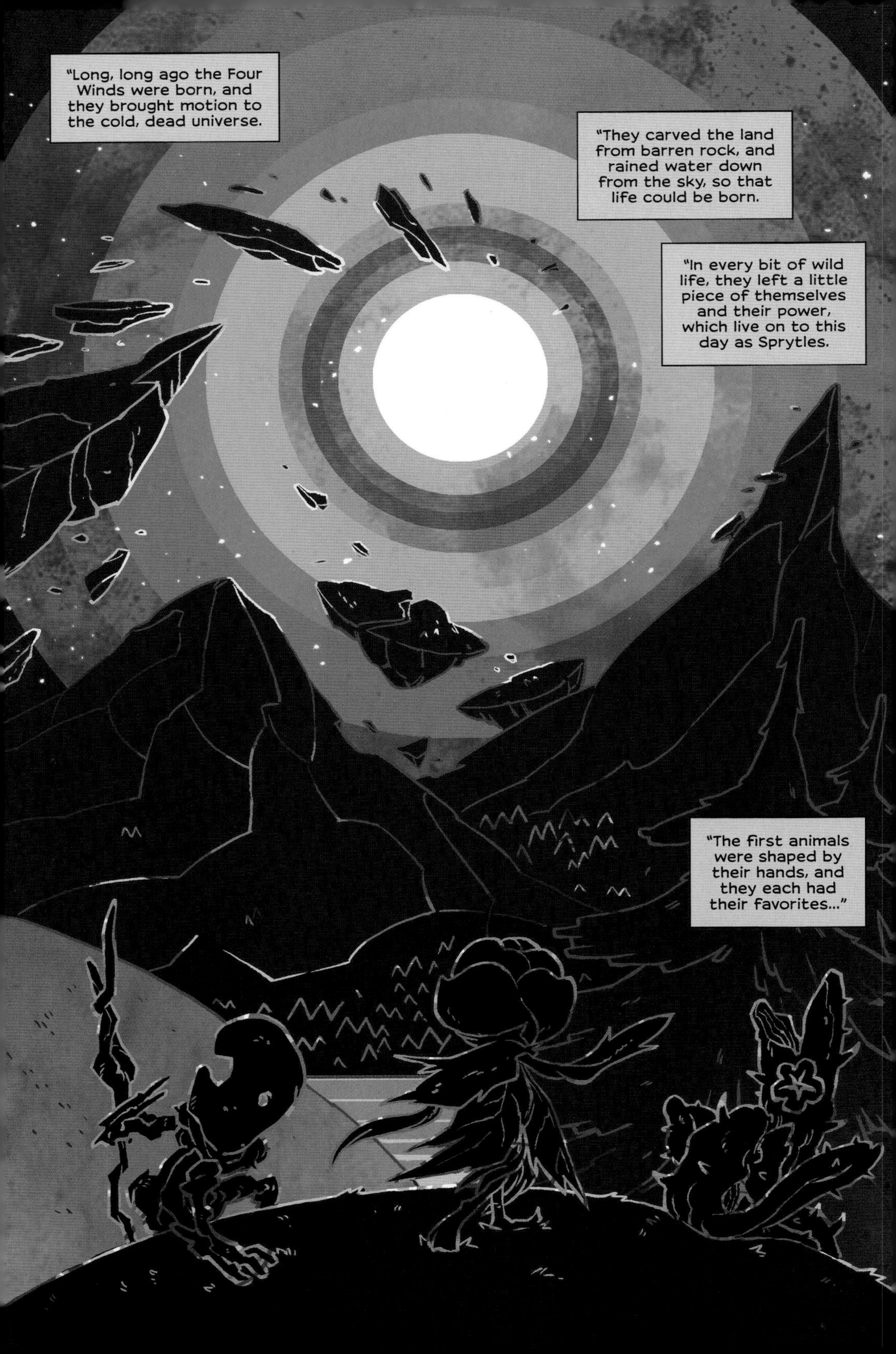
"Long, long ago the Four Winds were born, and they brought motion to the cold, dead universe.
"They carved the land from barren rock, and rained water down from the sky, so that life could be born.
"In every bit of wild life, they left a little piece of themselves and their power, which live on to this day as Sprytles.
"The first animals were shaped by their hands, and they each had their favorites..."

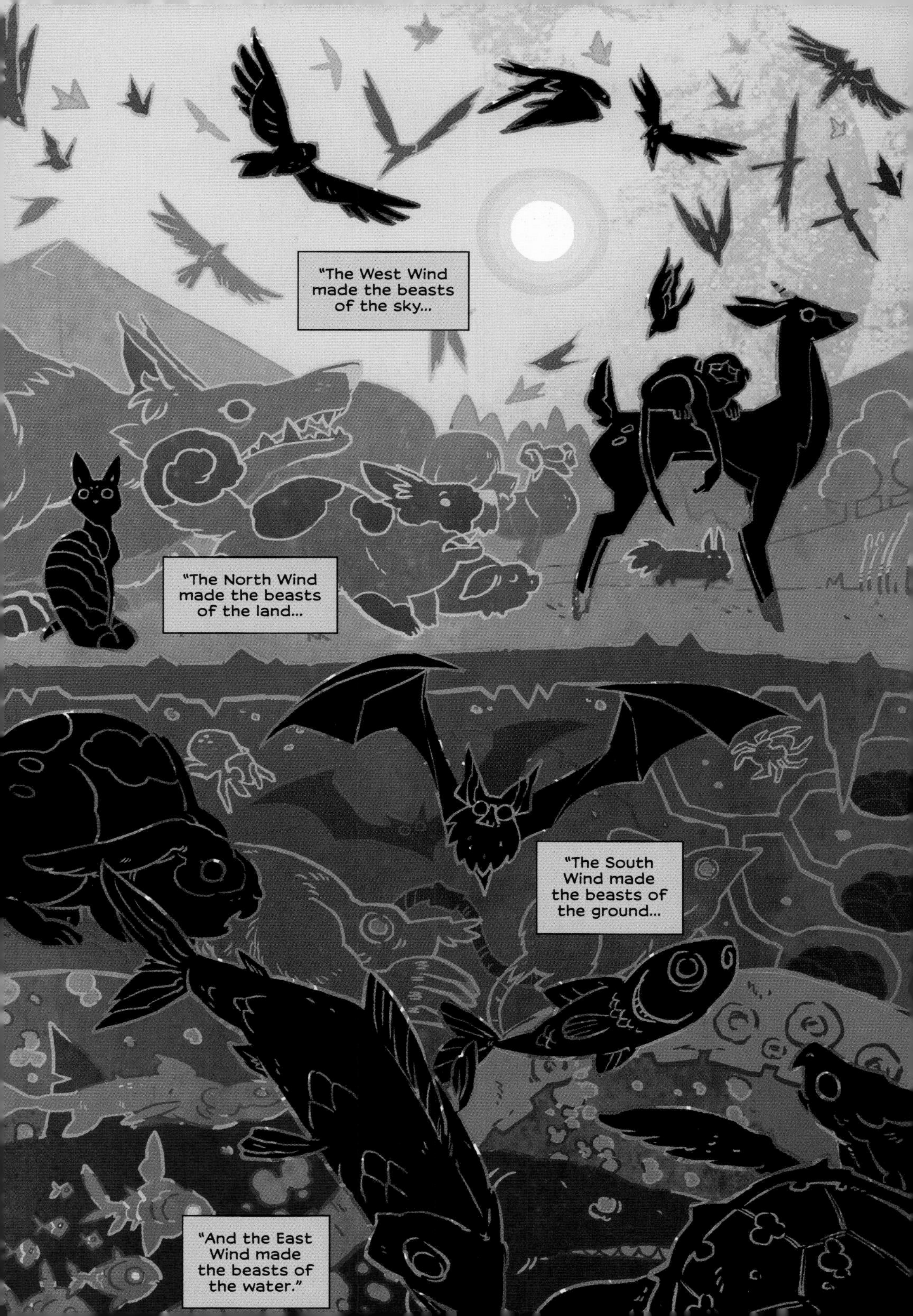
"The West Wind made the beasts of the sky...
"The North Wind made the beasts of the land...
"The South Wind made the beasts of the ground...
"And the East Wind made the beasts of the water."

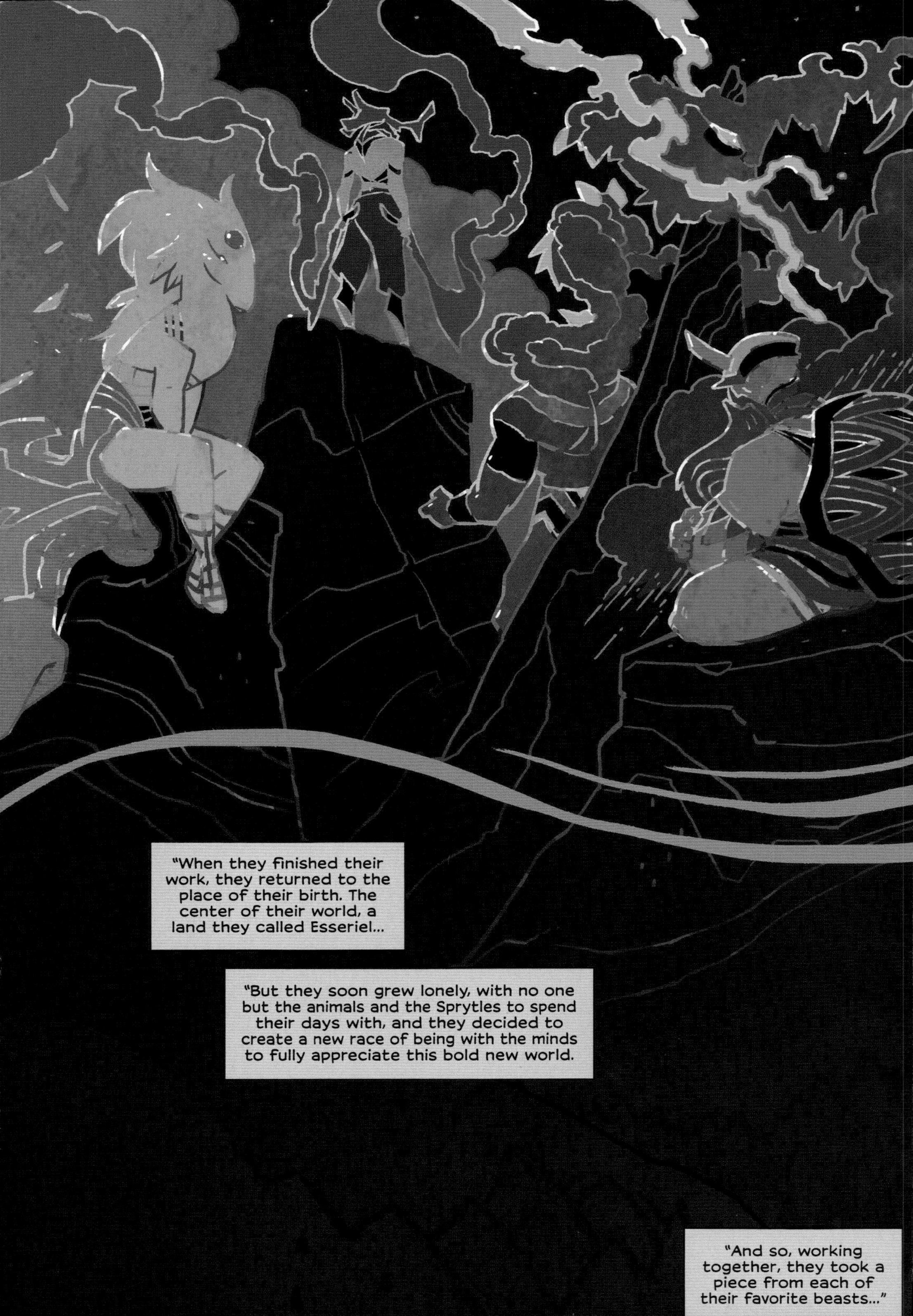
"When they finished their work, they returned to the place of their birth. The center of their world, a land they called Esseriel...
"But they soon grew lonely, with no one but the animals and the Sprytles to spend their days with, and they decided to create a new race of being with the minds to fully appreciate this bold new world.
"And so, working together, they took a piece from each of their favorite beasts..."

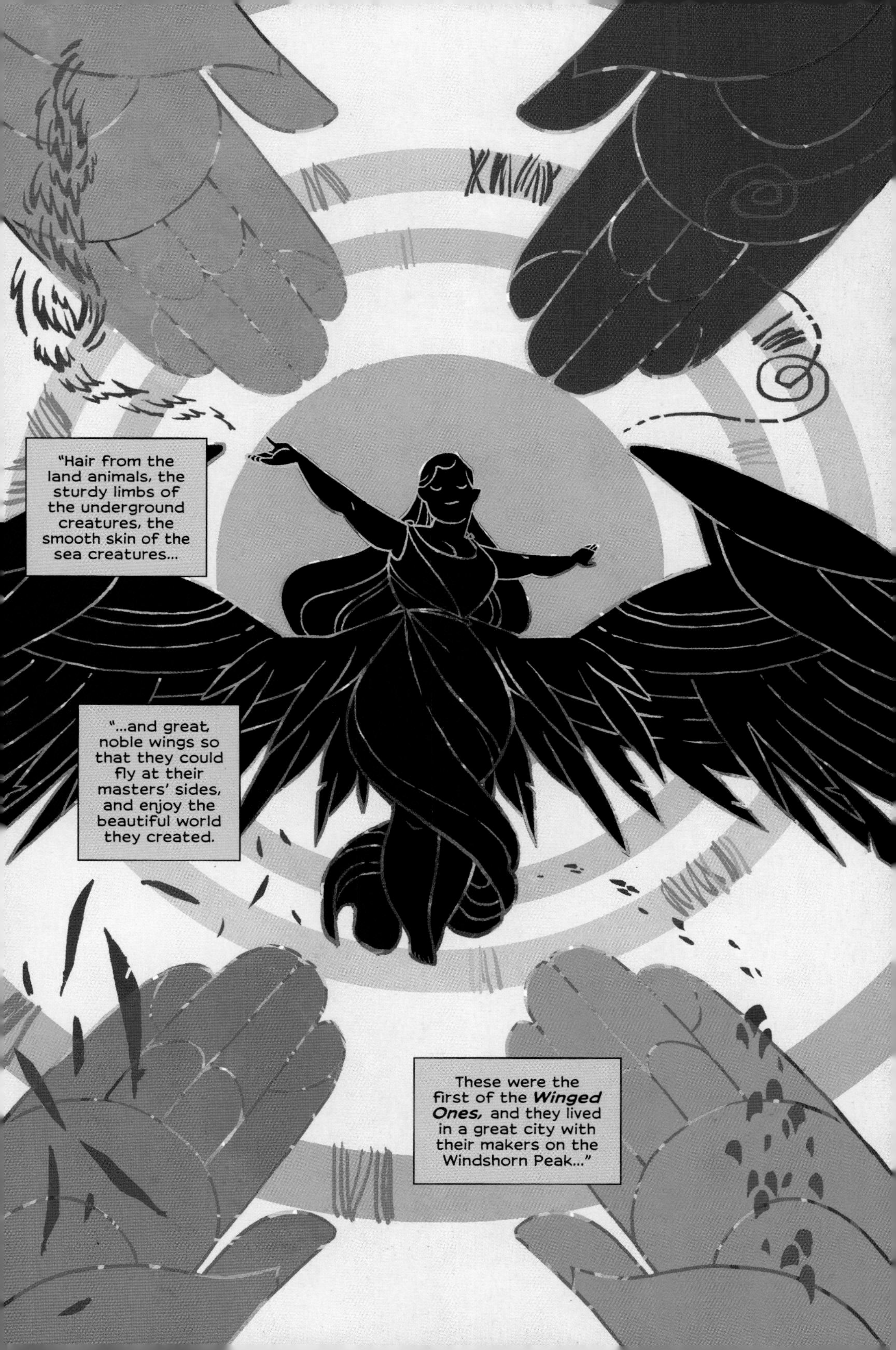
"Hair from the land animals, the sturdy limbs of the underground creatures, the smooth skin of the sea creatures...
"...and great, noble wings so that they could fly at their masters' sides, and enjoy the beautiful world they created.
These were the first of the ***Winged Ones,*** and they lived in a great city with their makers on the Windshorn Peak..."

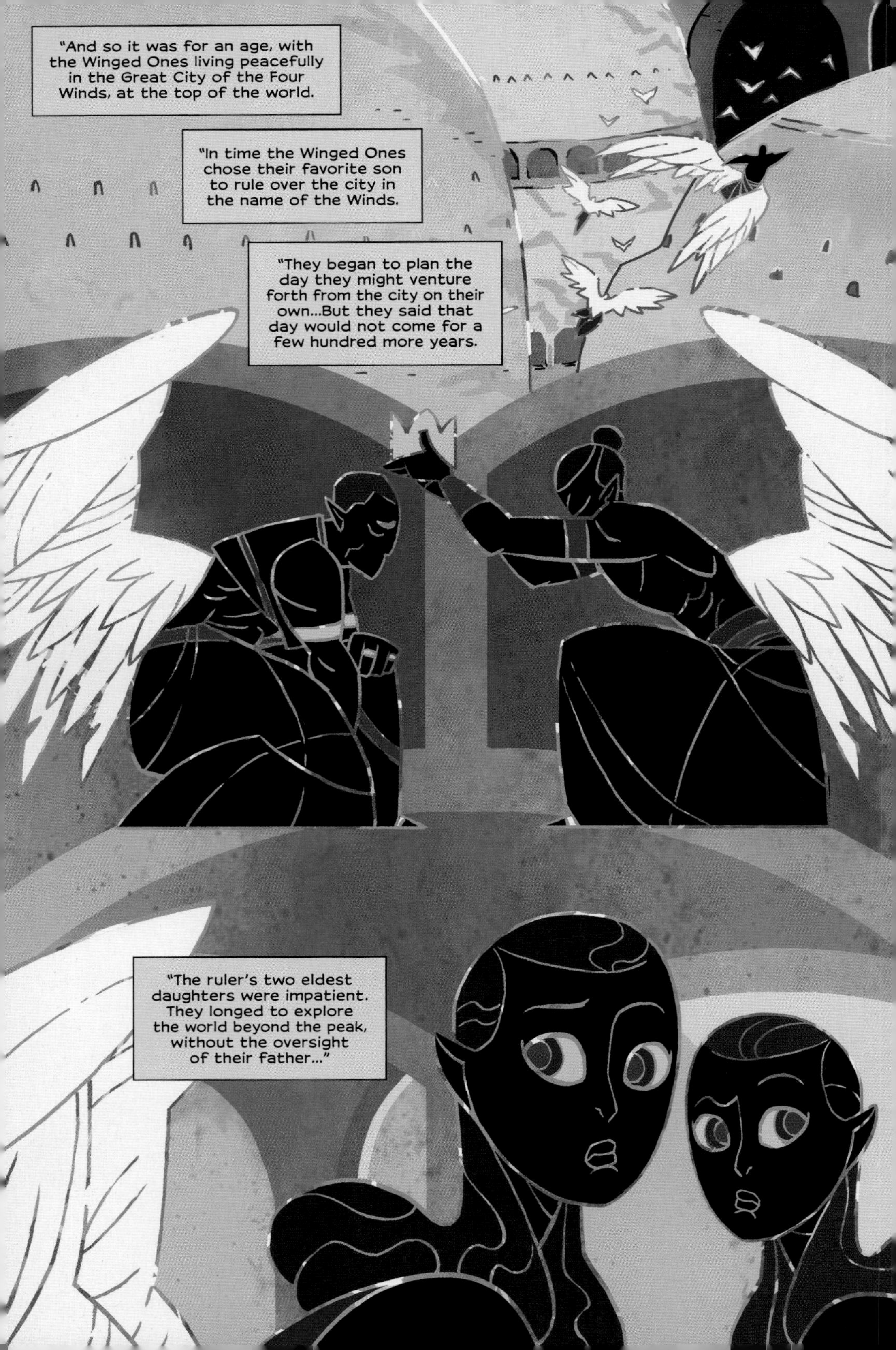
"And so it was for an age, with the Winged Ones living peacefully in the Great City of the Four Winds, at the top of the world.
"In time the Winged Ones chose their favorite son to rule over the city in the name of the Winds.
"They began to plan the day they might venture forth from the city on their own...But they said that day would not come for a few hundred more years.
"The ruler's two eldest daughters were impatient. They longed to explore the world beyond the peak, without the oversight of their father..."

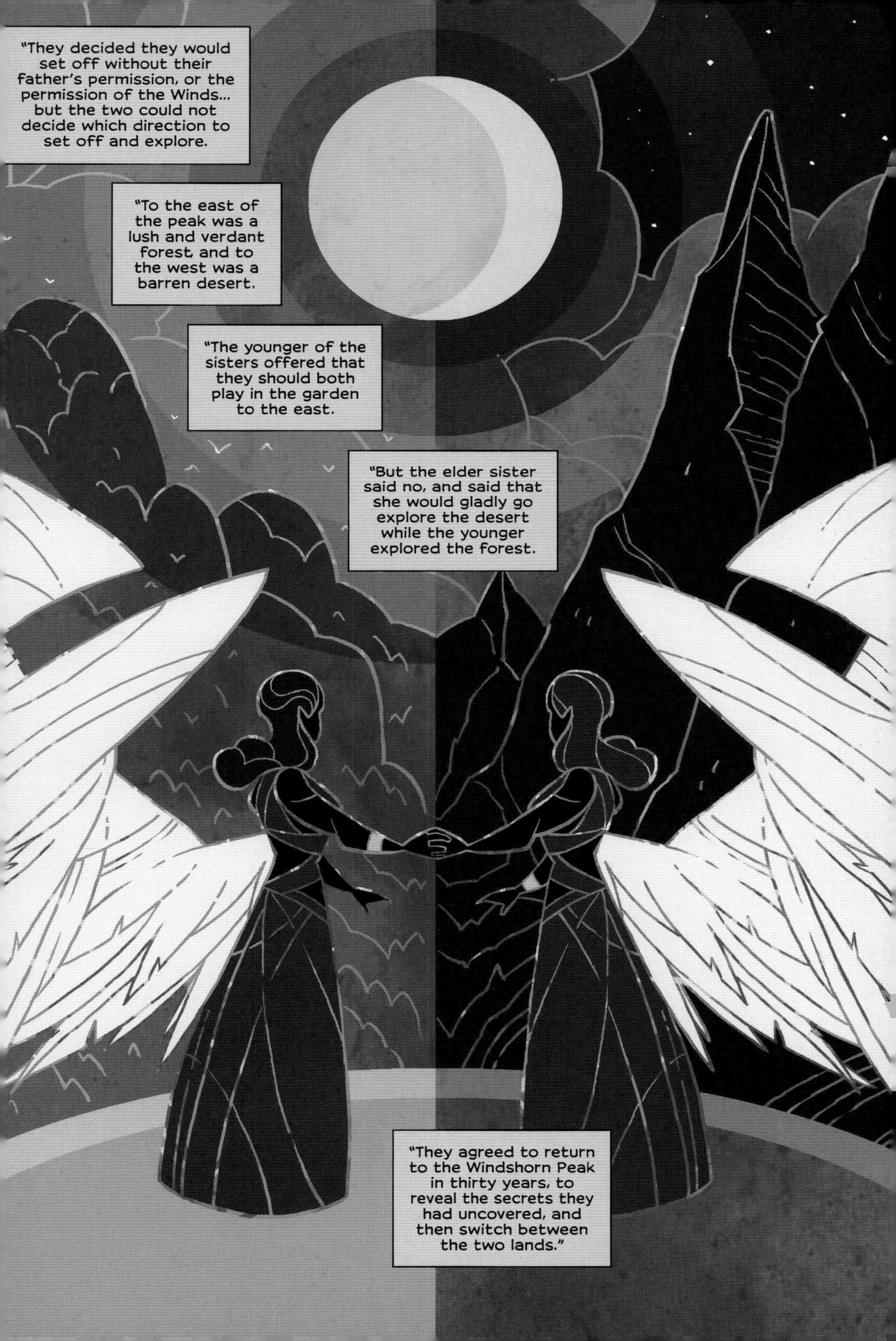
"They decided they would set off without their father's permission, or the permission of the Winds... but the two could not decide which direction to set off and explore.
"To the east of the peak was a lush and verdant forest, and to the west was a barren desert.
"The younger of the sisters offered that they should both play in the garden to the east.
"But the elder sister said no, and said that she would gladly go explore the desert while the younger explored the forest.
"They agreed to return to the Windshorn Peak in thirty years, to reveal the secrets they had uncovered, and then switch between the two lands."

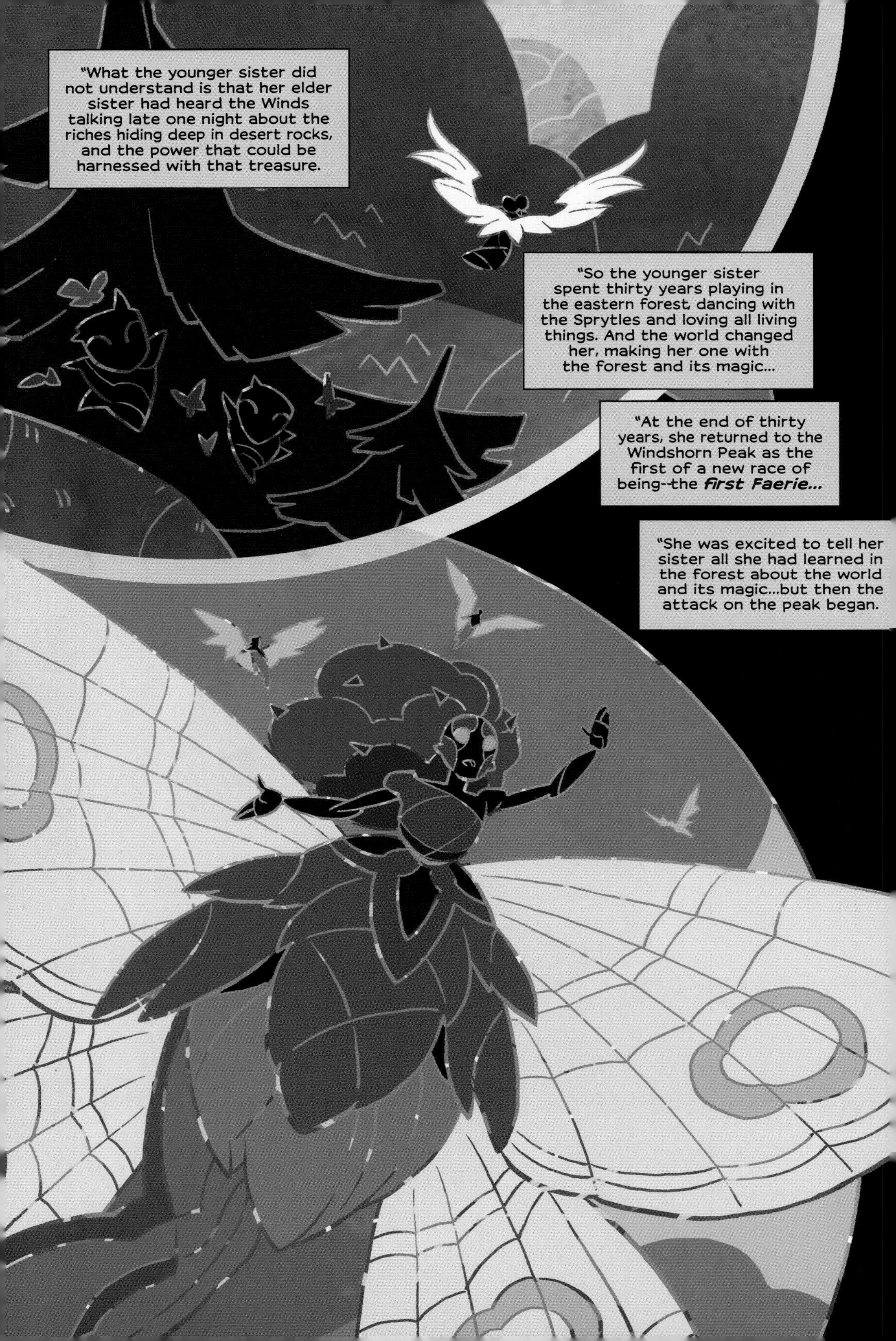
"What the younger sister did not understand is that her elder sister had heard the Winds talking late one night about the riches hiding deep in desert rocks, and the power that could be harnessed with that treasure.
"So the younger sister spent thirty years playing in the eastern forest, dancing with the Sprytles and loving all living things. And the world changed her, making her one with the forest and its magic...
"At the end of thirty years, she returned to the Windshorn Peak as the first of a new race of being--the *first Faerie...*
"She was excited to tell her sister all she had learned in the forest about the world and its magic...but then the attack on the peak began.

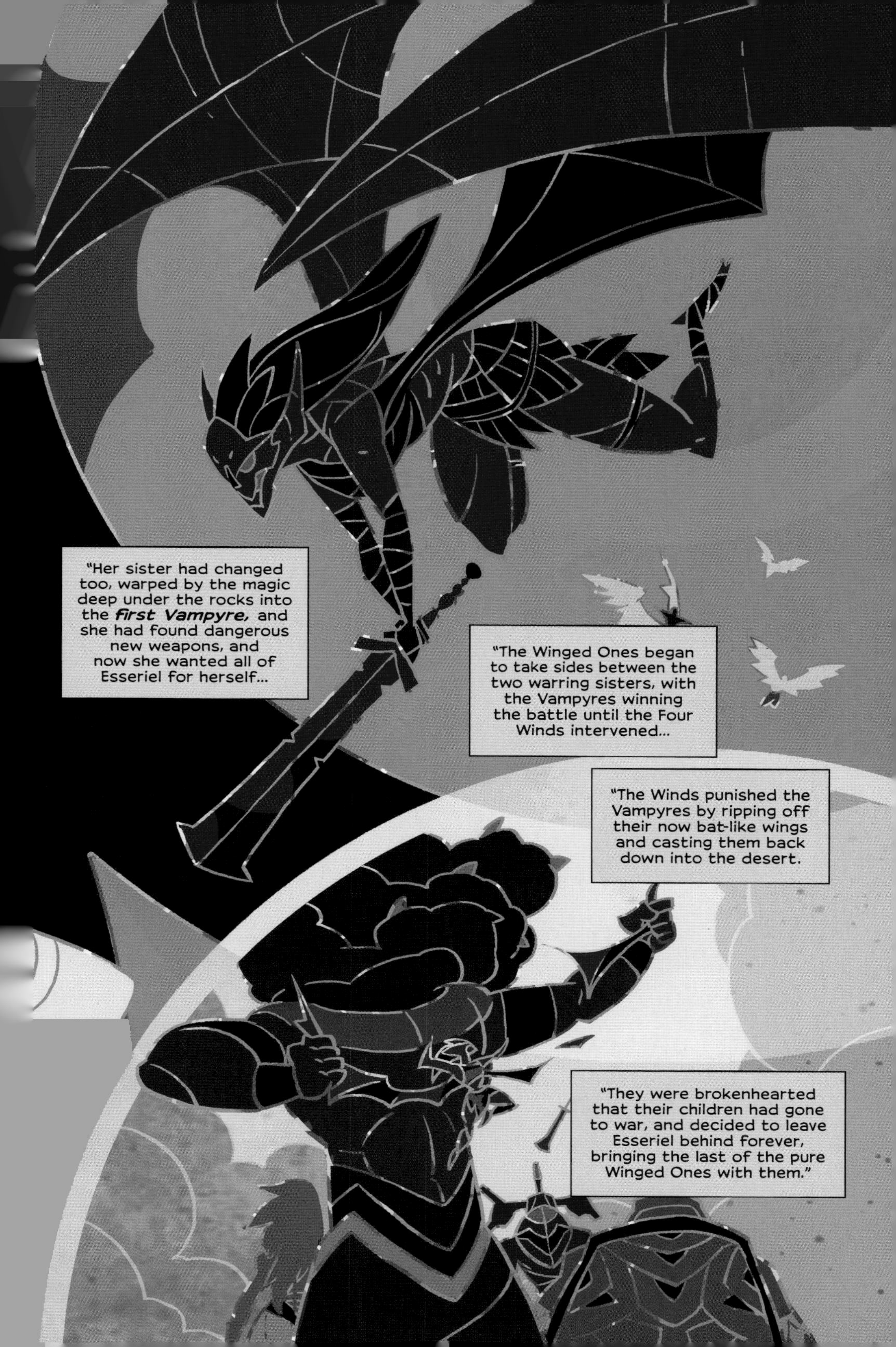
"Her sister had changed too, warped by the magic deep under the rocks into the ***first Vampyre,*** and she had found dangerous new weapons, and now she wanted all of Esseriel for herself...
"The Winged Ones began to take sides between the two warring sisters, with the Vampyres winning the battle until the Four Winds intervened...
"The Winds punished the Vampyres by ripping off their now bat-like wings and casting them back down into the desert.
"They were brokenhearted that their children had gone to war, and decided to leave Esseriel behind forever, bringing the last of the pure Winged Ones with them."

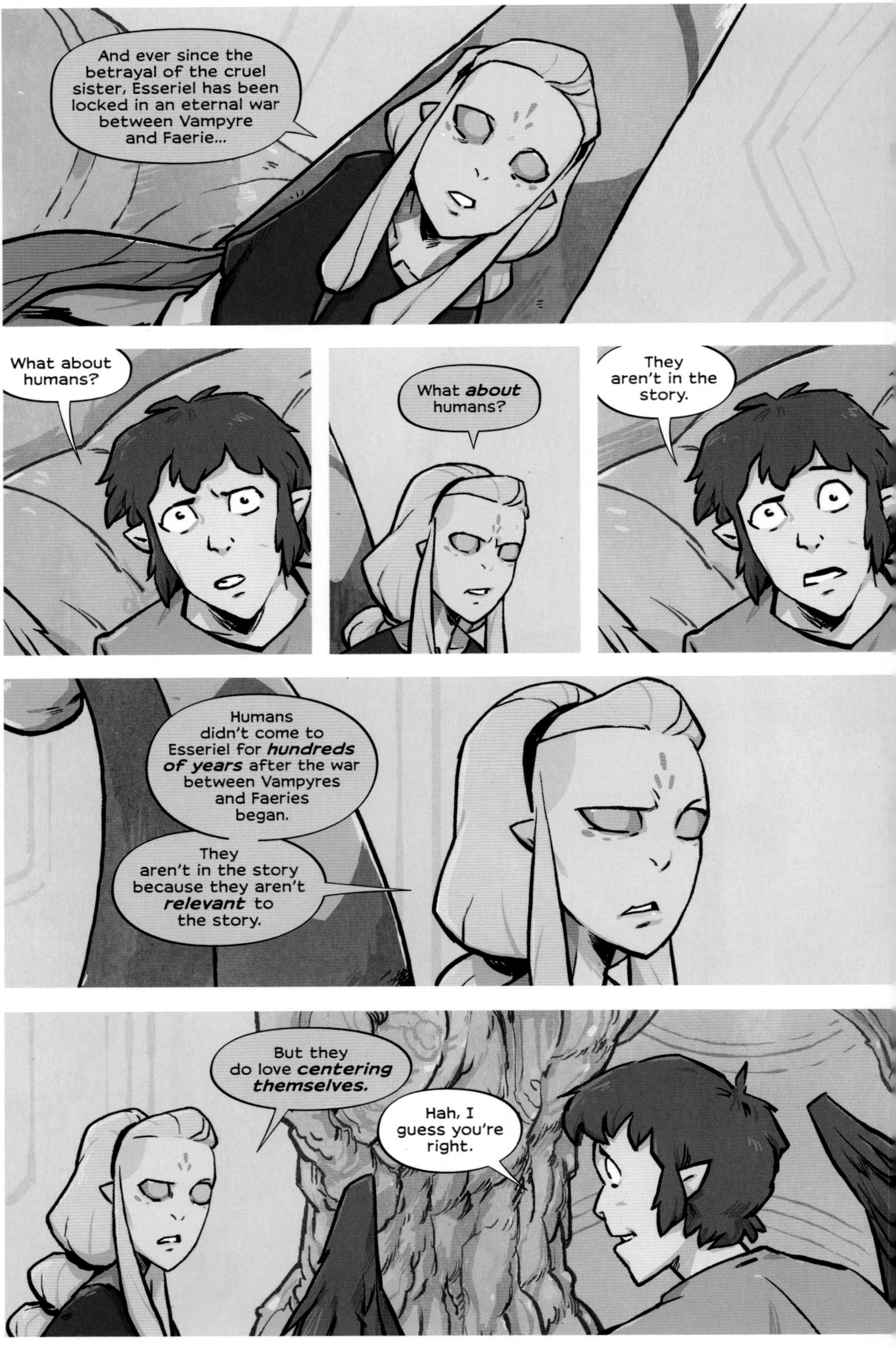

And ever since the betrayal of the cruel sister, Esseriel has been locked in an eternal war between Vampyre and Faerie...
What about humans?
What *about* humans?
They aren't in the story.
Humans didn't come to Esseriel for ***hundreds of years*** after the war between Vampyres and Faeries began.
They aren't in the story because they aren't ***relevant*** to the story.
But they do love ***centering themselves.***
Hah, I guess you're right.

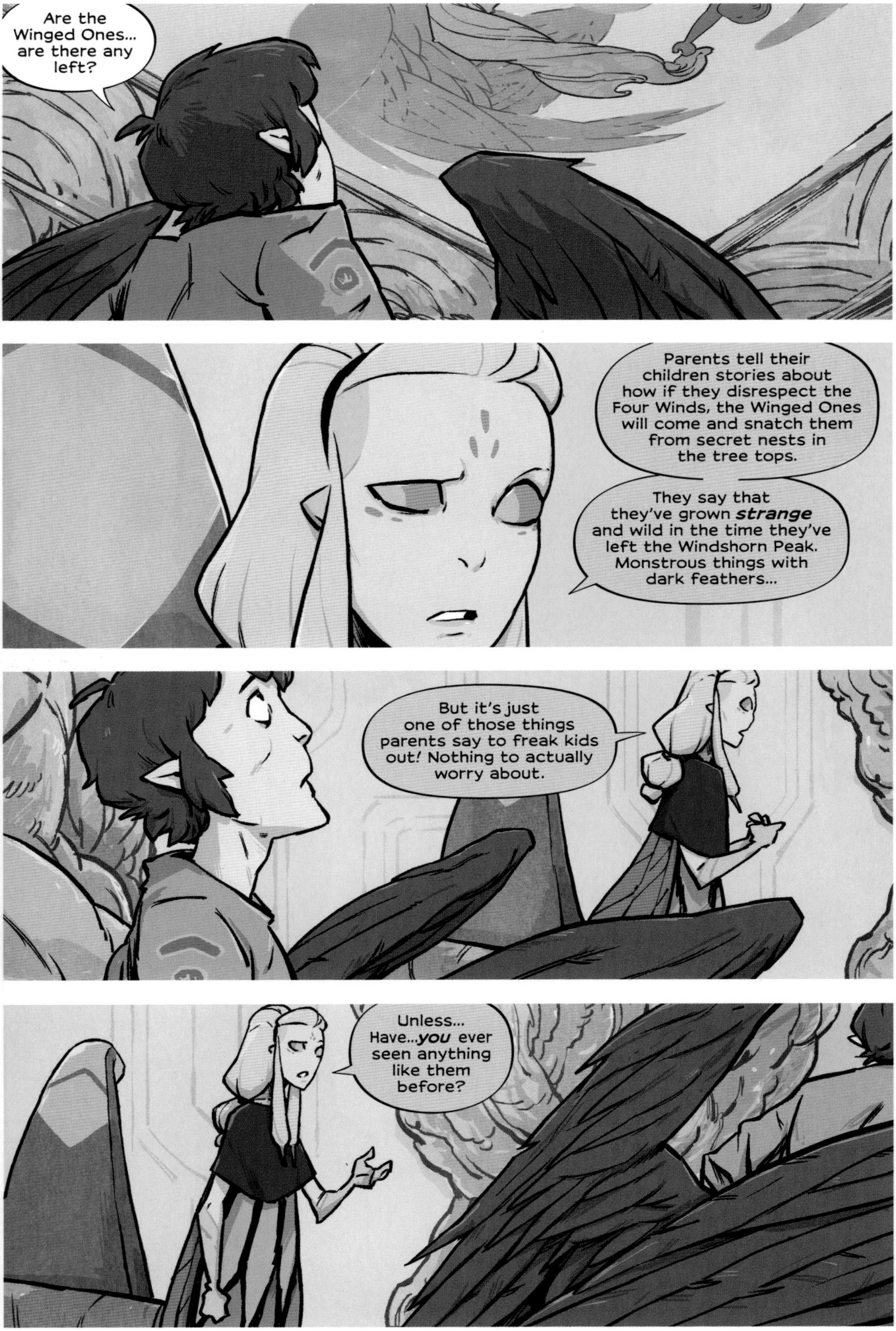

Are the Winged Ones... are there any left?
Parents tell their children stories about how if they disrespect the Four Winds, the Winged Ones will come and snatch them from secret nests in the tree tops.
They say that they've grown ***strange*** and wild in the time they've left the Windshorn Peak. Monstrous things with dark feathers...
But it's just one of those things parents say to freak kids out! Nothing to actually worry about.
Unless... Have...***you*** ever seen anything like them before?

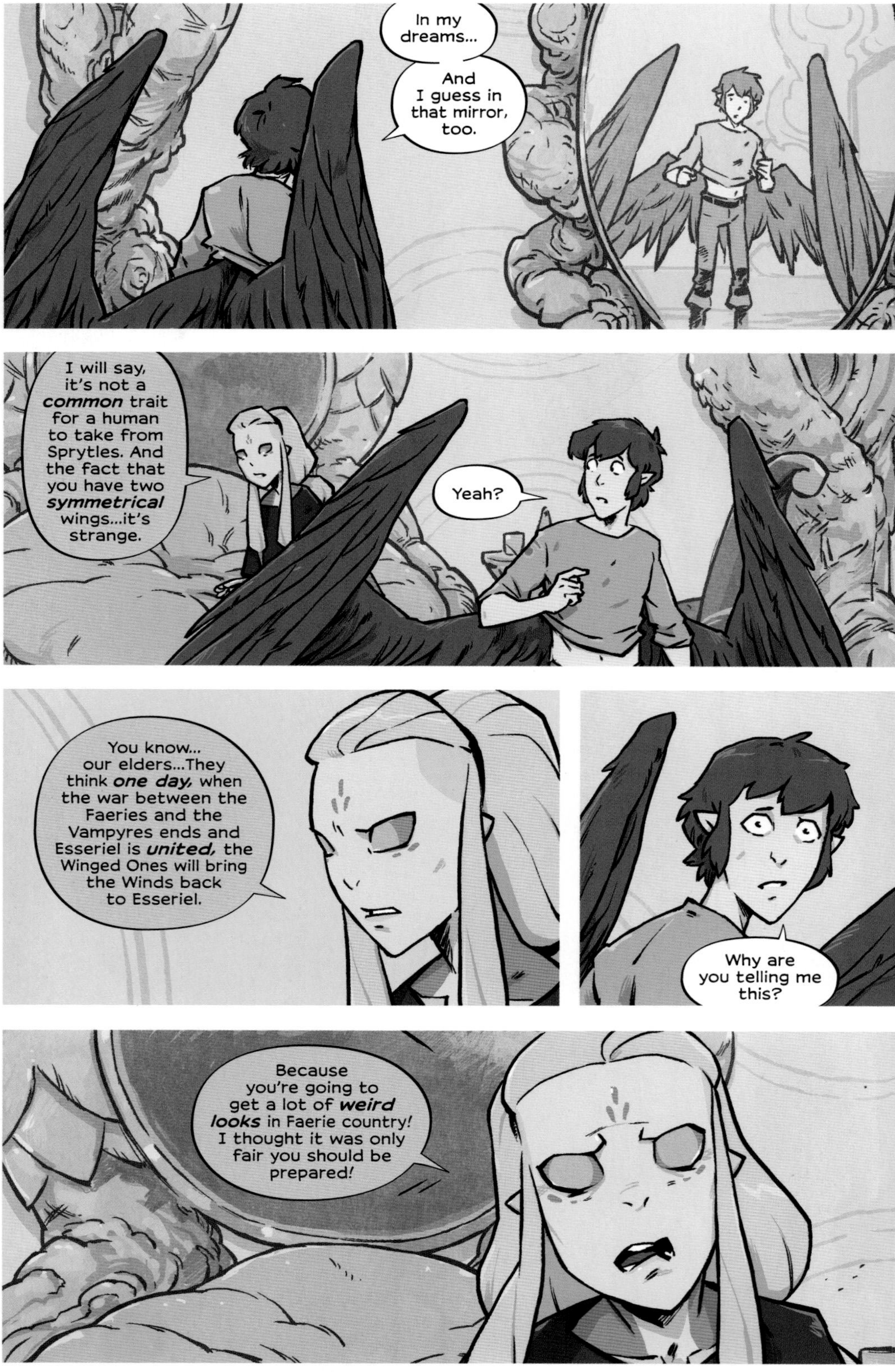
In my dreams...
And I guess in that mirror, too.
I will say, it's not a ***common*** trait for a human to take from Sprytles. And the fact that you have two ***symmetrical*** wings...it's strange.
Yeah?
You know... our elders...They think ***one day,*** when the war between the Faeries and the Vampyres ends and Esseriel is ***united,*** the Winged Ones will bring the Winds back to Esseriel.
Why are you telling me this?
Because you're going to get a lot of ***weird looks*** in Faerie country! I thought it was only fair you should be prepared!

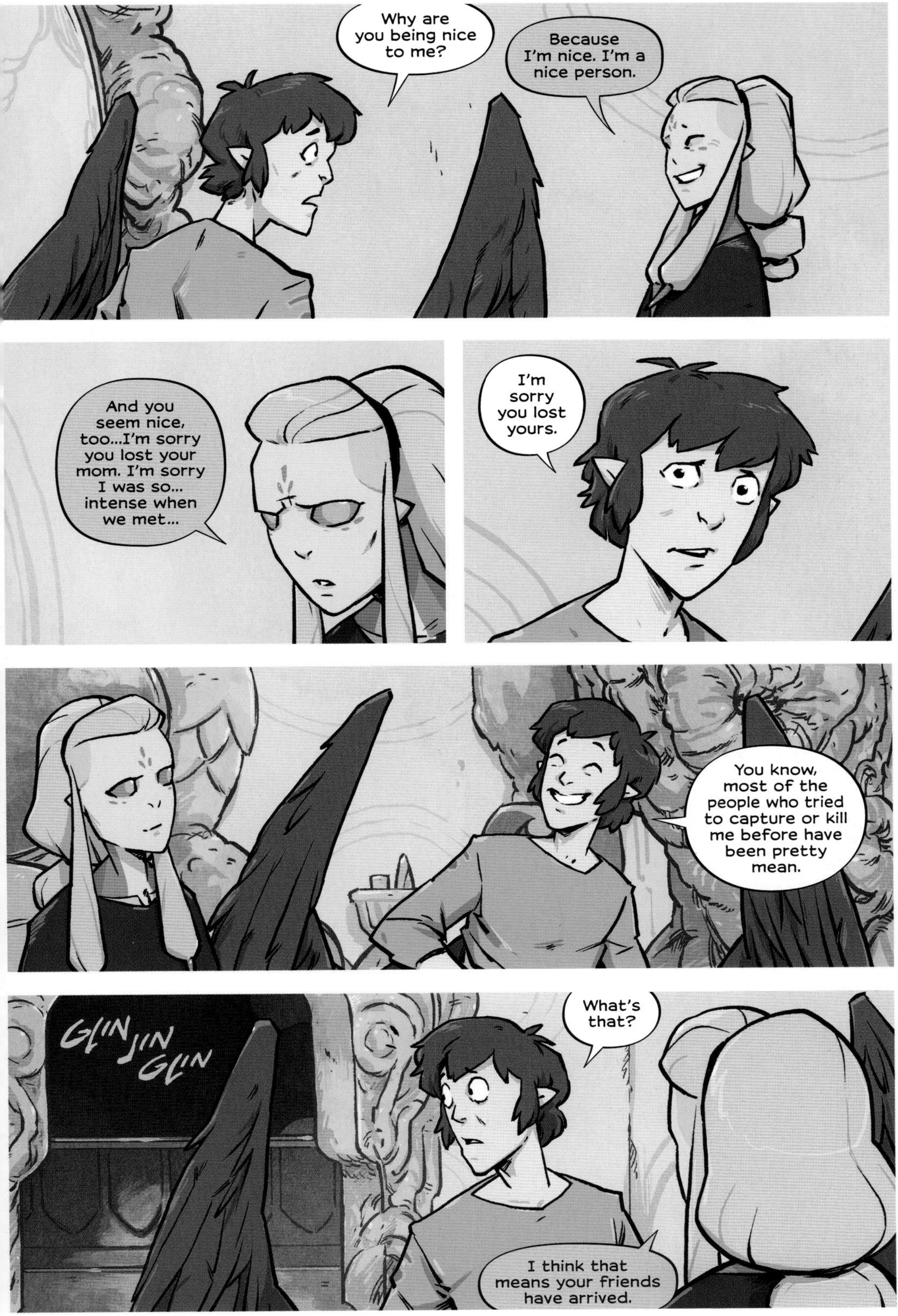
Why are you being nice to me?
Because I'm nice. I'm a nice person.
And you seem nice, too...I'm sorry you lost your mom. I'm sorry I was so... intense when we met...
I'm sorry you lost yours.
You know, most of the people who tried to capture or kill me before have been pretty mean.
GLIN JIN GLIN
What's that?
I think that means your friends have arrived.

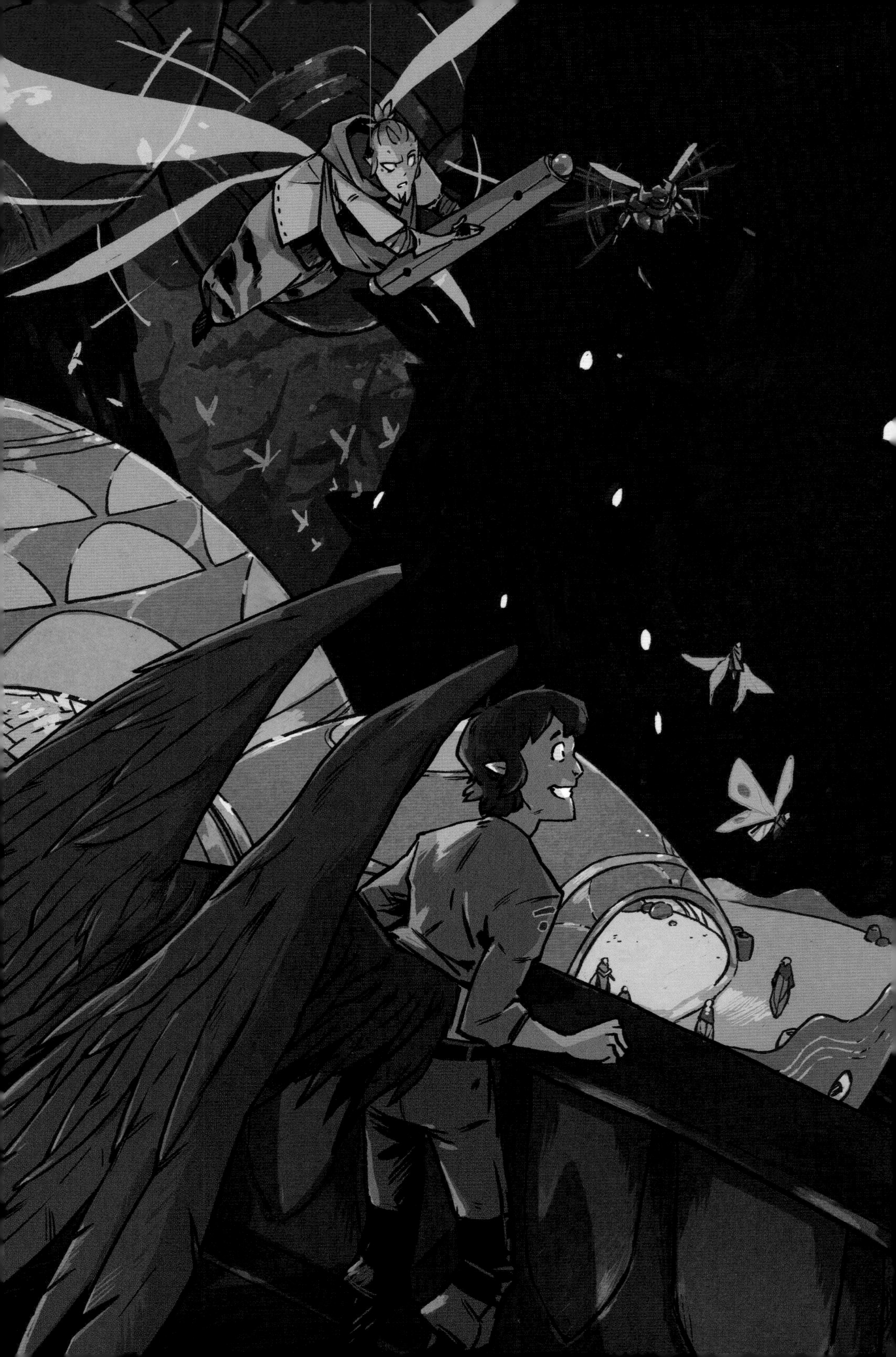

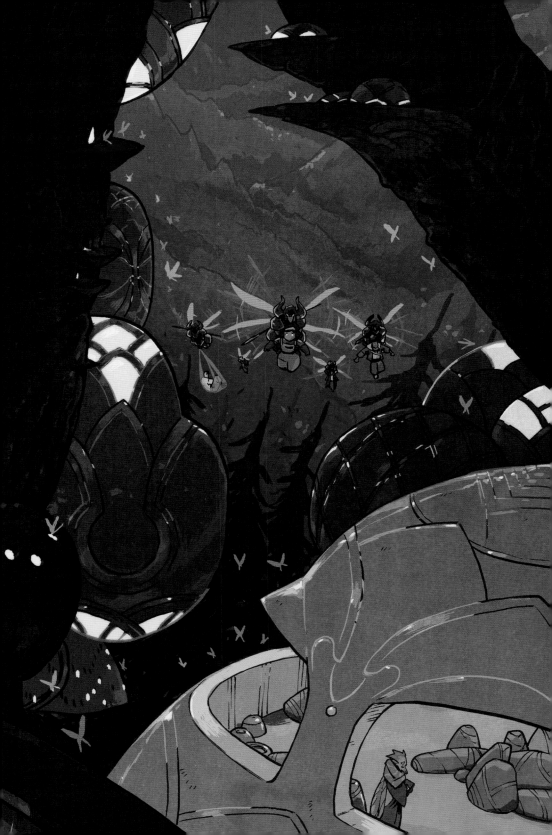

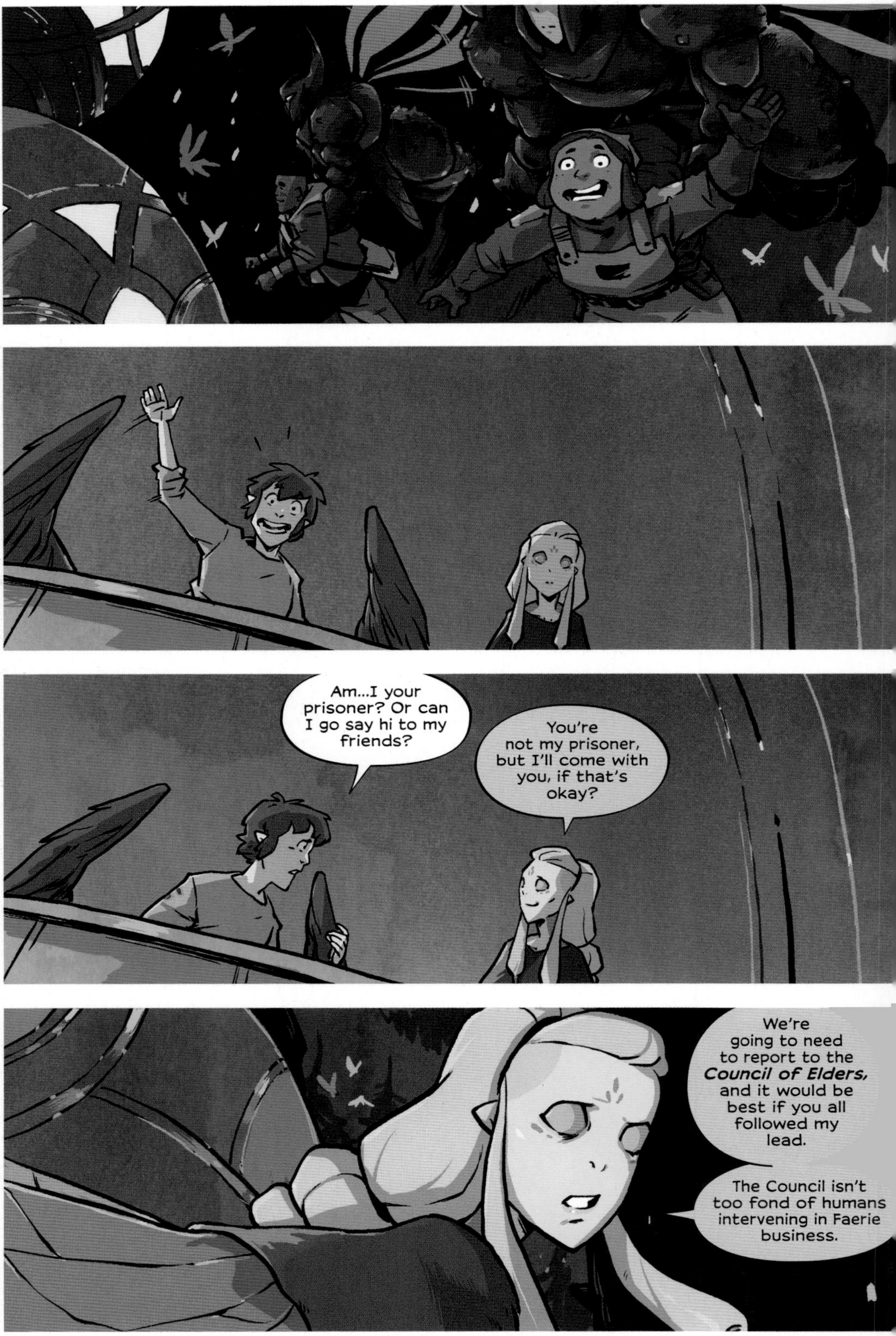

Am...I your prisoner? Or can I go say hi to my friends?
You're not my prisoner, but I'll come with you, if that's okay?
We're going to need to report to the *Council of Elders,* and it would be best if you all followed my lead.
The Council isn't too fond of humans intervening in Faerie business.

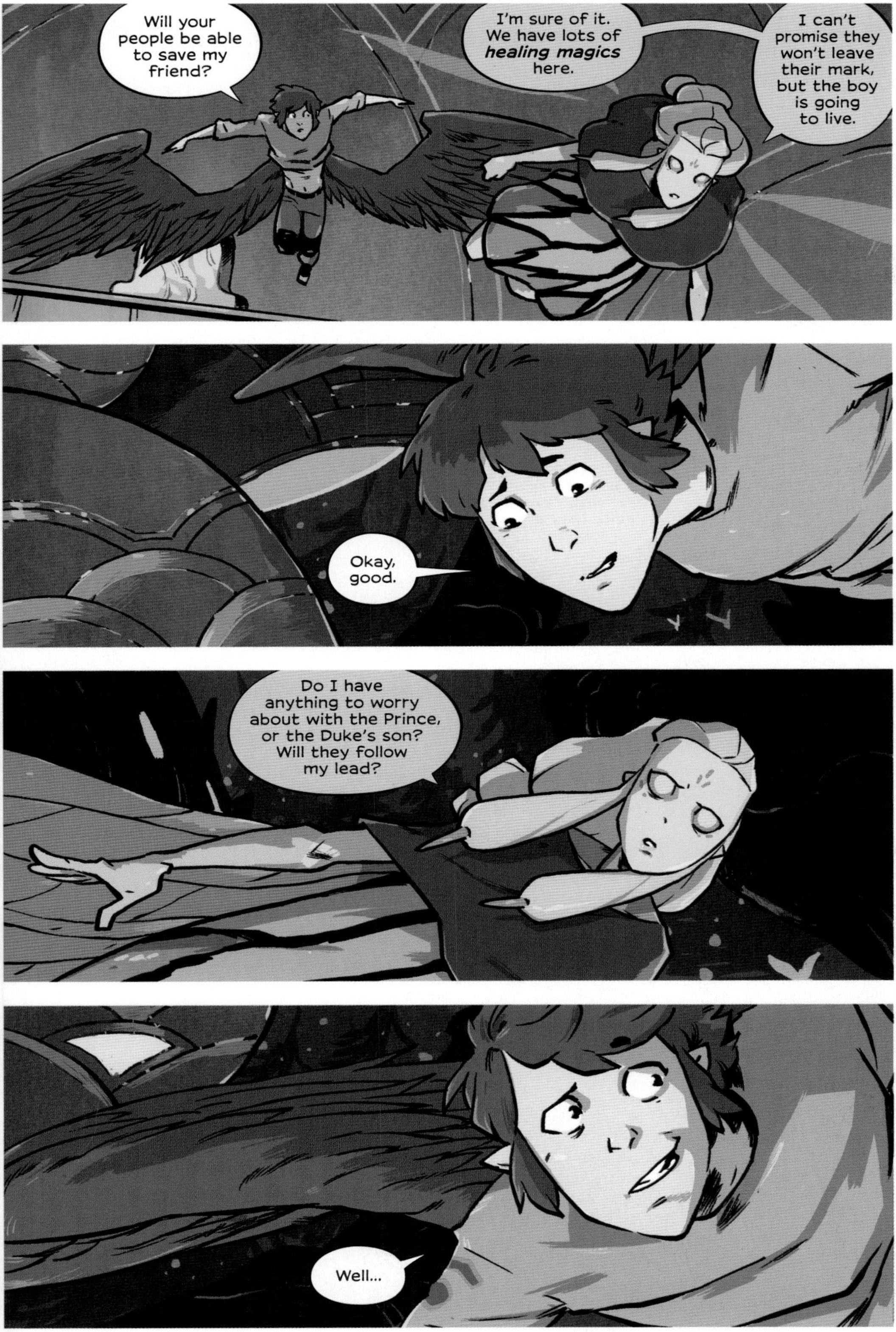

Will your people be able to save my friend?
I'm sure of it. We have lots of *healing magics* here.
I can't promise they won't leave their mark, but the boy is going to live.
Okay, good.
Do I have anything to worry about with the Prince, or the Duke's son? Will they follow my lead?
Well...

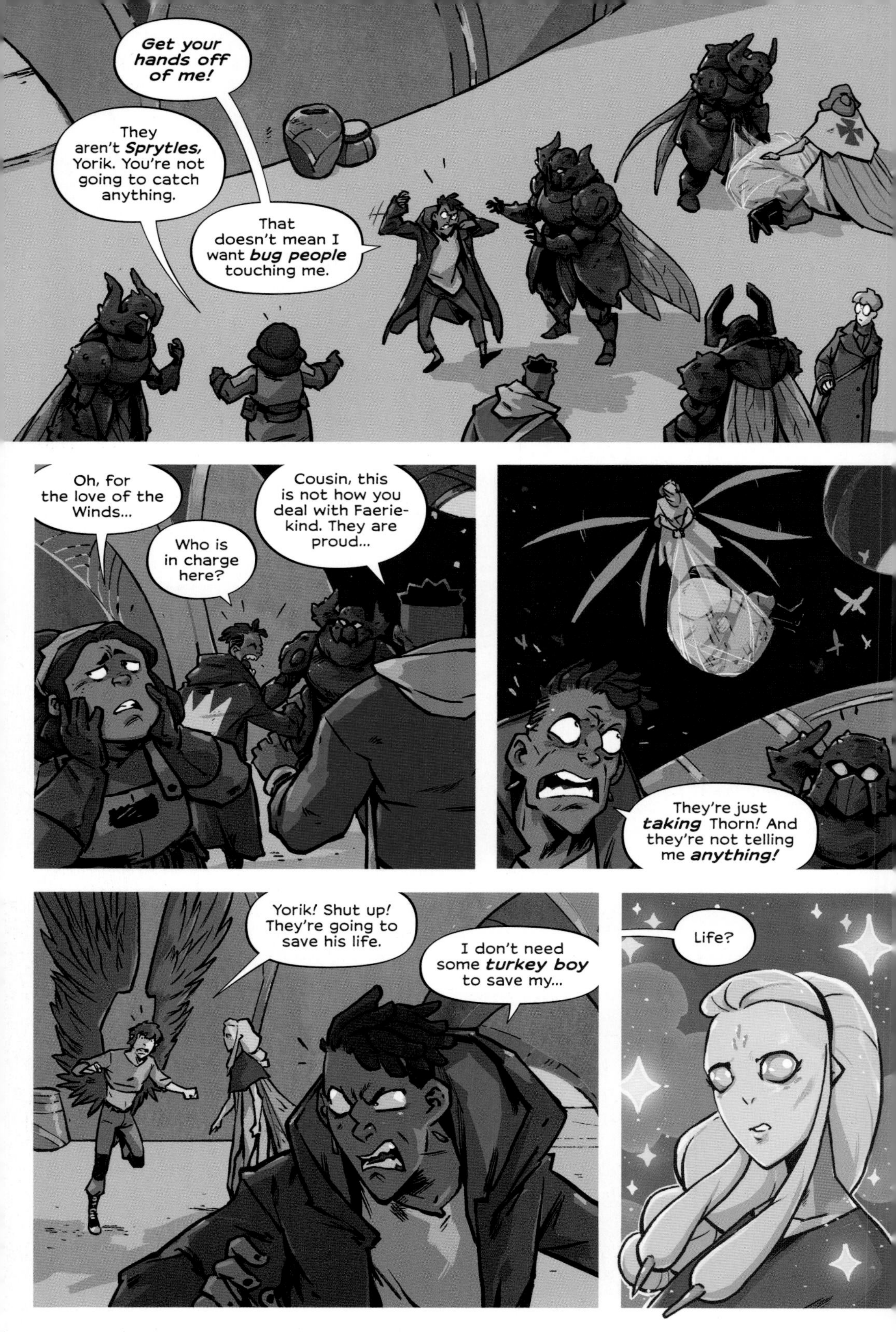
Get your hands off of me!
They aren't Sprytles, Yorik. You're not going to catch anything.
That doesn't mean I want bug people touching me.
Oh, for the love of the Winds...
Who is in charge here?
Cousin, this is not how you deal with Faerie-kind. They are proud...
They're just taking Thorn! And they're not telling me anything!
Yorik! Shut up! They're going to save his life.
I don't need some turkey boy to save my...
Life?

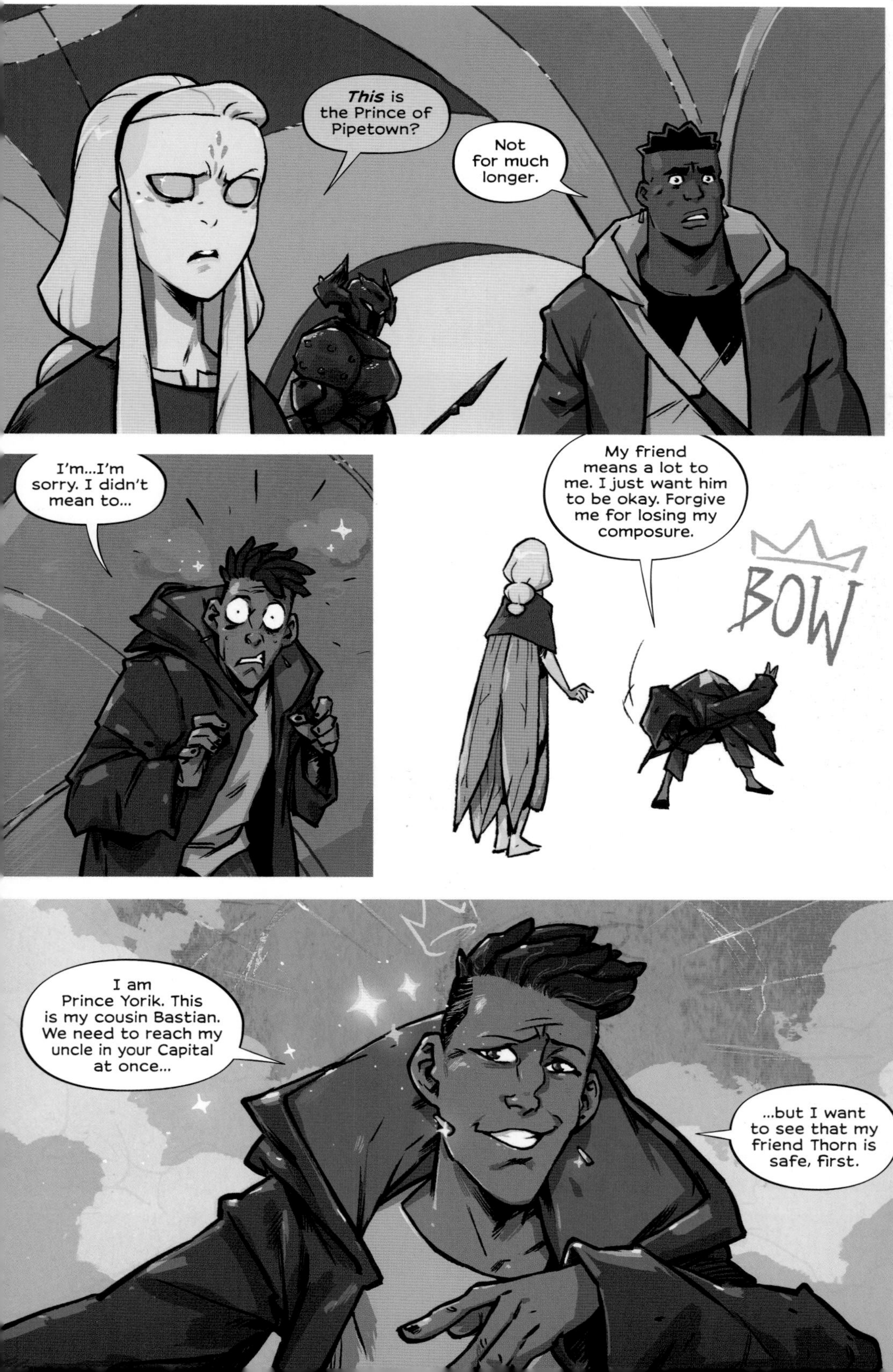
This is the Prince of Pipetown?
Not for much longer.
I'm...I'm sorry. I didn't mean to...
My friend means a lot to me. I just want him to be okay. Forgive me for losing my composure.
BOW
I am Prince Yorik. This is my cousin Bastian. We need to reach my uncle in your Capital at once...
...but I want to see that my friend Thorn is safe, first.

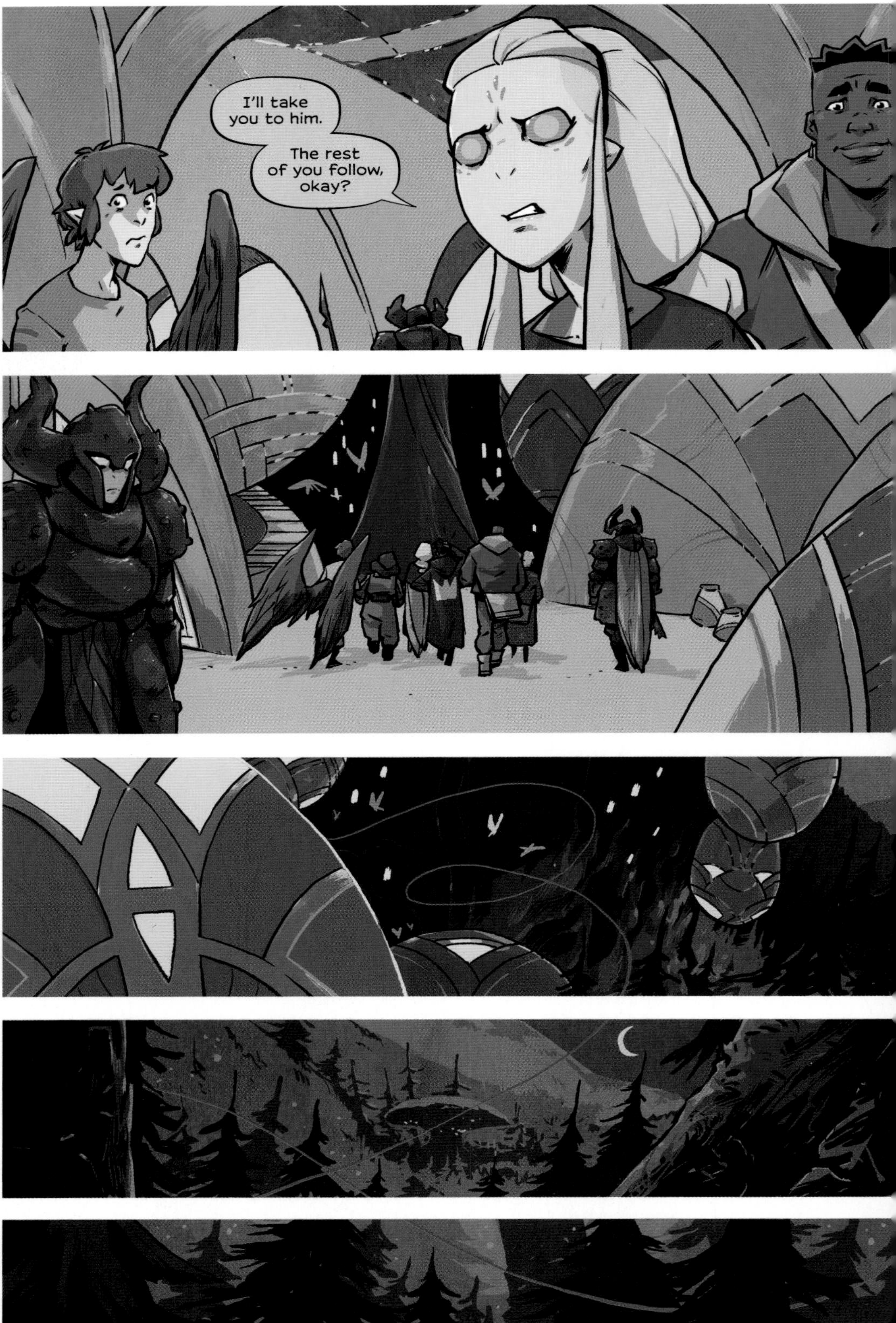
I'll take you to him.
The rest of you follow, okay?

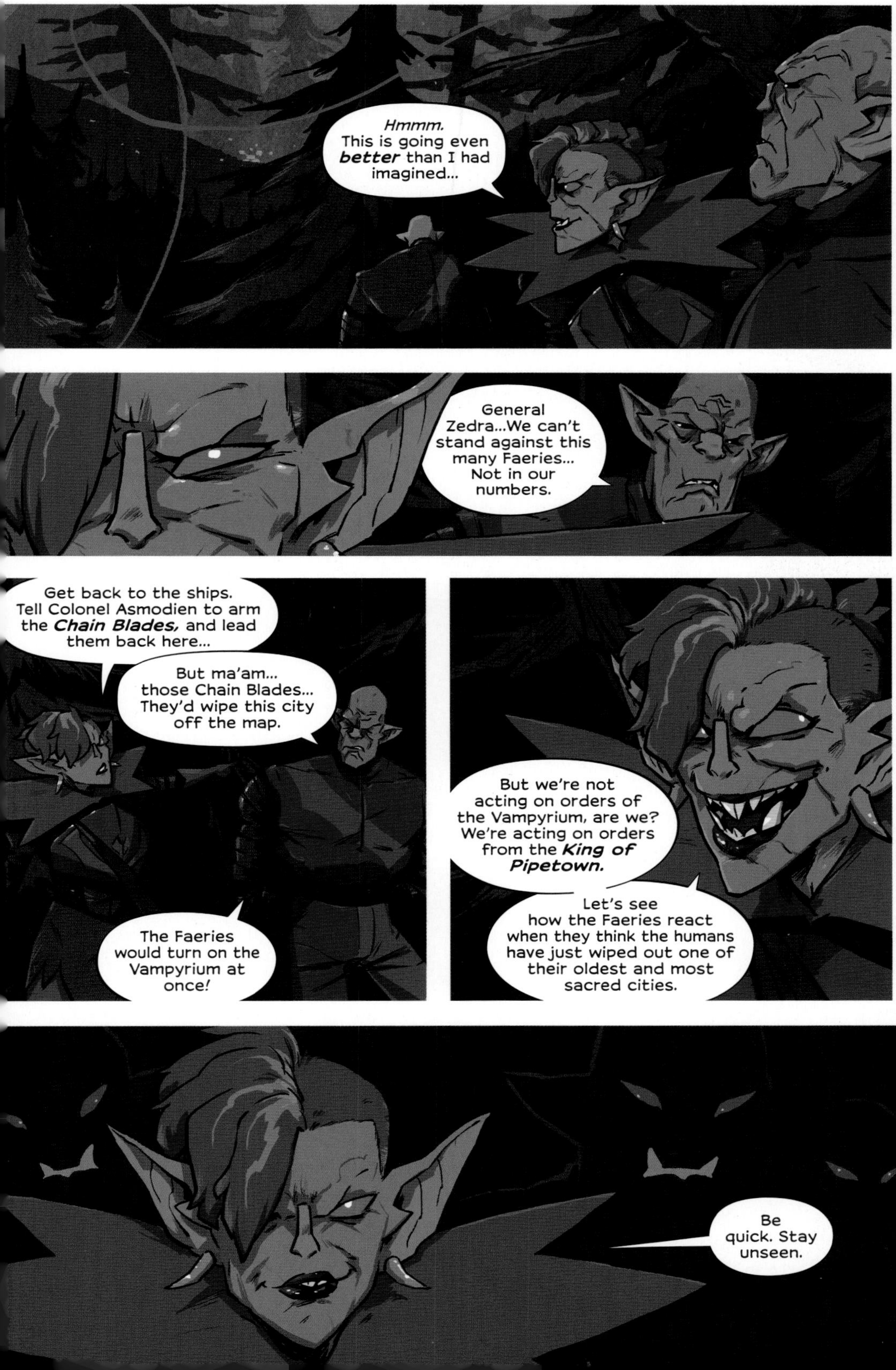
Hmmm. This is going even ***better*** than I had imagined...
General Zedra...We can't stand against this many Faeries... Not in our numbers.
Get back to the ships. Tell Colonel Asmodien to arm the ***Chain Blades,*** and lead them back here...
But ma'am... those Chain Blades... They'd wipe this city off the map.
The Faeries would turn on the Vampyrium at once!
But we're not acting on orders of the Vampyrium, are we? We're acting on orders from the ***King of Pipetown.***
Let's see how the Faeries react when they think the humans have just wiped out one of their oldest and most sacred cities.
Be quick. Stay unseen.

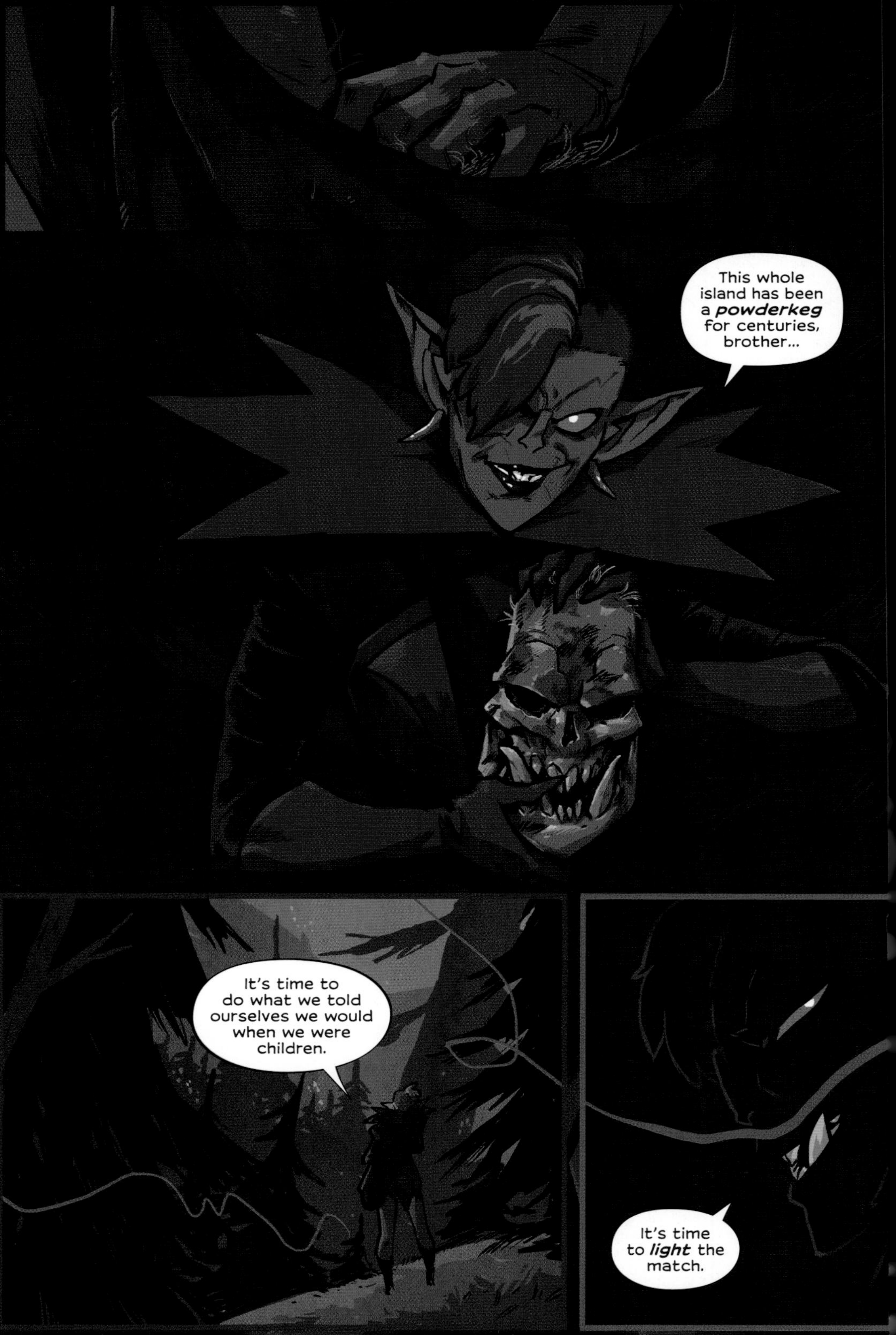
This whole island has been a ***powderkeg*** for centuries, brother...
It's time to do what we told ourselves we would when we were children.
It's time to ***light*** the match.

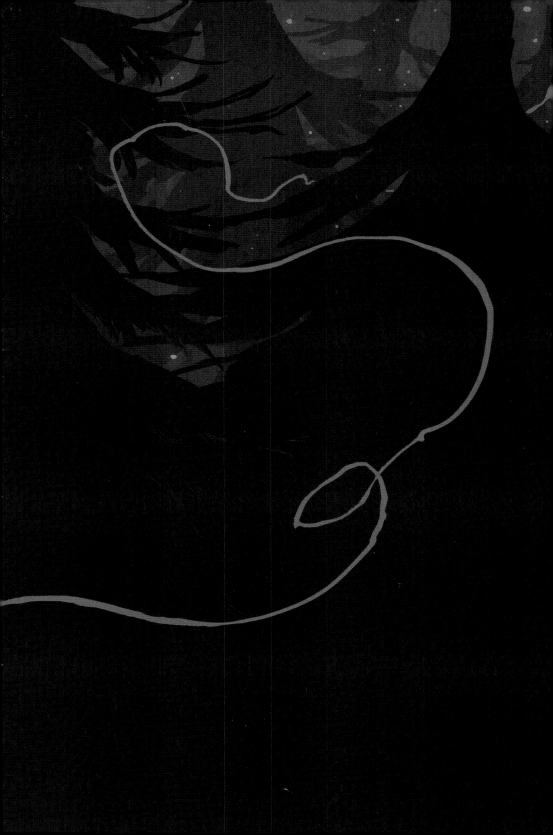

CHAPTER FOUR
ESSERIEL UNITED

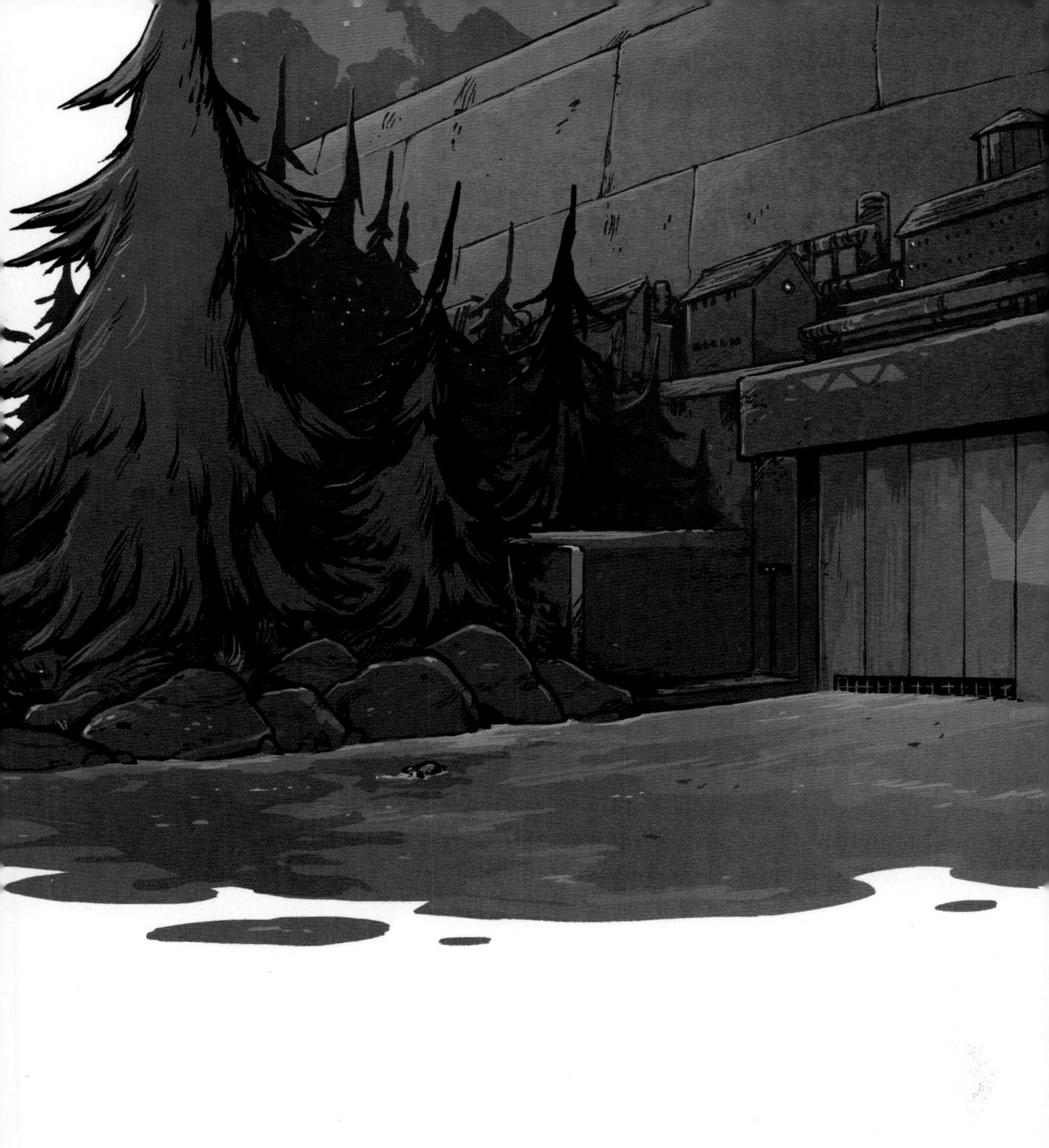

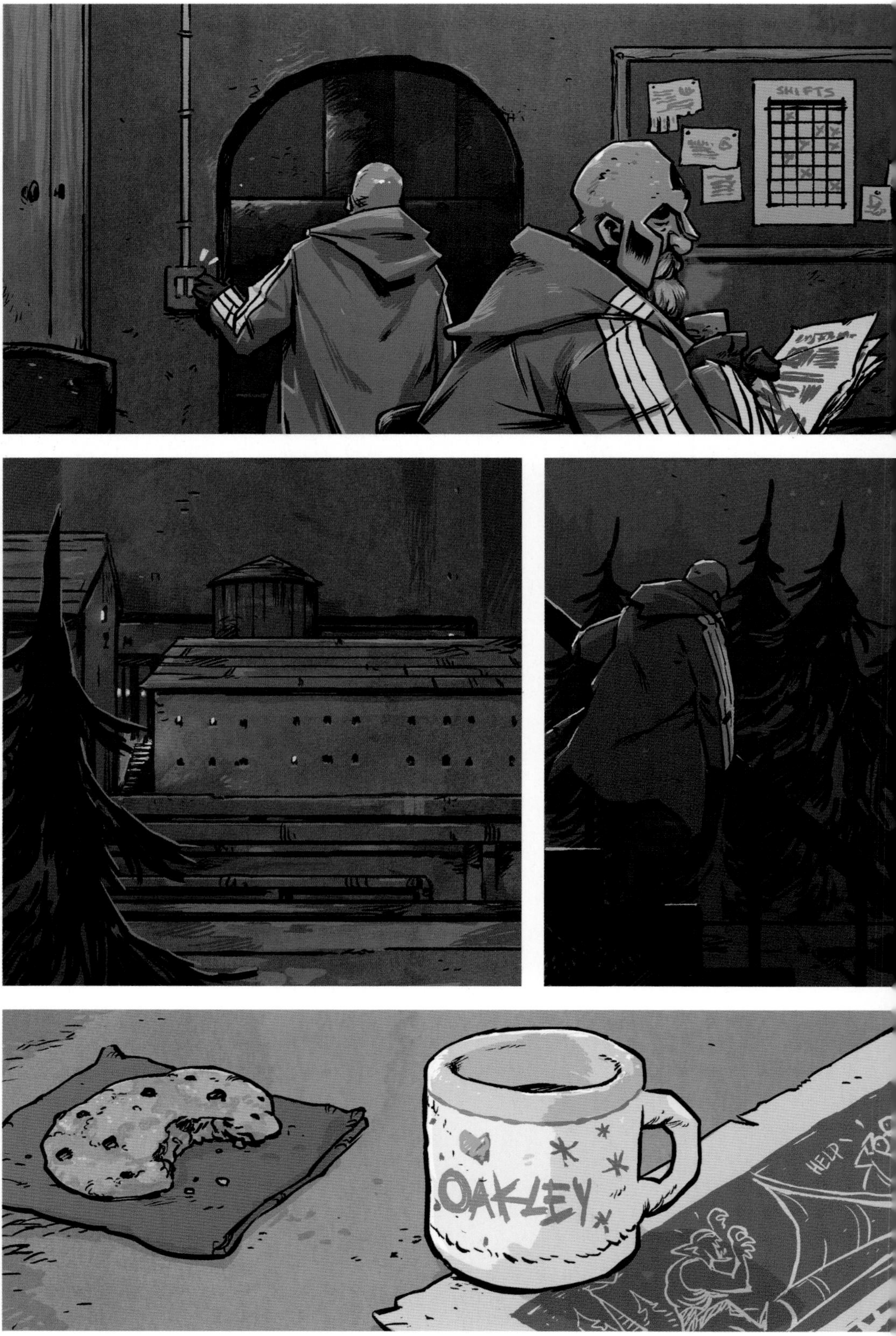
SHIFTS
OAKLEY
HELP!

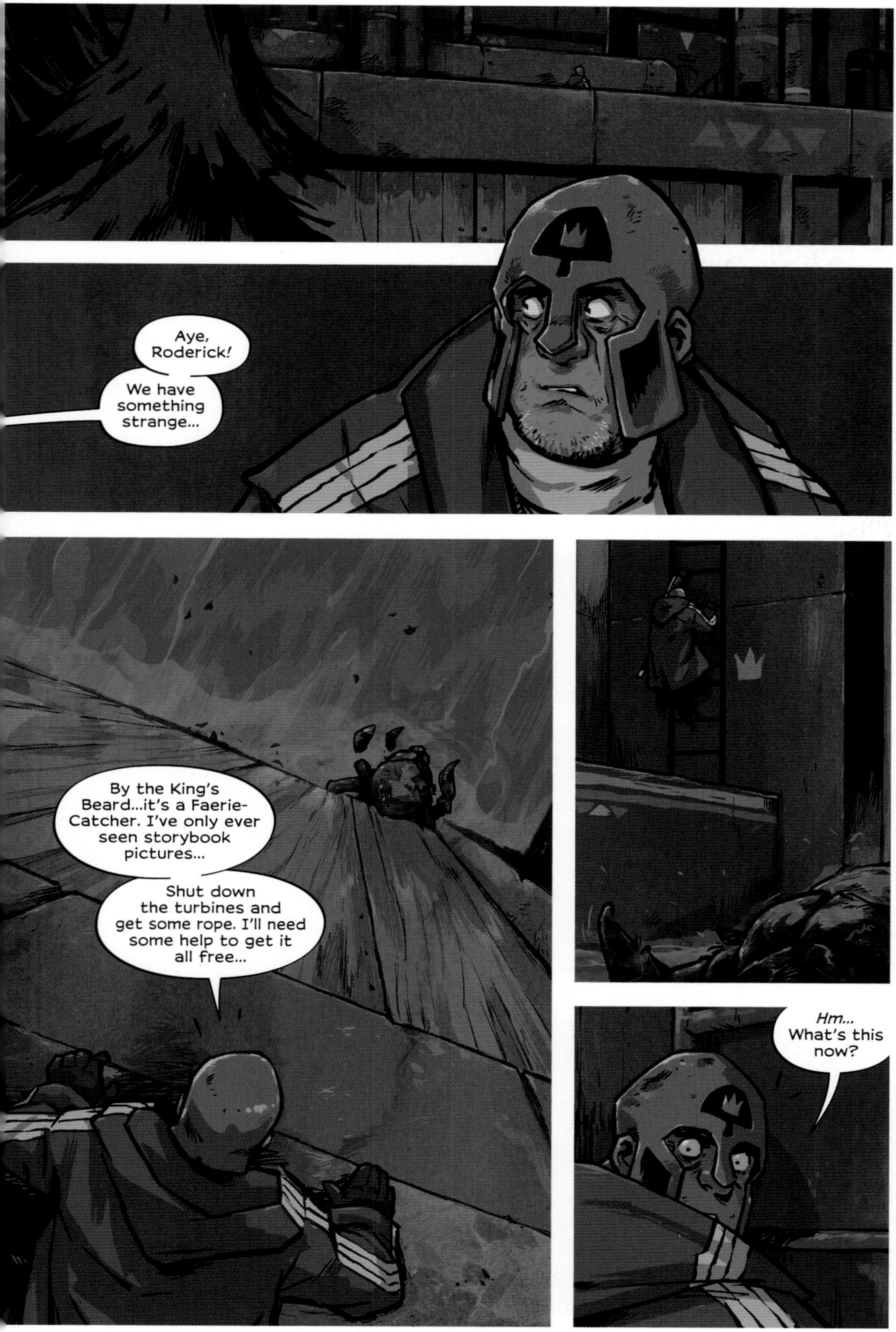
Aye, Roderick!
We have something strange...
By the King's Beard...it's a Faerie-Catcher. I've only ever seen storybook pictures...
Shut down the turbines and get some rope. I'll need some help to get it all free...
Hm... What's this now?

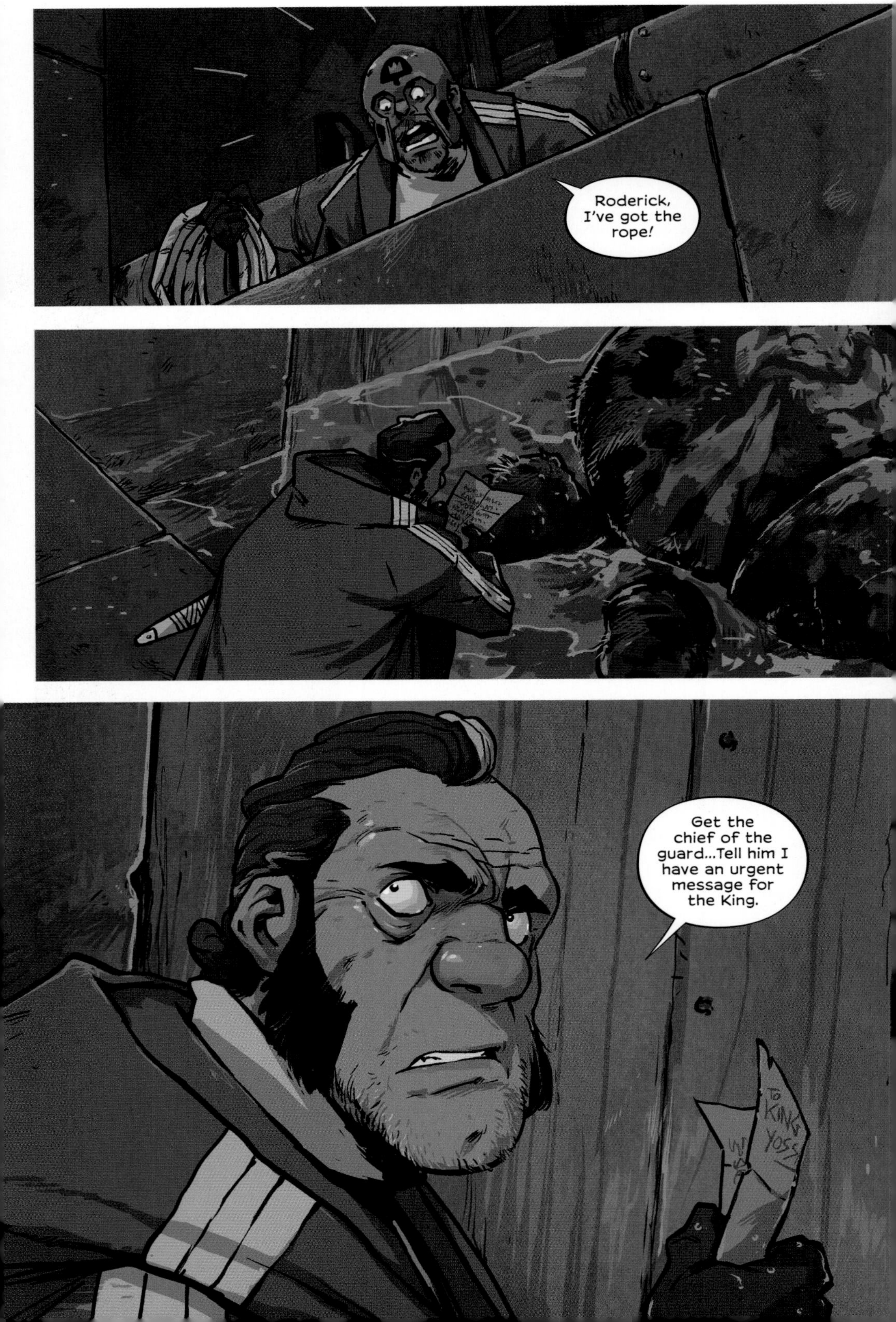
Roderick, I've got the rope!
Get the chief of the guard...Tell him I have an urgent message for the King.
TO KING YOSS

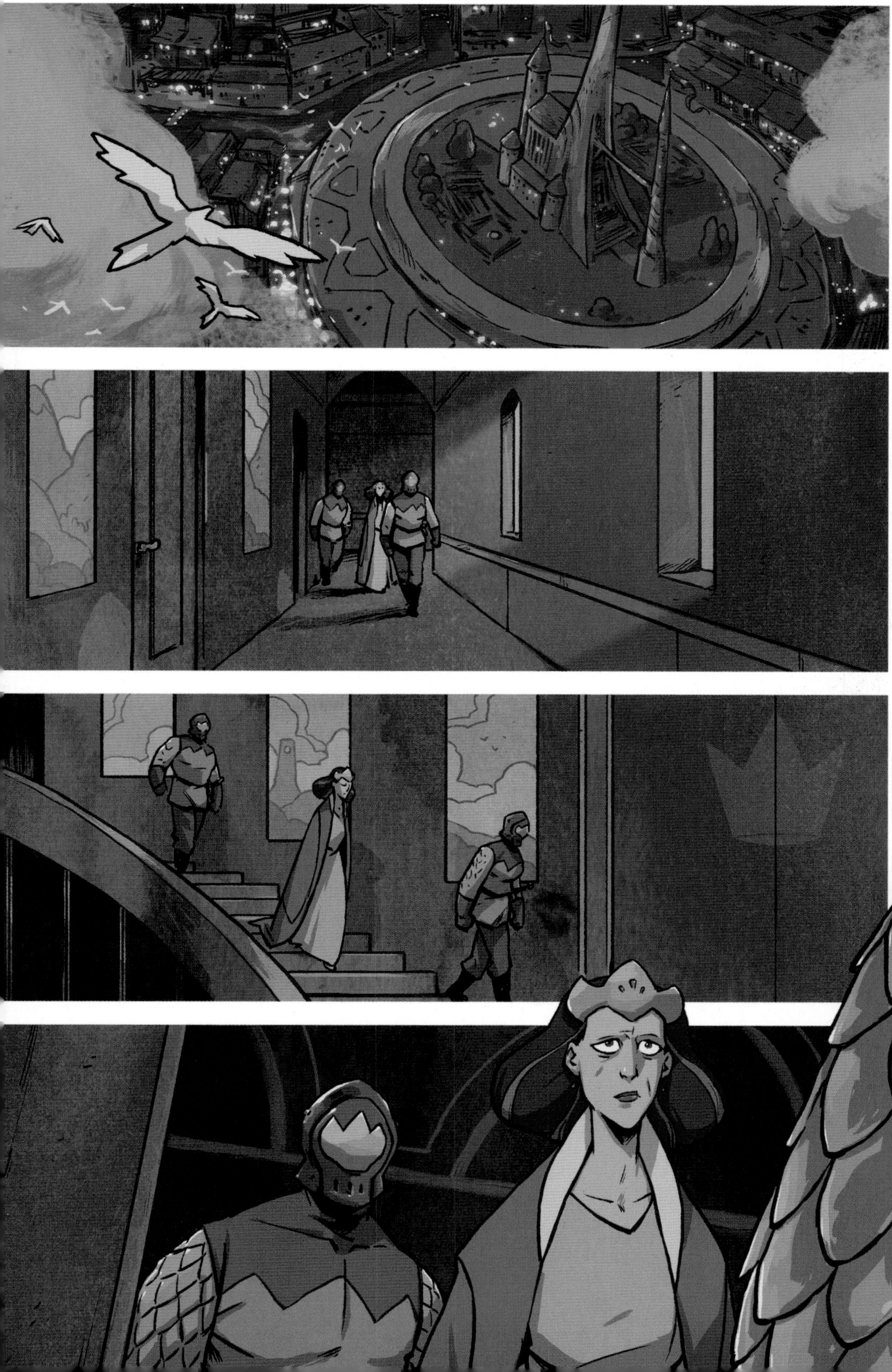

What is the meaning of this, my love?

I think you know, turtledove.

I think you've been waiting for this day for years and years.

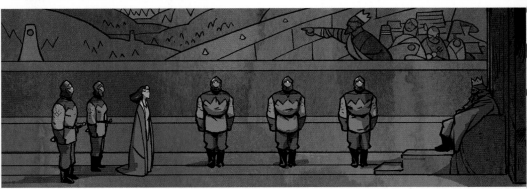

Say what you've been clearly dying to say to my face.

Your father put a *hate* in you so deep and powerful that it has *twisted* your mind against your family. Against your brother. Against your *son.*

It's killing you. And it will kill us all.

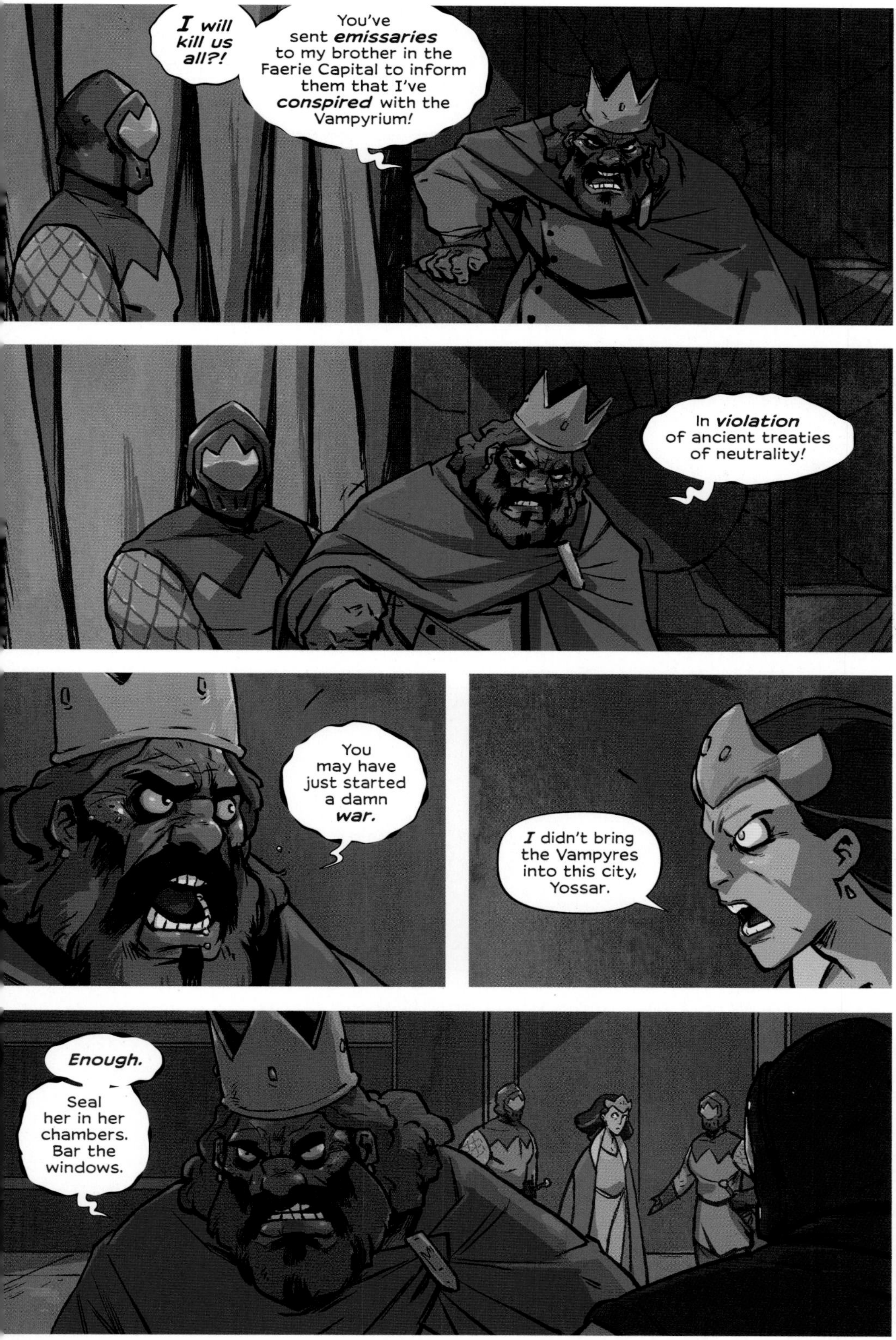
I will kill us all?!
You've sent emissaries to my brother in the Faerie Capital to inform them that I've conspired with the Vampyrium!
In violation of ancient treaties of neutrality!
You may have just started a damn war.
I didn't bring the Vampyres into this city, Yossar.
Enough.
Seal her in her chambers. Bar the windows.

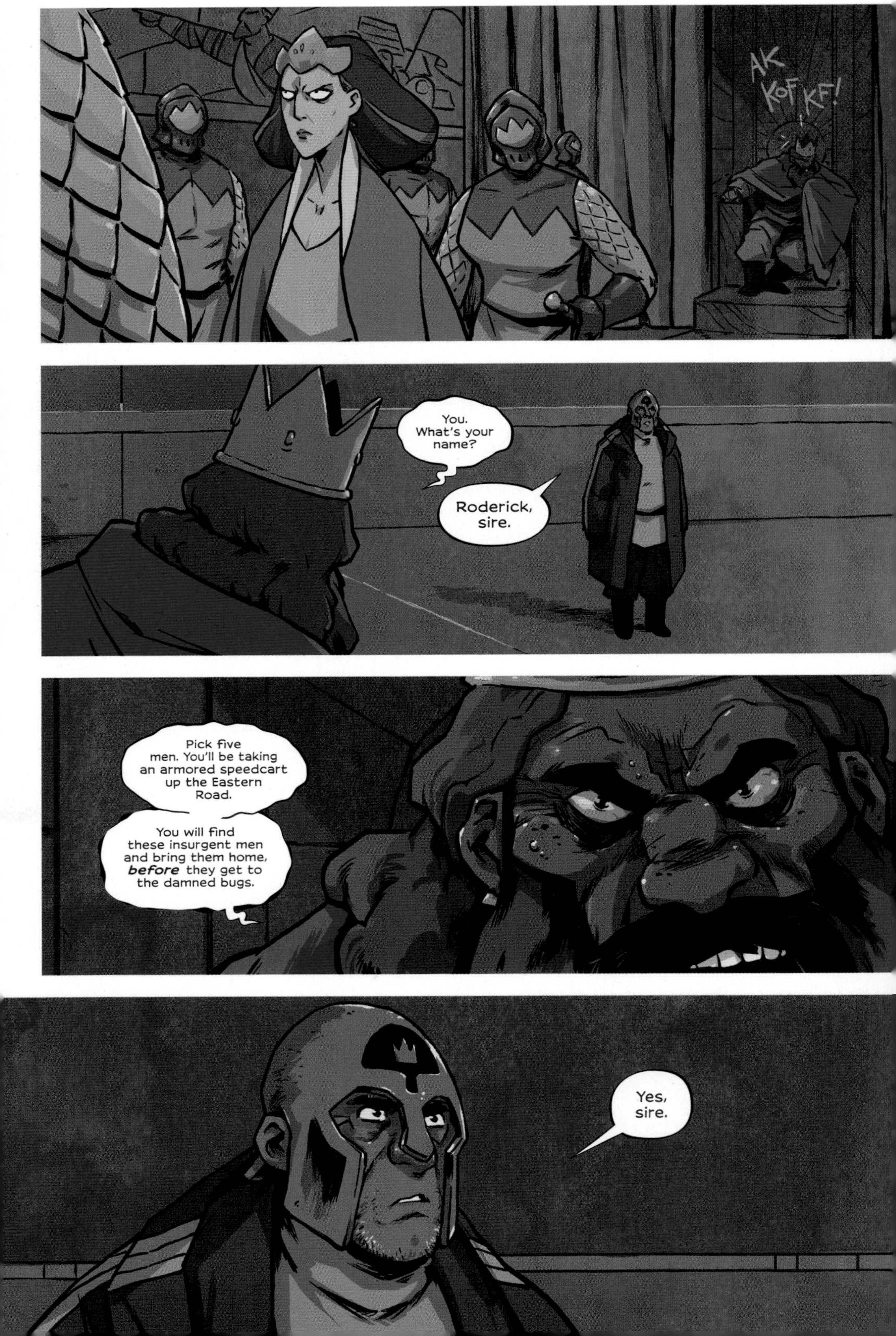
AK KOF KF!
You. What's your name?
Roderick, sire.
Pick five men. You'll be taking an armored speedcart up the Eastern Road.
You will find these insurgent men and bring them home, *before* they get to the damned bugs.
Yes, sire.

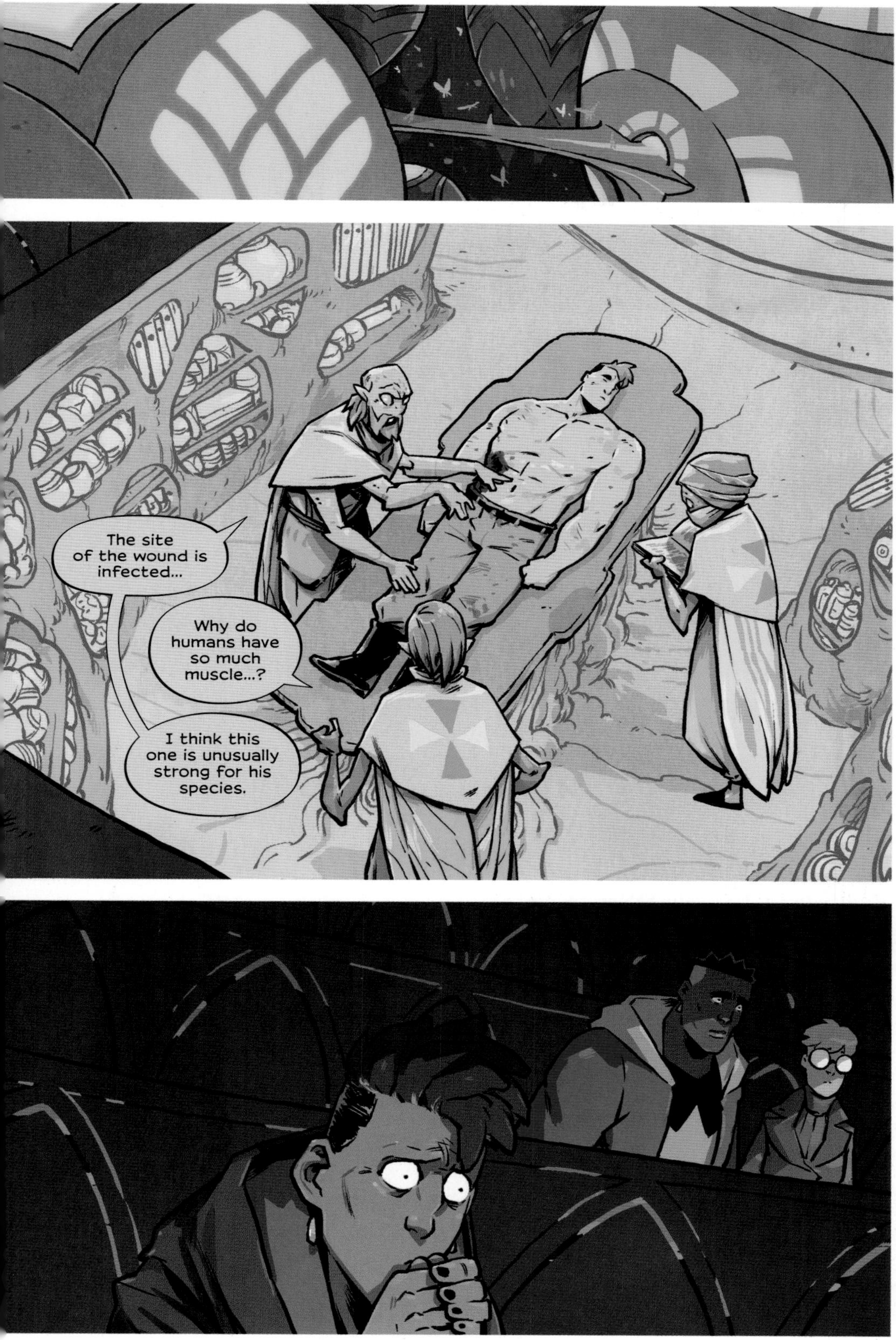

The site of the wound is infected...
Why do humans have so much muscle...?
I think this one is unusually strong for his species.

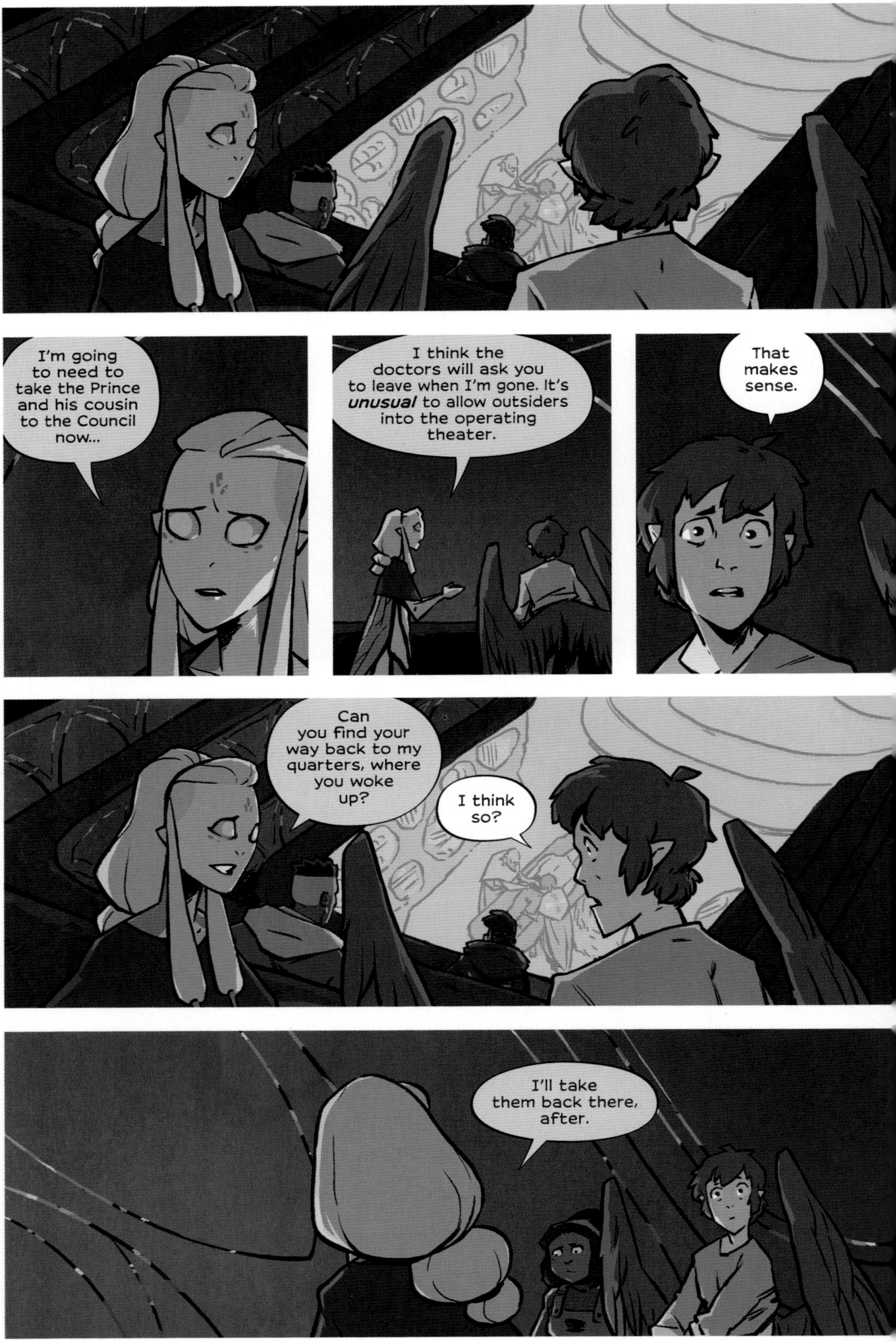
I'm going to need to take the Prince and his cousin to the Council now...
I think the doctors will ask you to leave when I'm gone. It's *unusual* to allow outsiders into the operating theater.
That makes sense.
Can you find your way back to my quarters, where you woke up?
I think so?
I'll take them back there, after.

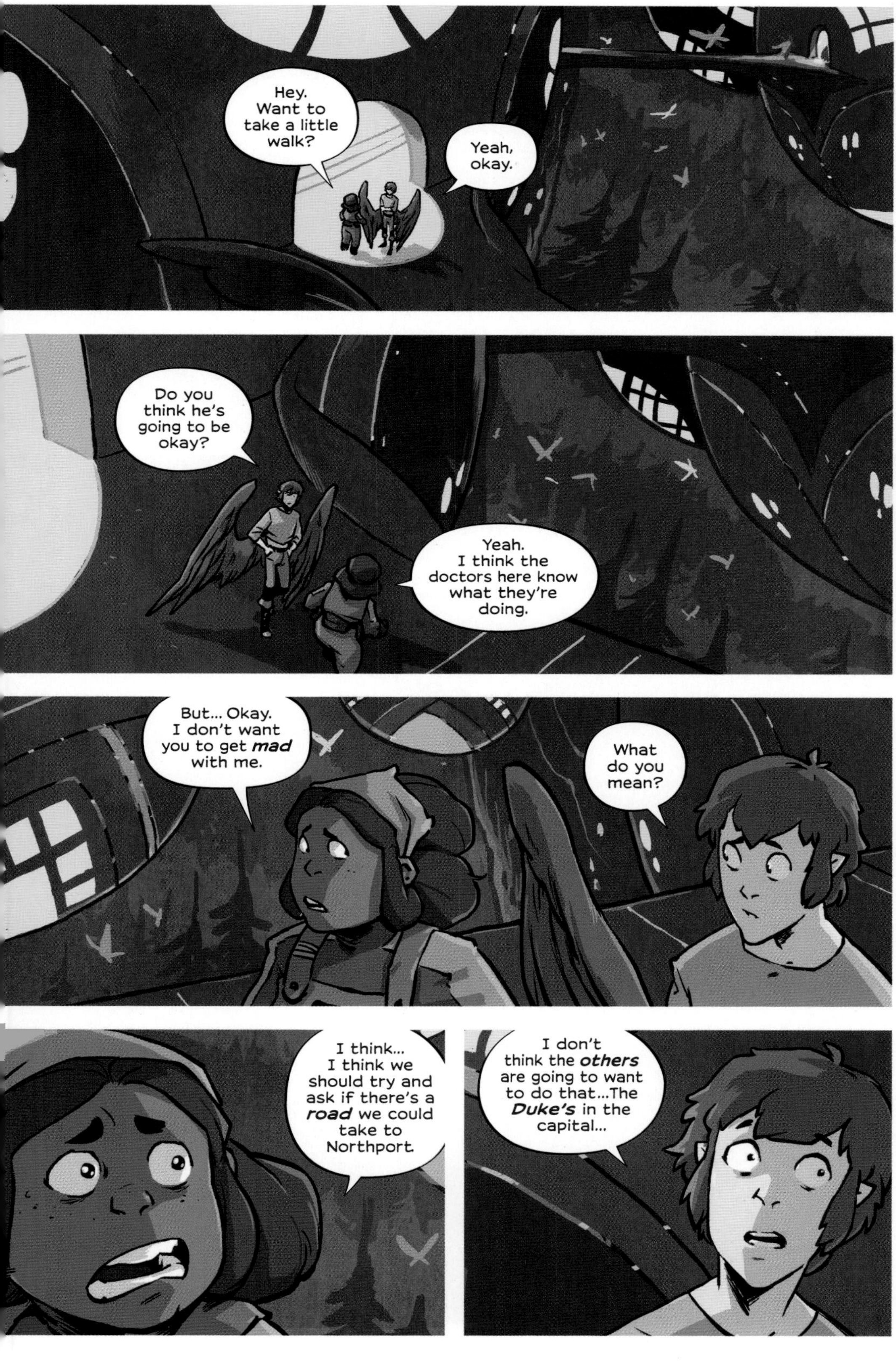

Hey. Want to take a little walk?
Yeah, okay.
Do you think he's going to be okay?
Yeah. I think the doctors here know what they're doing.
But... Okay. I don't want you to get *mad* with me.
What do you mean?
I think... I think we should try and ask if there's a *road* we could take to Northport.
I don't think the *others* are going to want to do that...The *Duke's* in the capital...

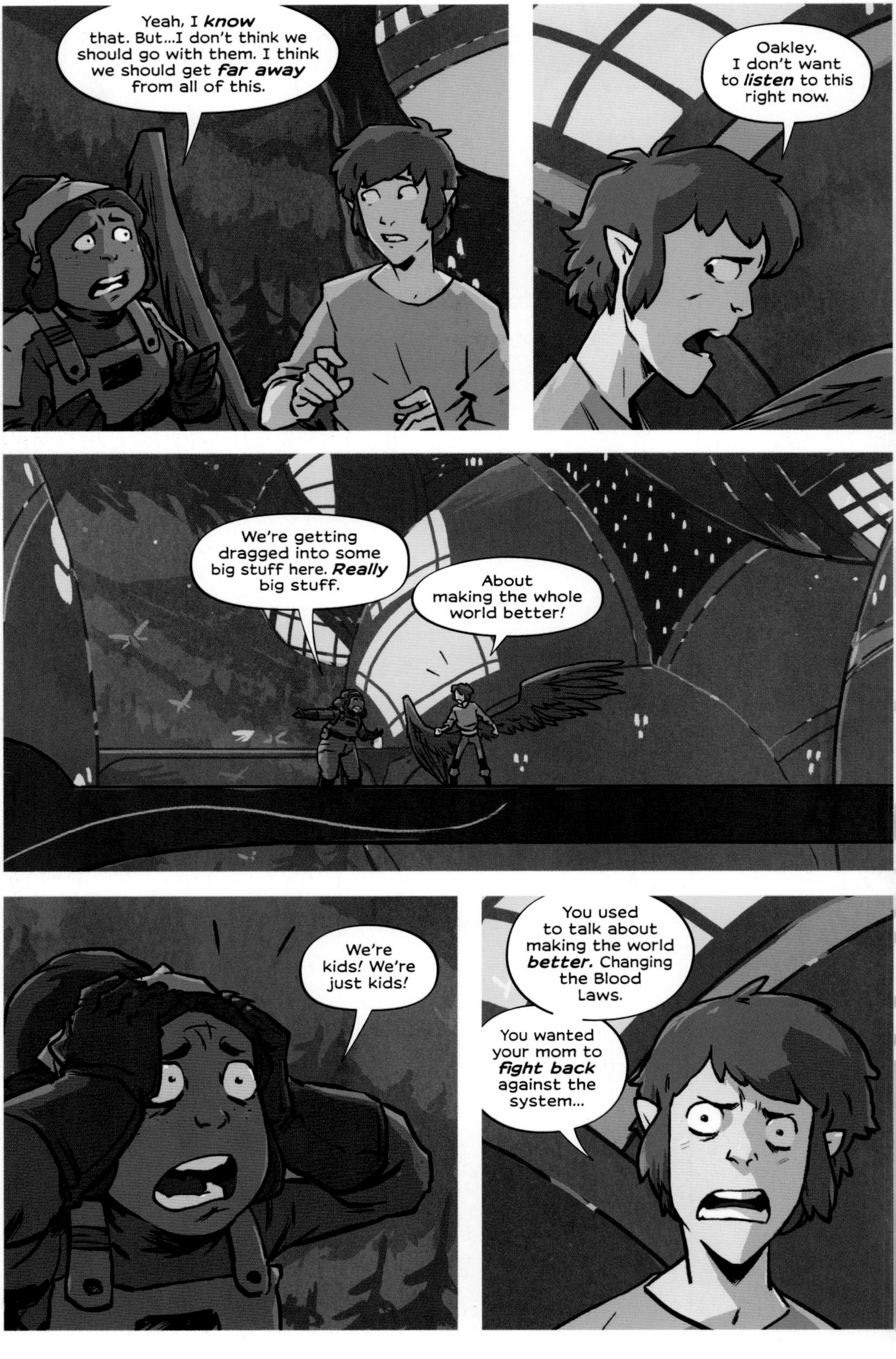
Yeah, I *know* that. But...I don't think we should go with them. I think we should get *far away* from all of this.
Oakley. I don't want to *listen* to this right now.
We're getting dragged into some big stuff here. *Really* big stuff.
About making the whole world better!
We're kids! We're just kids!
You used to talk about making the world *better.* Changing the Blood Laws.
You wanted your mom to *fight back* against the system...

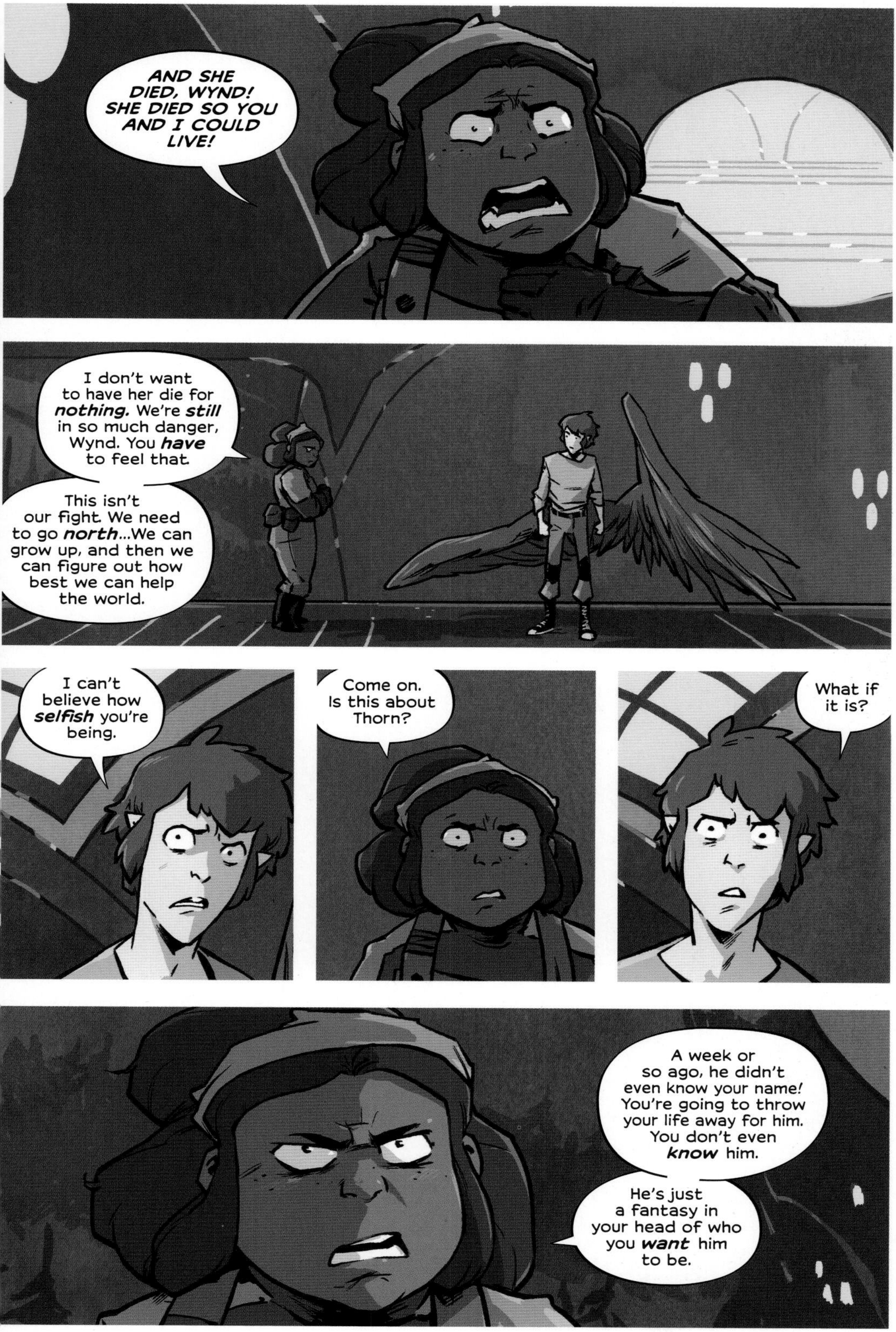
AND SHE DIED, WYND! SHE DIED SO YOU AND I COULD LIVE!
I don't want to have her die for *nothing.* We're *still* in so much danger, Wynd. You *have* to feel that.
This isn't our fight. We need to go *north*...We can grow up, and then we can figure out how best we can help the world.
I can't believe how *selfish* you're being.
Come on. Is this about Thorn?
What if it is?
A week or so ago, he didn't even know your name! You're going to throw your life away for him. You don't even *know* him.
He's just a fantasy in your head of who you *want* him to be.

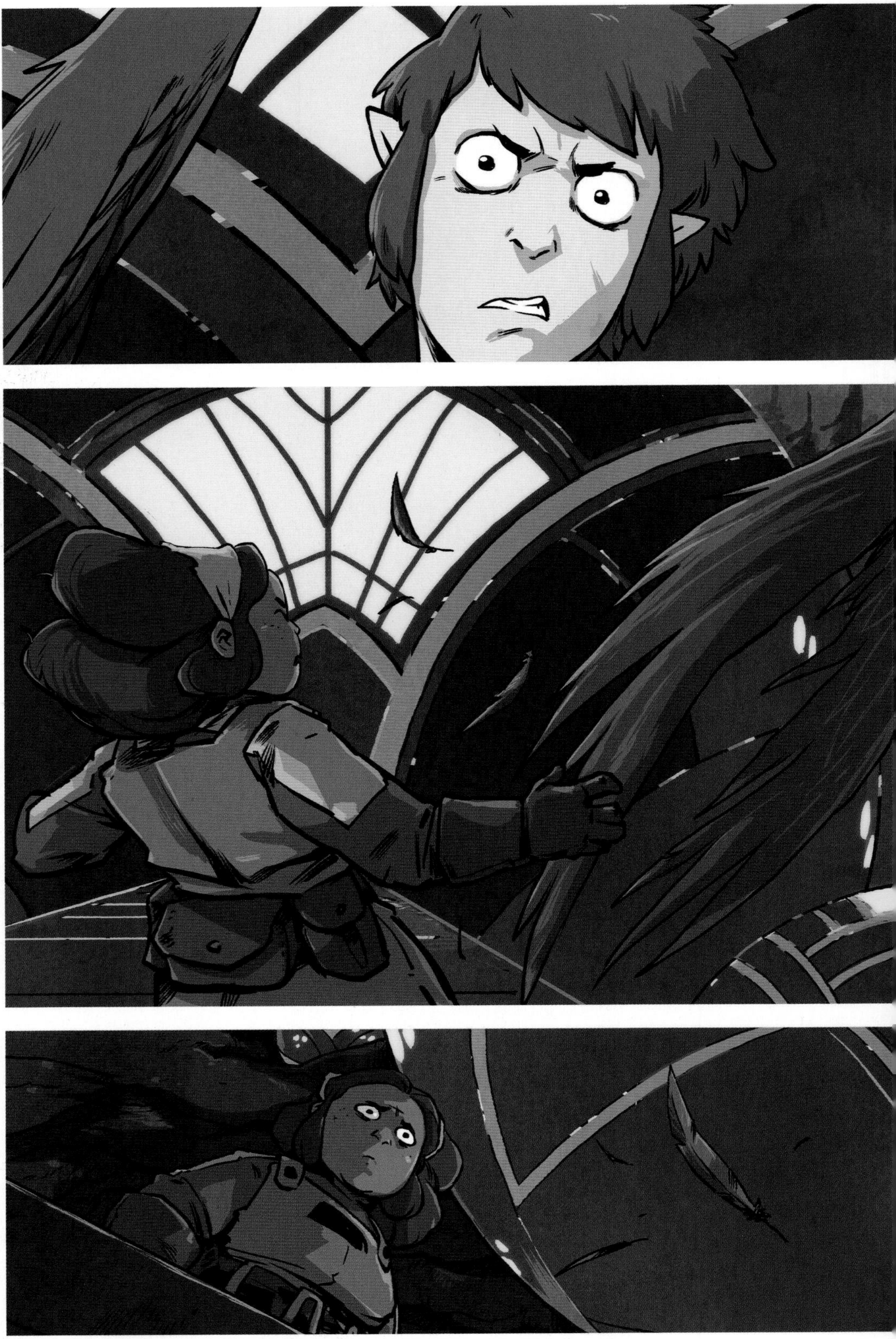

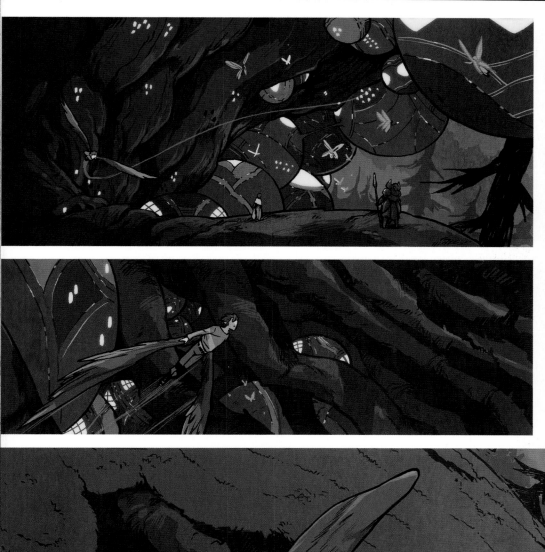

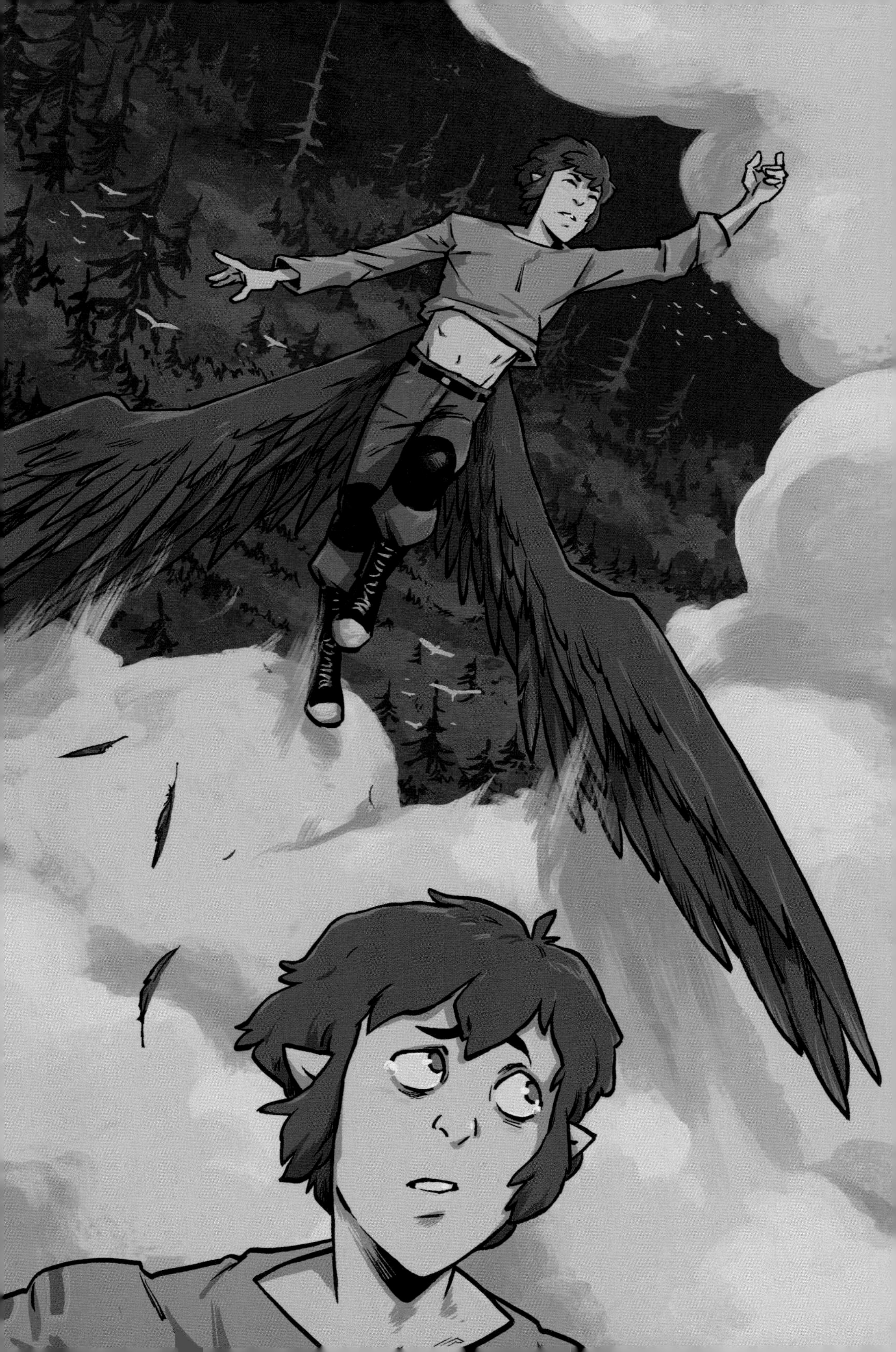

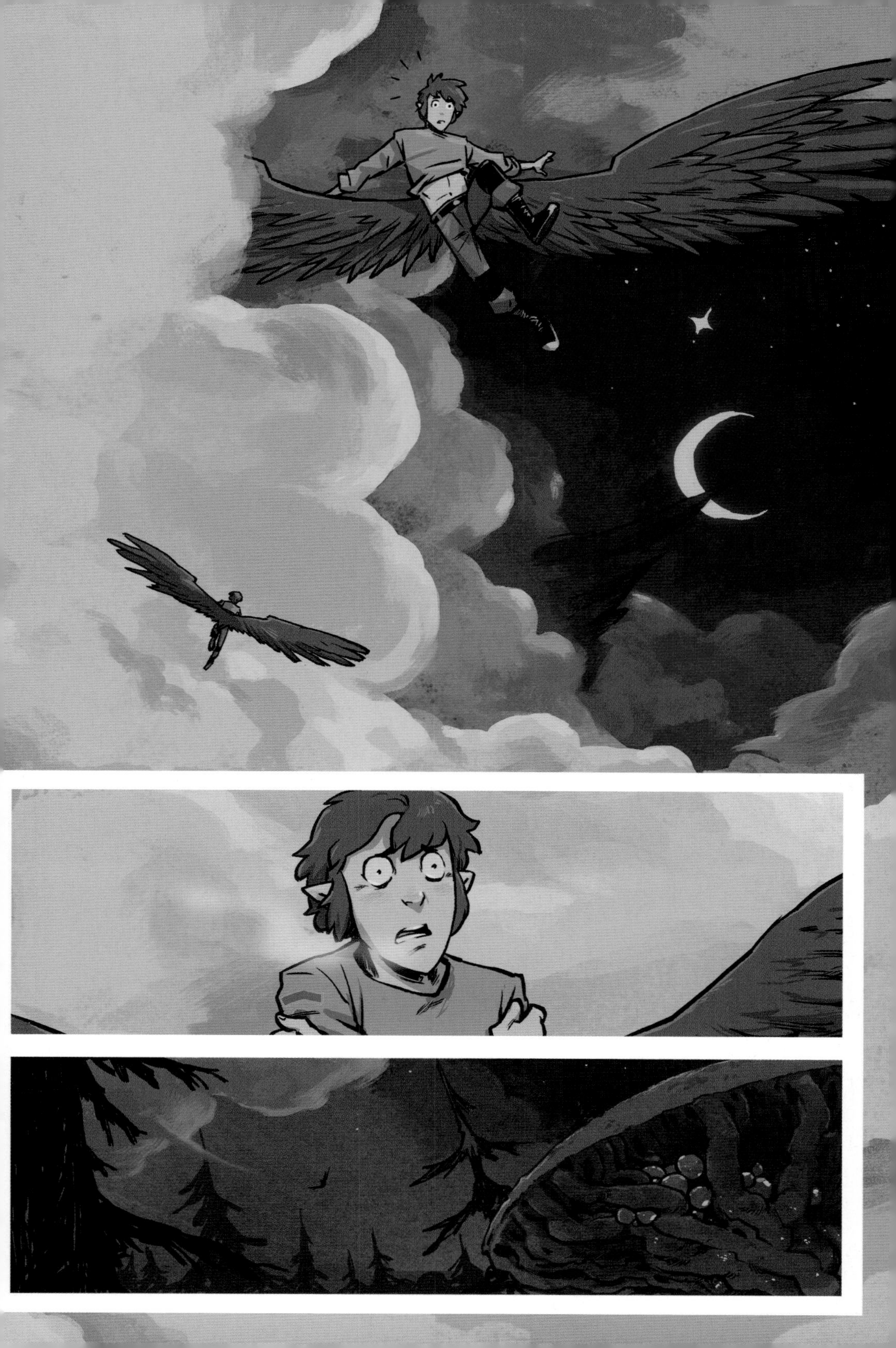

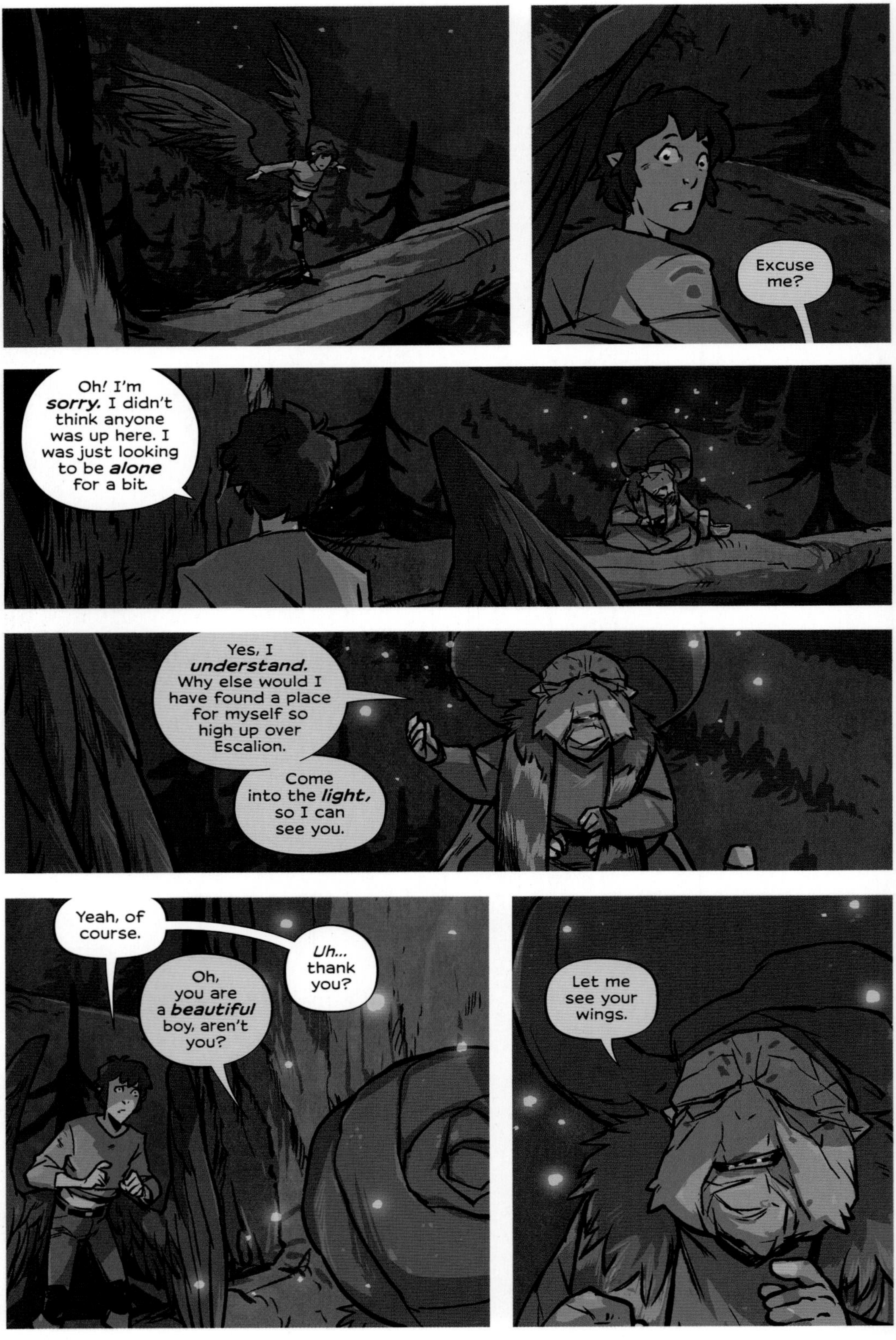
Excuse me?
Oh! I'm *sorry.* I didn't think anyone was up here. I was just looking to be *alone* for a bit.
Yes, I *understand.* Why else would I have found a place for myself so high up over Escalion.
Come into the *light,* so I can see you.
Yeah, of course.
Oh, you are a *beautiful* boy, aren't you?
Uh... thank you?
Let me see your wings.

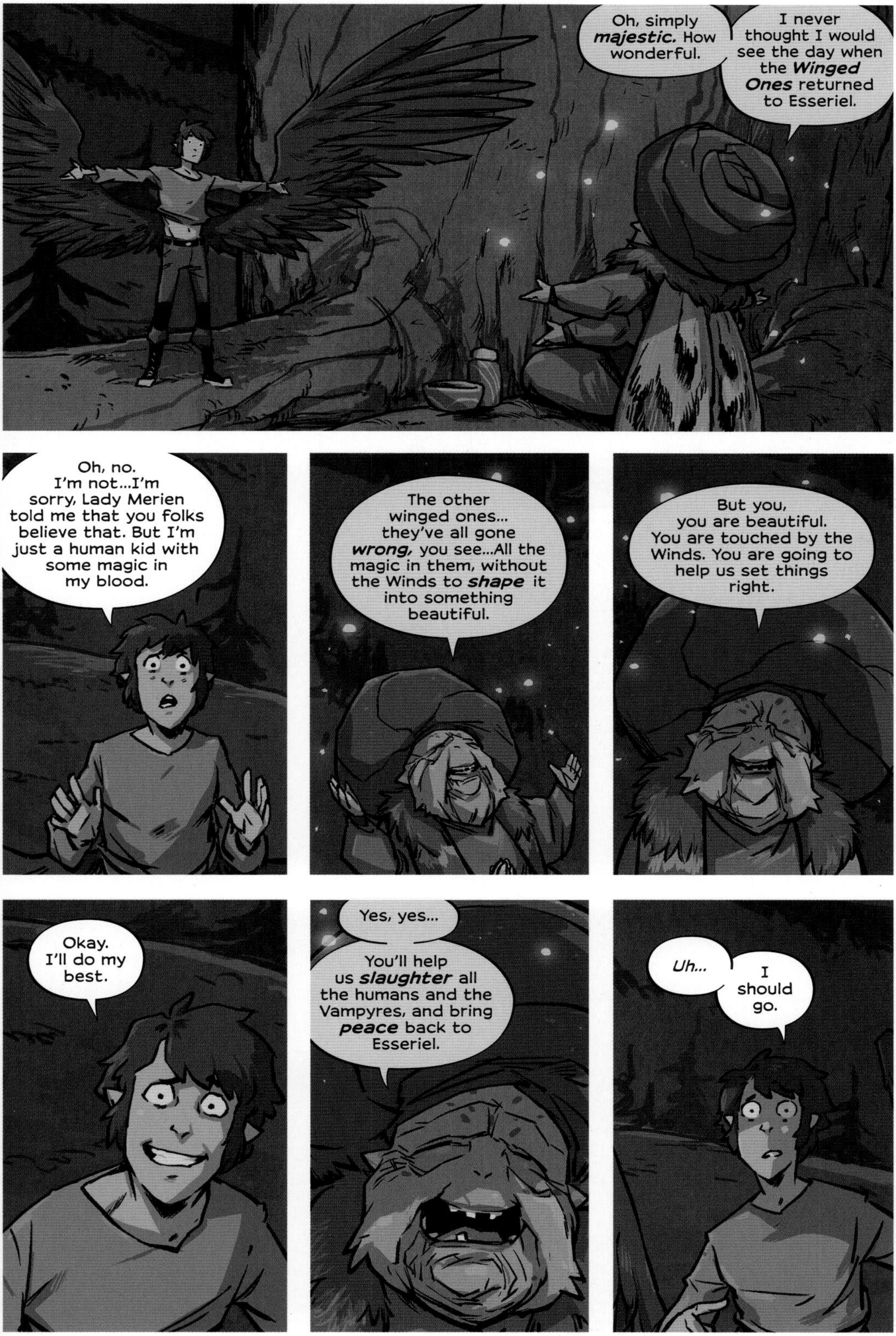
Oh, simply majestic. How wonderful.
I never thought I would see the day when the Winged Ones returned to Esseriel.
Oh, no. I'm not...I'm sorry, Lady Merien told me that you folks believe that. But I'm just a human kid with some magic in my blood.
The other winged ones... they've all gone wrong, you see...All the magic in them, without the Winds to shape it into something beautiful.
But you, you are beautiful. You are touched by the Winds. You are going to help us set things right.
Okay. I'll do my best.
Yes, yes...
You'll help us slaughter all the humans and the Vampyres, and bring peace back to Esseriel.
Uh...
I should go.

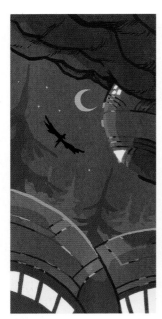

Friends, my cousin and I are not here to bring you any trouble--

And yet that is *all* you humans seem capable of bringing to the Weird Woods.

Counselor, I don't think that is fair...

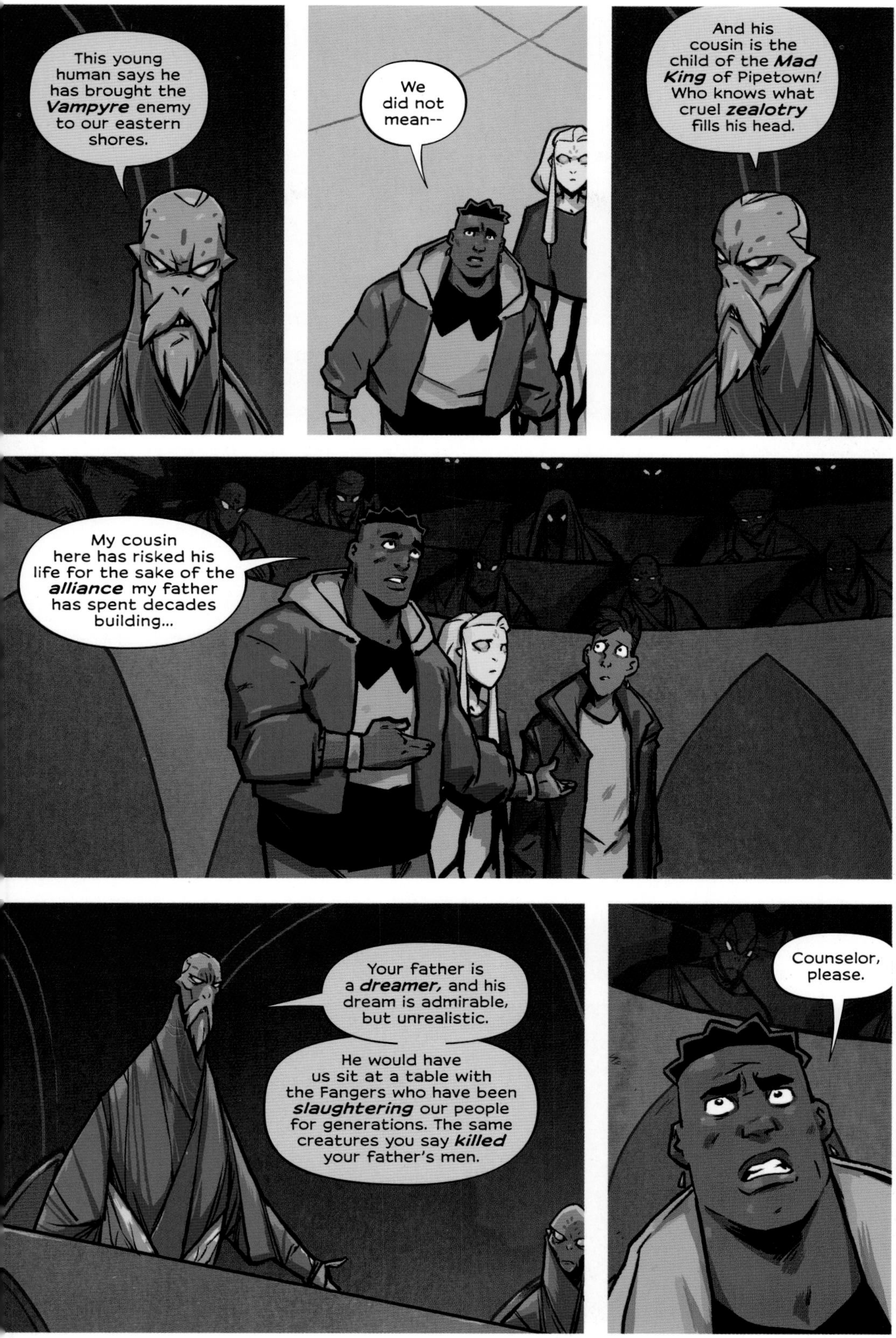
This young human says he has brought the *Vampyre* enemy to our eastern shores.
We did not mean--
And his cousin is the child of the *Mad King* of Pipetown! Who knows what cruel *zealotry* fills his head.
My cousin here has risked his life for the sake of the *alliance* my father has spent decades building...
Your father is a *dreamer,* and his dream is admirable, but unrealistic.
He would have us sit at a table with the Fangers who have been *slaughtering* our people for generations. The same creatures you say *killed* your father's men.
Counselor, please.

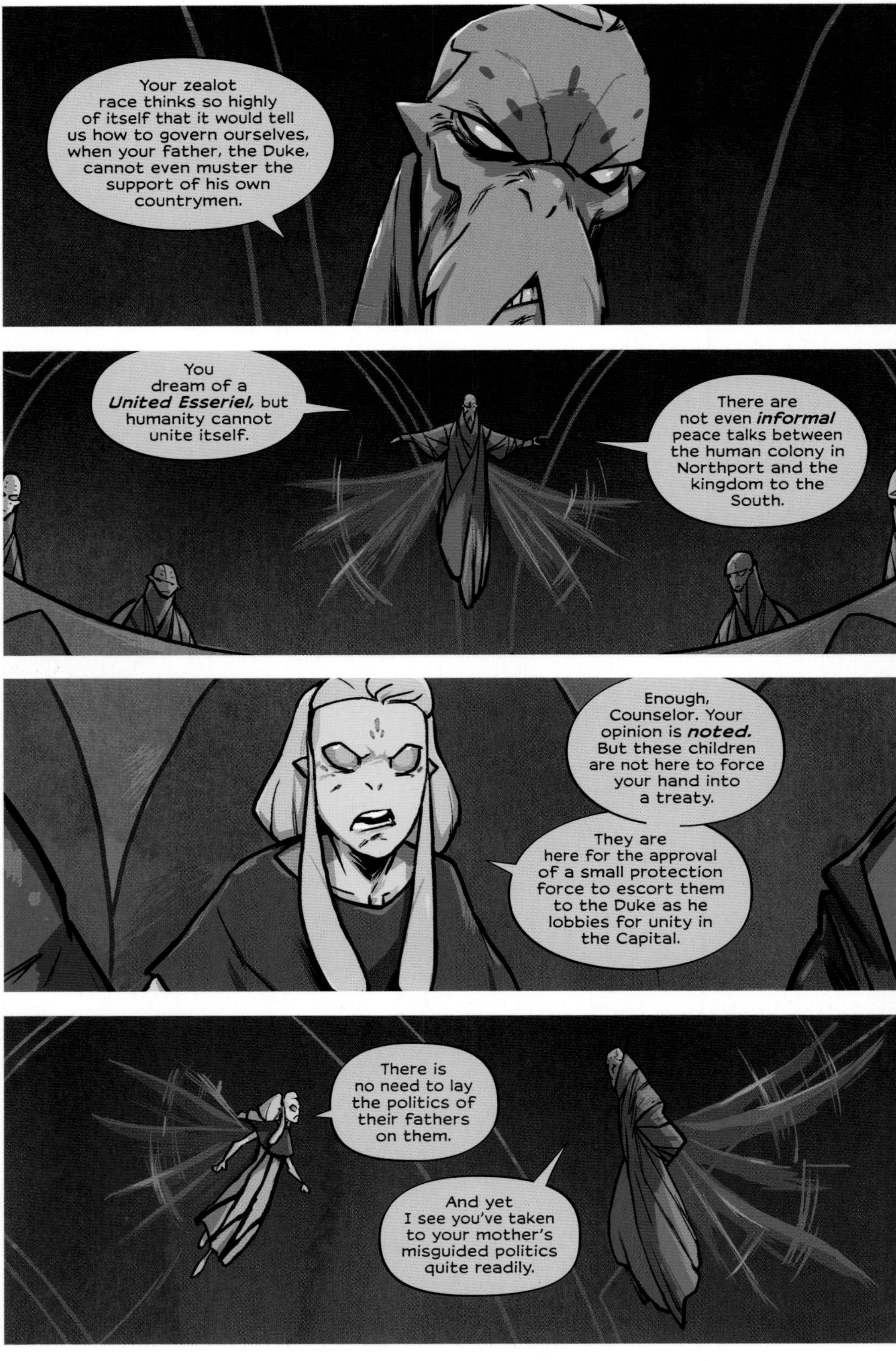
Your zealot race thinks so highly of itself that it would tell us how to govern ourselves, when your father, the Duke, cannot even muster the support of his own countrymen.
You dream of a ***United Esseriel,*** but humanity cannot unite itself.
There are not even ***informal*** peace talks between the human colony in Northport and the kingdom to the South.
Enough, Counselor. Your opinion is ***noted.*** But these children are not here to force your hand into a treaty.
They are here for the approval of a small protection force to escort them to the Duke as he lobbies for unity in the Capital.
There is no need to lay the politics of their fathers on them.
And yet I see you've taken to your mother's misguided politics quite readily.

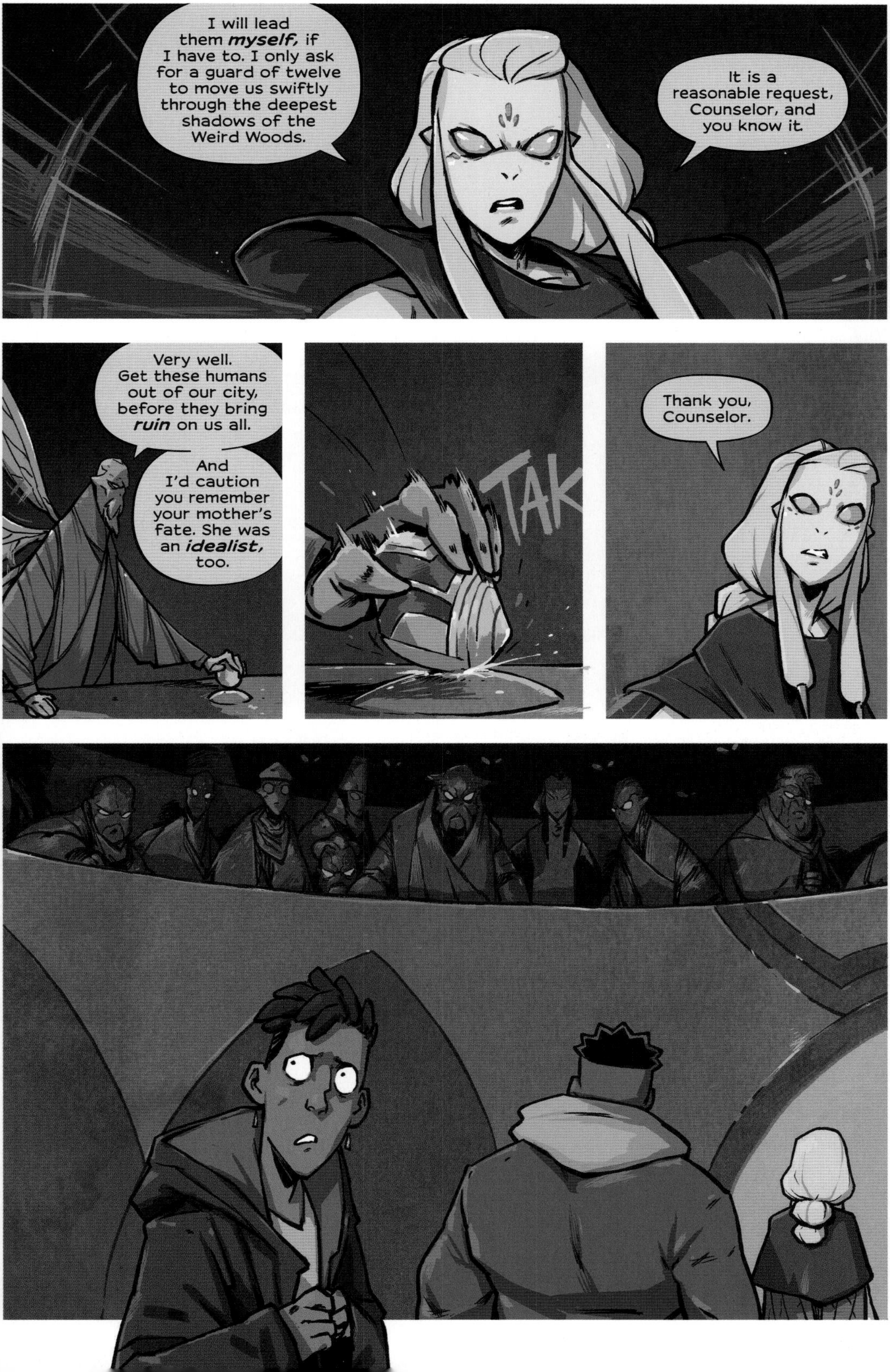
I will lead them *myself,* if I have to. I only ask for a guard of twelve to move us swiftly through the deepest shadows of the Weird Woods.
It is a reasonable request, Counselor, and you know it.
Very well. Get these humans out of our city, before they bring *ruin* on us all.
And I'd caution you remember your mother's fate. She was an *idealist,* too.
TAK
Thank you, Counselor.

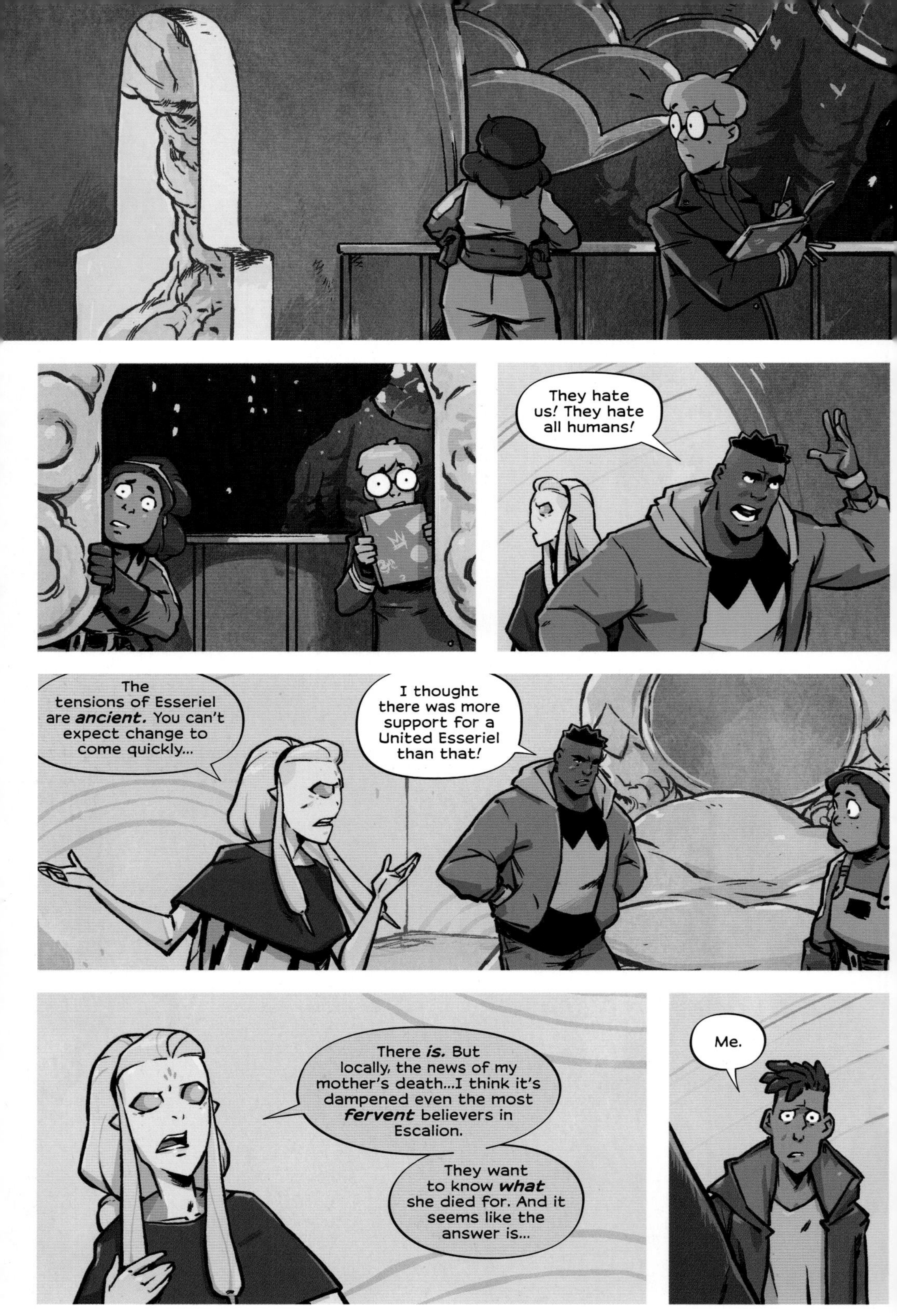
They hate us! They hate all humans!
The tensions of Esseriel are ***ancient.*** You can't expect change to come quickly...
I thought there was more support for a United Esseriel than that!
There ***is.*** But locally, the news of my mother's death...I think it's dampened even the most ***fervent*** believers in Escalion.
They want to know ***what*** she died for. And it seems like the answer is...
Me.

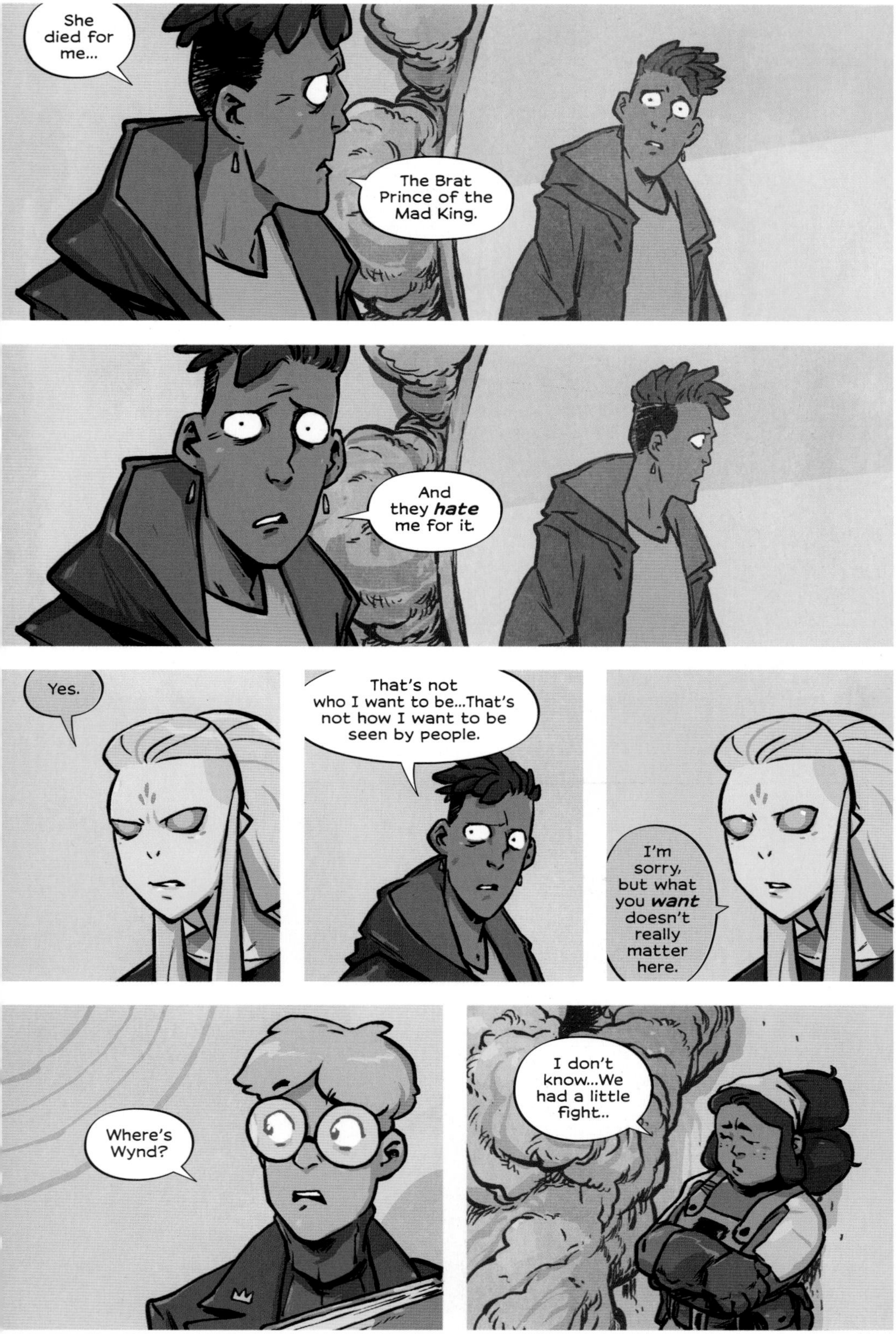
She died for me...
The Brat Prince of the Mad King.
And they *hate* me for it.
Yes.
That's not who I want to be...That's not how I want to be seen by people.
I'm sorry, but what you *want* doesn't really matter here.
Where's Wynd?
I don't know...We had a little fight..

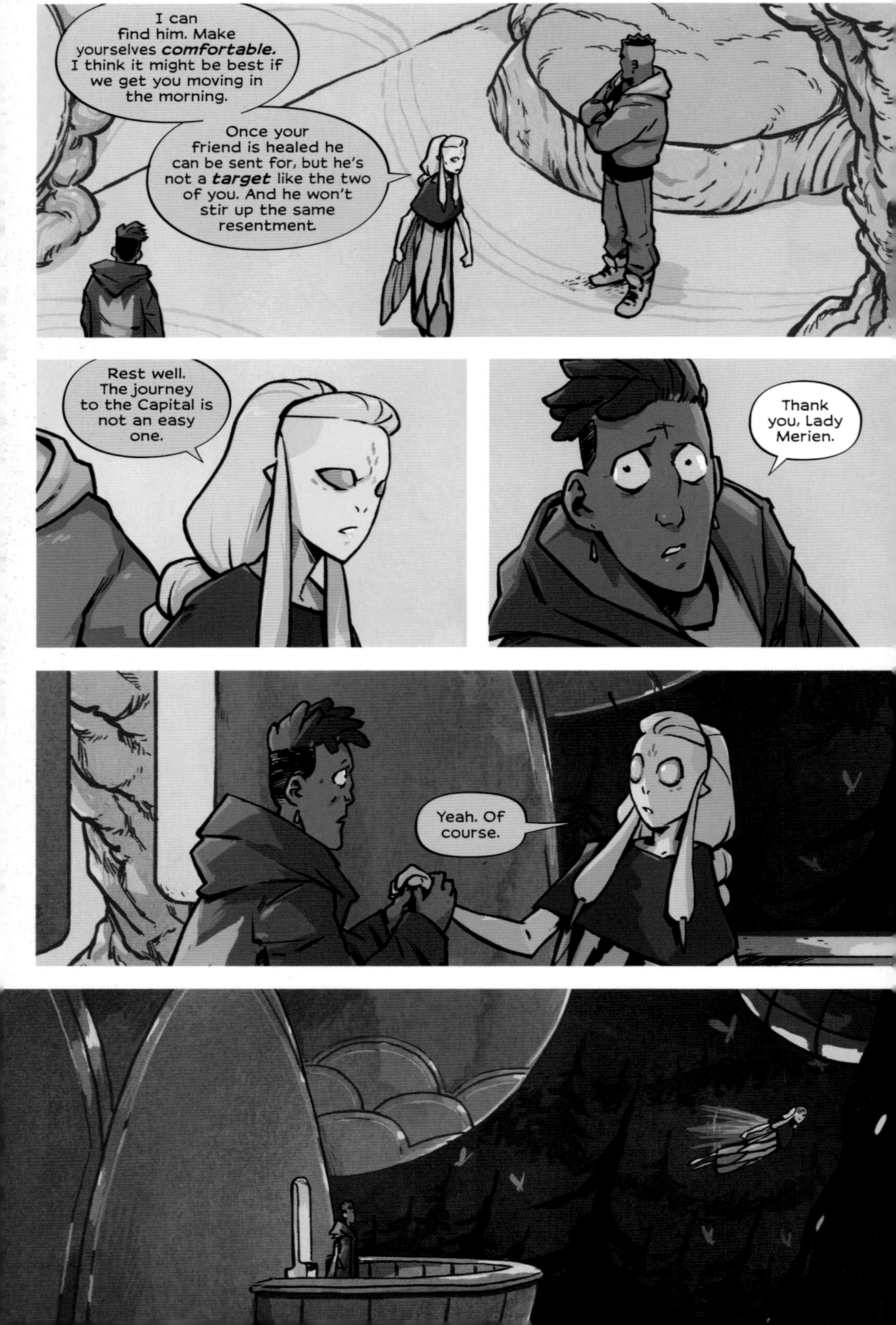

I can find him. Make yourselves **comfortable.** I think it might be best if we get you moving in the morning.
Once your friend is healed he can be sent for, but he's not a ***target*** like the two of you. And he won't stir up the same resentment.
Rest well. The journey to the Capital is not an easy one.
Thank you, Lady Merien.
Yeah. Of course.

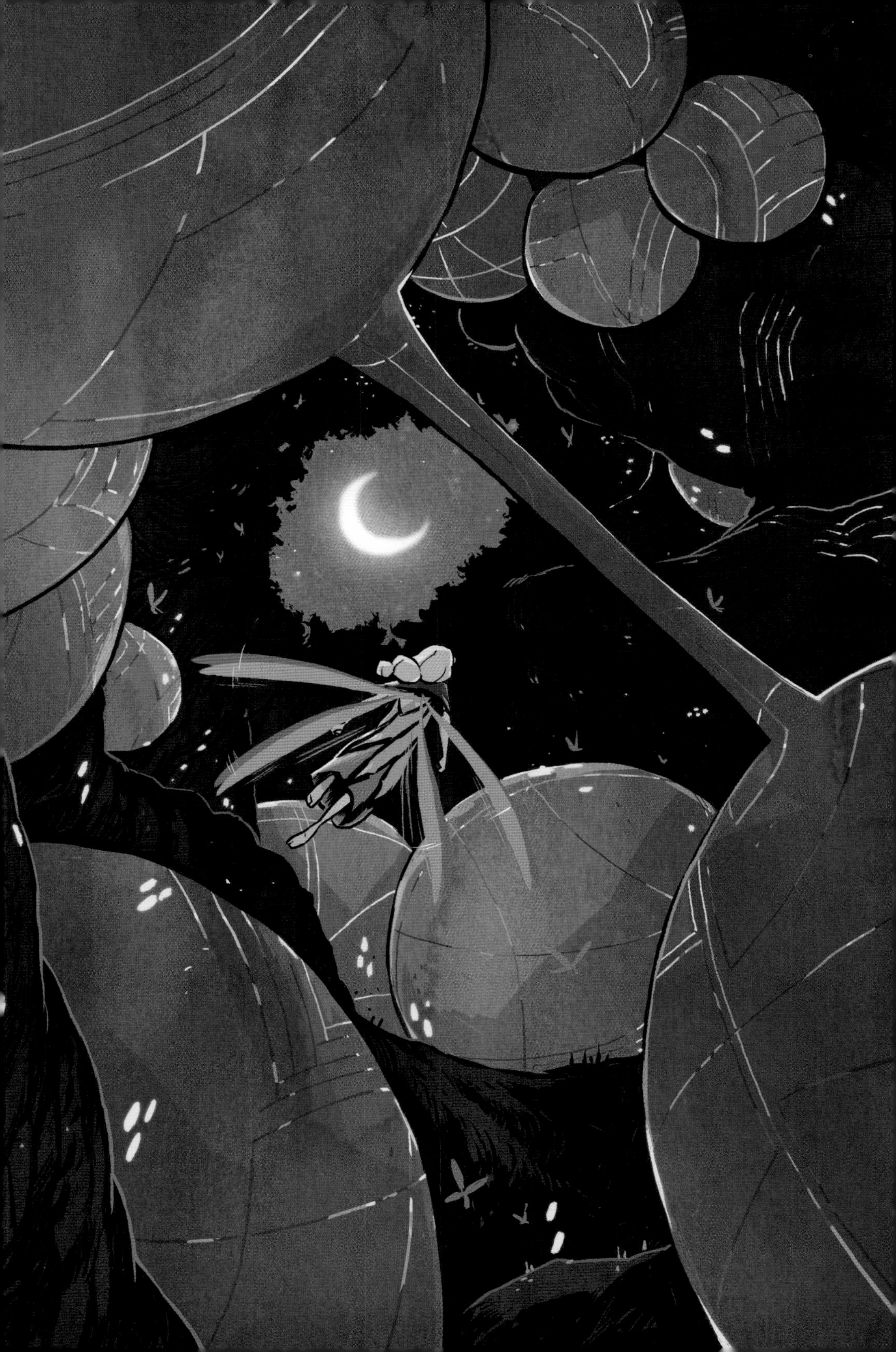

CHAPTER FIVE
THE FALL

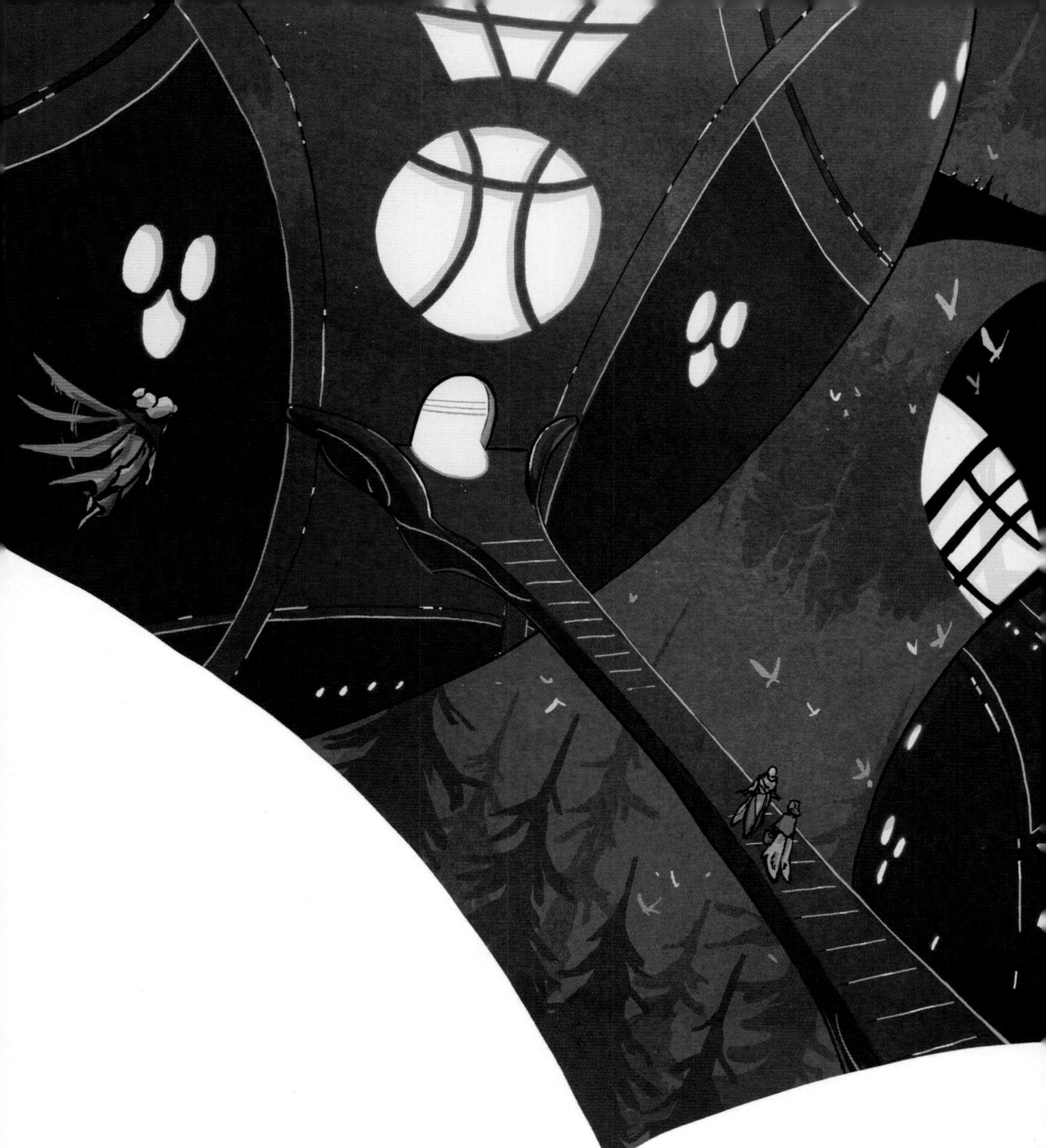

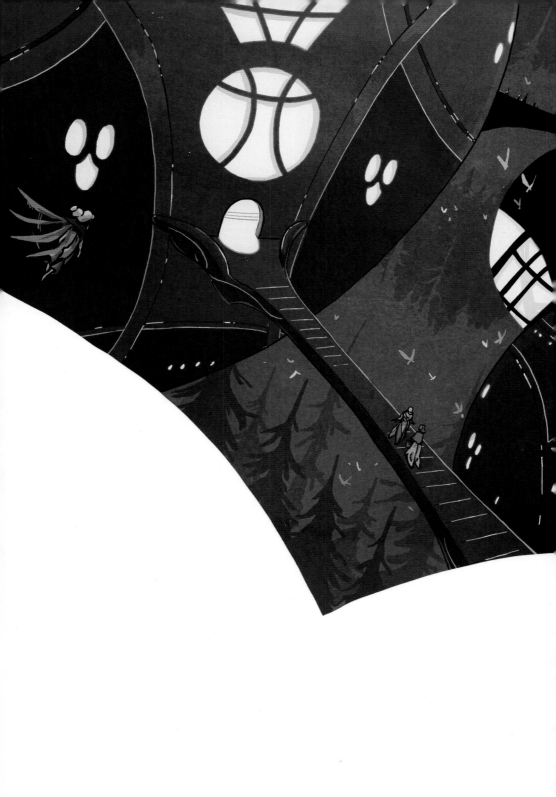

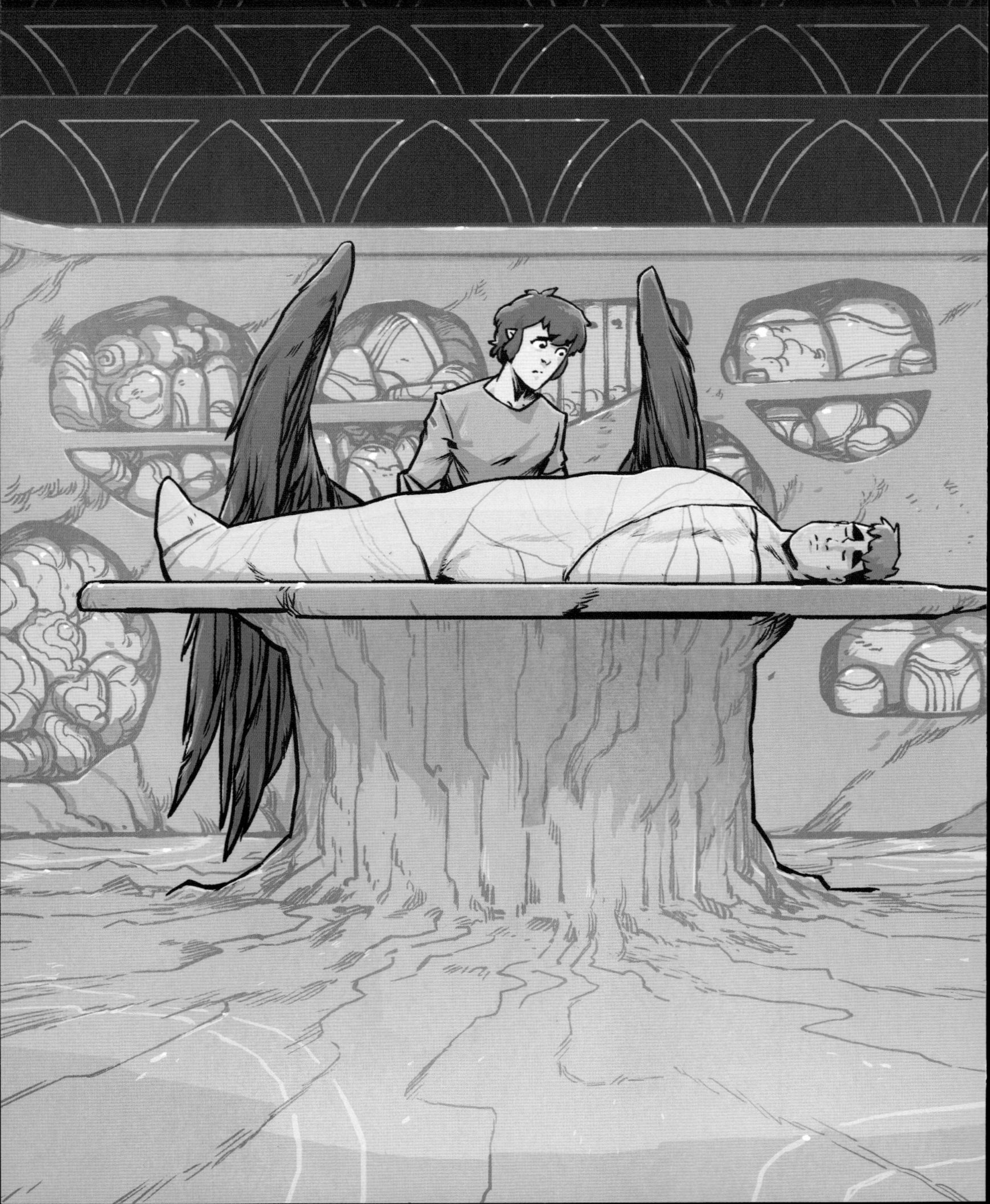

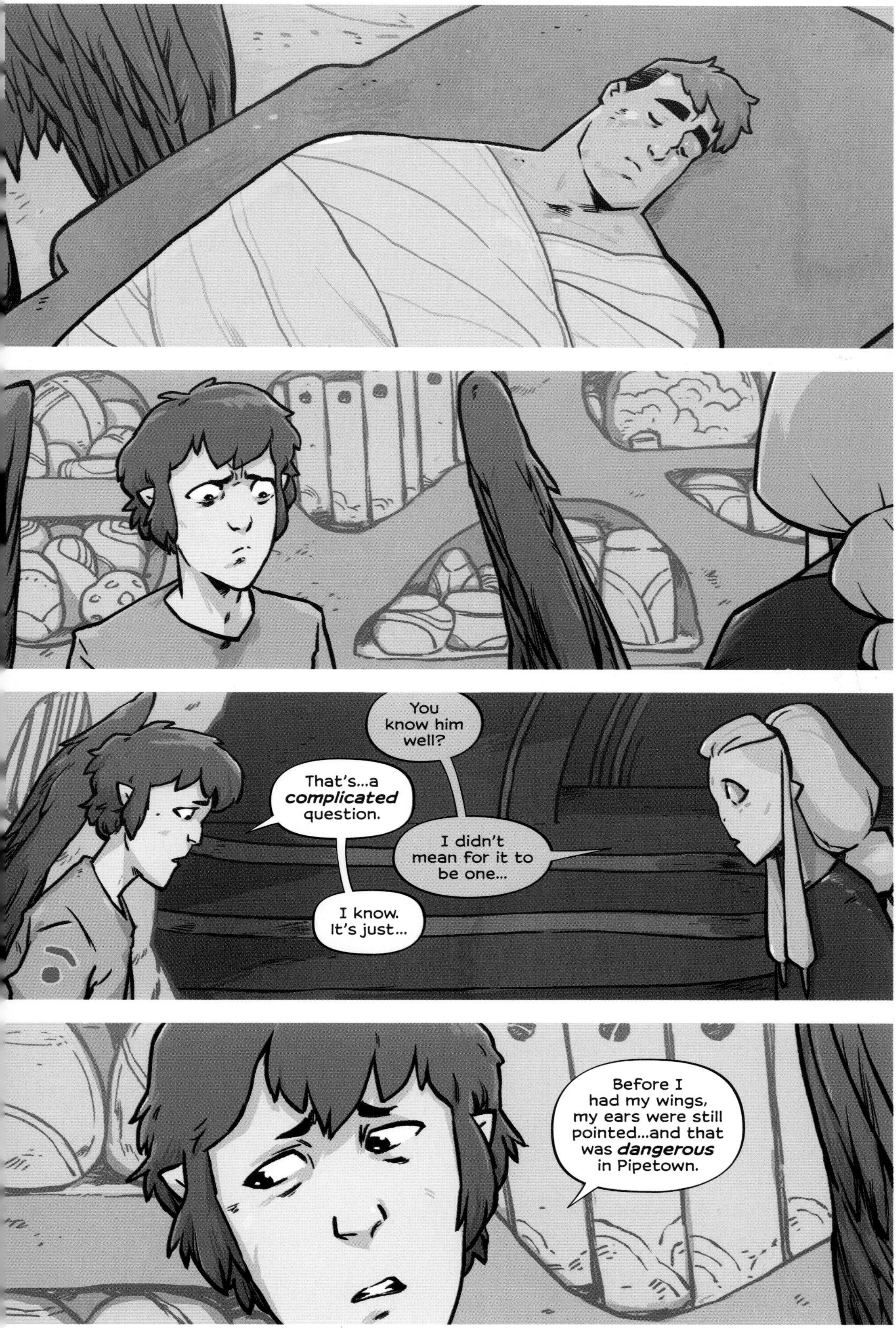
You know him well?
That's...a *complicated* question.
I didn't mean for it to be one...
I know. It's just...
Before I had my wings, my ears were still pointed...and that was *dangerous* in Pipetown.

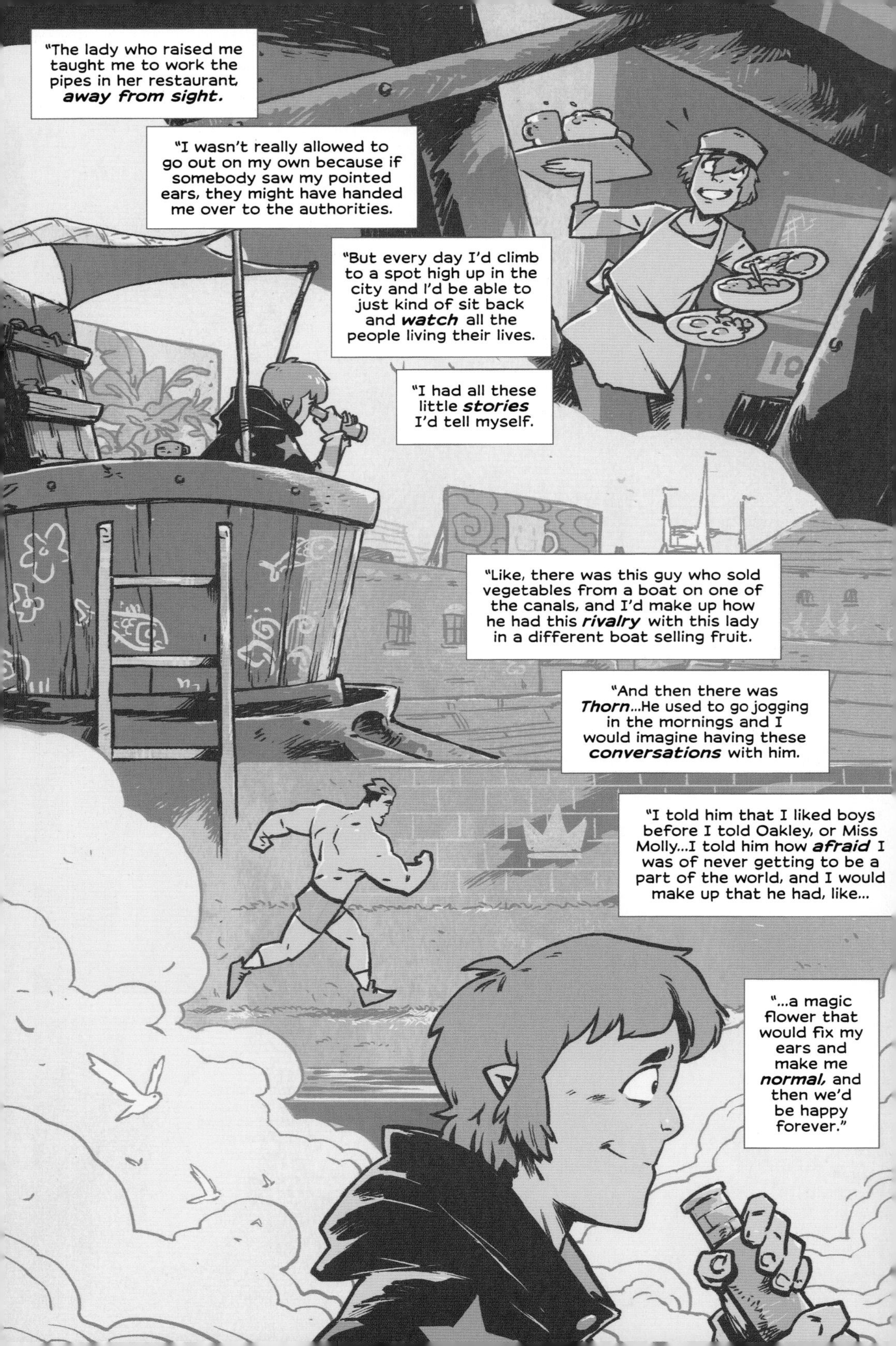
"The lady who raised me taught me to work the pipes in her restaurant, ***away from sight.***
"I wasn't really allowed to go out on my own because if somebody saw my pointed ears, they might have handed me over to the authorities.
"But every day I'd climb to a spot high up in the city and I'd be able to just kind of sit back and ***watch*** all the people living their lives.
"I had all these little ***stories*** I'd tell myself.
"Like, there was this guy who sold vegetables from a boat on one of the canals, and I'd make up how he had this ***rivalry*** with this lady in a different boat selling fruit.
"And then there was ***Thorn***...He used to go jogging in the mornings and I would imagine having these ***conversations*** with him.
"I told him that I liked boys before I told Oakley, or Miss Molly...I told him how ***afraid*** I was of never getting to be a part of the world, and I would make up that he had, like...
"...a magic flower that would fix my ears and make me ***normal,*** and then we'd be happy forever."

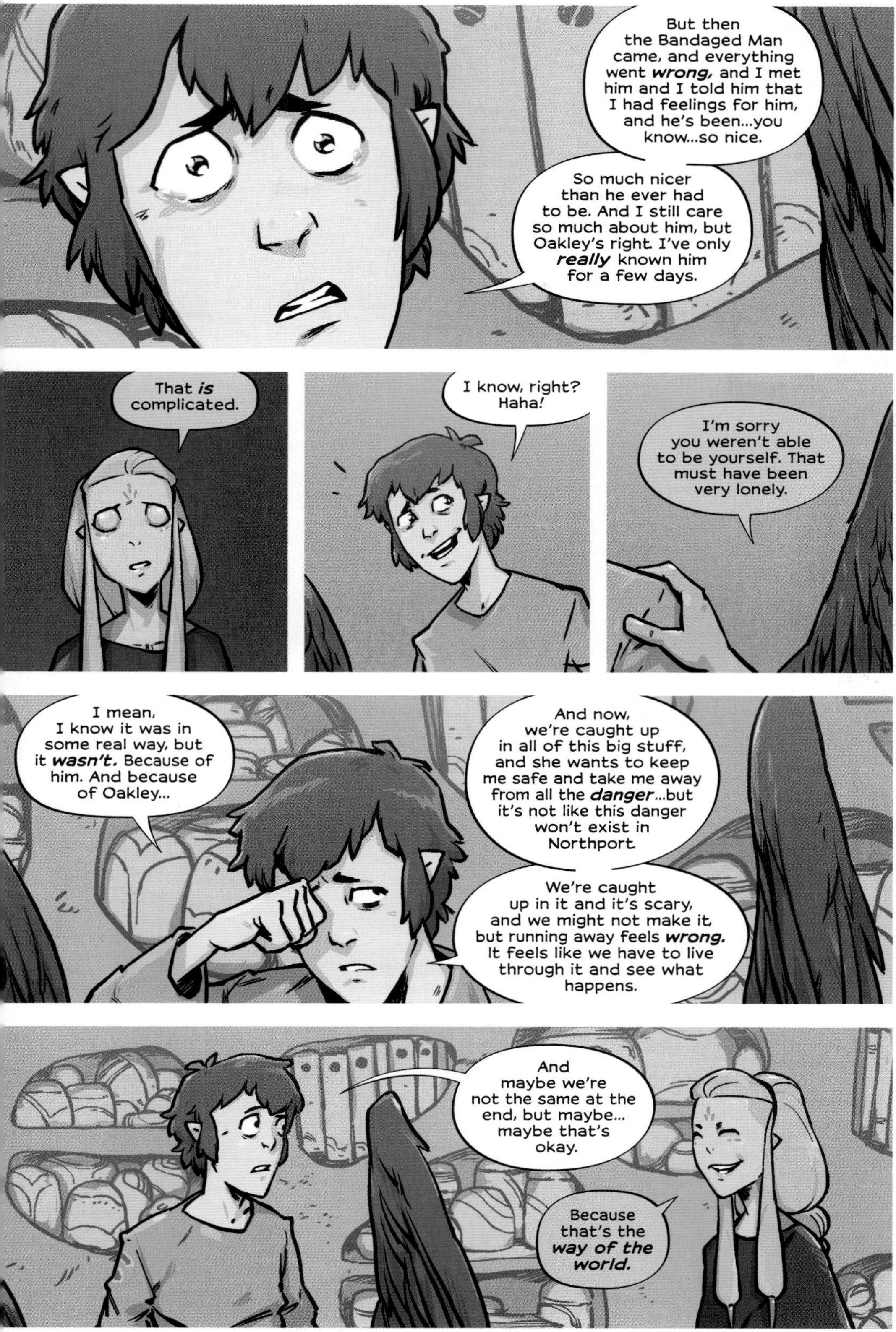

But then the Bandaged Man came, and everything went *wrong,* and I met him and I told him that I had feelings for him, and he's been...you know...so nice.
So much nicer than he ever had to be. And I still care so much about him, but Oakley's right. I've only *really* known him for a few days.
That *is* complicated.
I know, right? Haha!
I'm sorry you weren't able to be yourself. That must have been very lonely.
I mean, I know it was in some real way, but it *wasn't.* Because of him. And because of Oakley...
And now, we're caught up in all of this big stuff, and she wants to keep me safe and take me away from all the *danger*...but it's not like this danger won't exist in Northport.
We're caught up in it and it's scary, and we might not make it, but running away feels *wrong.* It feels like we have to live through it and see what happens.
And maybe we're not the same at the end, but maybe... maybe that's okay.
Because that's the *way of the world.*

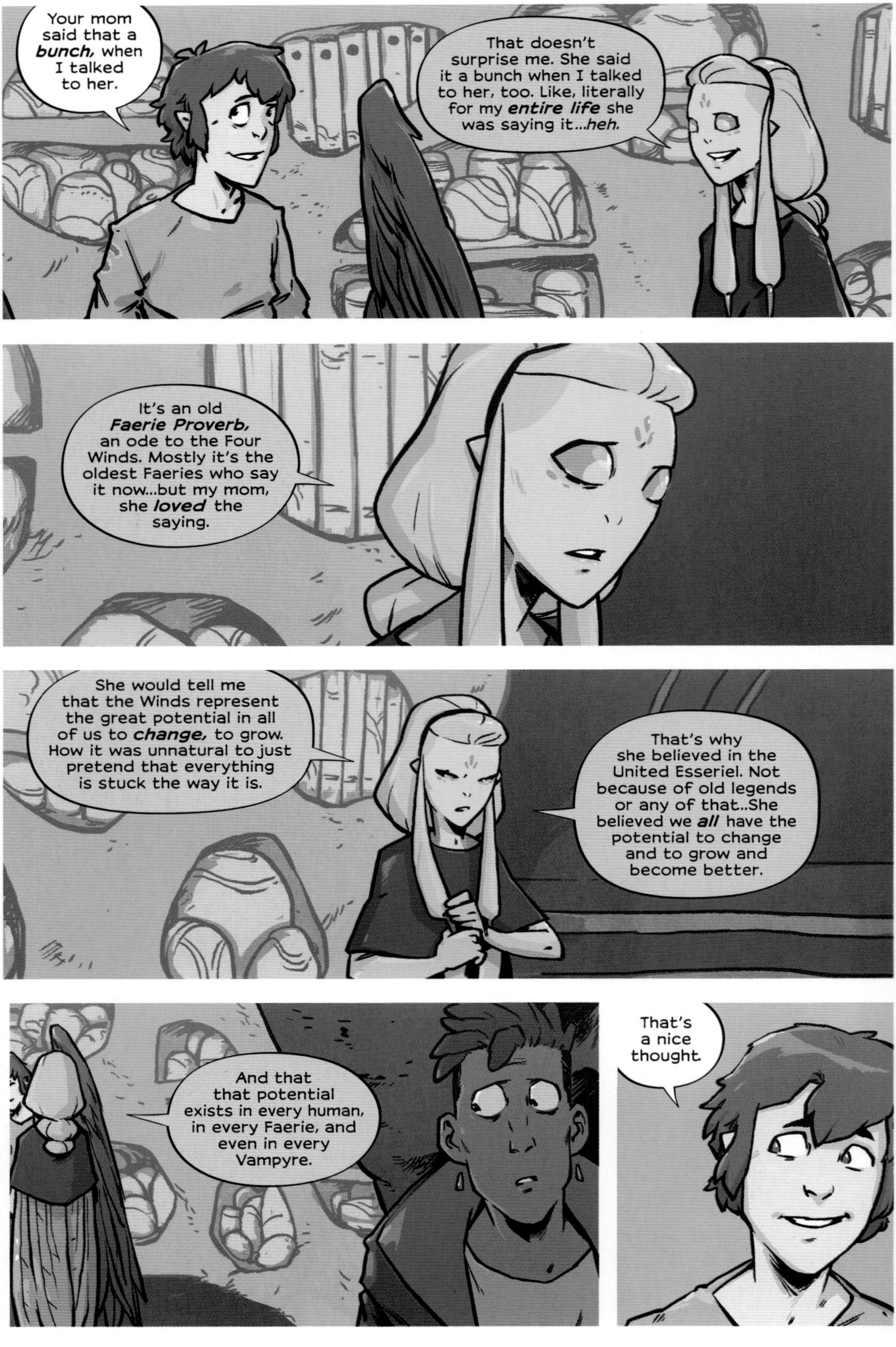
Your mom said that a *bunch,* when I talked to her.
That doesn't surprise me. She said it a bunch when I talked to her, too. Like, literally for my *entire life* she was saying it...*heh.*
It's an old *Faerie Proverb,* an ode to the Four Winds. Mostly it's the oldest Faeries who say it now...but my mom, she *loved* the saying.
She would tell me that the Winds represent the great potential in all of us to *change,* to grow. How it was unnatural to just pretend that everything is stuck the way it is.
That's why she believed in the United Esseriel. Not because of old legends or any of that...She believed we *all* have the potential to change and to grow and become better.
And that that potential exists in every human, in every Faerie, and even in every Vampyre.
That's a nice thought.

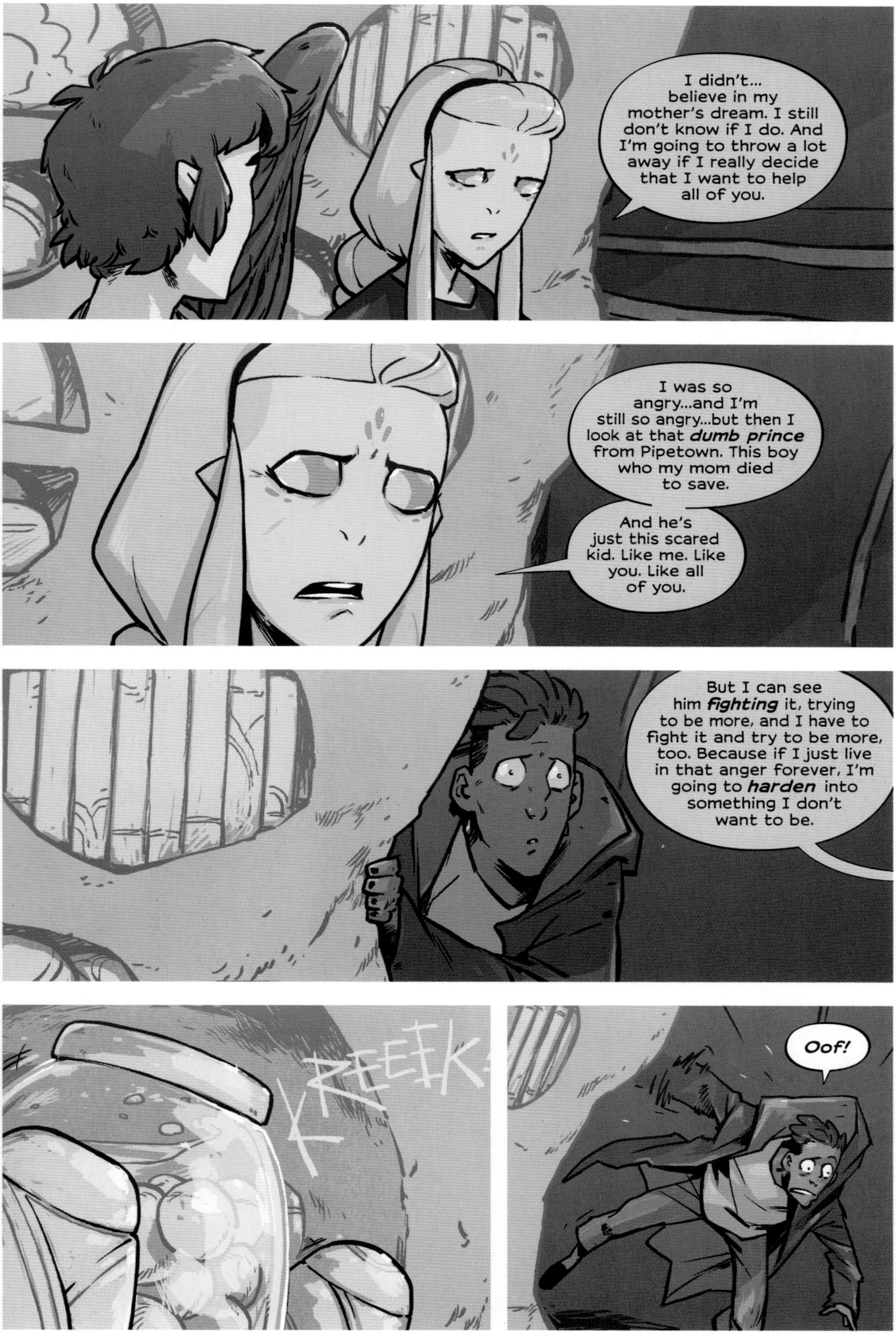

I didn't... believe in my mother's dream. I still don't know if I do. And I'm going to throw a lot away if I really decide that I want to help all of you.
I was so angry...and I'm still so angry...but then I look at that *dumb prince* from Pipetown. This boy who my mom died to save.
And he's just this scared kid. Like me. Like you. Like all of you.
But I can see him *fighting* it, trying to be more, and I have to fight it and try to be more, too. Because if I just live in that anger forever, I'm going to *harden* into something I don't want to be.
KREEEK
Oof!

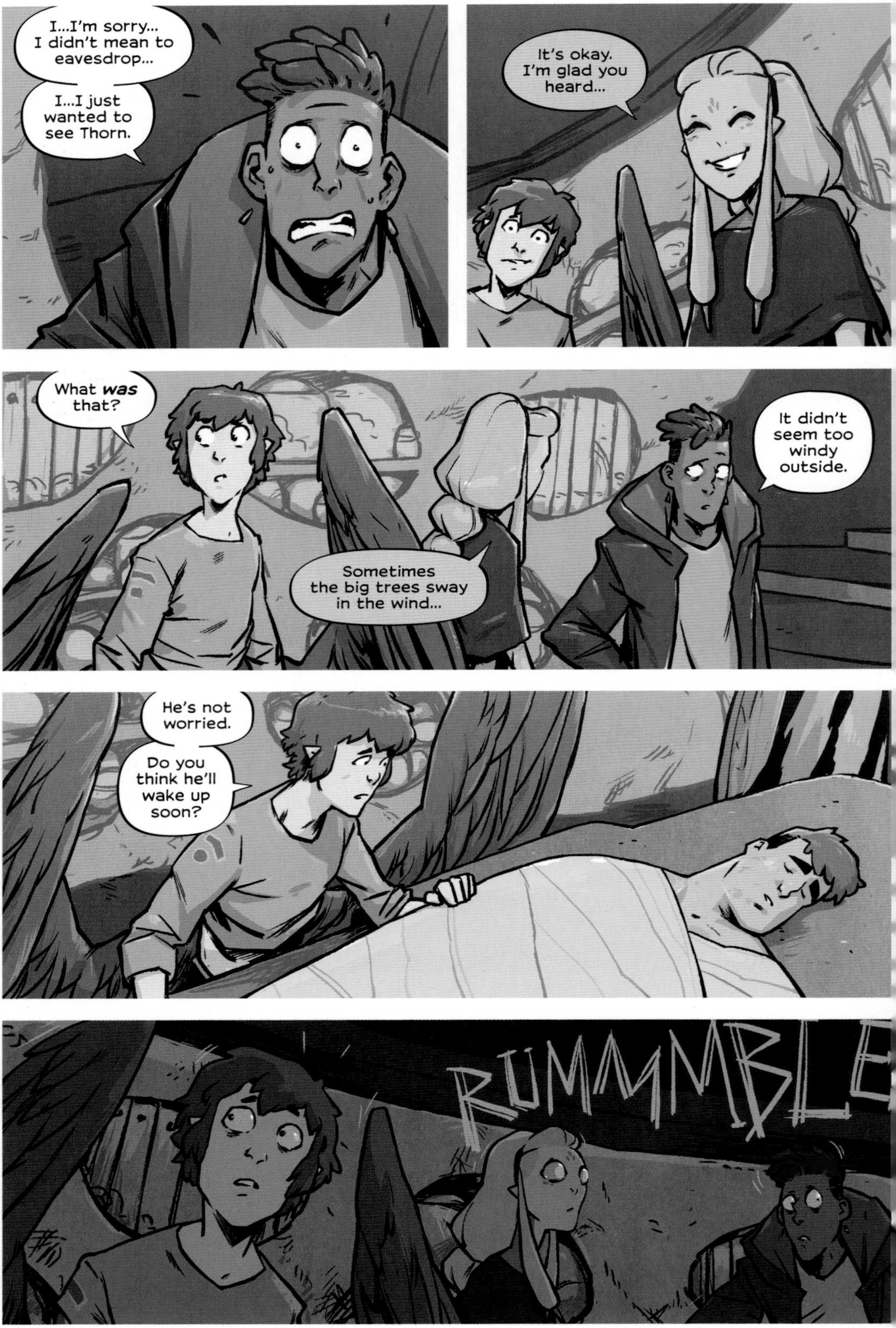
I...I'm sorry... I didn't mean to eavesdrop...
I...I just wanted to see Thorn.
It's okay. I'm glad you heard...
What *was* that?
Sometimes the big trees sway in the wind...
It didn't seem too windy outside.
He's not worried.
Do you think he'll wake up soon?
RUMMMBLE

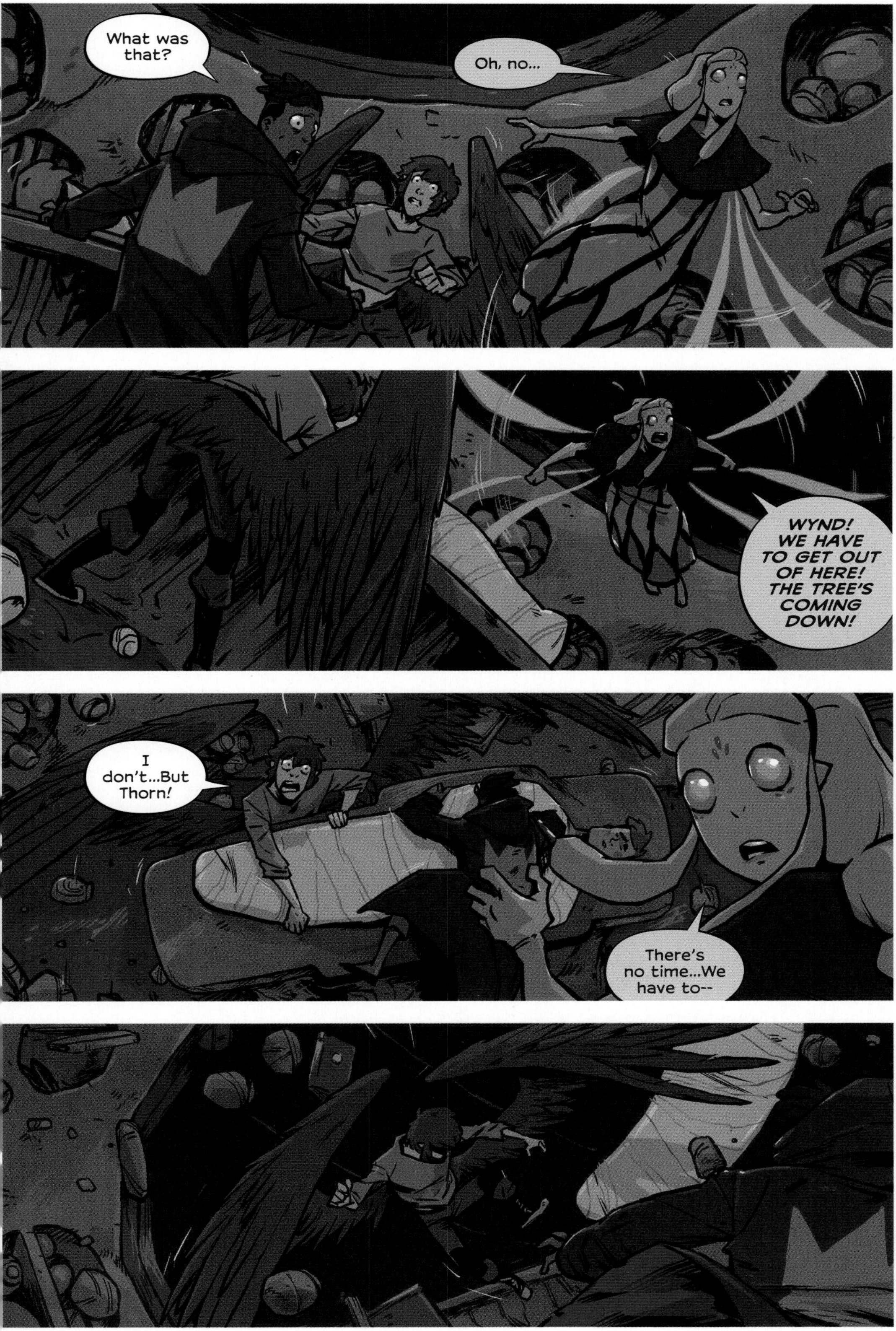

What was that?
Oh, no...
WYND! WE HAVE TO GET OUT OF HERE! THE TREE'S COMING DOWN!
I don't...But Thorn!
There's no time...We have to--

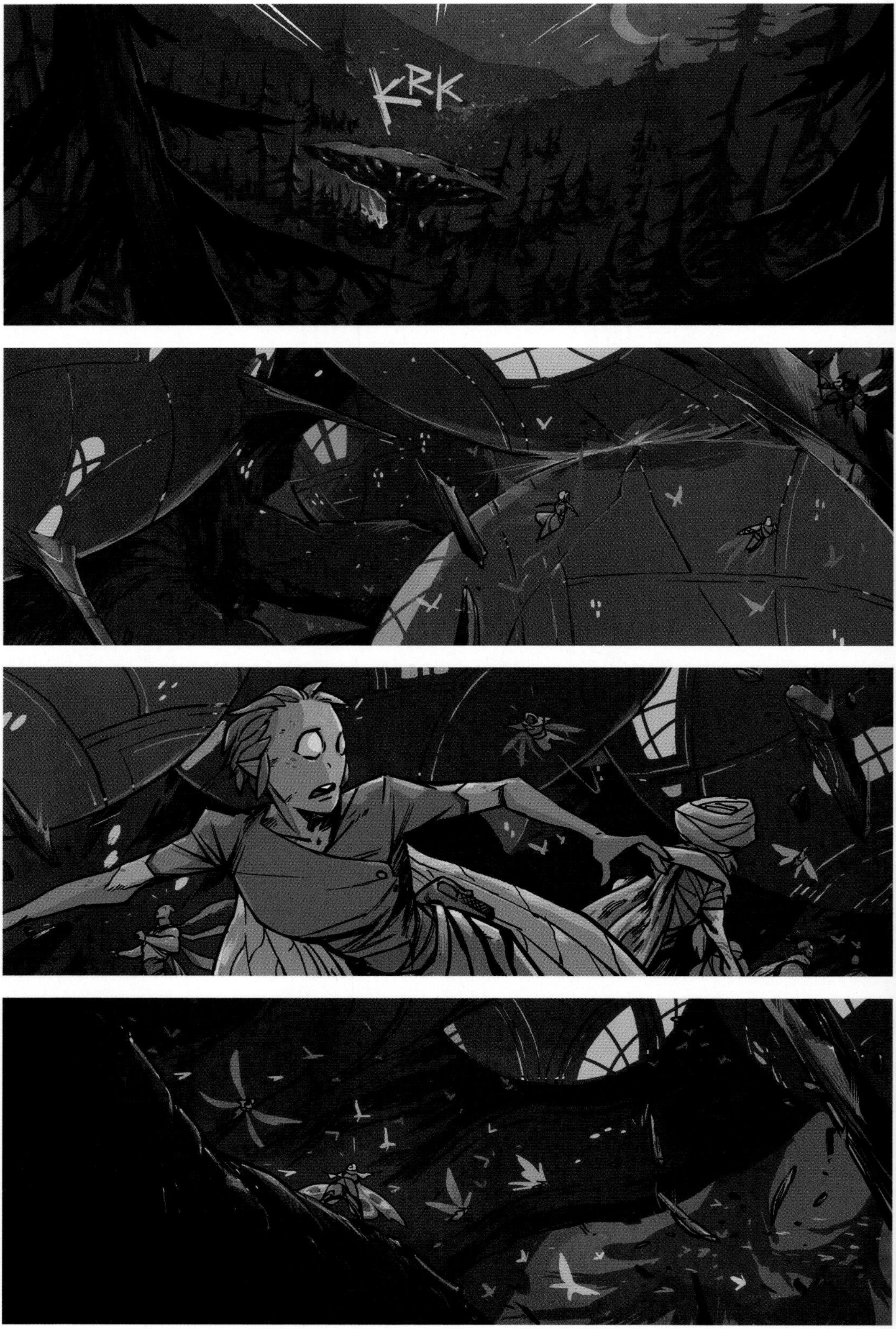
KRK

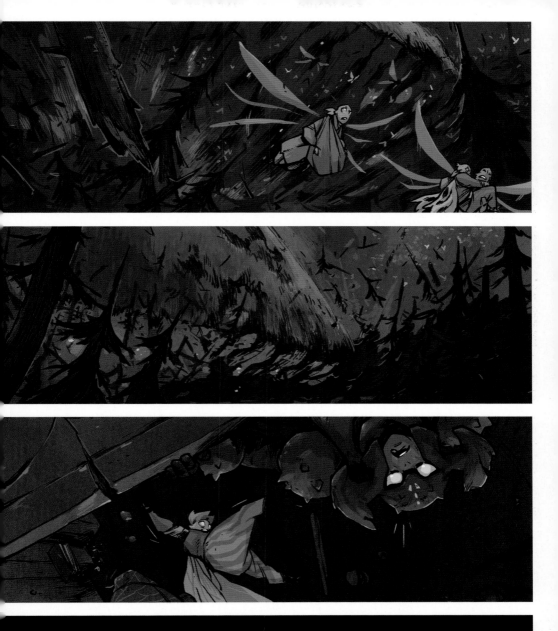

DOOM

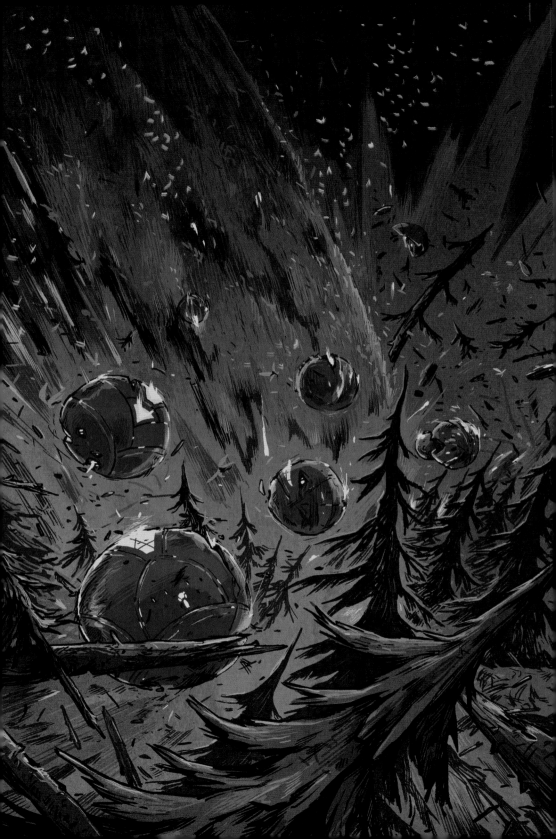

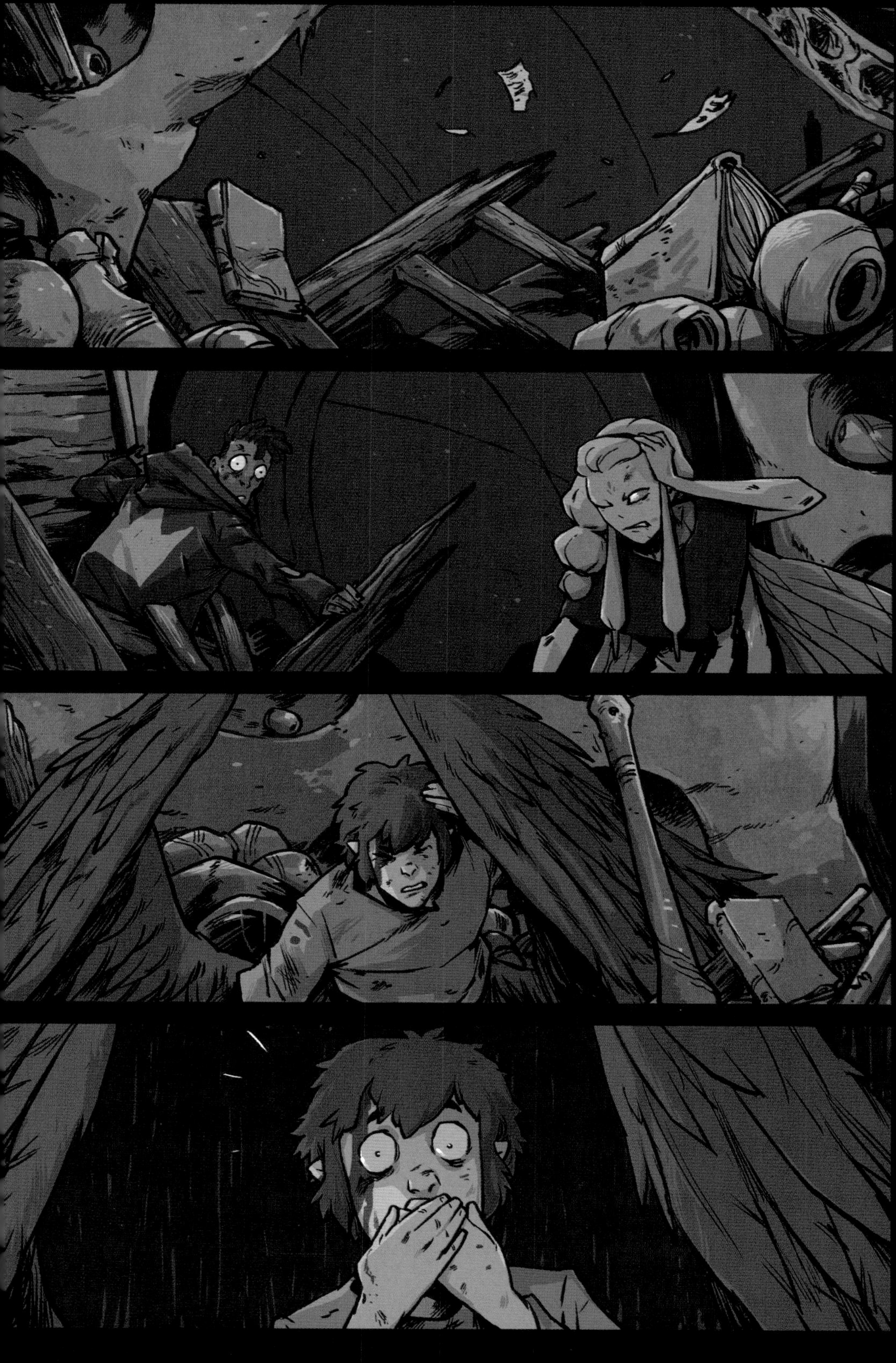

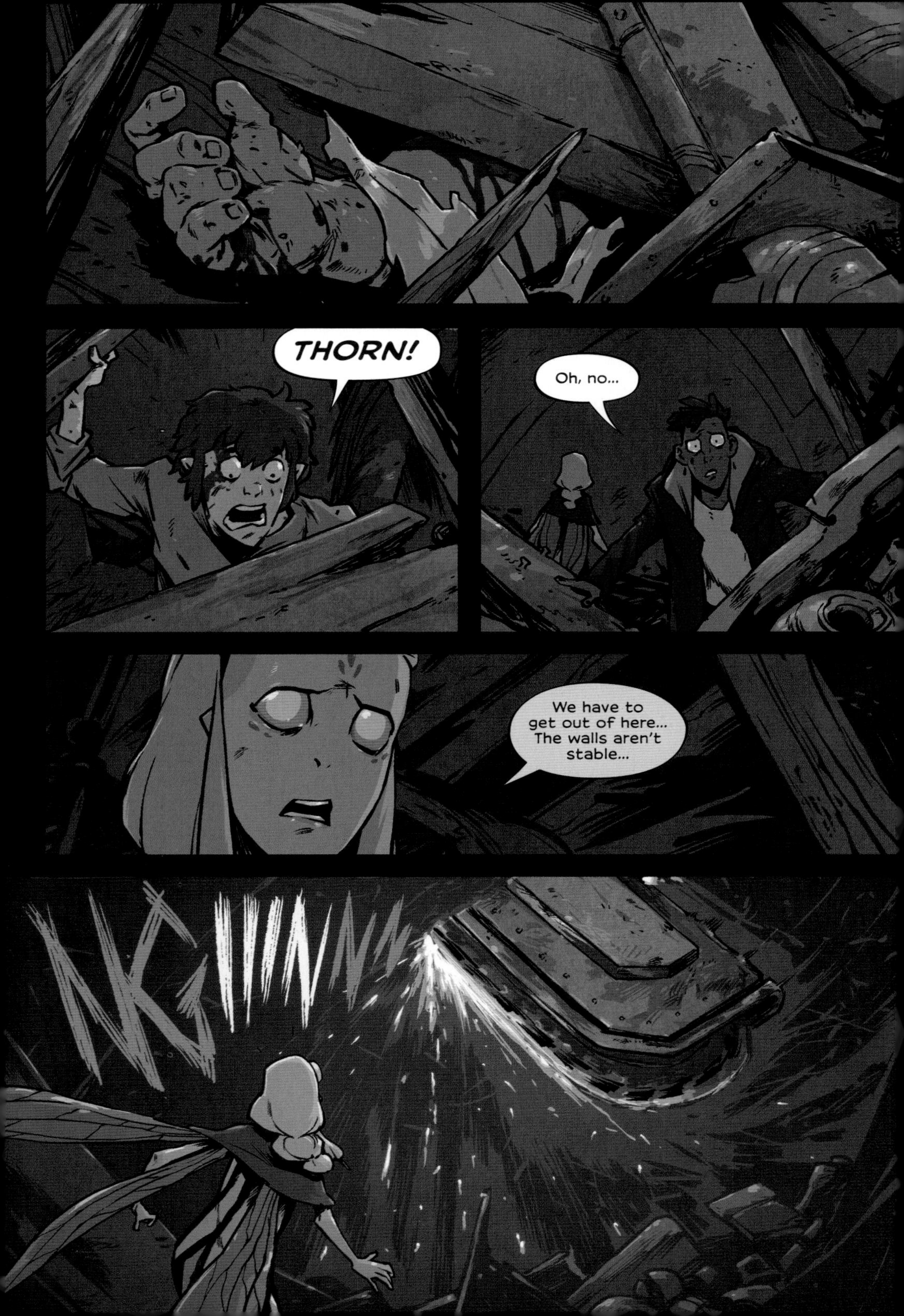
THORN!
Oh, no...
We have to get out of here... The walls aren't stable...
NGIINN

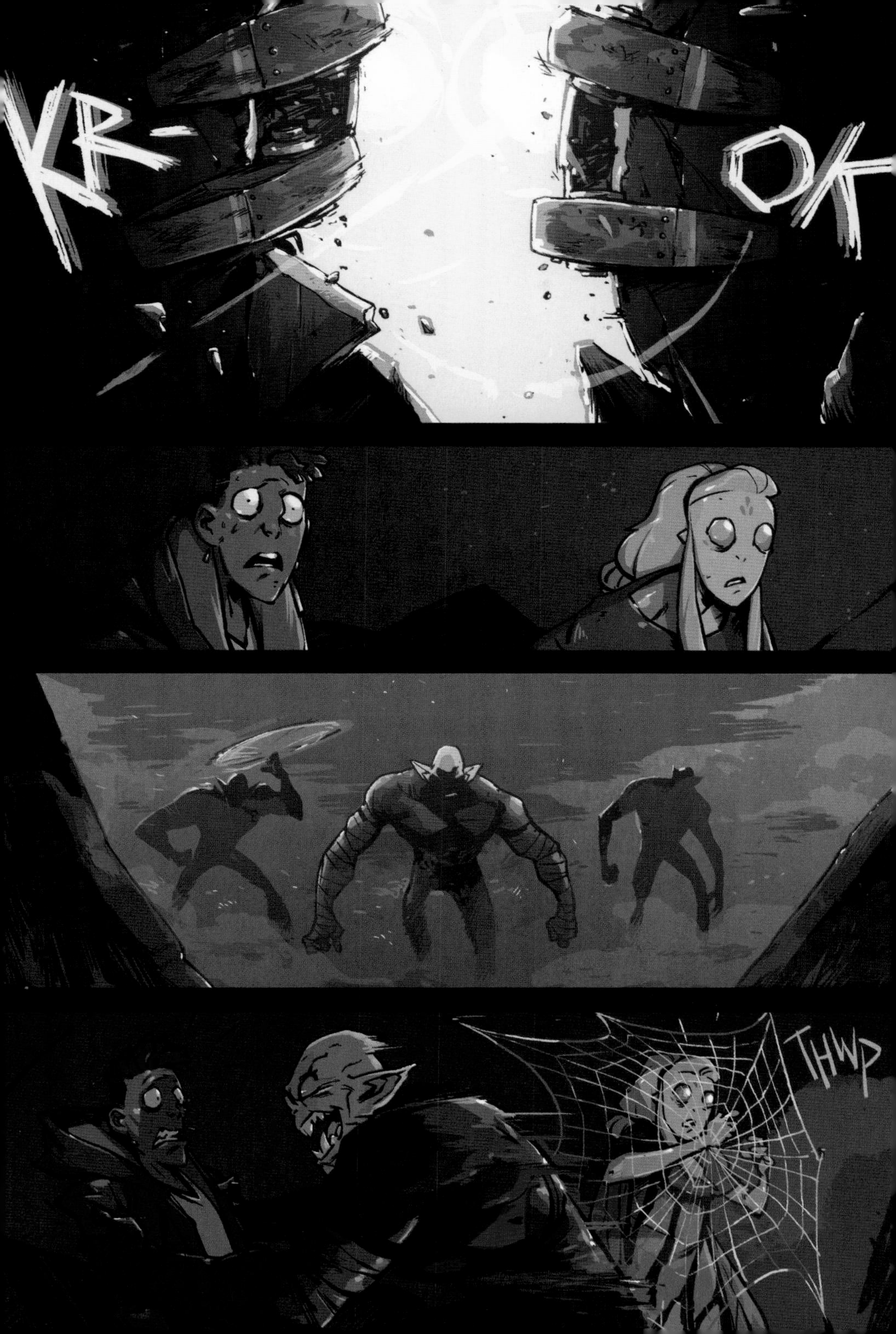
KR-
OK
THWP

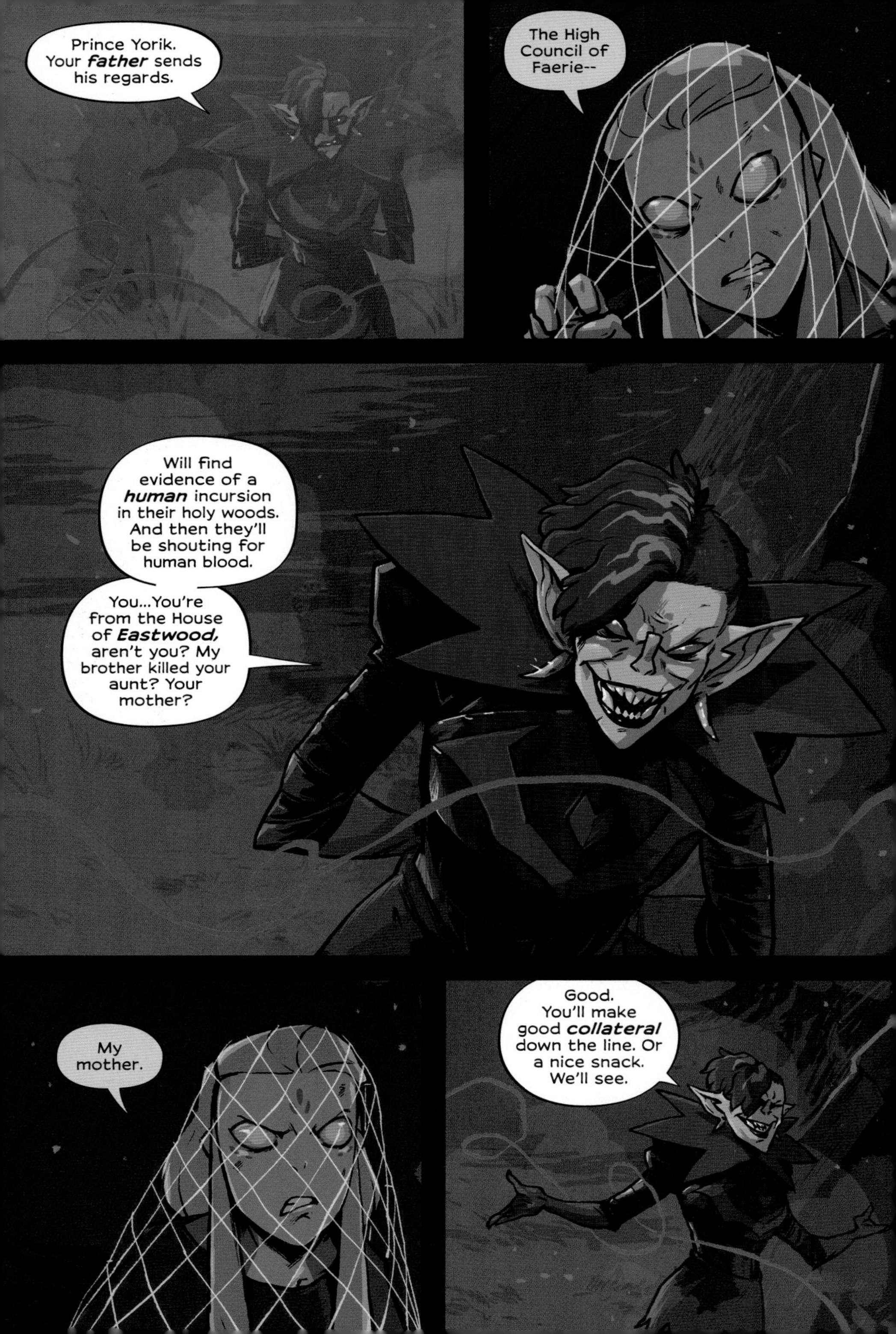
Prince Yorik. Your *father* sends his regards.
The High Council of Faerie--
Will find evidence of a *human* incursion in their holy woods. And then they'll be shouting for human blood.
You...You're from the House of *Eastwood,* aren't you? My brother killed your aunt? Your mother?
My mother.
Good. You'll make good *collateral* down the line. Or a nice snack. We'll see.

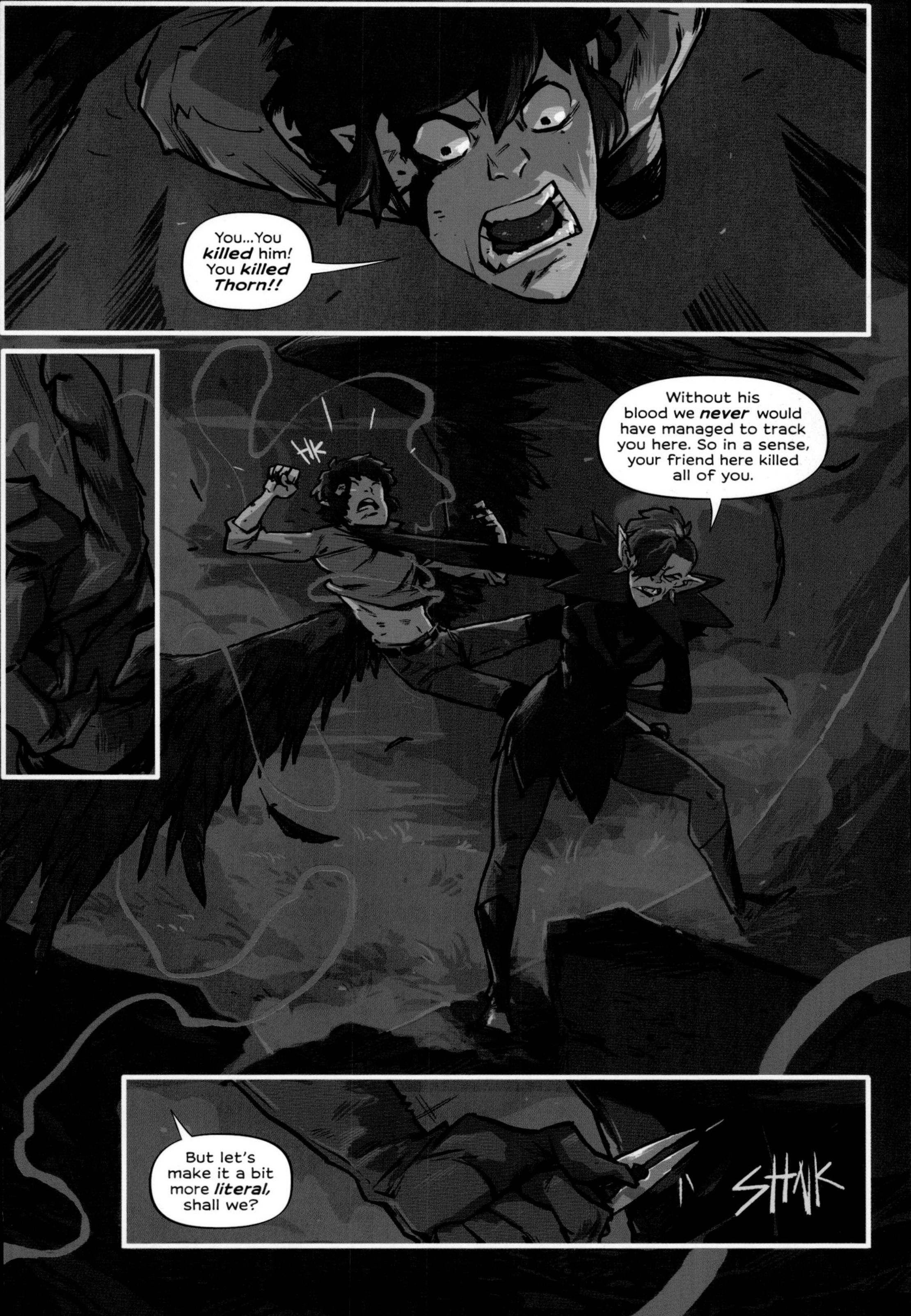
You...You *killed* him! You *killed* Thorn!!
HK
Without his blood we ***never*** would have managed to track you here. So in a sense, your friend here killed all of you.
But let's make it a bit more *literal,* shall we?
SHNK

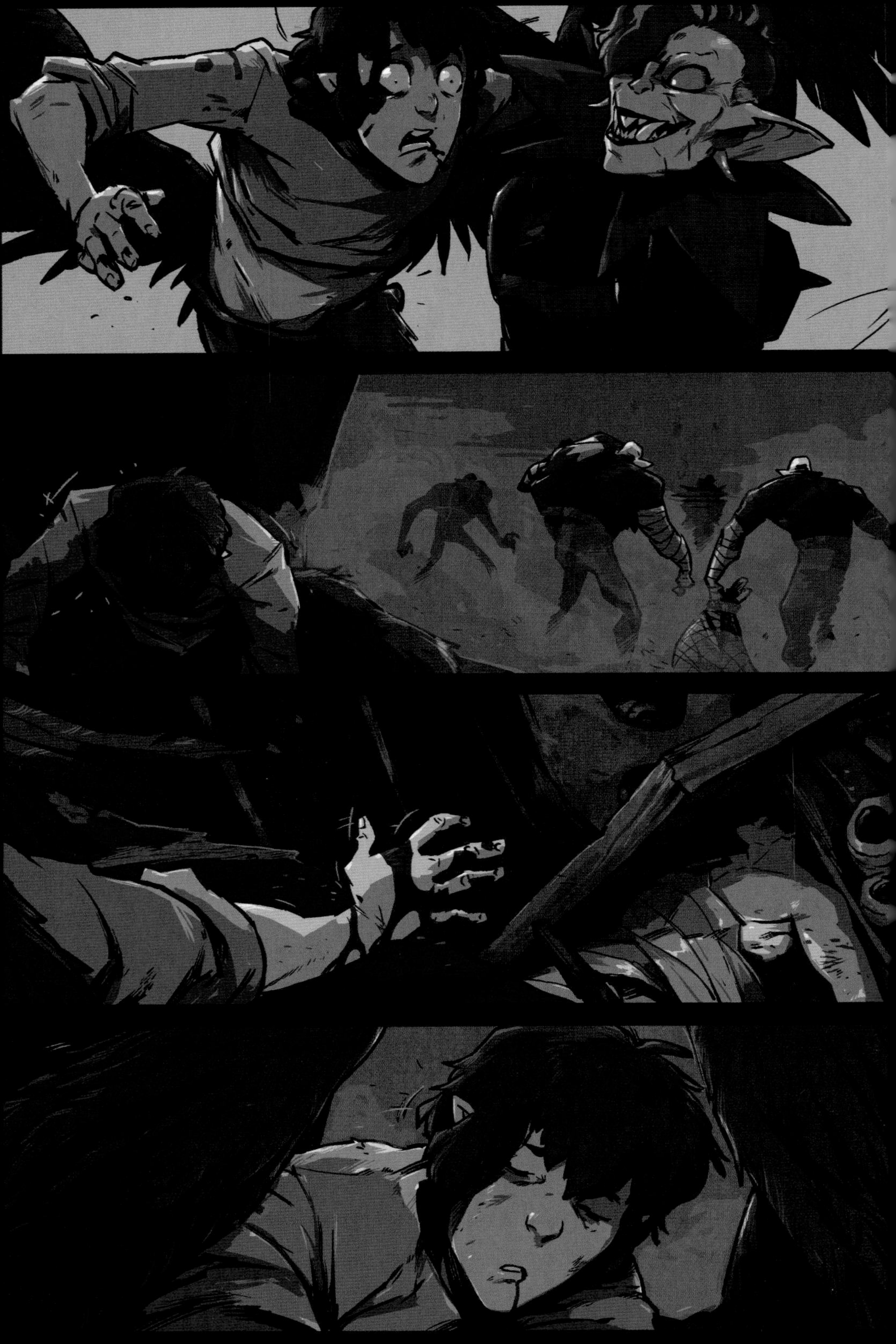

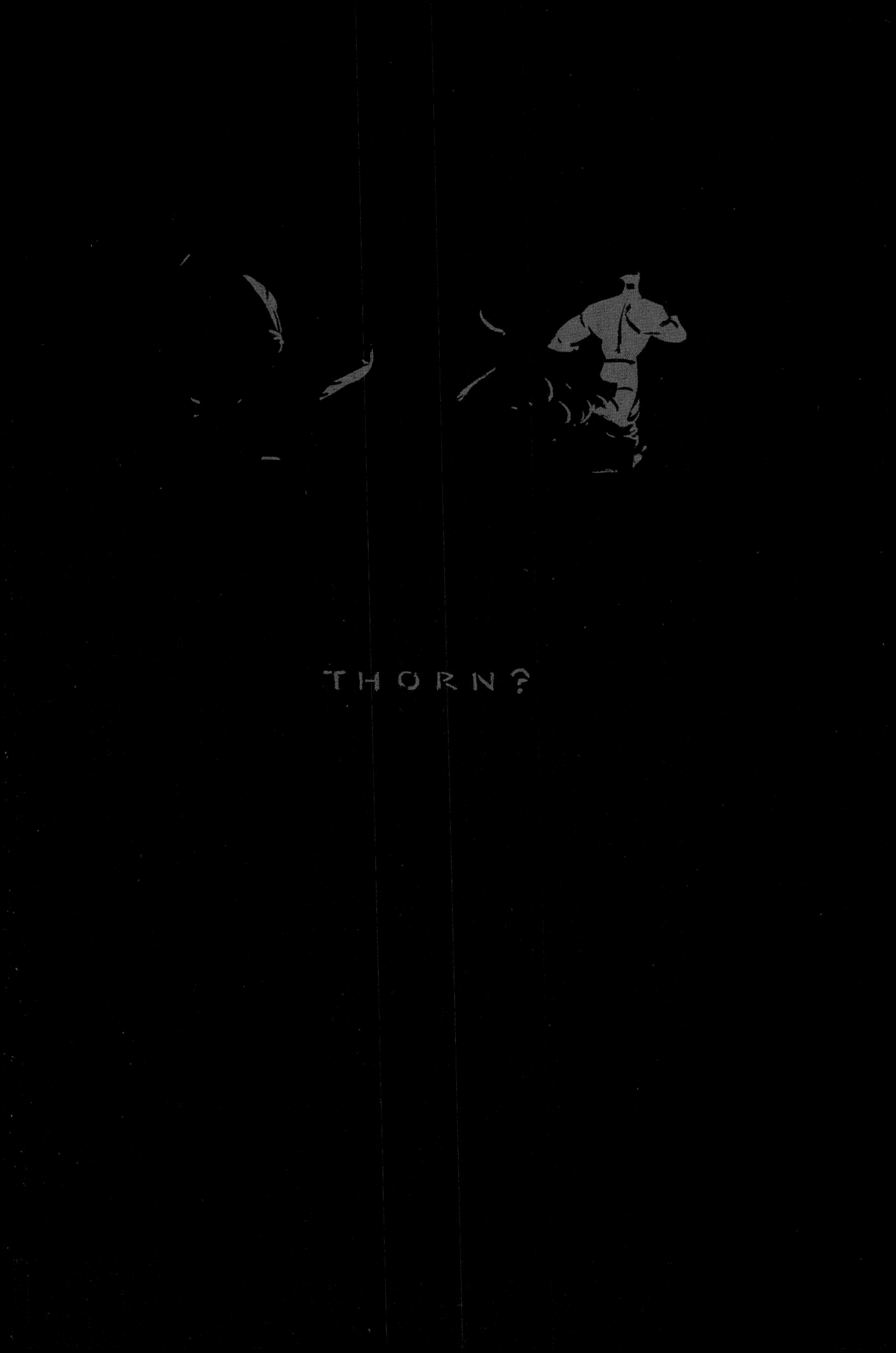
THORN?

CHAPTER SIX
TOUCHED BY MAGIC

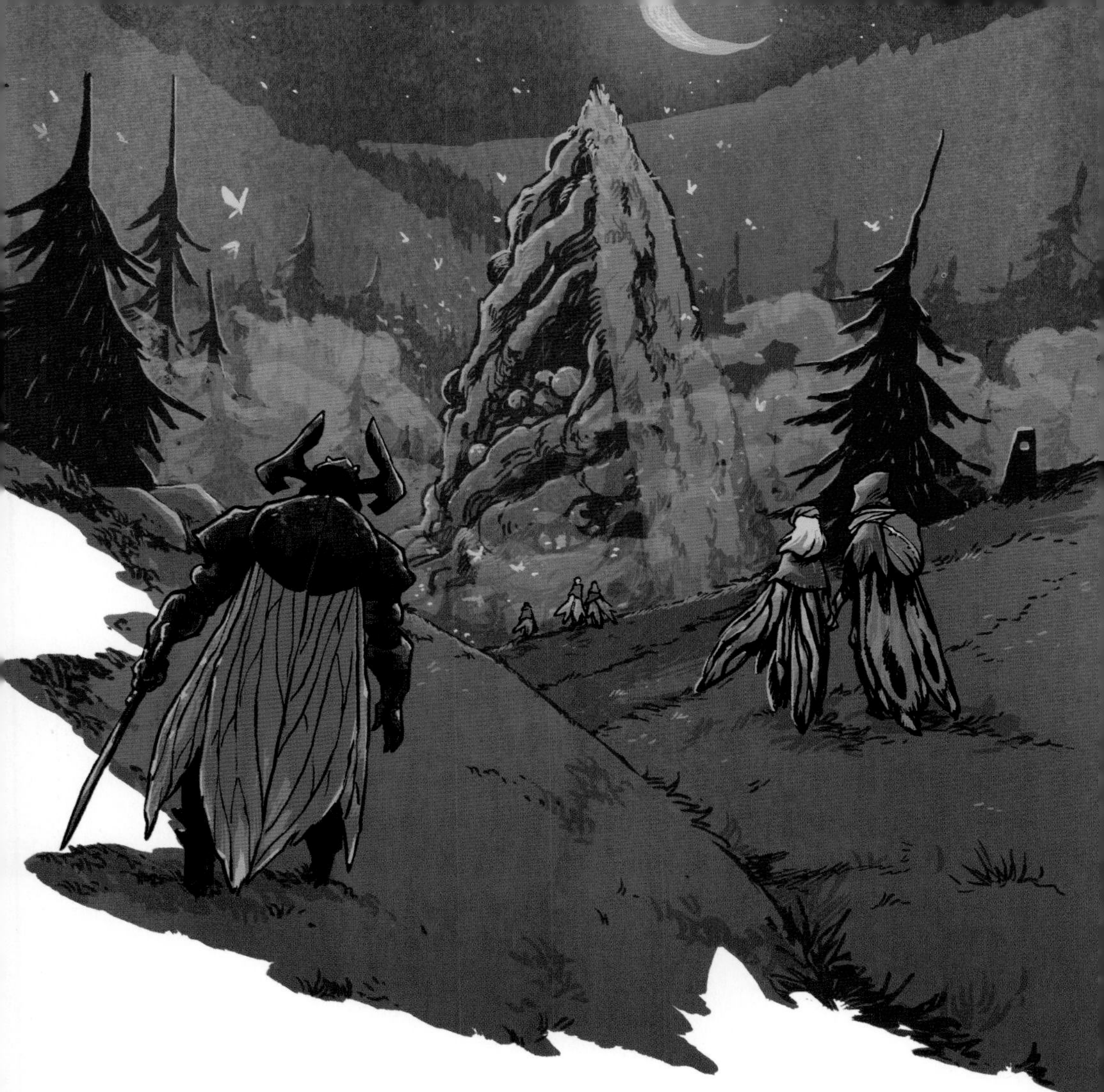

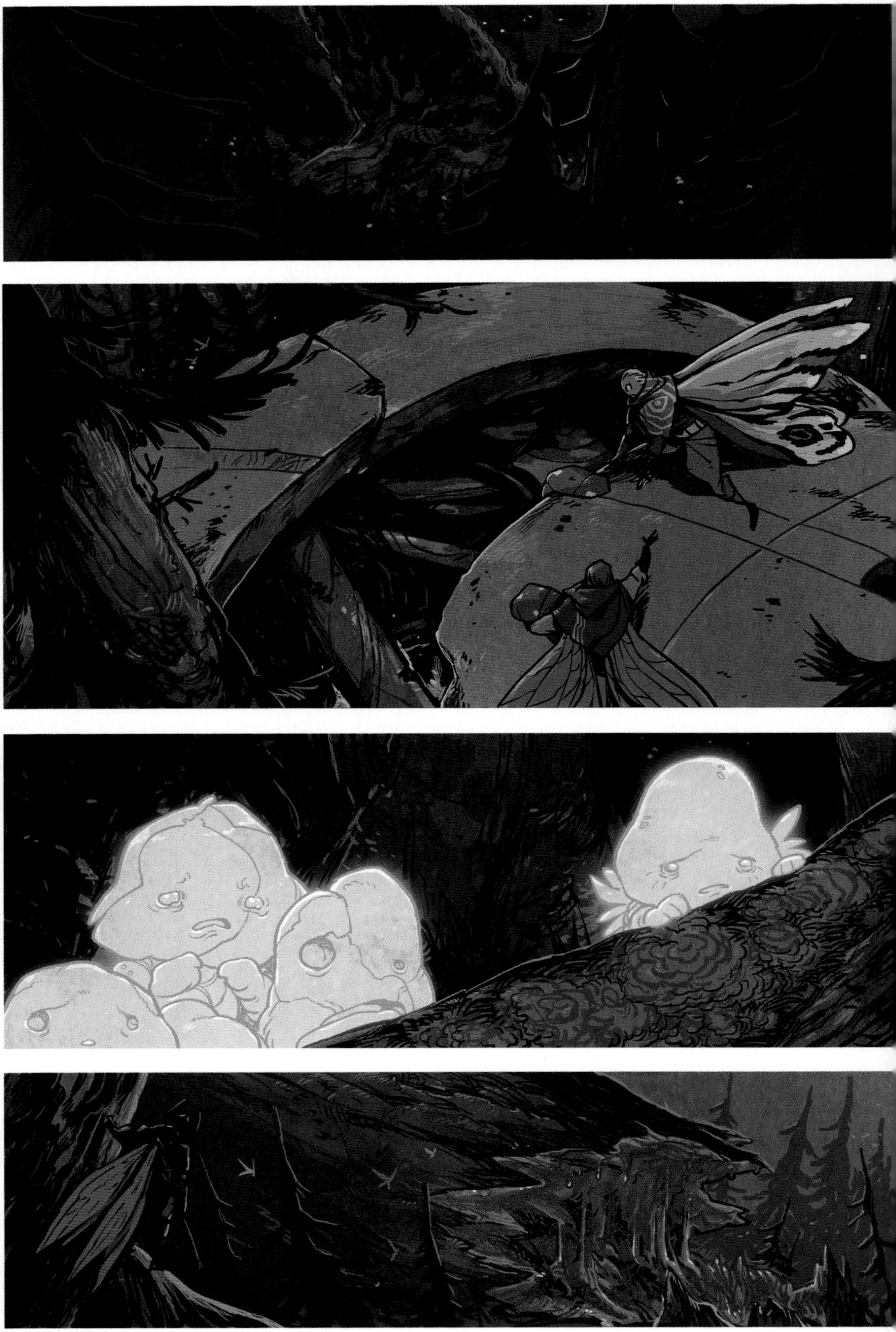

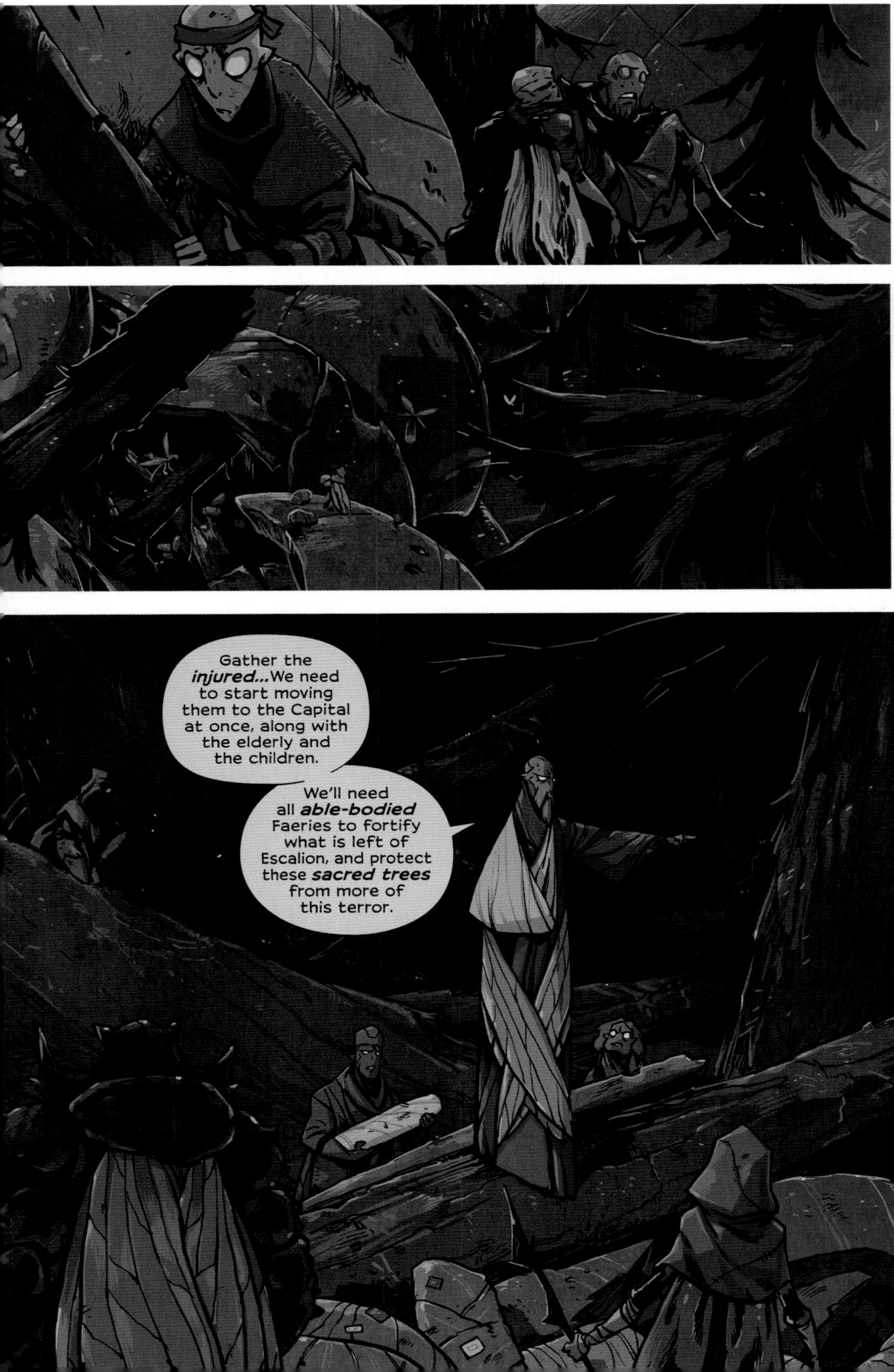
Gather the *injured...* We need to start moving them to the Capital at once, along with the elderly and the children.
We'll need all *able-bodied* Faeries to fortify what is left of Escalion, and protect these *sacred trees* from more of this terror.

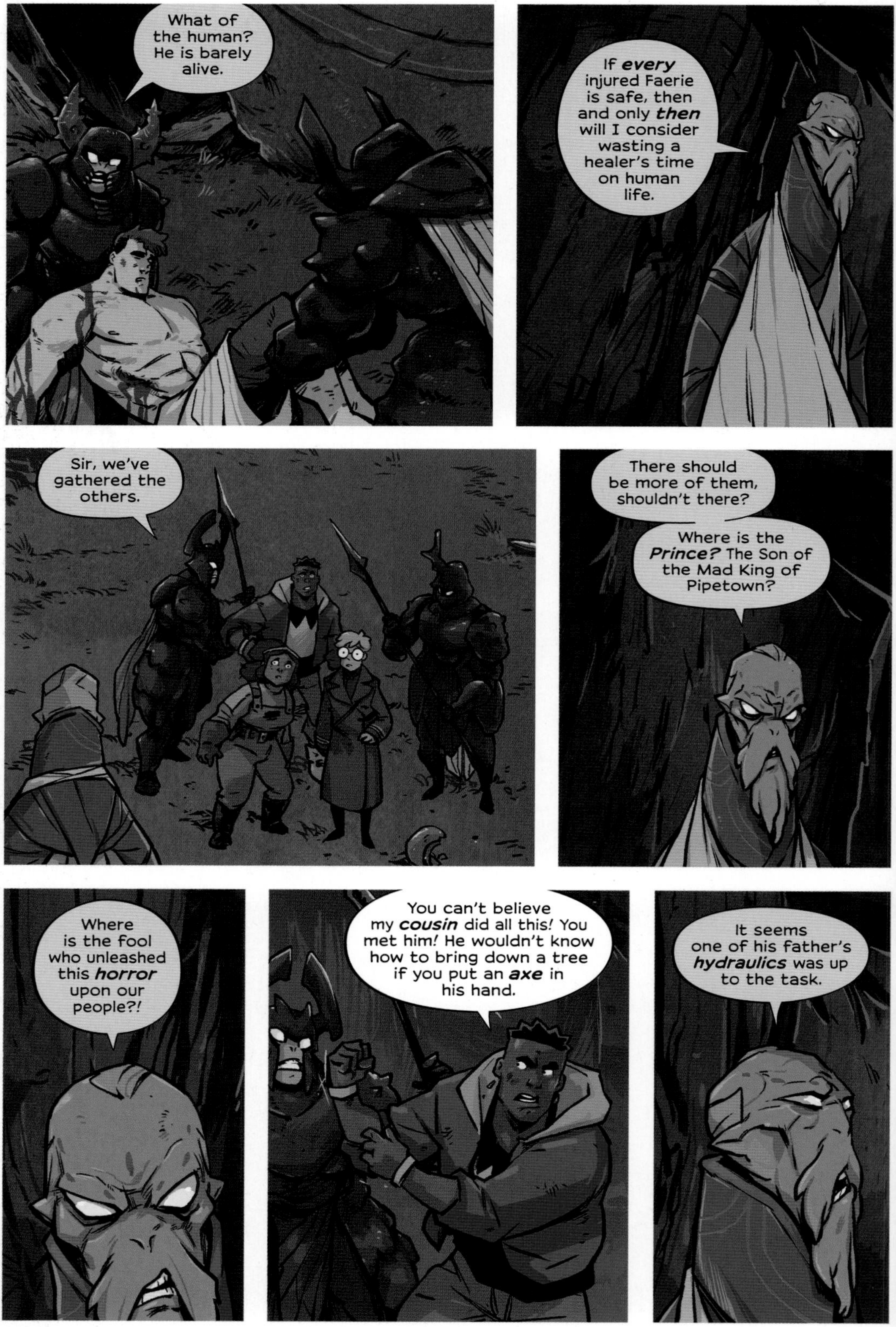
What of the human? He is barely alive.
If *every* injured Faerie is safe, then and only *then* will I consider wasting a healer's time on human life.
Sir, we've gathered the others.
There should be more of them, shouldn't there?
Where is the *Prince?* The Son of the Mad King of Pipetown?
Where is the fool who unleashed this *horror* upon our people?!
You can't believe my *cousin* did all this! You met him! He wouldn't know how to bring down a tree if you put an *axe* in his hand.
It seems one of his father's *hydraulics* was up to the task.

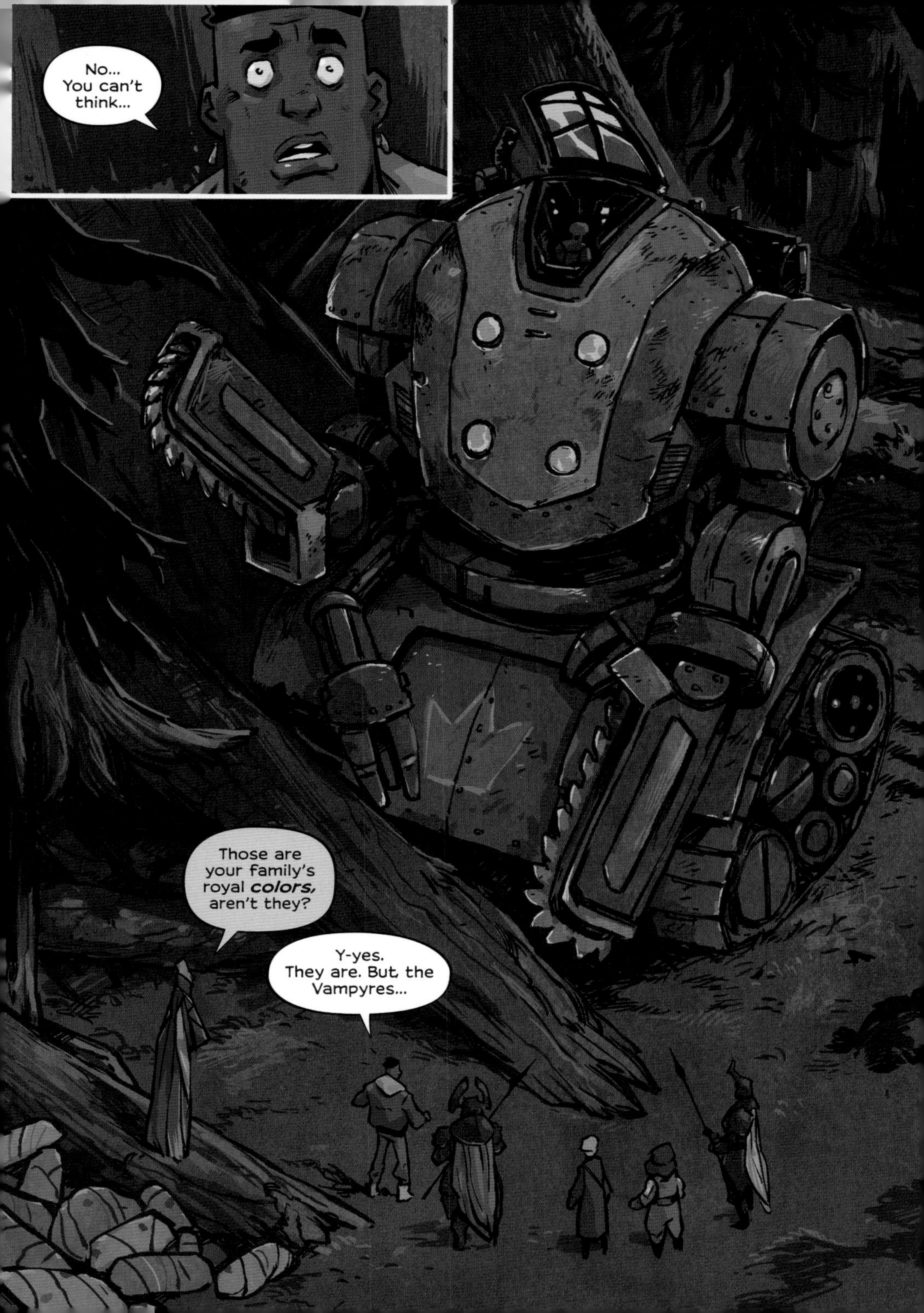
No...
You can't
think...
Those are
your family's
royal *colors,*
aren't they?
Y-yes.
They are. But, the
Vampyres...

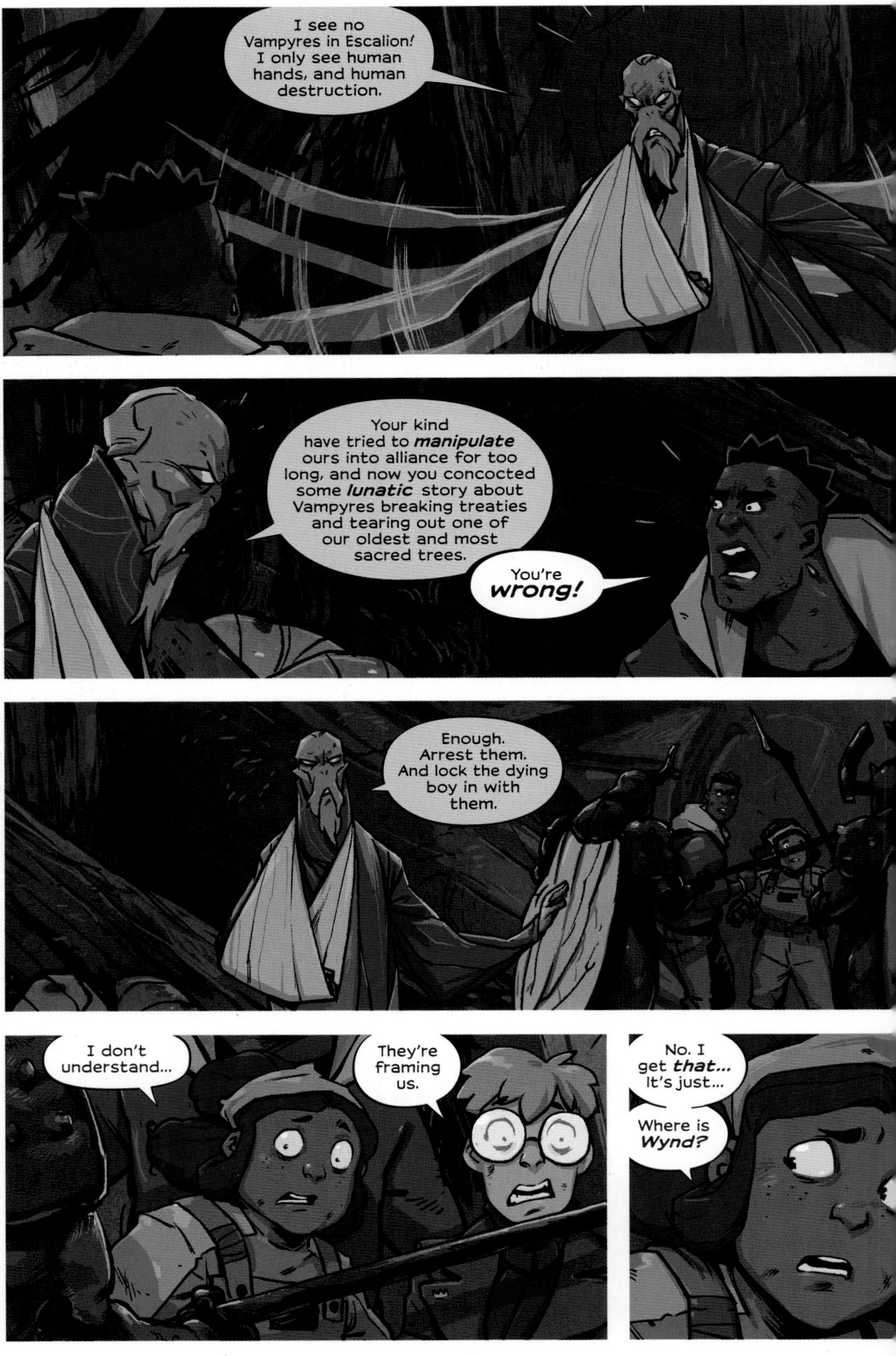

I see no Vampyres in Escalion! I only see human hands, and human destruction.
Your kind have tried to *manipulate* ours into alliance for too long, and now you concocted some *lunatic* story about Vampyres breaking treaties and tearing out one of our oldest and most sacred trees.
You're **wrong!**
Enough. Arrest them. And lock the dying boy in with them.
I don't understand...
They're framing us.
No. I get ***that...*** It's just...
Where is ***Wynd?***

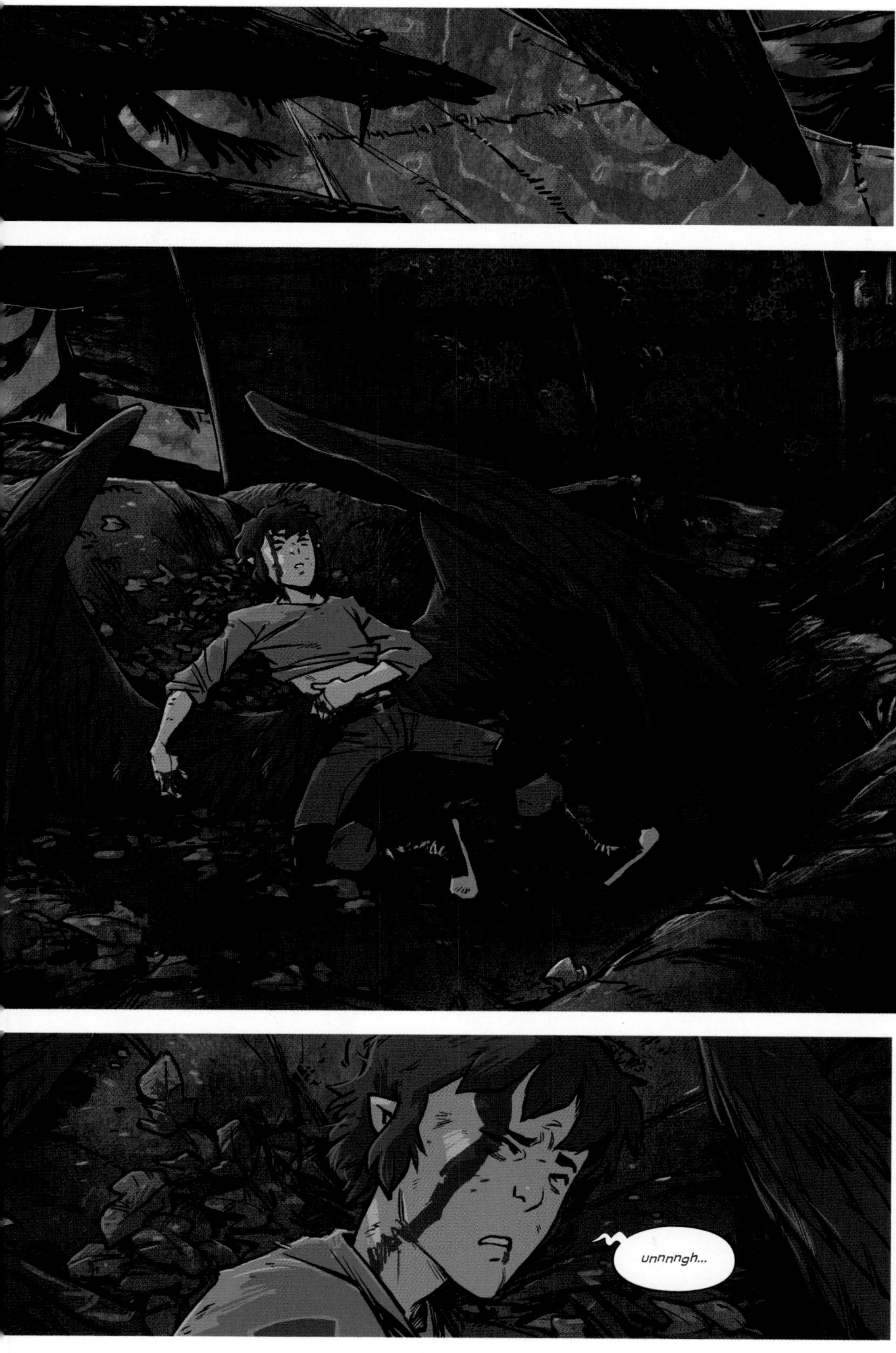
unnnngh...

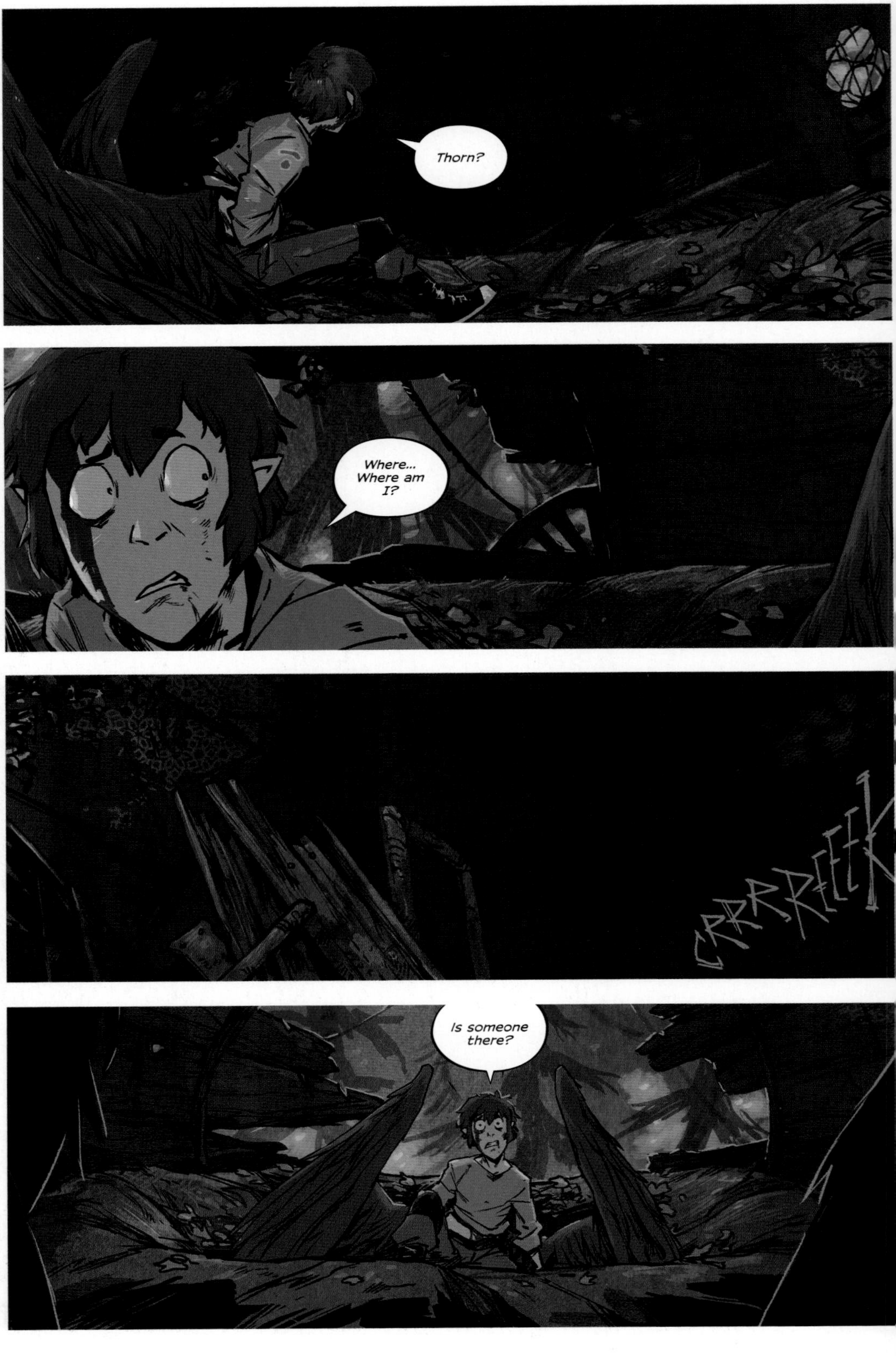
Thorn?
Where... Where am I?
CRRRREEEK
Is someone there?

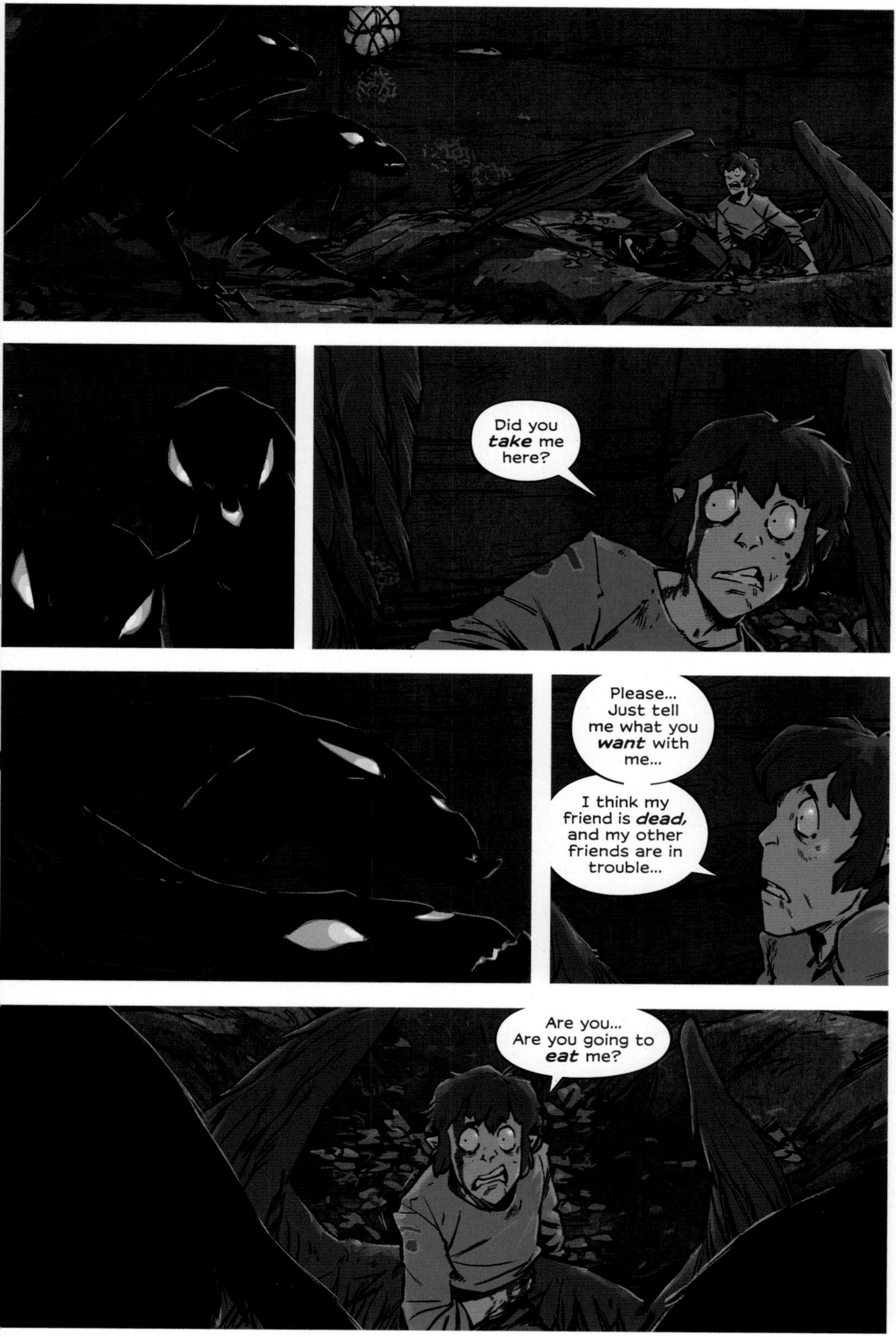
Did you *take* me here?
Please... Just tell me what you *want* with me...
I think my friend is *dead,* and my other friends are in trouble...
Are you... Are you going to *eat* me?

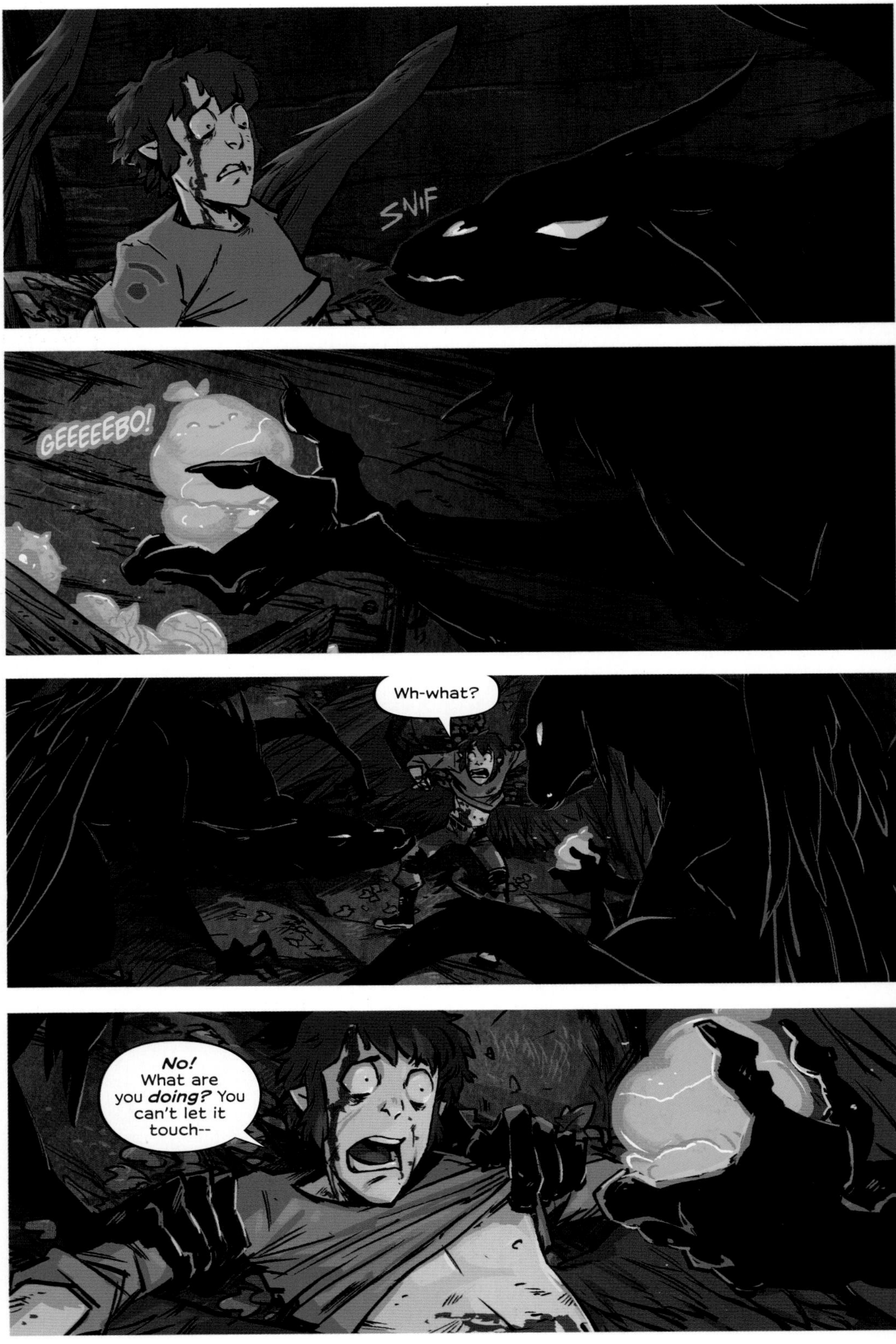
SNIF
GEEEEEBO!
Wh-what?
No! What are you *doing?* You can't let it touch--

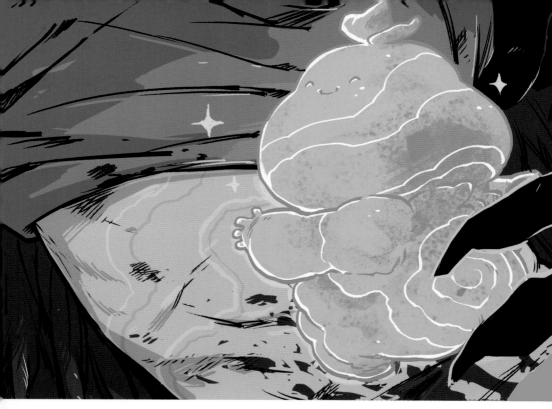

Oh.

Ohhh...

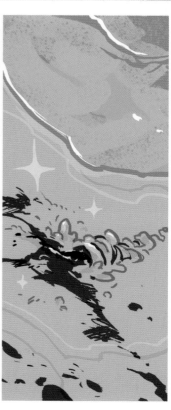

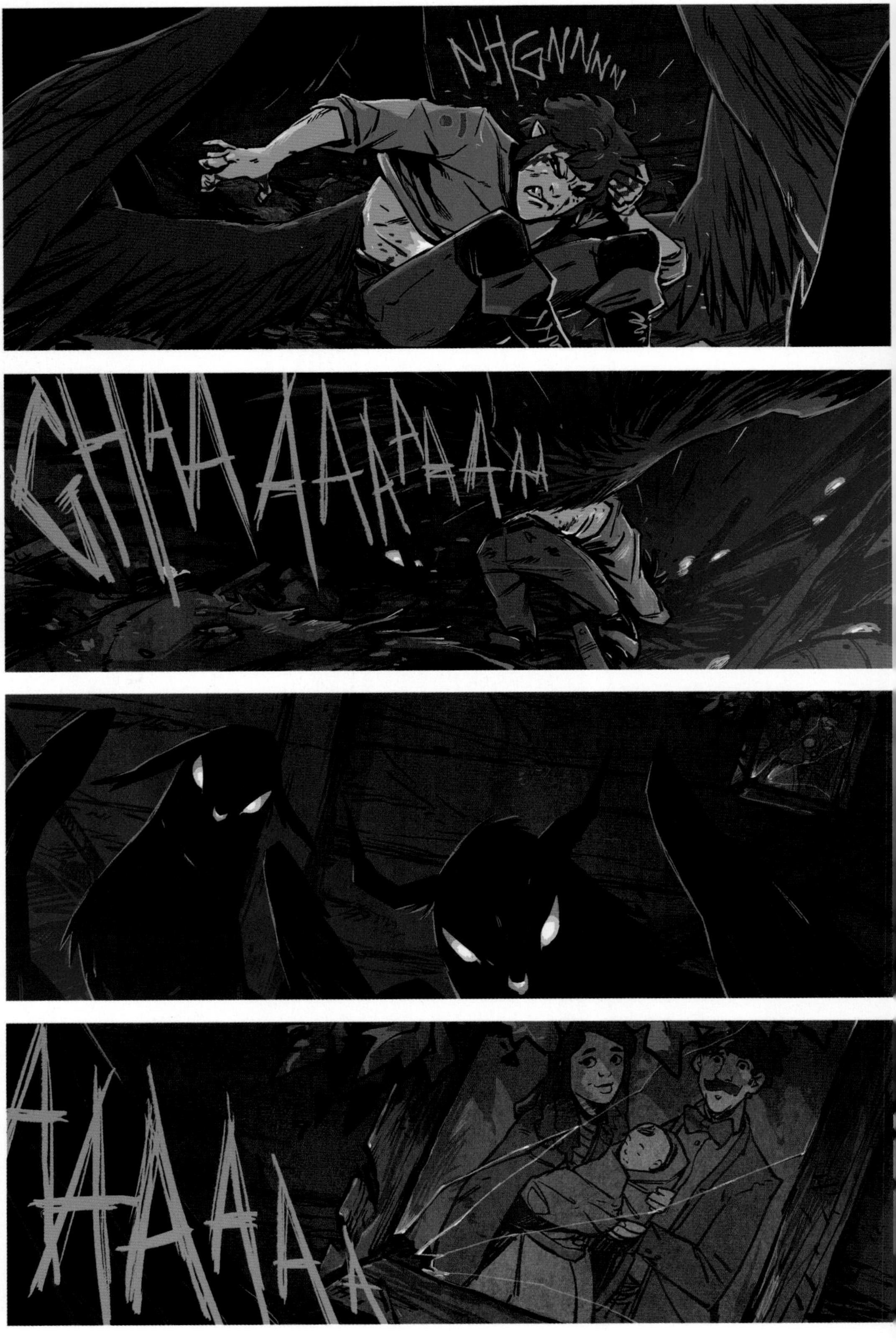
NHGNNNNN
GHAAAAAAAA
AHAAAAA

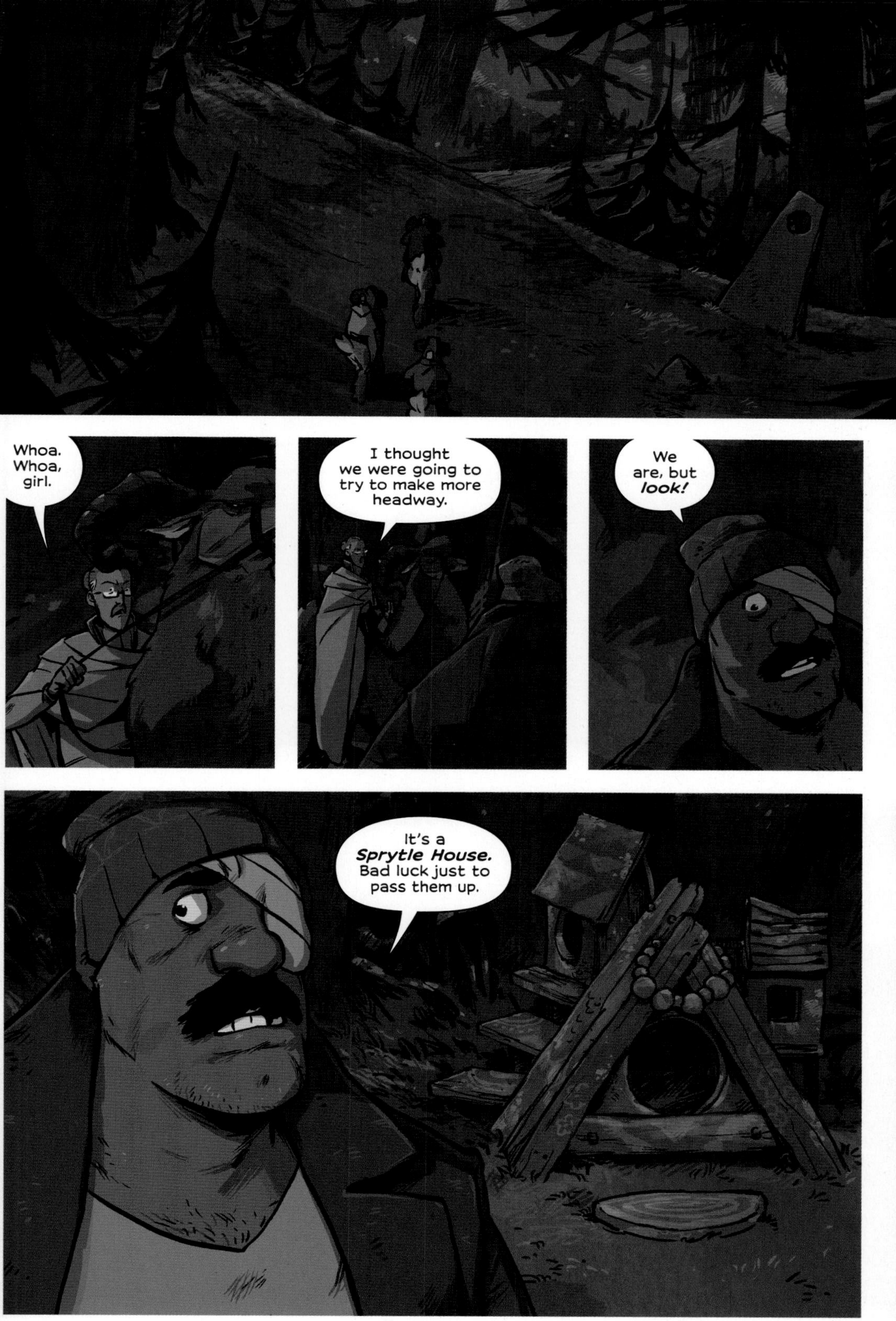
Whoa. Whoa, girl.
I thought we were going to try to make more headway.
We are, but *look!*
It's a ***Sprytle House.*** Bad luck just to pass them up.

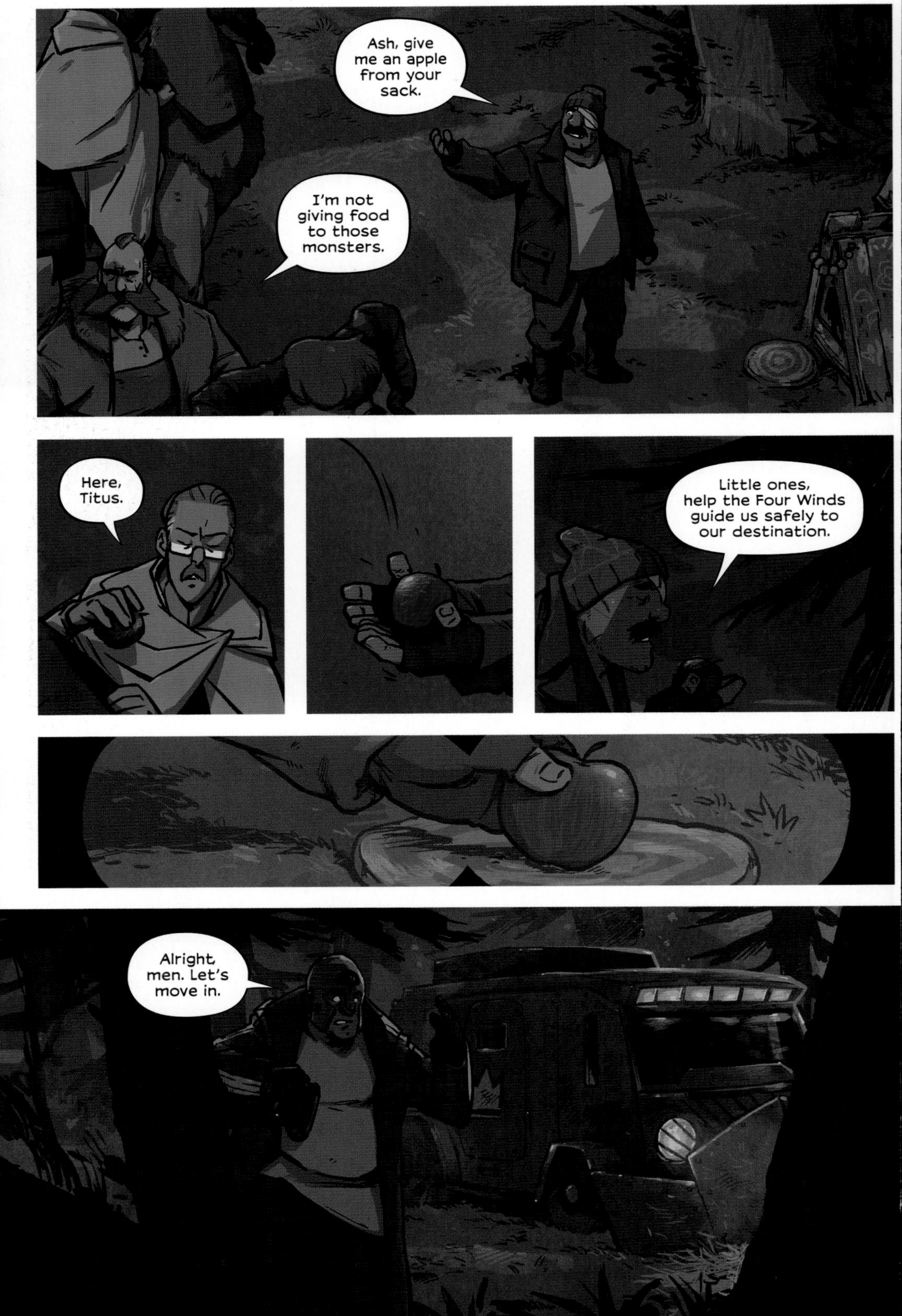
Ash, give me an apple from your sack.
I'm not giving food to those monsters.
Here, Titus.
Little ones, help the Four Winds guide us safely to our destination.
Alright, men. Let's move in.

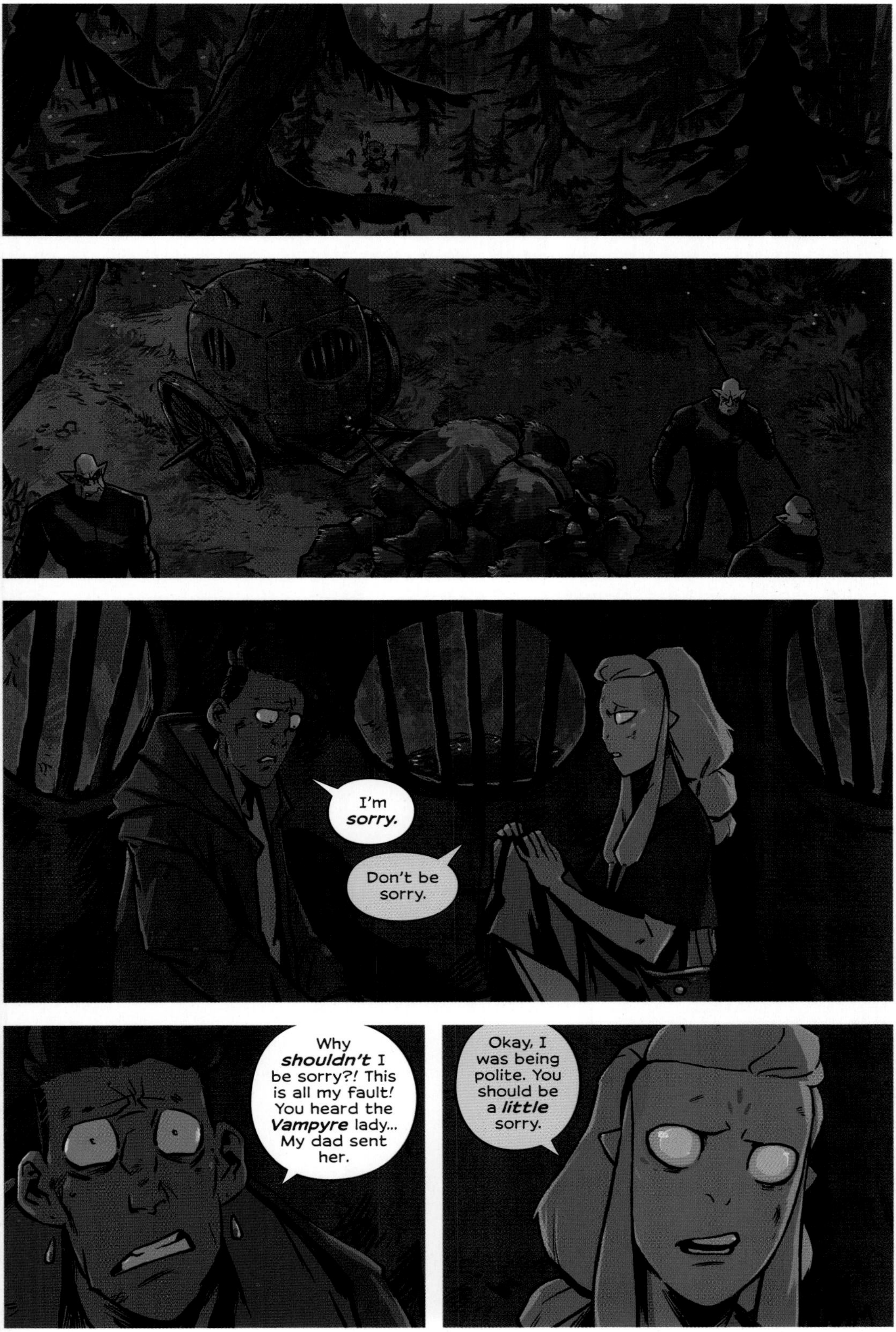
I'm *sorry.*
Don't be sorry.
Why *shouldn't* I be sorry?! This is all my fault! You heard the *Vampyre* lady... My dad sent her.
Okay, I was being polite. You should be a *little* sorry.

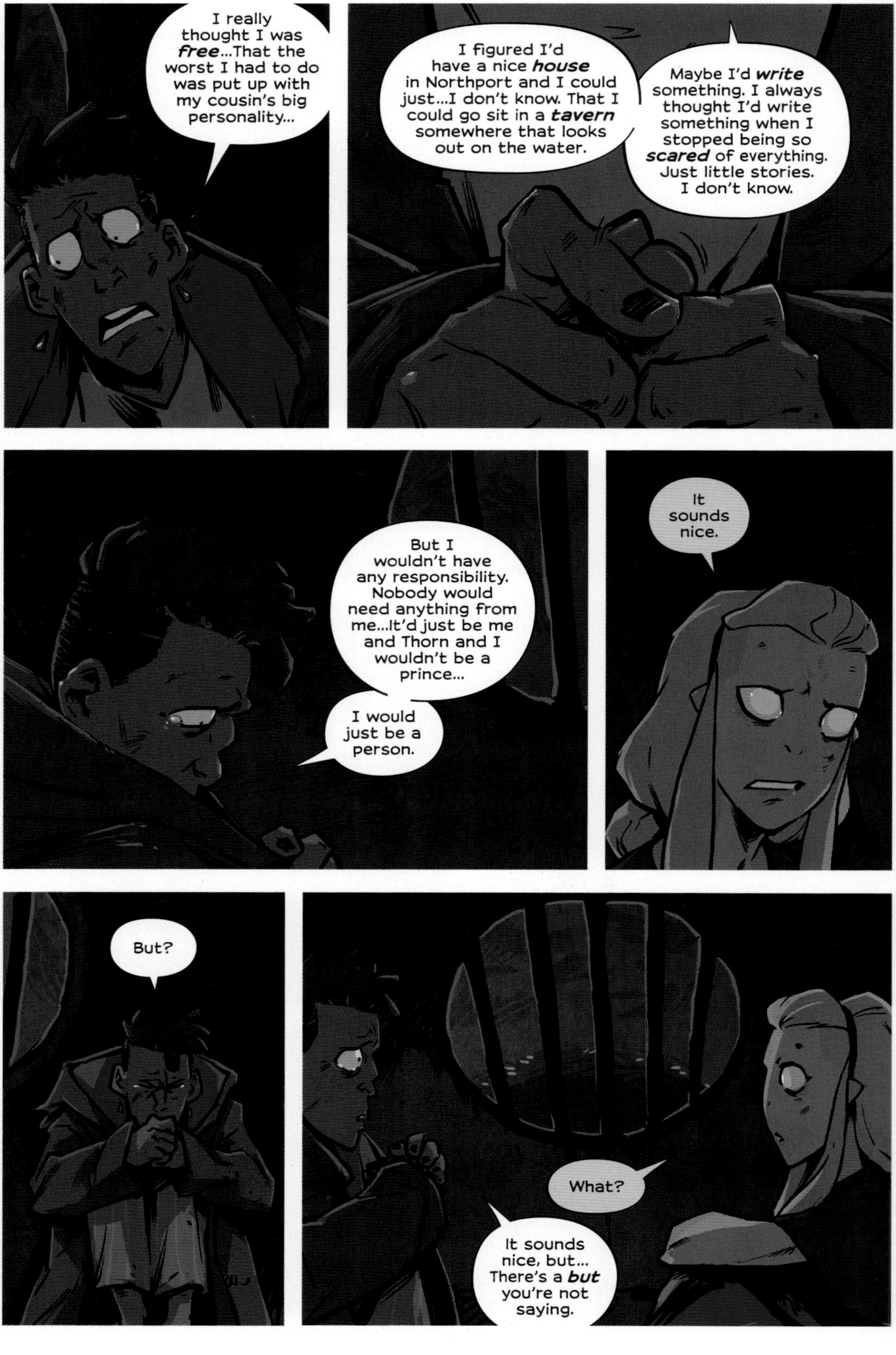
I really thought I was *free*...That the worst I had to do was put up with my cousin's big personality...
I figured I'd have a nice *house* in Northport and I could just...I don't know. That I could go sit in a *tavern* somewhere that looks out on the water.
Maybe I'd *write* something. I always thought I'd write something when I stopped being so *scared* of everything. Just little stories. I don't know.
But I wouldn't have any responsibility. Nobody would need anything from me...It'd just be me and Thorn and I wouldn't be a prince...
I would just be a person.
It sounds nice.
But?
What?
It sounds nice, but... There's a *but* you're not saying.

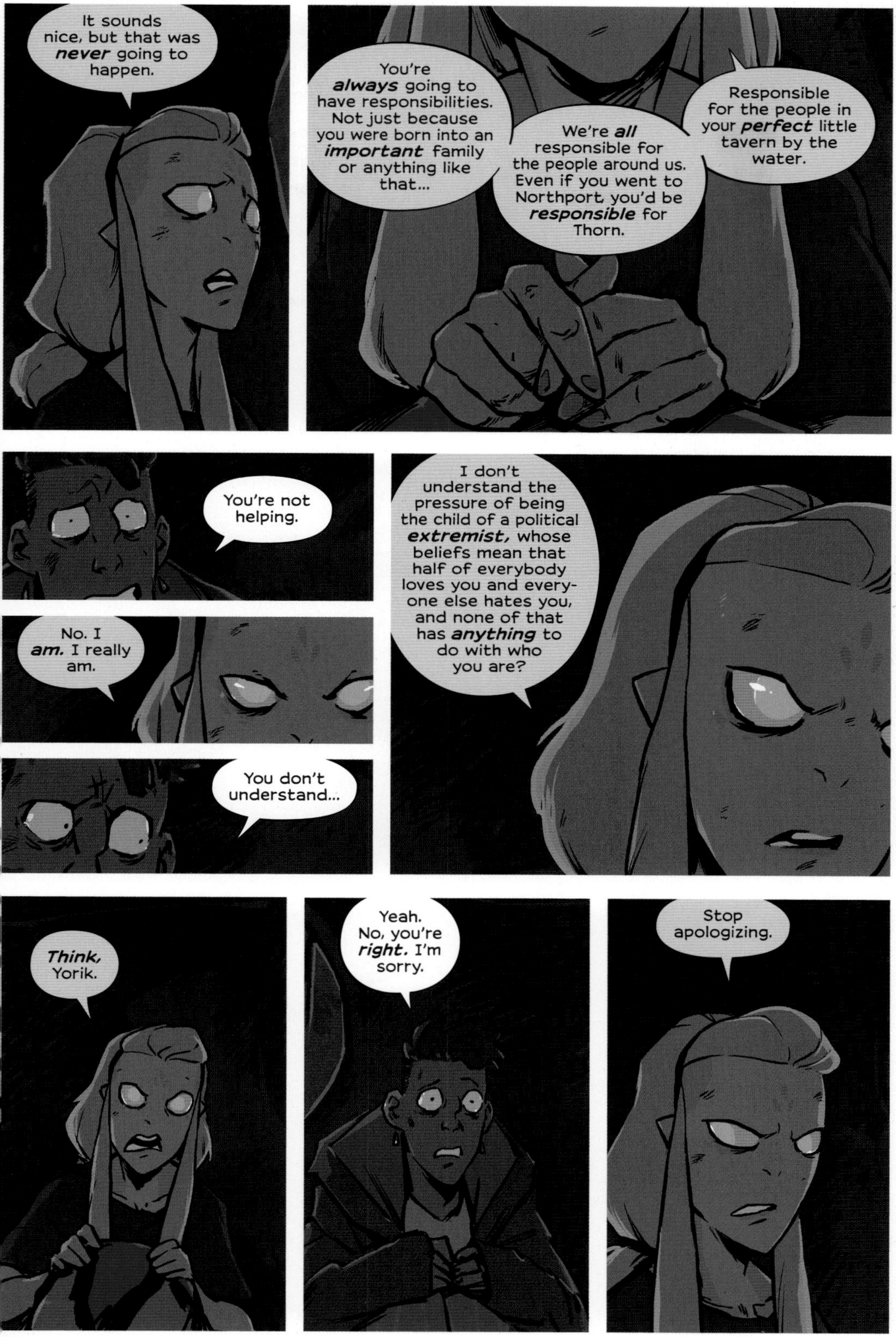
It sounds nice, but that was *never* going to happen.
You're *always* going to have responsibilities. Not just because you were born into an *important* family or anything like that...
We're *all* responsible for the people around us. Even if you went to Northport you'd be *responsible* for Thorn.
Responsible for the people in your *perfect* little tavern by the water.
You're not helping.
No. I *am.* I really am.
You don't understand...
I don't understand the pressure of being the child of a political *extremist,* whose beliefs mean that half of everybody loves you and everyone else hates you, and none of that has *anything* to do with who you are?
Think, Yorik.
Yeah. No, you're *right.* I'm sorry.
Stop apologizing.

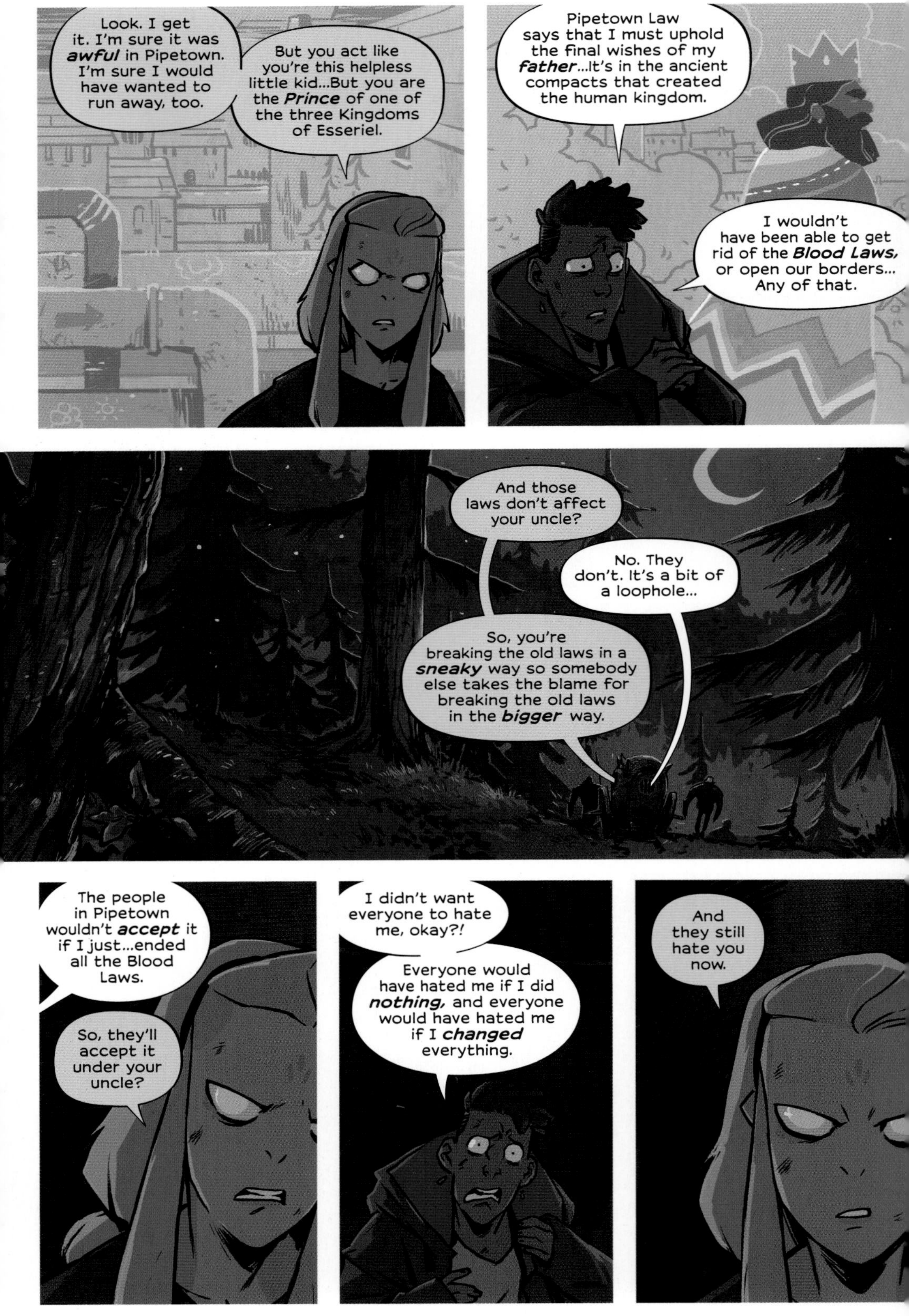

Look. I get it. I'm sure it was *awful* in Pipetown. I'm sure I would have wanted to run away, too.
But you act like you're this helpless little kid...But you are the *Prince* of one of the three Kingdoms of Esseriel.
Pipetown Law says that I must uphold the final wishes of my *father*...It's in the ancient compacts that created the human kingdom.
I wouldn't have been able to get rid of the *Blood Laws,* or open our borders... Any of that.
And those laws don't affect your uncle?
No. They don't. It's a bit of a loophole...
So, you're breaking the old laws in a *sneaky* way so somebody else takes the blame for breaking the old laws in the *bigger* way.
The people in Pipetown wouldn't *accept* it if I just...ended all the Blood Laws.
So, they'll accept it under your uncle?
I didn't want everyone to hate me, okay?!
Everyone would have hated me if I did *nothing,* and everyone would have hated me if I *changed* everything.
And they still hate you now.

I know! You don't think I know that?!

In Escalion you said you didn't want people to see you that way.

So, what do *you* want?

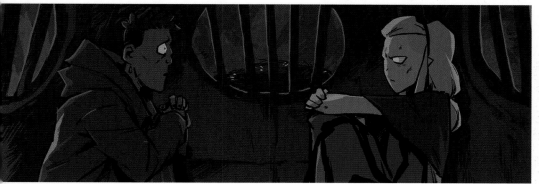

It doesn't matter any-more. My father won.

Your father winning means you'll be *King.* So I think what you want matters tremendously, now.

So, what do you *want,* Yorik?

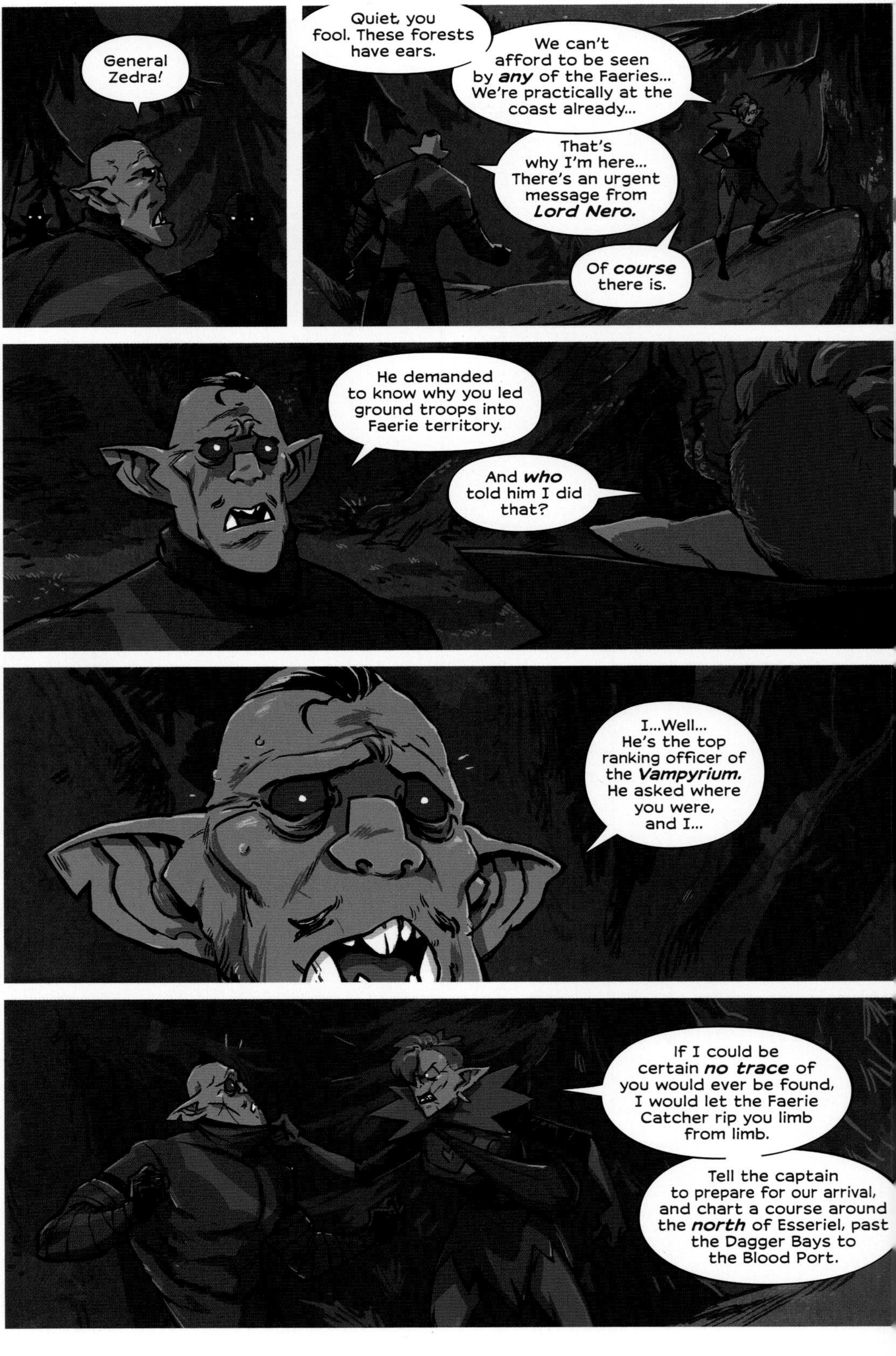
General Zedra!
Quiet, you fool. These forests have ears.
We can't afford to be seen by *any* of the Faeries... We're practically at the coast already...
That's why I'm here... There's an urgent message from ***Lord Nero.***
Of ***course*** there is.
He demanded to know why you led ground troops into Faerie territory.
And ***who*** told him I did that?
I...Well... He's the top ranking officer of the ***Vampyrium.*** He asked where you were, and I...
If I could be certain ***no trace*** of you would ever be found, I would let the Faerie Catcher rip you limb from limb.
Tell the captain to prepare for our arrival, and chart a course around the ***north*** of Esseriel, past the Dagger Bays to the Blood Port.

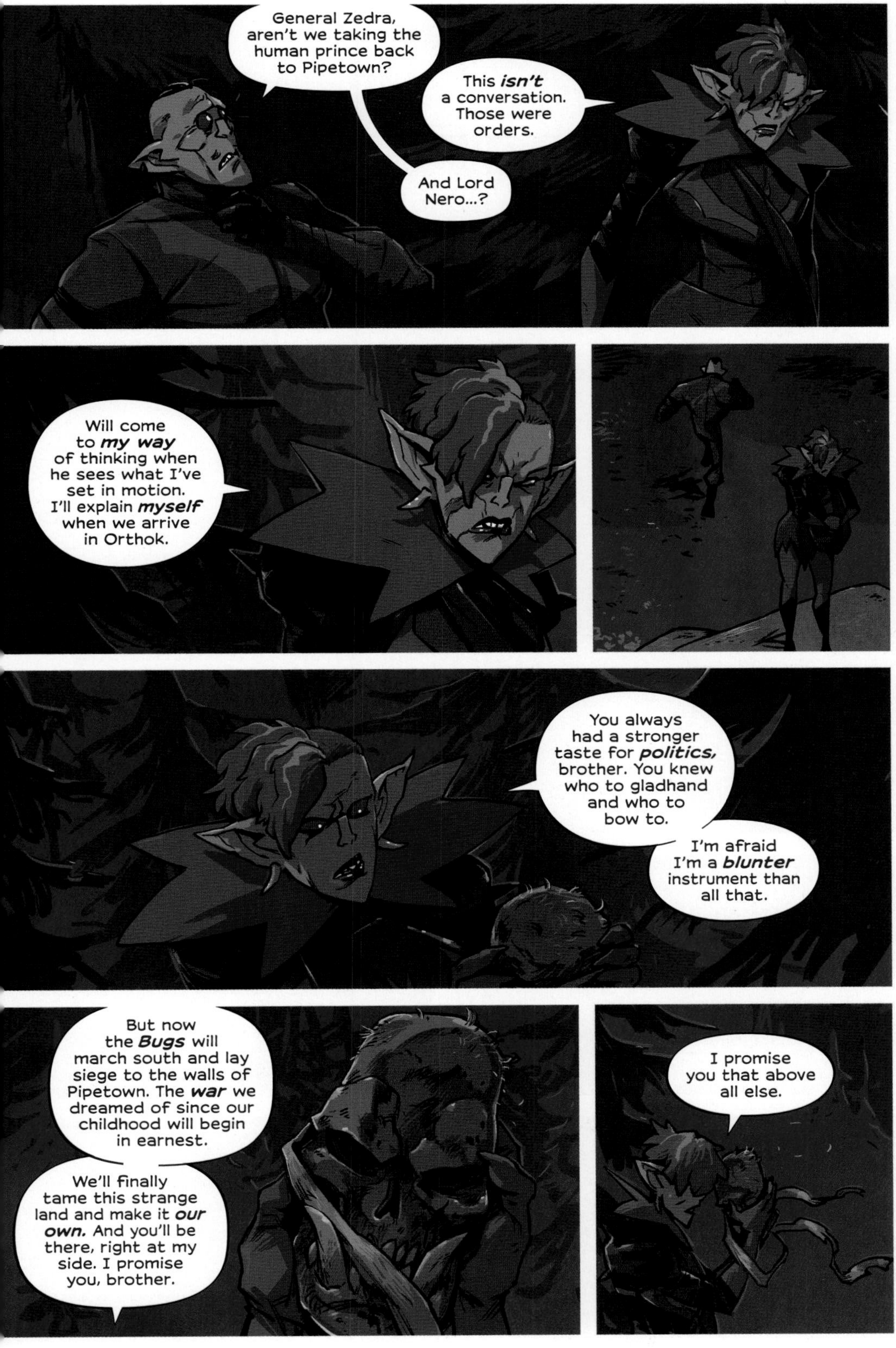
General Zedra, aren't we taking the human prince back to Pipetown?
This *isn't* a conversation. Those were orders.
And Lord Nero...?
Will come to *my way* of thinking when he sees what I've set in motion. I'll explain *myself* when we arrive in Orthok.
You always had a stronger taste for *politics,* brother. You knew who to gladhand and who to bow to.
I'm afraid I'm a *blunter* instrument than all that.
But now the *Bugs* will march south and lay siege to the walls of Pipetown. The *war* we dreamed of since our childhood will begin in earnest.
We'll finally tame this strange land and make it *our own.* And you'll be there, right at my side. I promise you, brother.
I promise you that above all else.

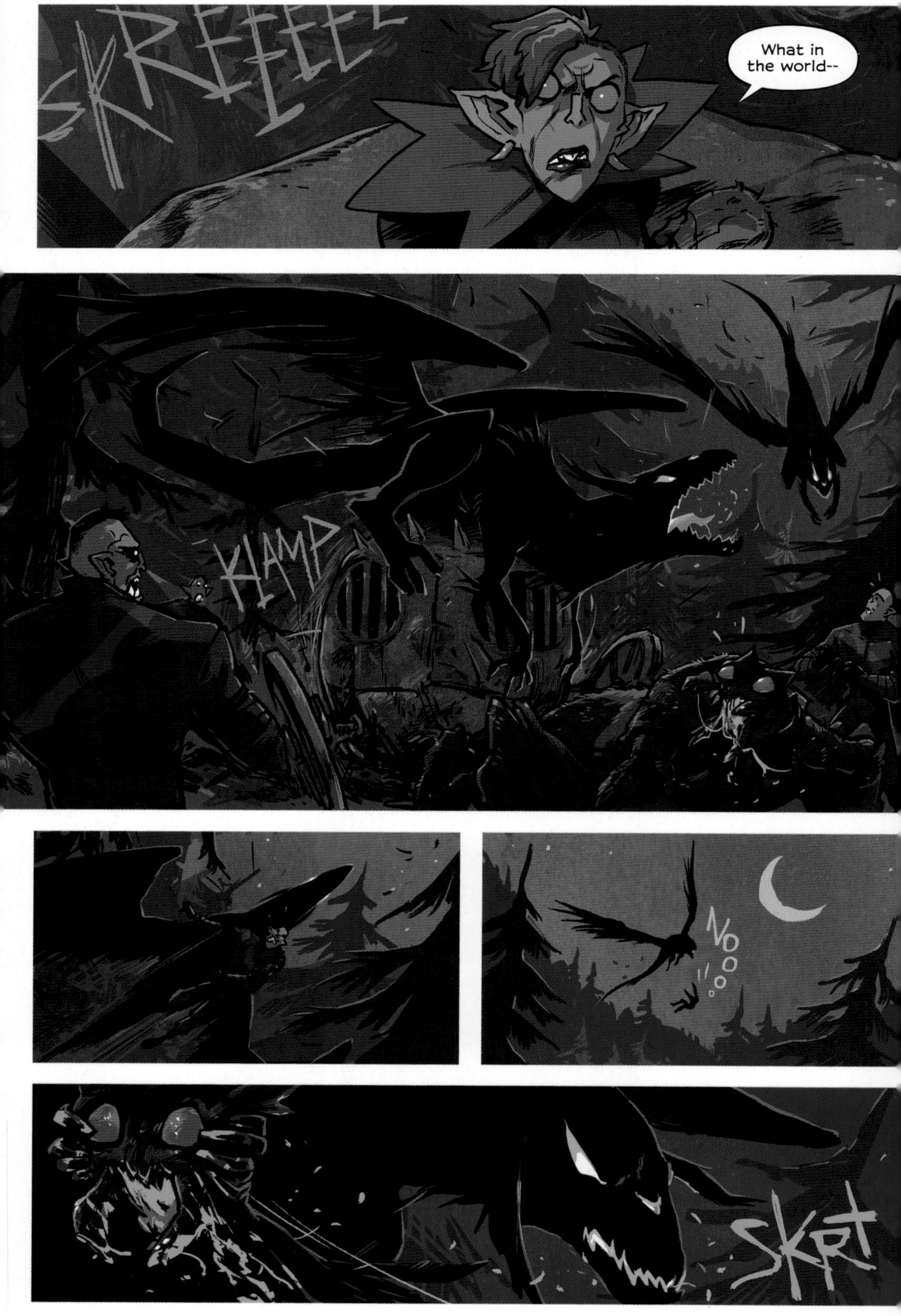
SKREEEEE
What in the world--
KLAMP
NOOOO!!
SKRT

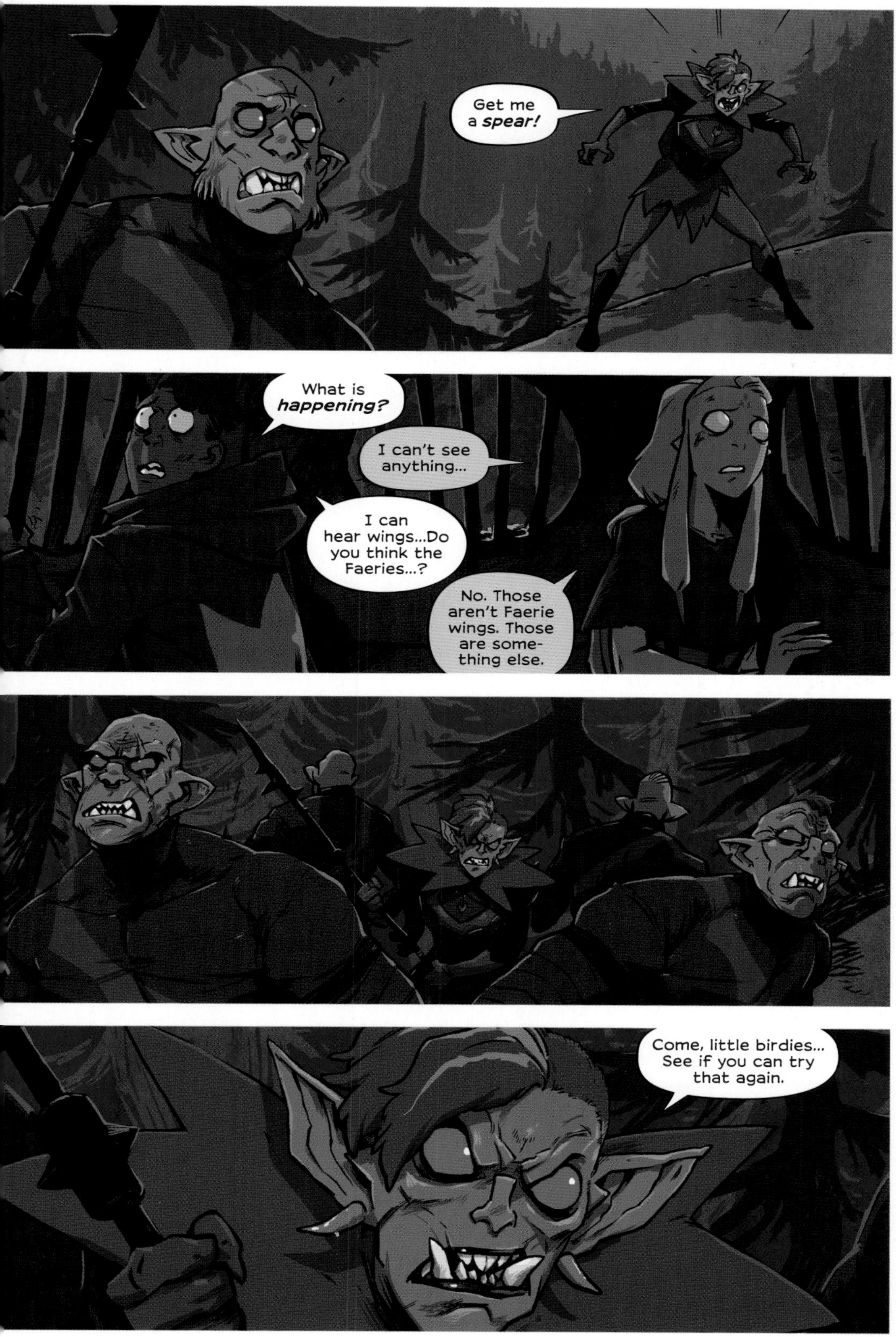

Get me a *spear!*
What is *happening?*
I can't see anything...
I can hear wings...Do you think the Faeries...?
No. Those aren't Faerie wings. Those are some-thing else.
Come, little birdies... See if you can try that again.

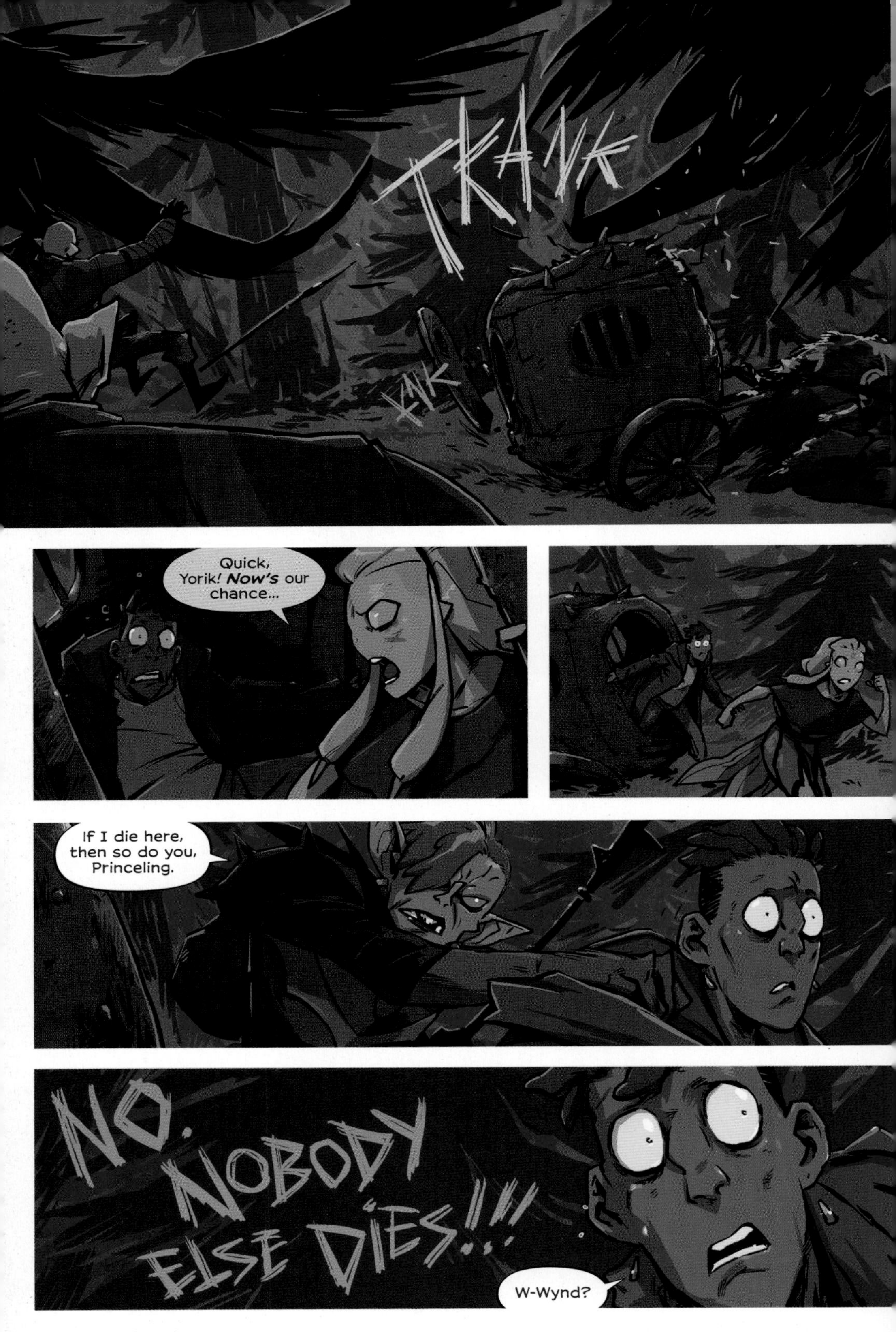
TKANK
KNK
Quick, Yorik! Now's our chance...
If I die here, then so do you, Princeling.
NO. NOBODY ELSE DIES!!!
W-Wynd?

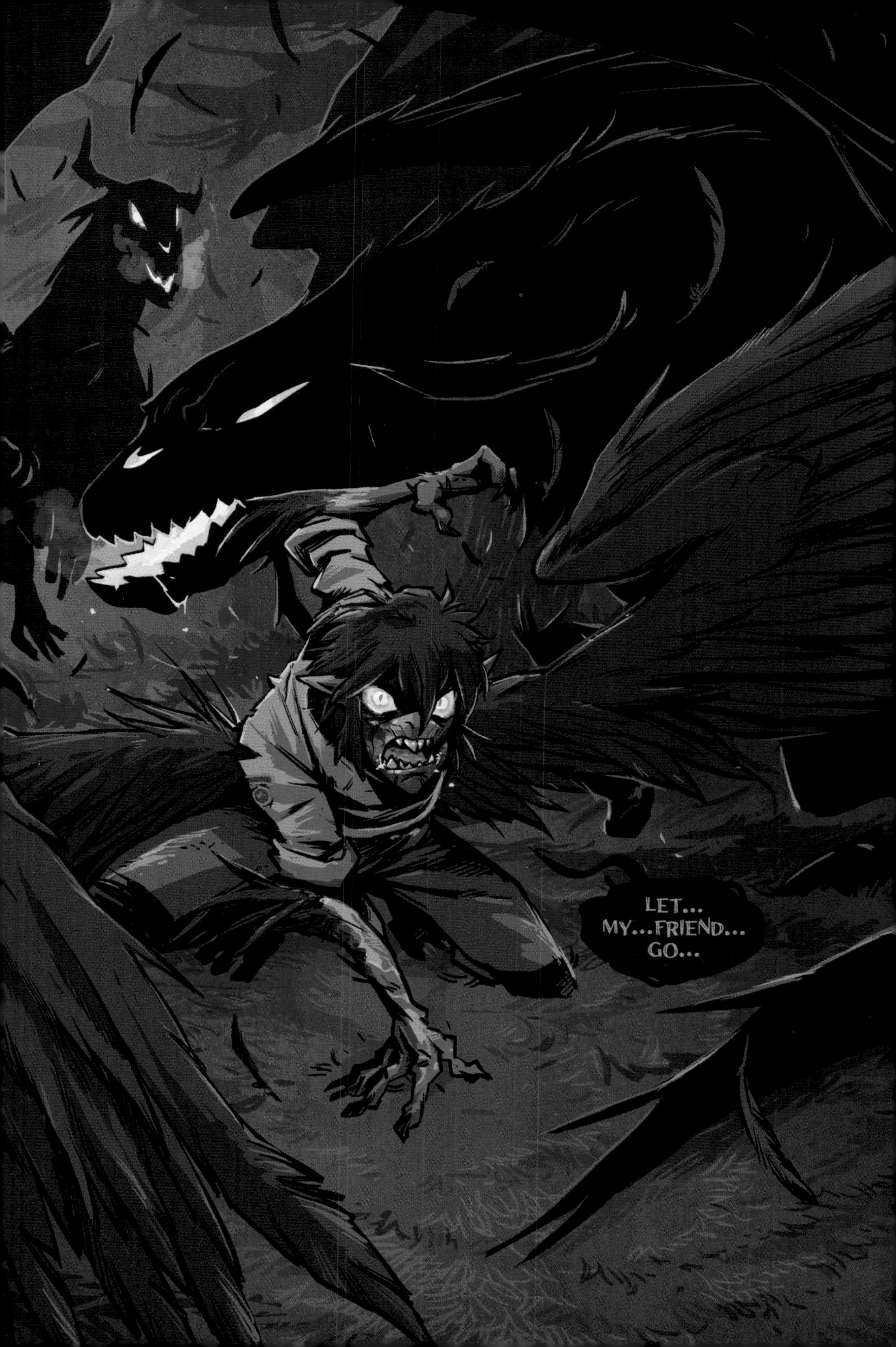
LET... MY...FRIEND... GO...

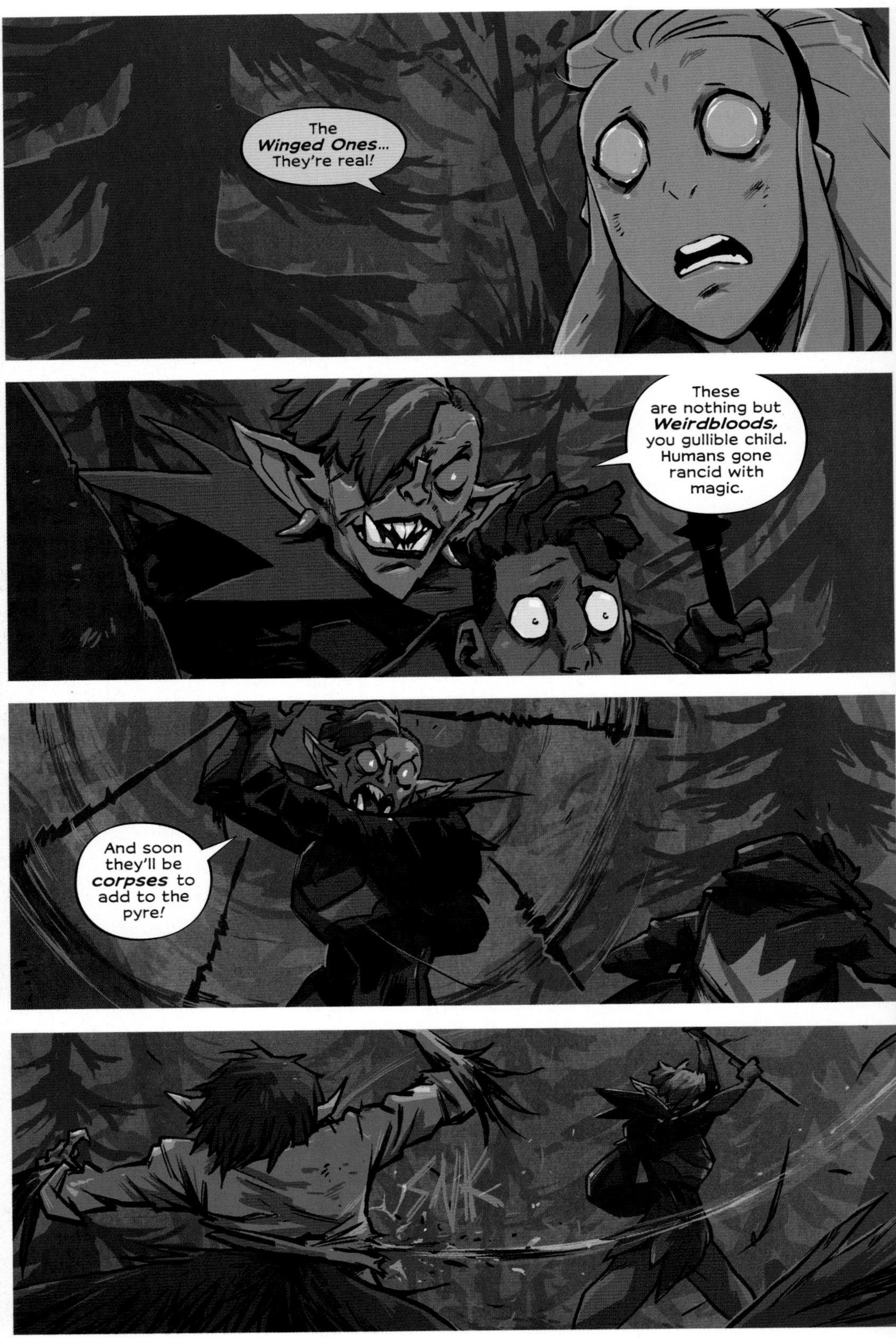
The *Winged Ones*... They're real!
These are nothing but *Weirdbloods,* you gullible child. Humans gone rancid with magic.
And soon they'll be *corpses* to add to the pyre!
SNIK

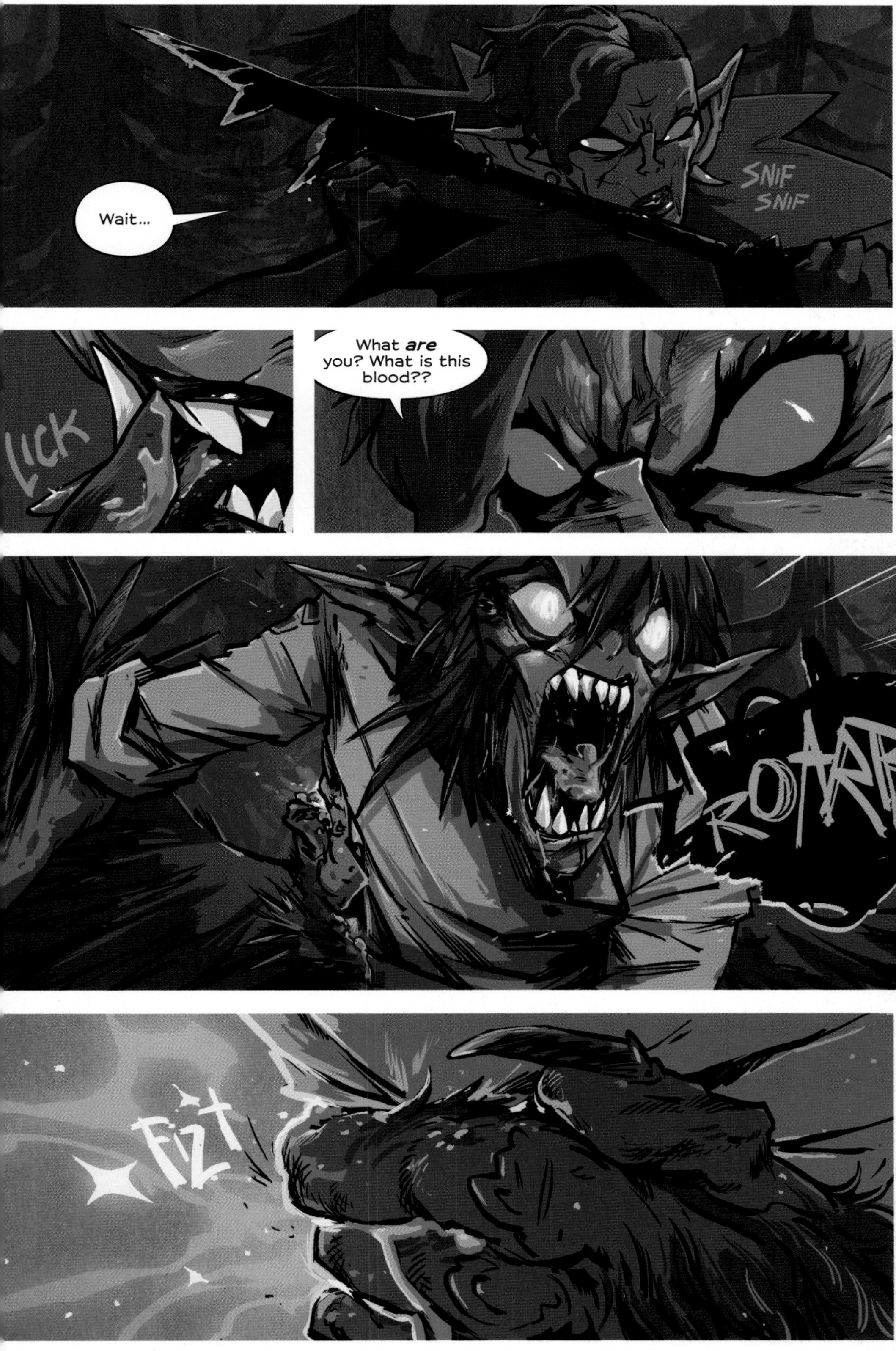

Wait...
SNIF
SNIF
LICK
What *are* you? What is this blood??
ROARR
FIZT

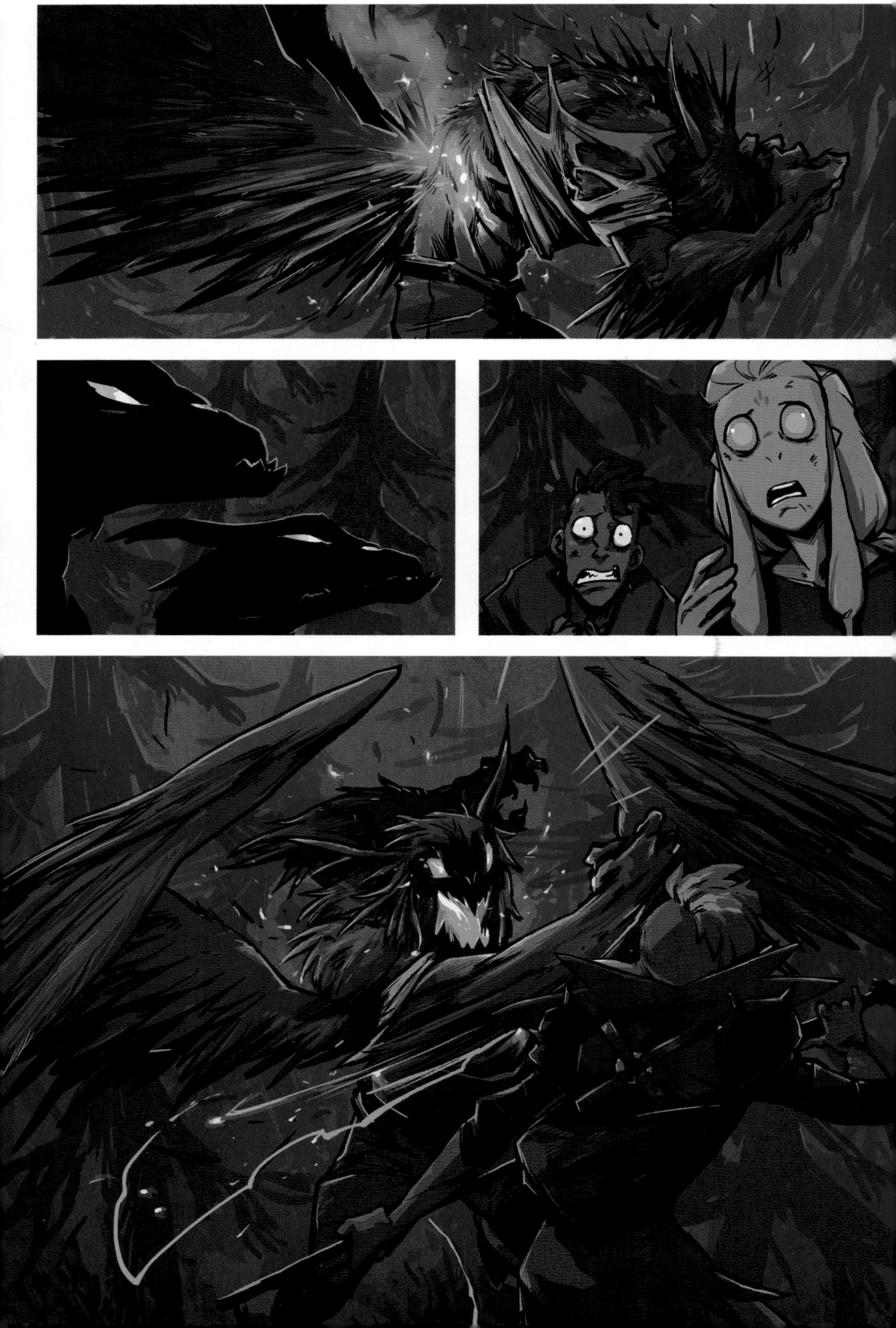

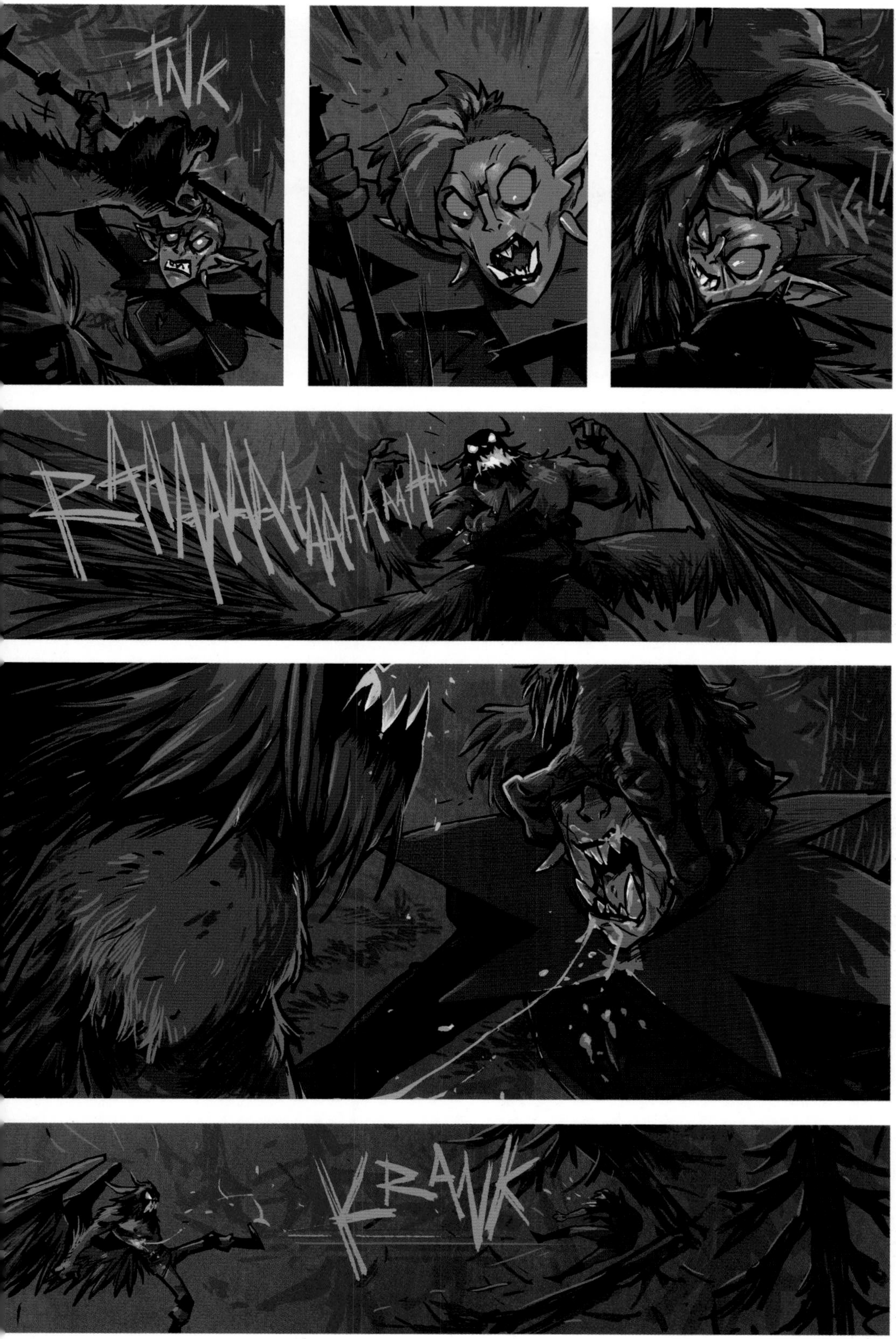

TNK
NG!!
RAAAAAAAaaaaaaaa
KRANK

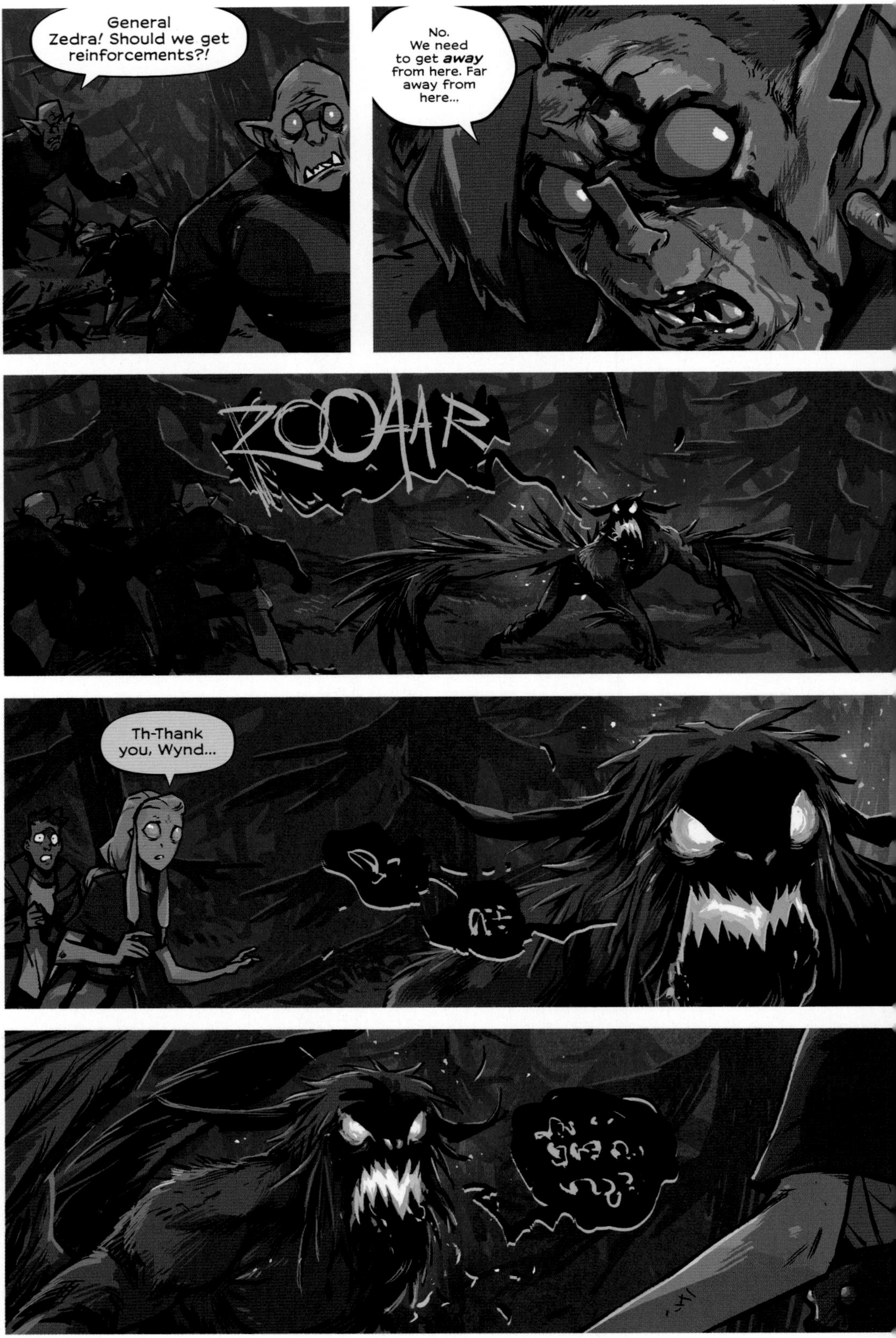
General Zedra! Should we get reinforcements?!
No. We need to get *away* from here. Far away from here...
ZOOAAR
Th-Thank you, Wynd...

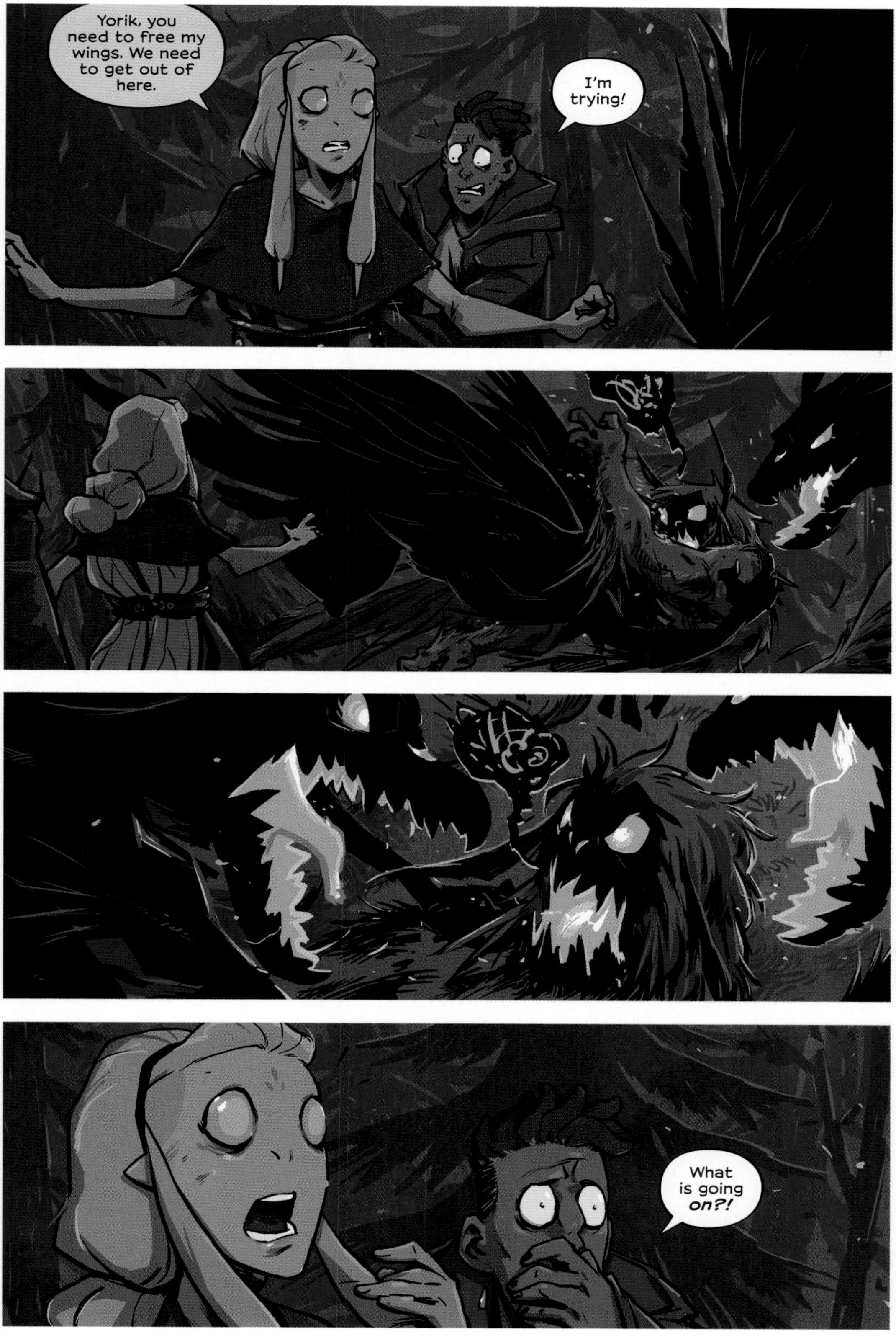
Yorik, you need to free my wings. We need to get out of here.
I'm trying!
What is going *on?!*

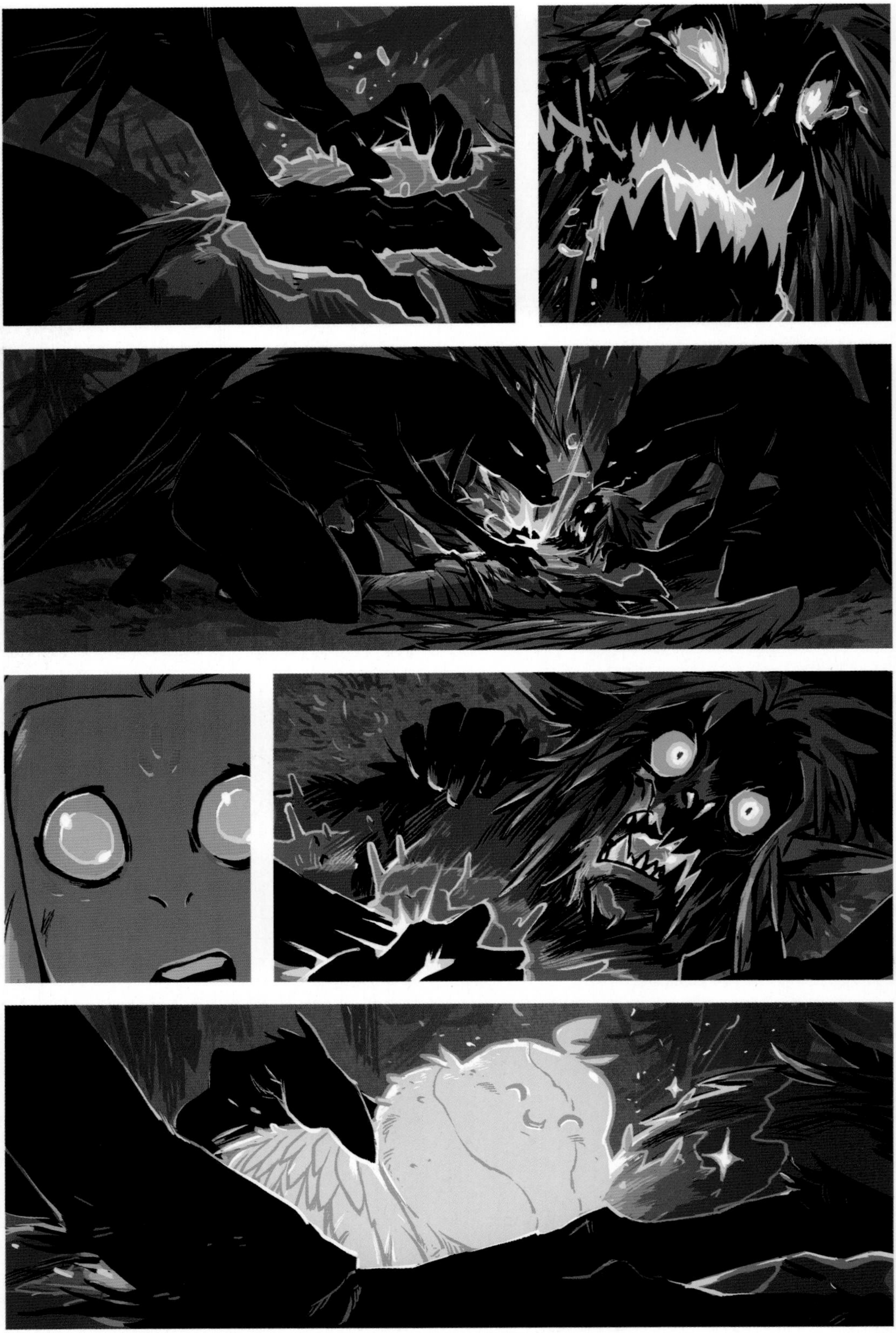

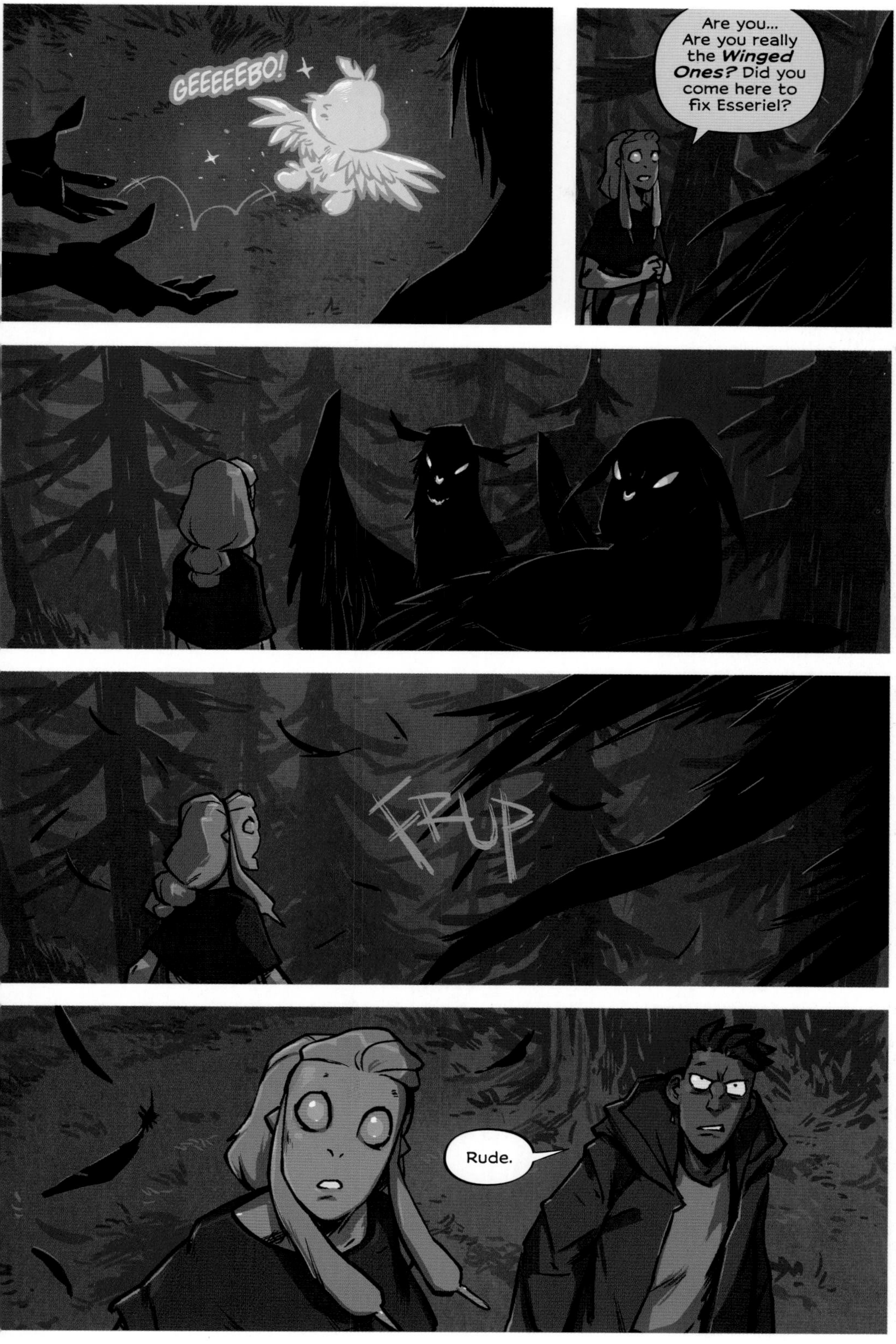
GEEEEEBO!
Are you... Are you really the ***Winged Ones?*** Did you come here to fix Esseriel?
FRUP
Rude.

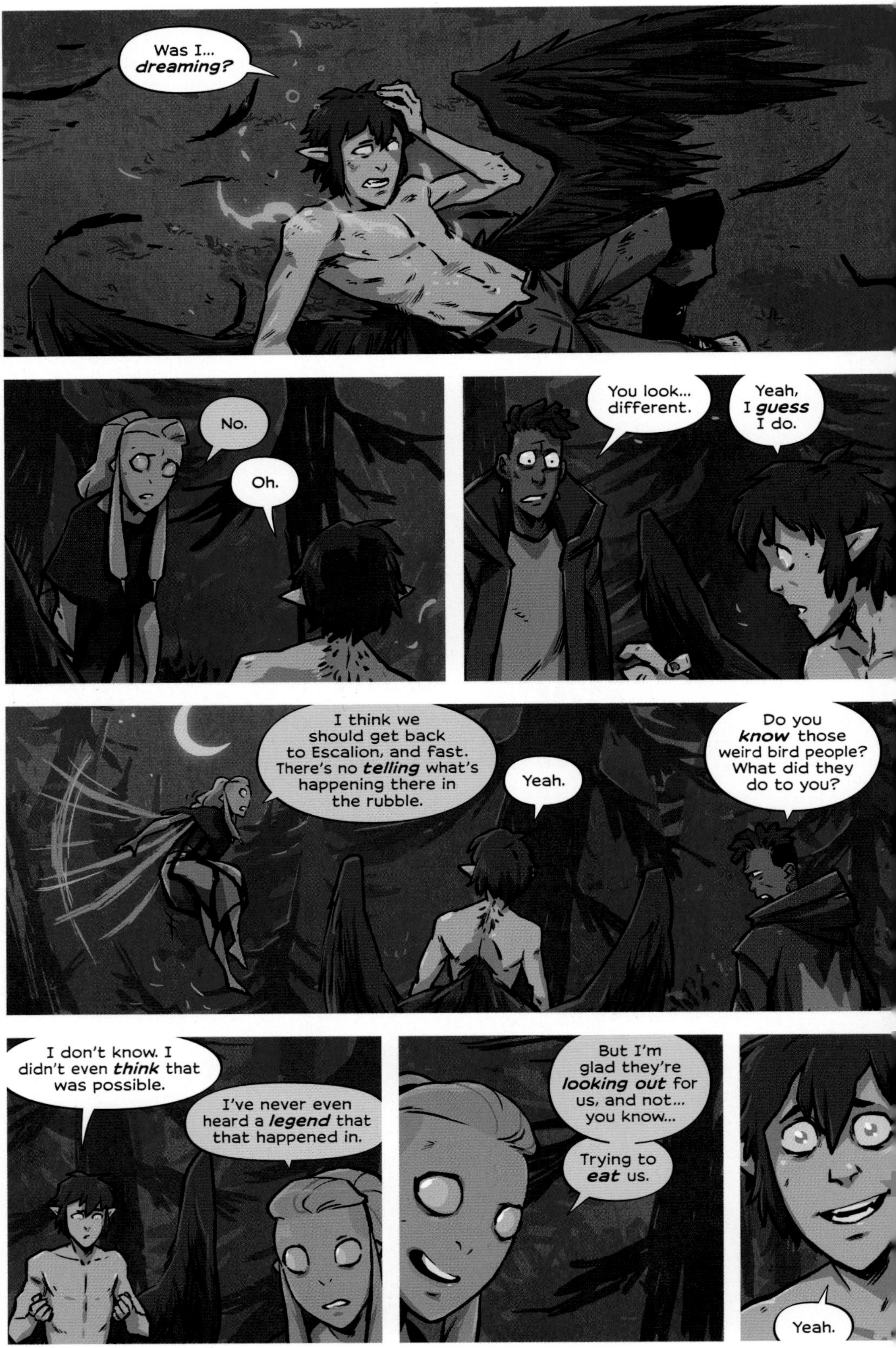
Was I... *dreaming?*
No.
Oh.
You look... different.
Yeah, I *guess* I do.
I think we should get back to Escalion, and fast. There's no *telling* what's happening there in the rubble.
Yeah.
Do you *know* those weird bird people? What did they do to you?
I don't know. I didn't even *think* that was possible.
I've never even heard a *legend* that that happened in.
But I'm glad they're *looking out* for us, and not... you know...
Trying to *eat* us.
Yeah.

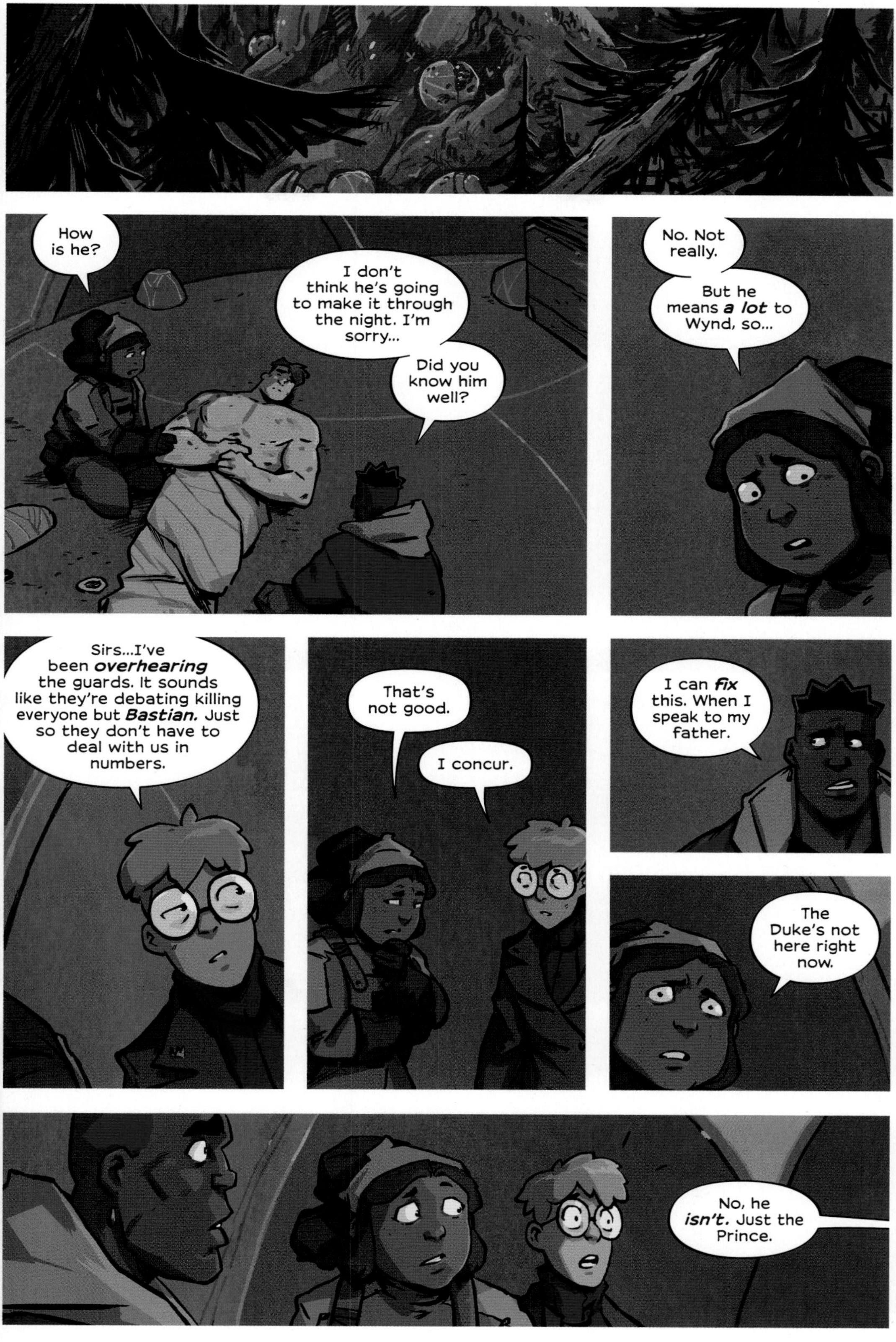
How is he?
I don't think he's going to make it through the night. I'm sorry...
Did you know him well?
No. Not really.
But he means *a lot* to Wynd, so...
Sirs...I've been *overhearing* the guards. It sounds like they're debating killing everyone but *Bastian.* Just so they don't have to deal with us in numbers.
That's not good.
I concur.
I can *fix* this. When I speak to my father.
The Duke's not here right now.
No, he *isn't.* Just the Prince.

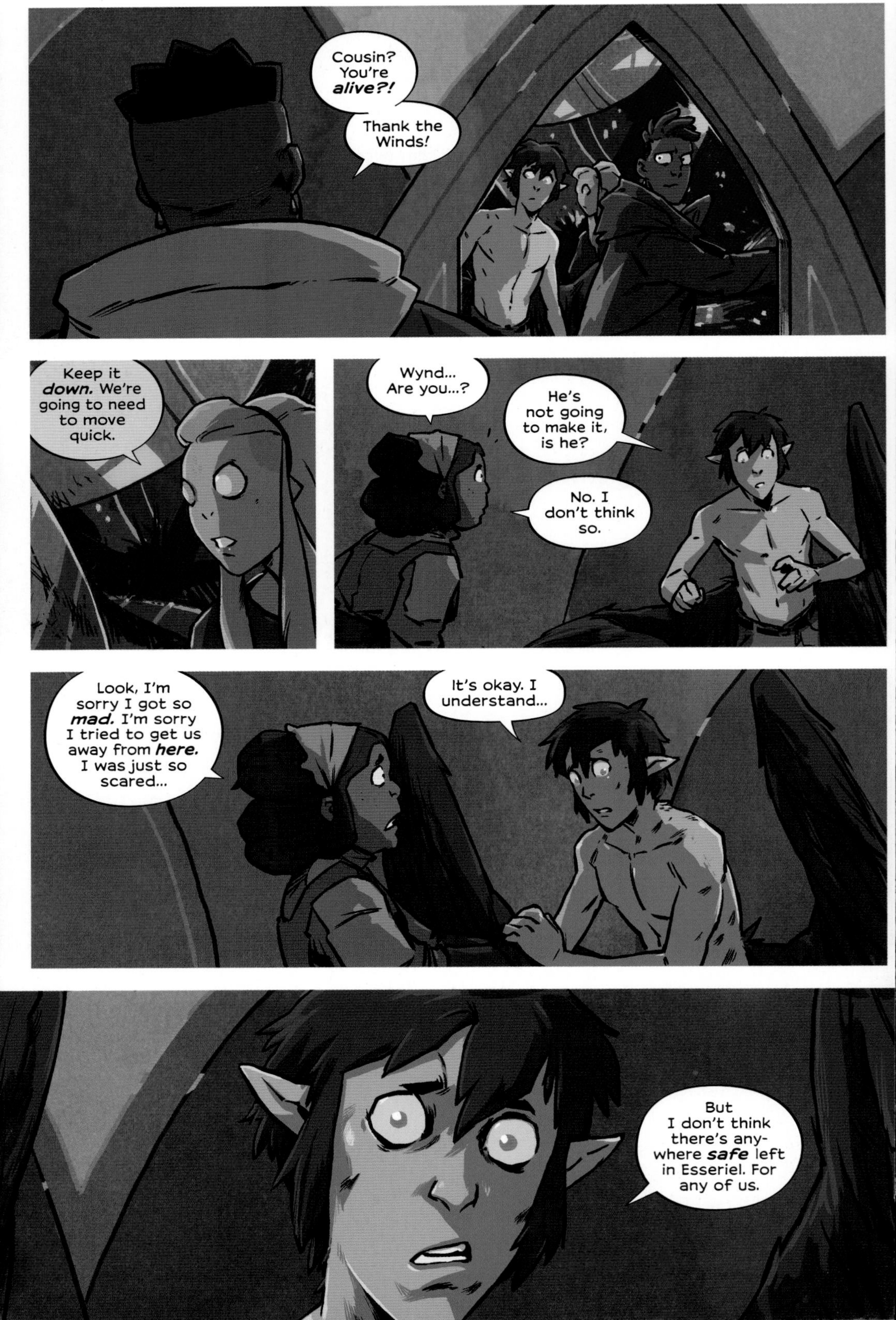

Cousin? You're *alive?!*
Thank the Winds!
Keep it *down.* We're going to need to move quick.
Wynd... Are you...?
He's not going to make it, is he?
No. I don't think so.
Look, I'm sorry I got so *mad.* I'm sorry I tried to get us away from *here.* I was just so scared...
It's okay. I understand...
But I don't think there's any-where *safe* left in Esseriel. For any of us.

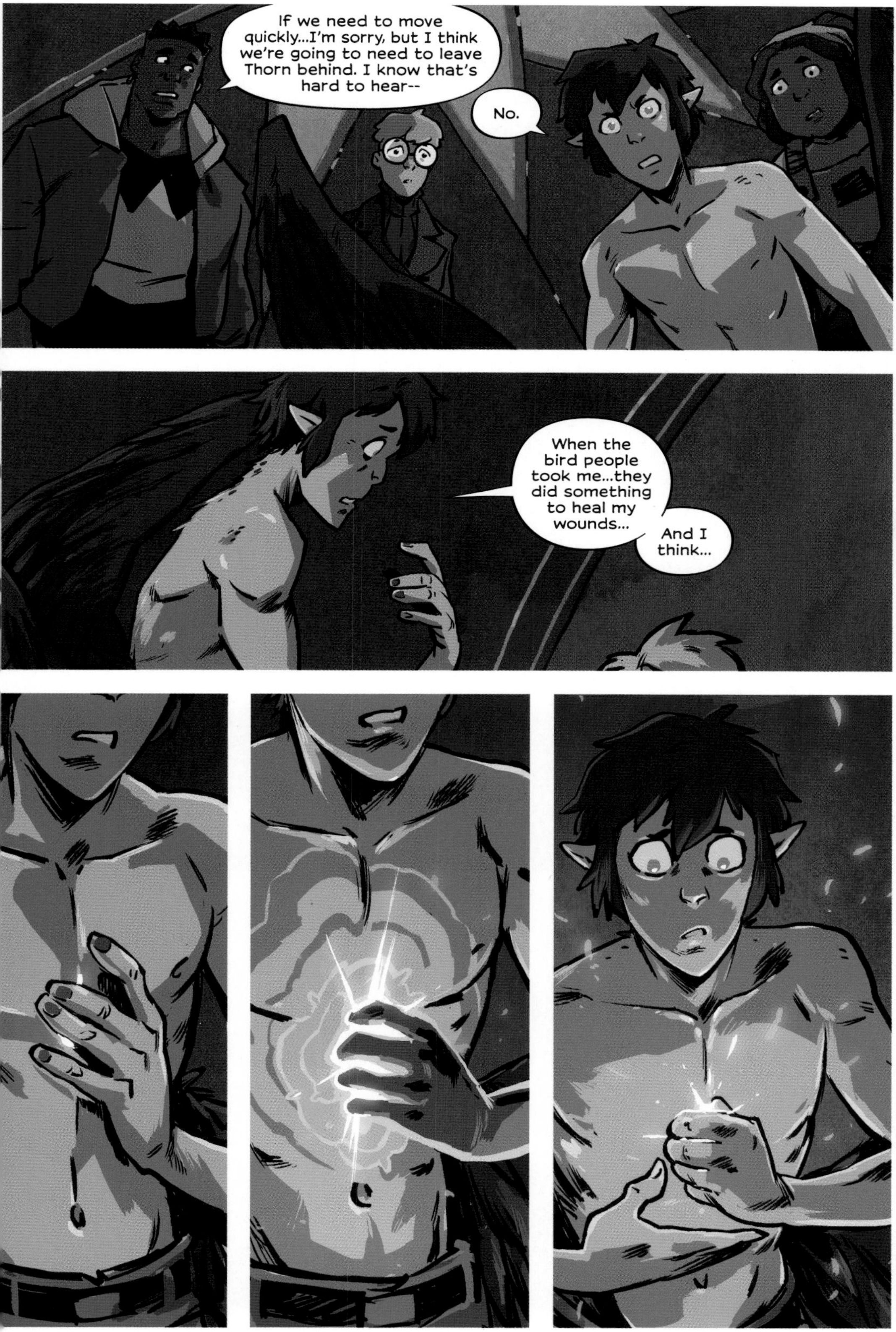
If we need to move quickly...I'm sorry, but I think we're going to need to leave Thorn behind. I know that's hard to hear--
No.
When the bird people took me...they did something to heal my wounds...
And I think...

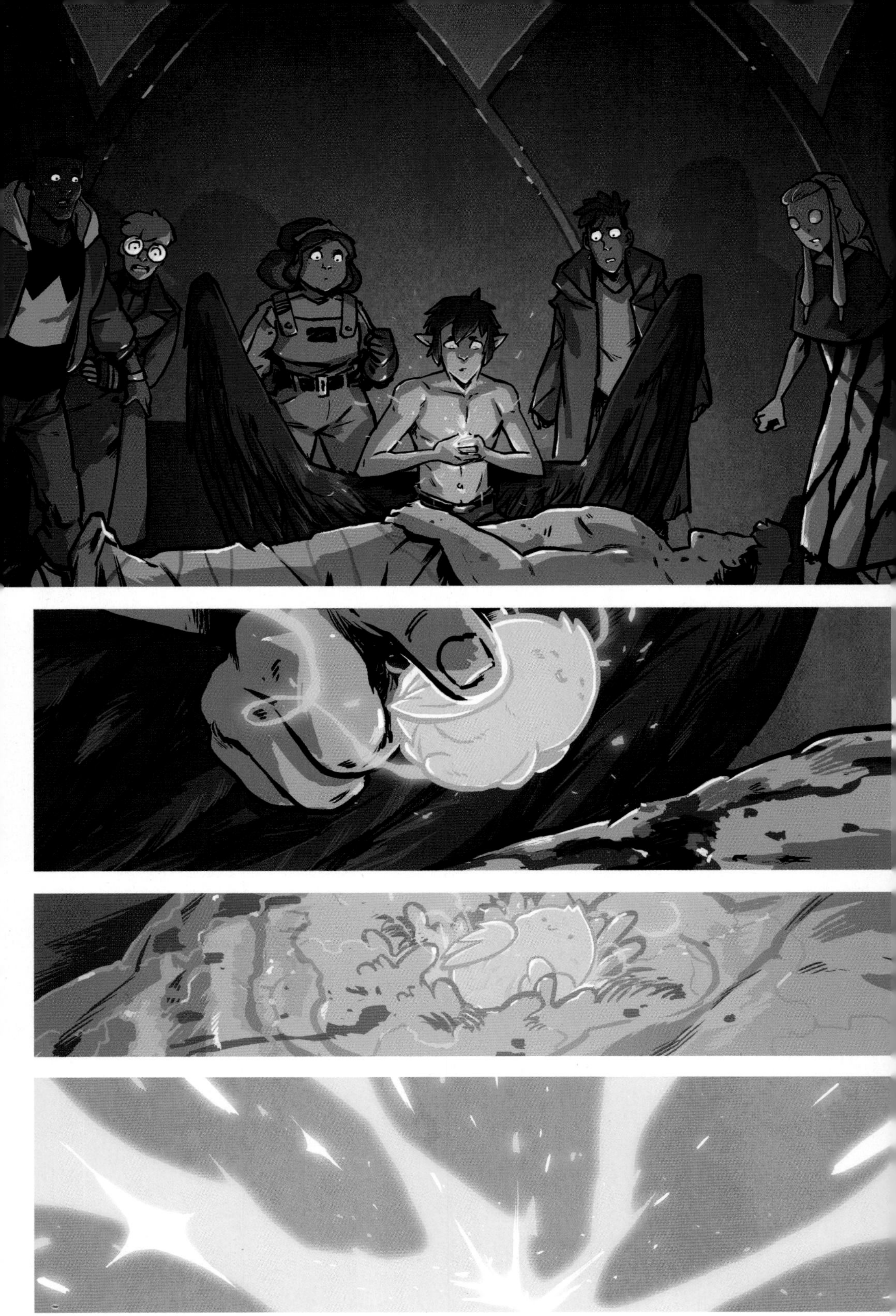

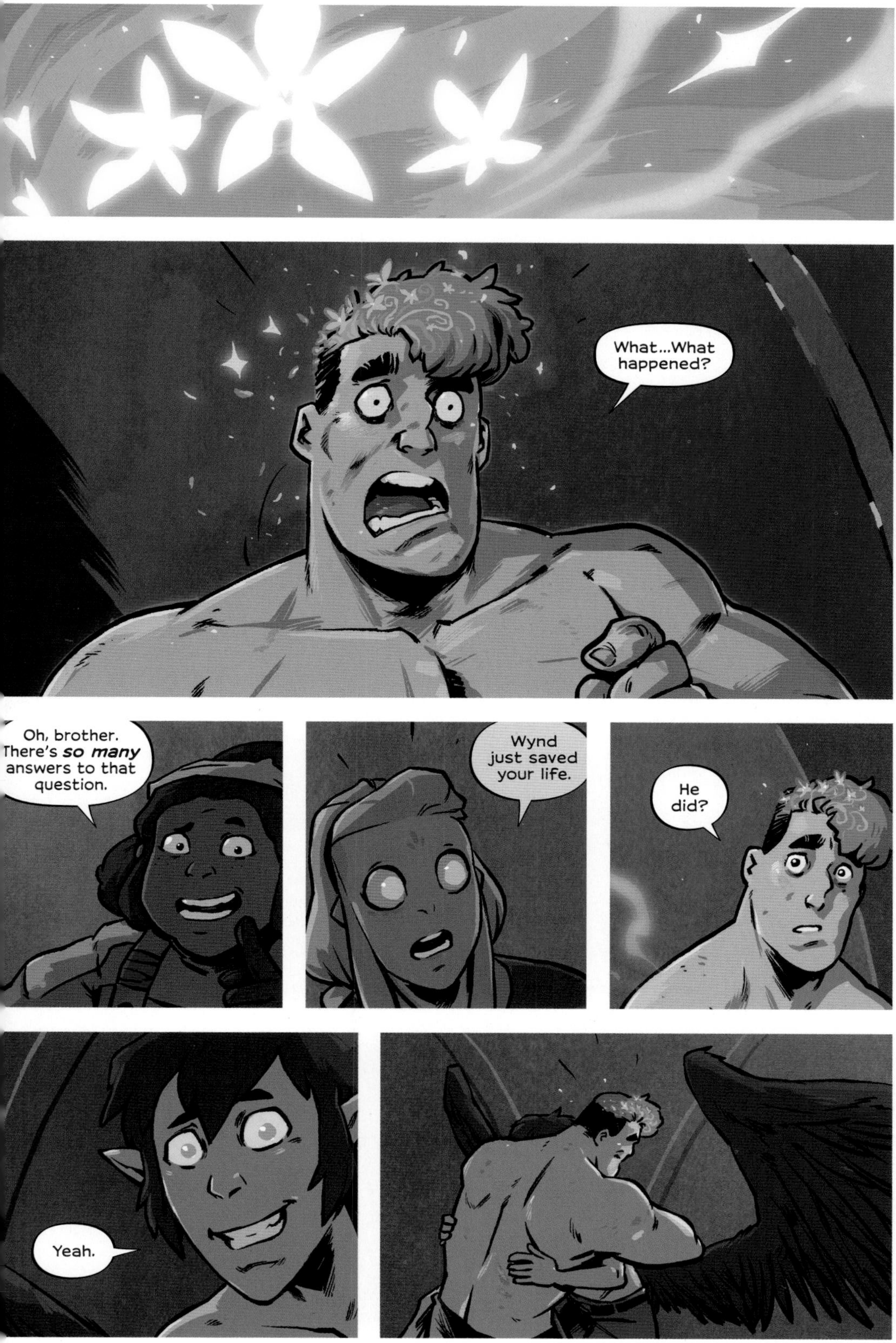
What...What happened?
Oh, brother. There's ***so many*** answers to that question.
Wynd just saved your life.
He did?
Yeah.

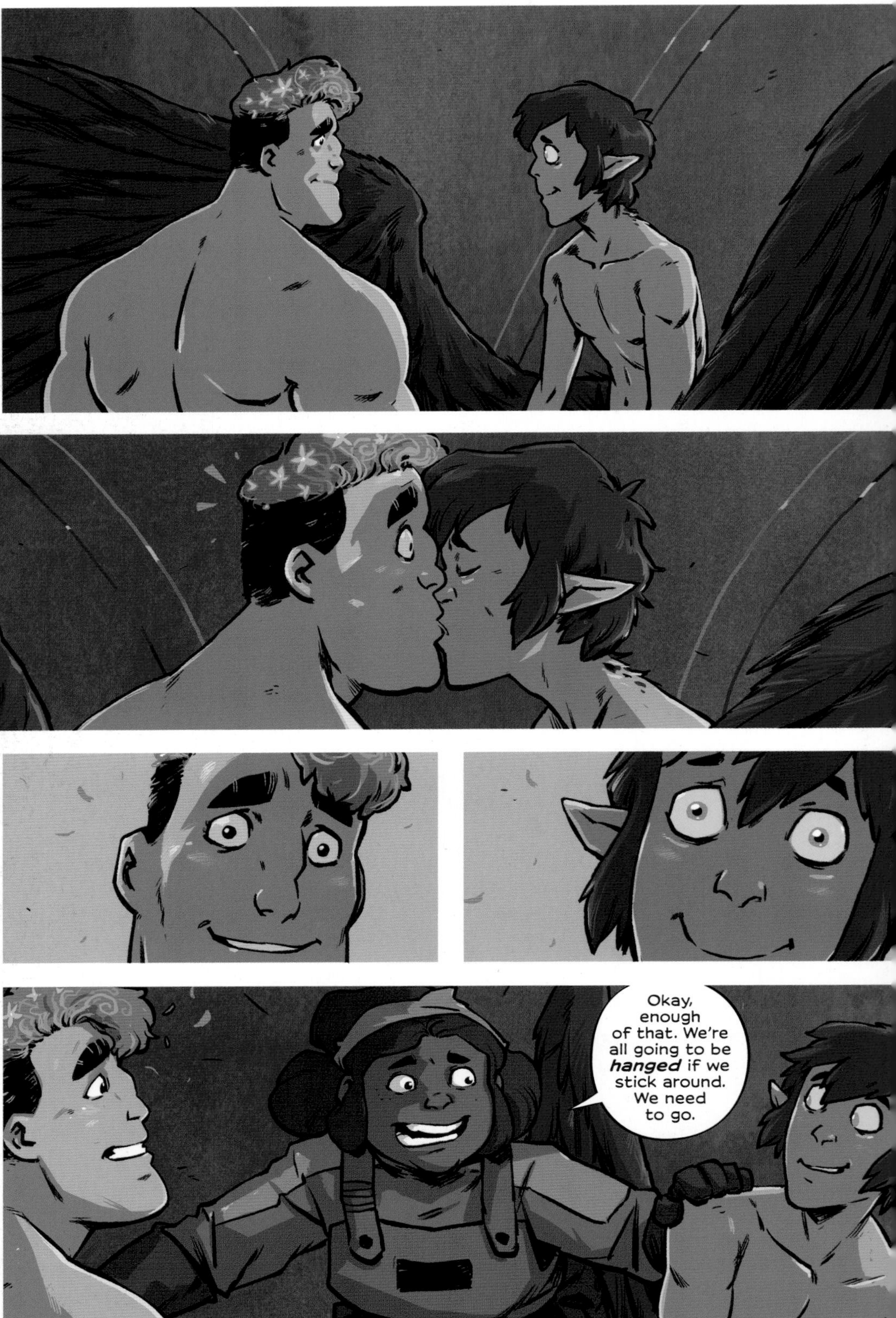
Okay, enough of that. We're all going to be ***hanged*** if we stick around. We need to go.

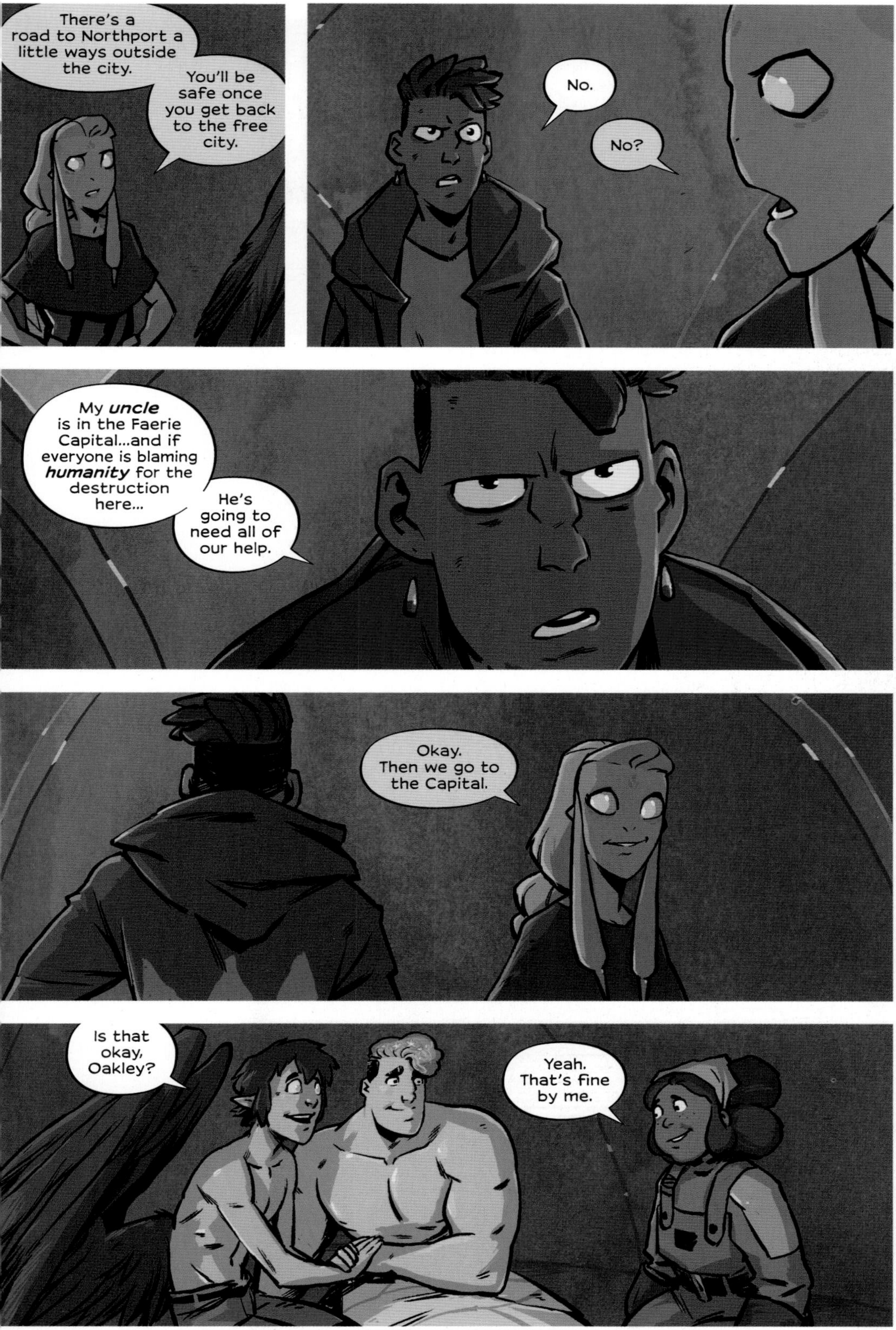
There's a road to Northport a little ways outside the city.
You'll be safe once you get back to the free city.
No.
No?
My *uncle* is in the Faerie Capital...and if everyone is blaming *humanity* for the destruction here...
He's going to need all of our help.
Okay. Then we go to the Capital.
Is that okay, Oakley?
Yeah. That's fine by me.

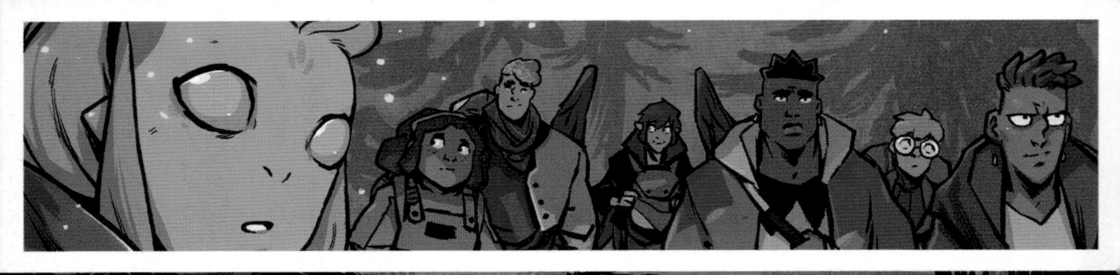
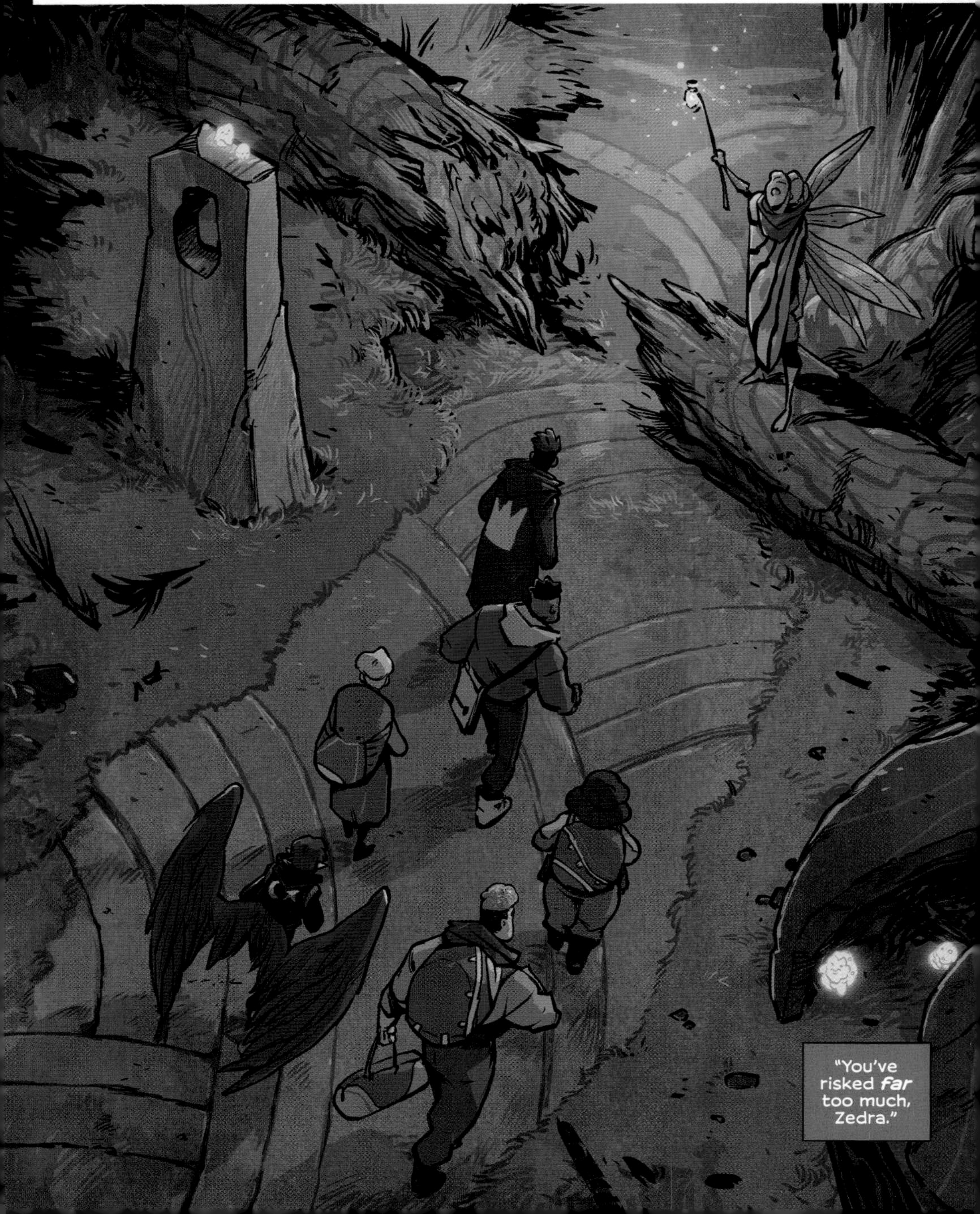
"You've
risked *far*
too much,
Zedra."

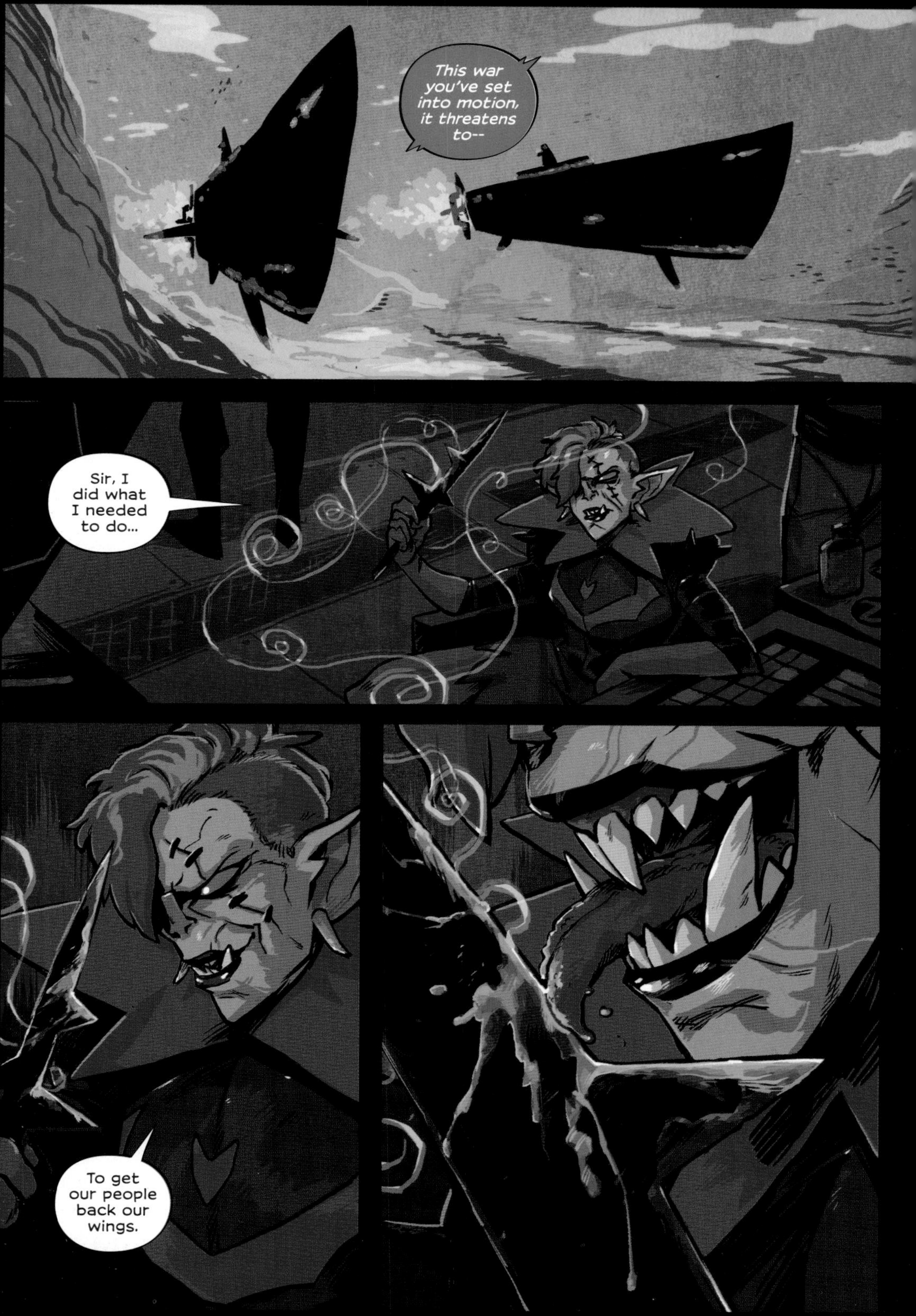
This war you've set into motion, it threatens to--
Sir, I did what I needed to do...
To get our people back our wings.

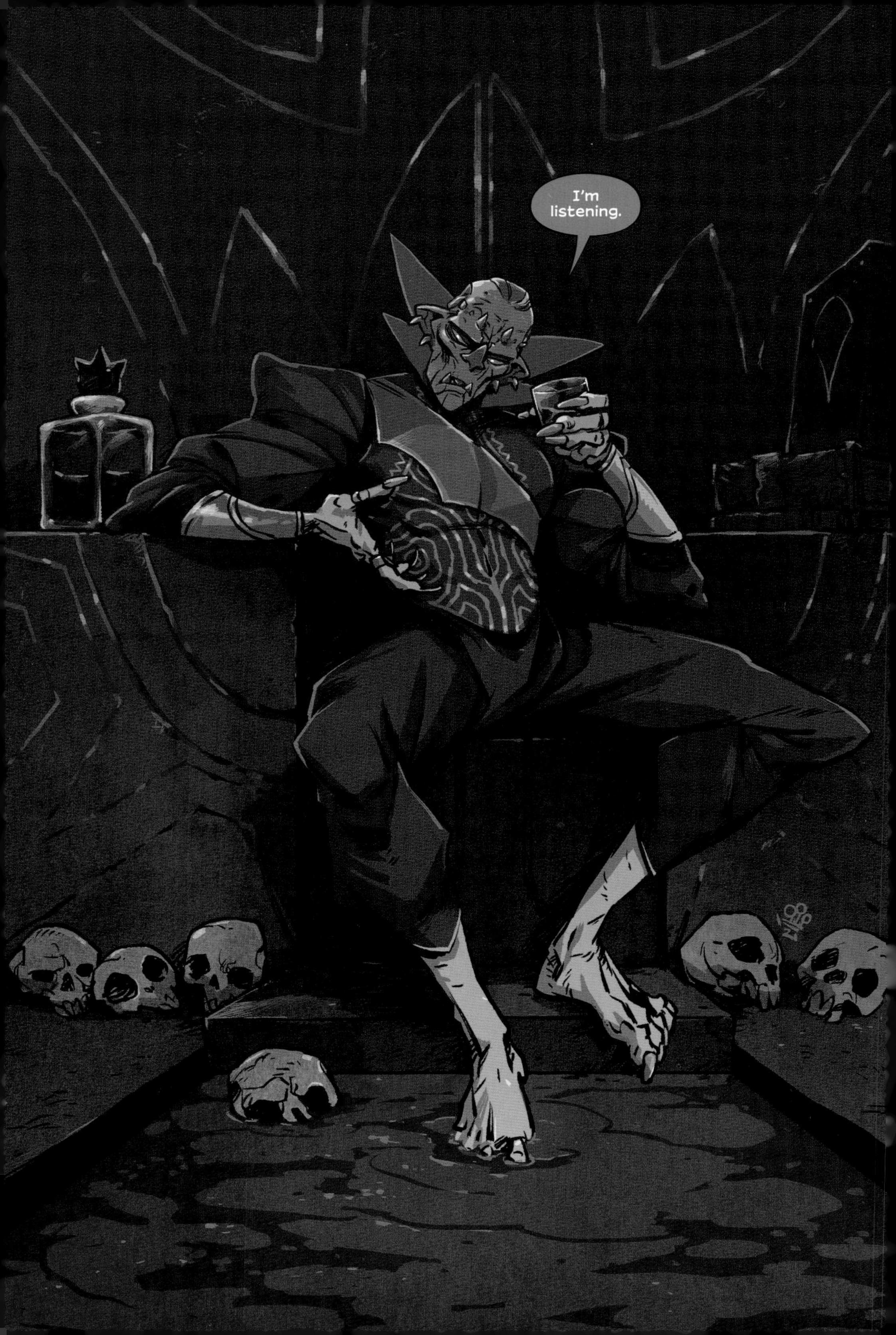
I'm listening.

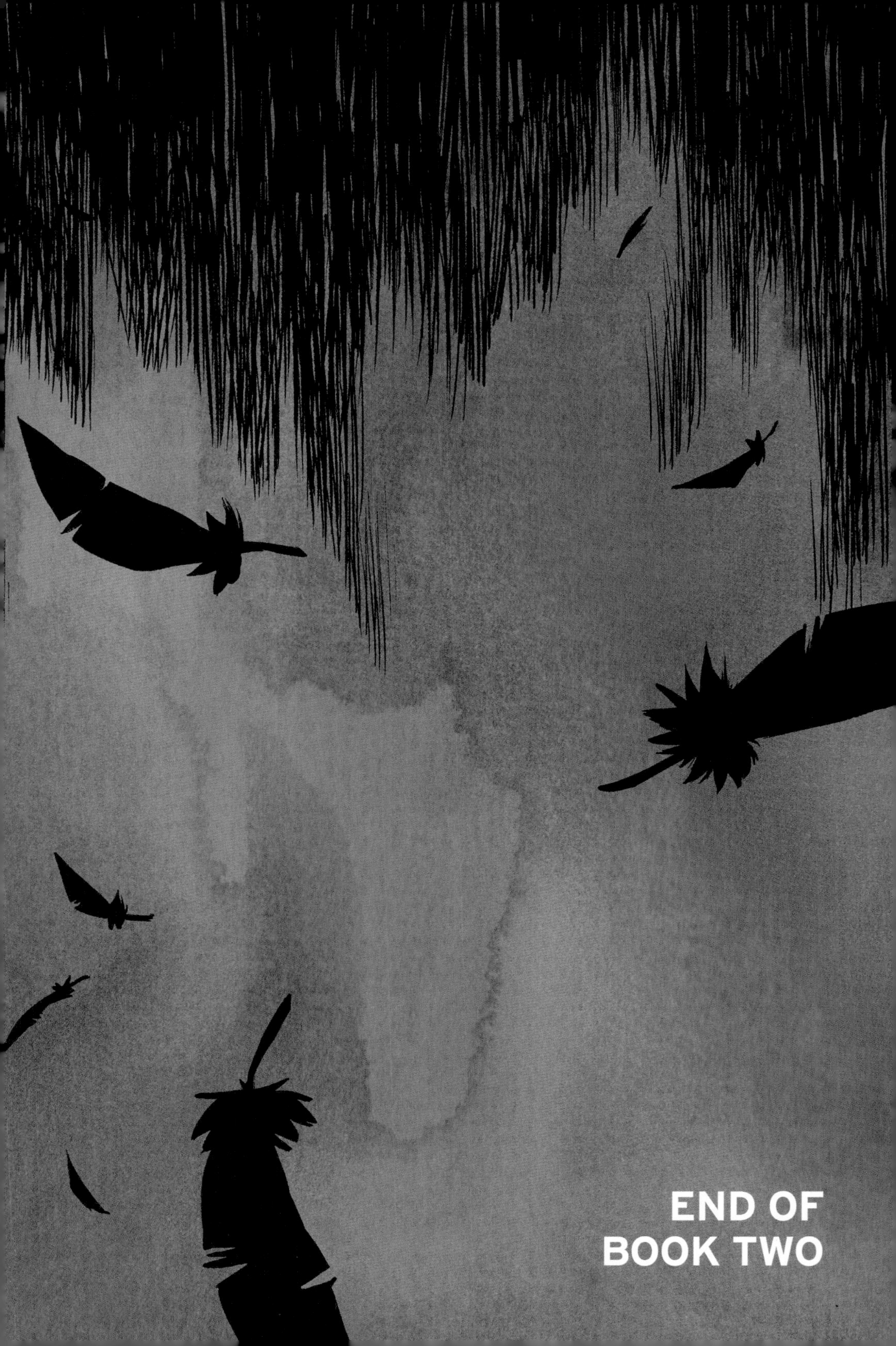
END OF
BOOK TWO

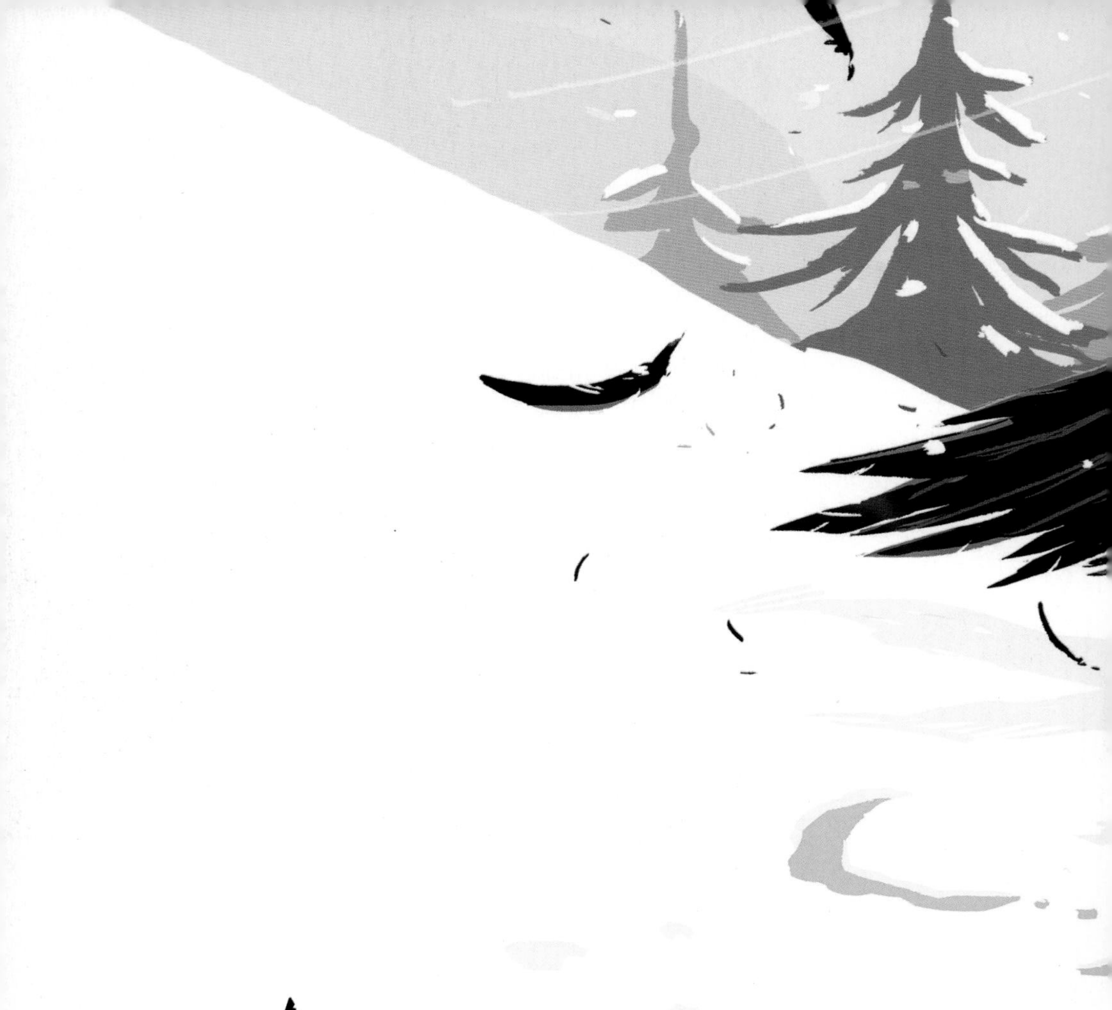

WYND

WILL RETURN IN

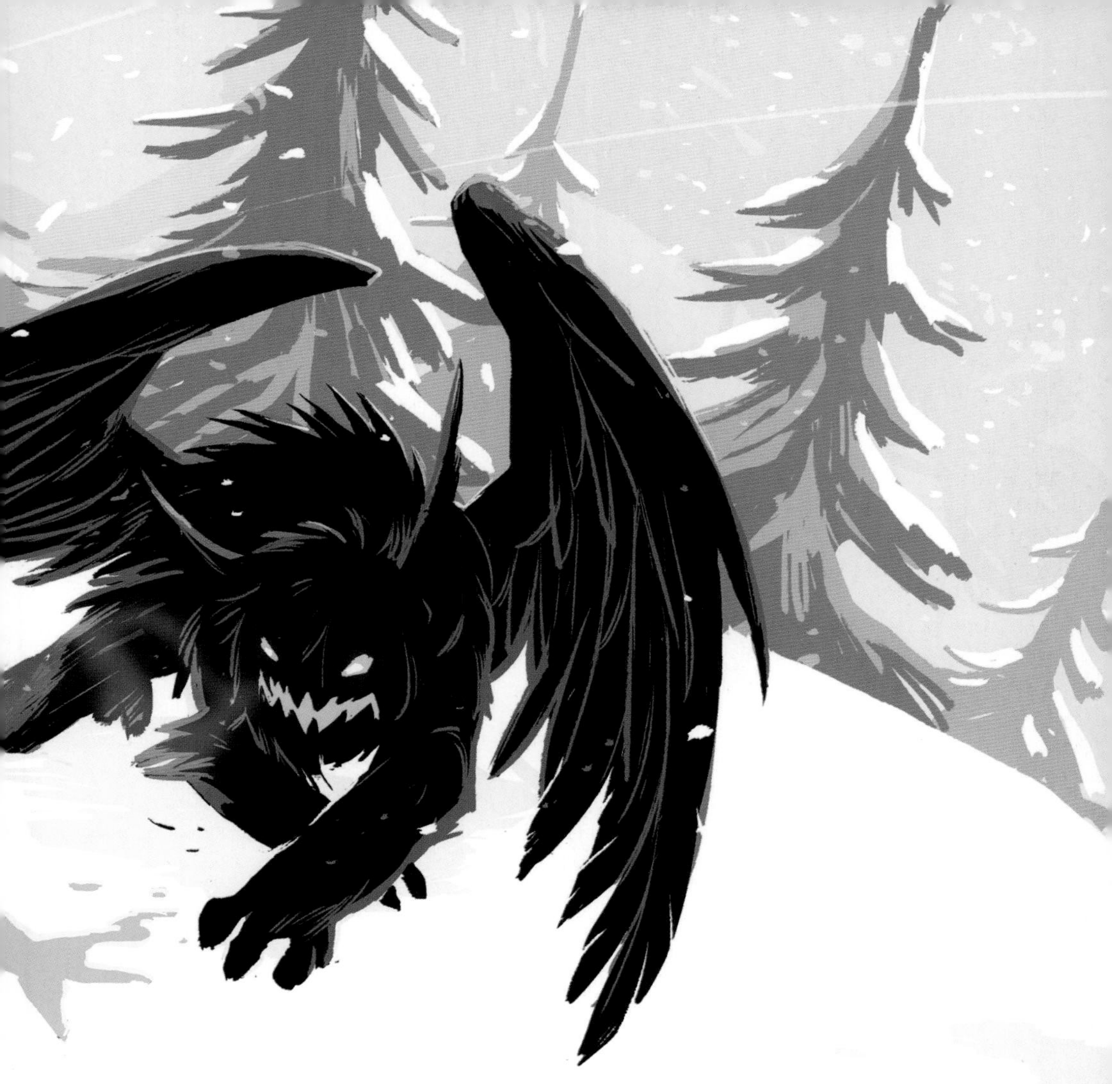

BOOK THREE:
THE THRONE IN THE SKY

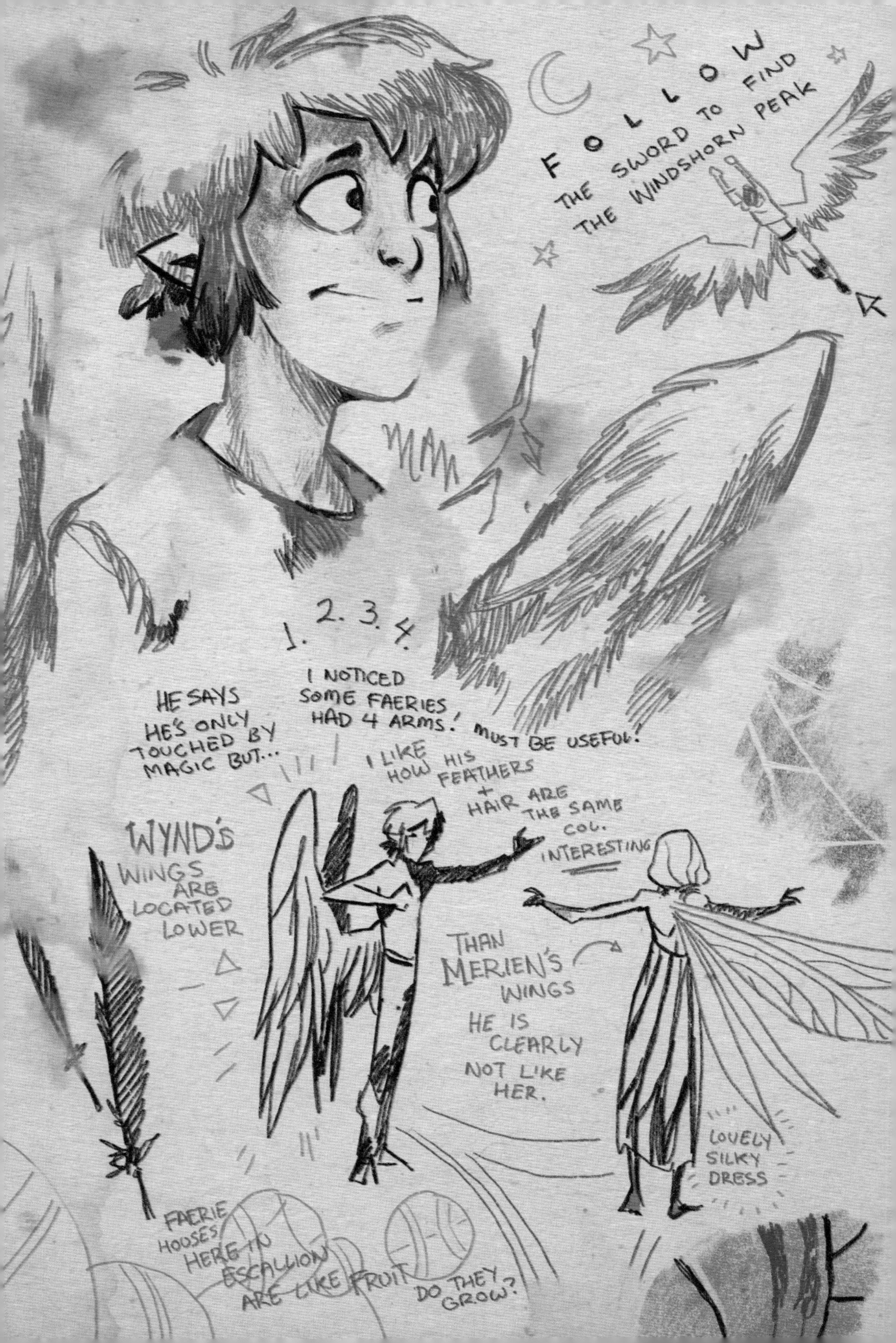
FOLLOW
THE SWORD TO FIND
THE WINDSHORN PEAK
1. 2. 3. 4.
HE SAYS HE'S ONLY TOUCHED BY MAGIC BUT...
I NOTICED SOME FAERIES HAD 4 ARMS! MUST BE USEFUL!
I LIKE HOW HIS FEATHERS + HAIR ARE THE SAME COL. INTERESTING
WYND'S WINGS ARE LOCATED LOWER
THAN MERIEN'S WINGS
HE IS CLEARLY NOT LIKE HER.
LOVELY SILKY DRESS
FAERIE HOUSES HERE IN ESCALLION ARE LIKE FRUIT
DO THEY GROW?

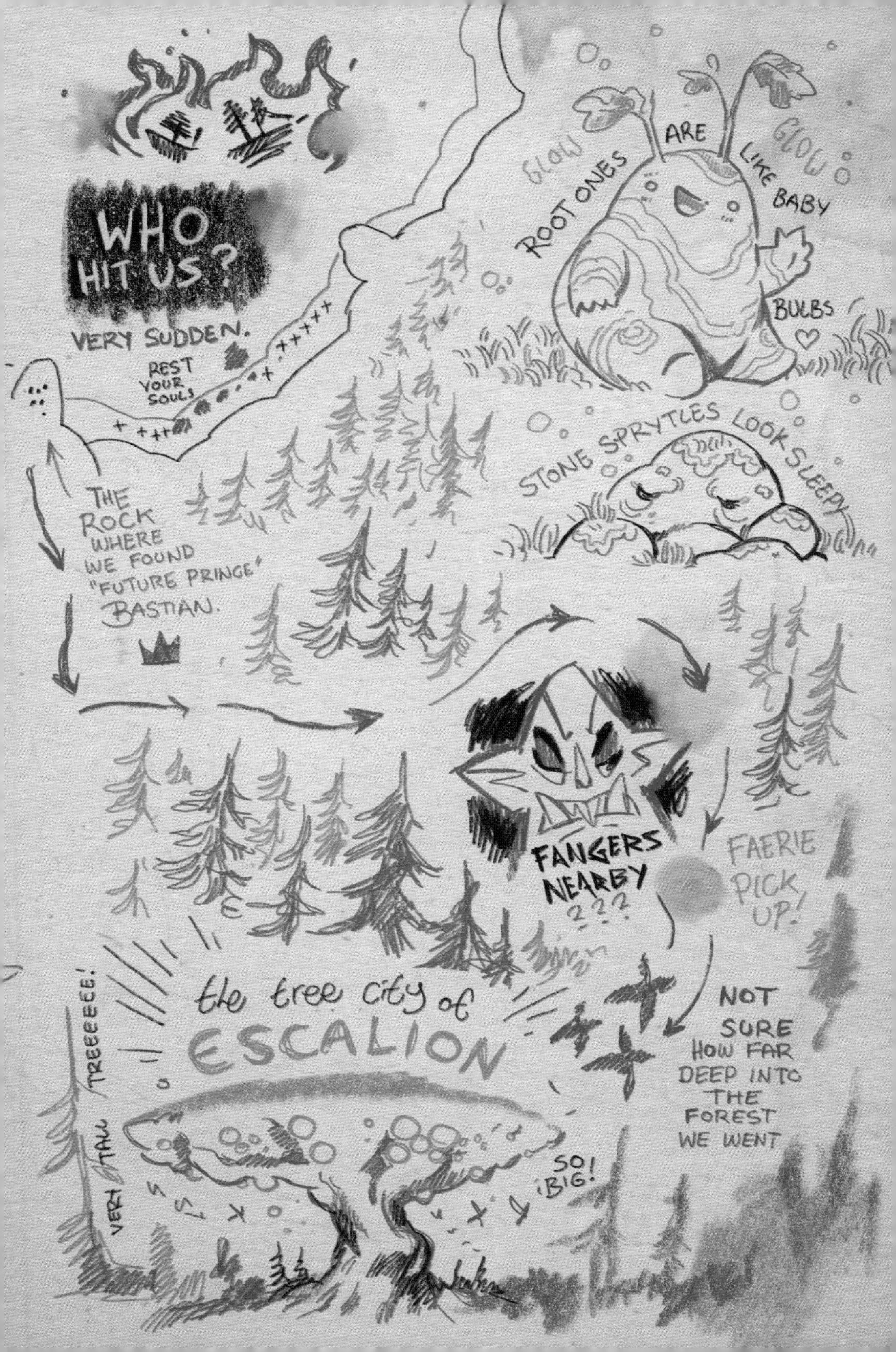
WHO HIT US?
VERY SUDDEN.
REST YOUR SOULS
ROOT ONES ARE LIKE BABY
GLOW GLOW
BULBS
STONE SPRYTLES LOOK SLEEPY
THE ROCK WHERE WE FOUND "FUTURE PRINCE" BASTIAN.
FANGERS NEARBY ???
FAERIE PICK UP!
the tree city of ESCALION
VERY TALL TREEEEEEE!
SO BIG!
NOT SURE HOW FAR DEEP INTO THE FOREST WE WENT

ISSUE #7 COVER BY
MICHAEL DIALYNAS

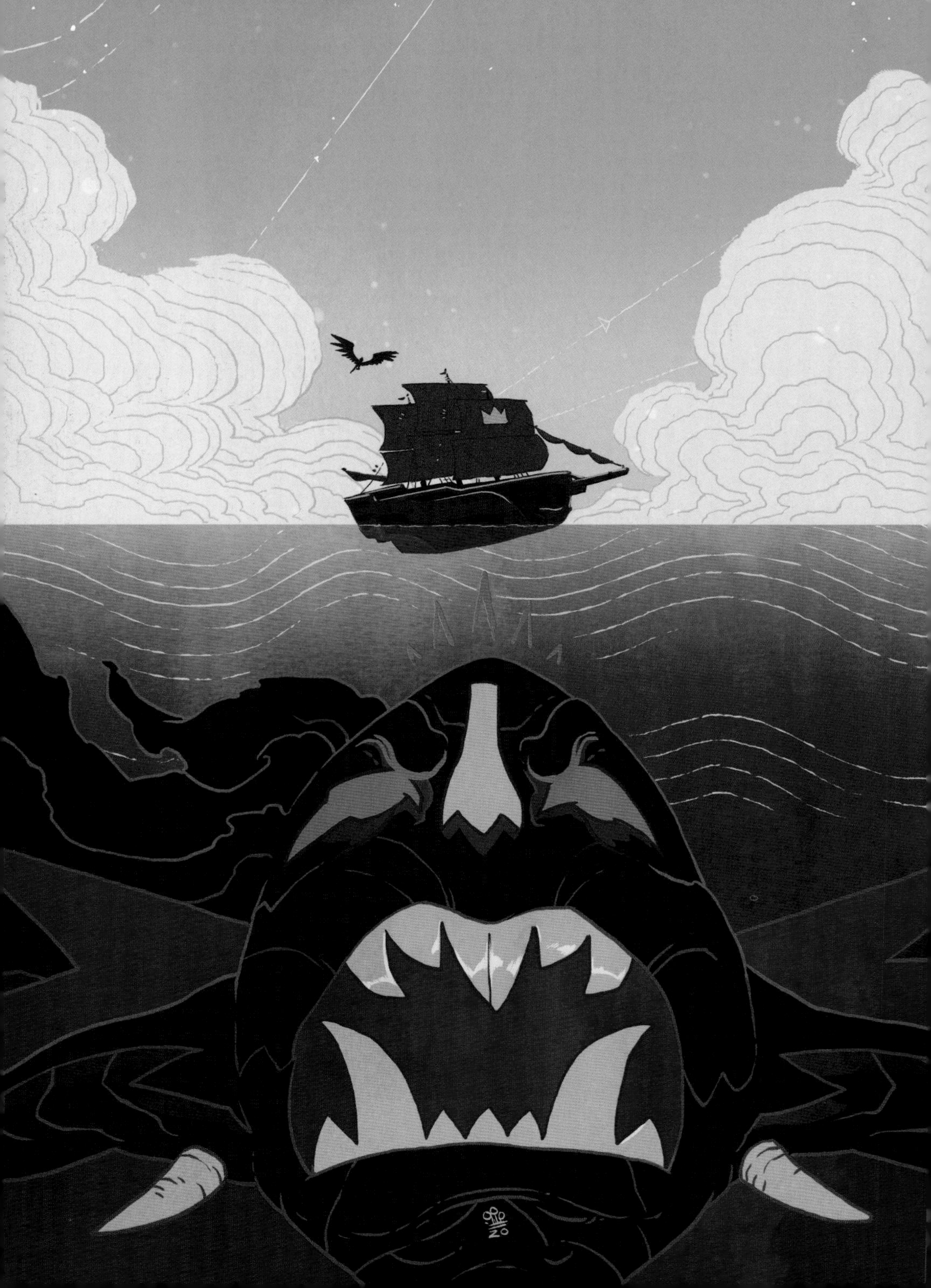

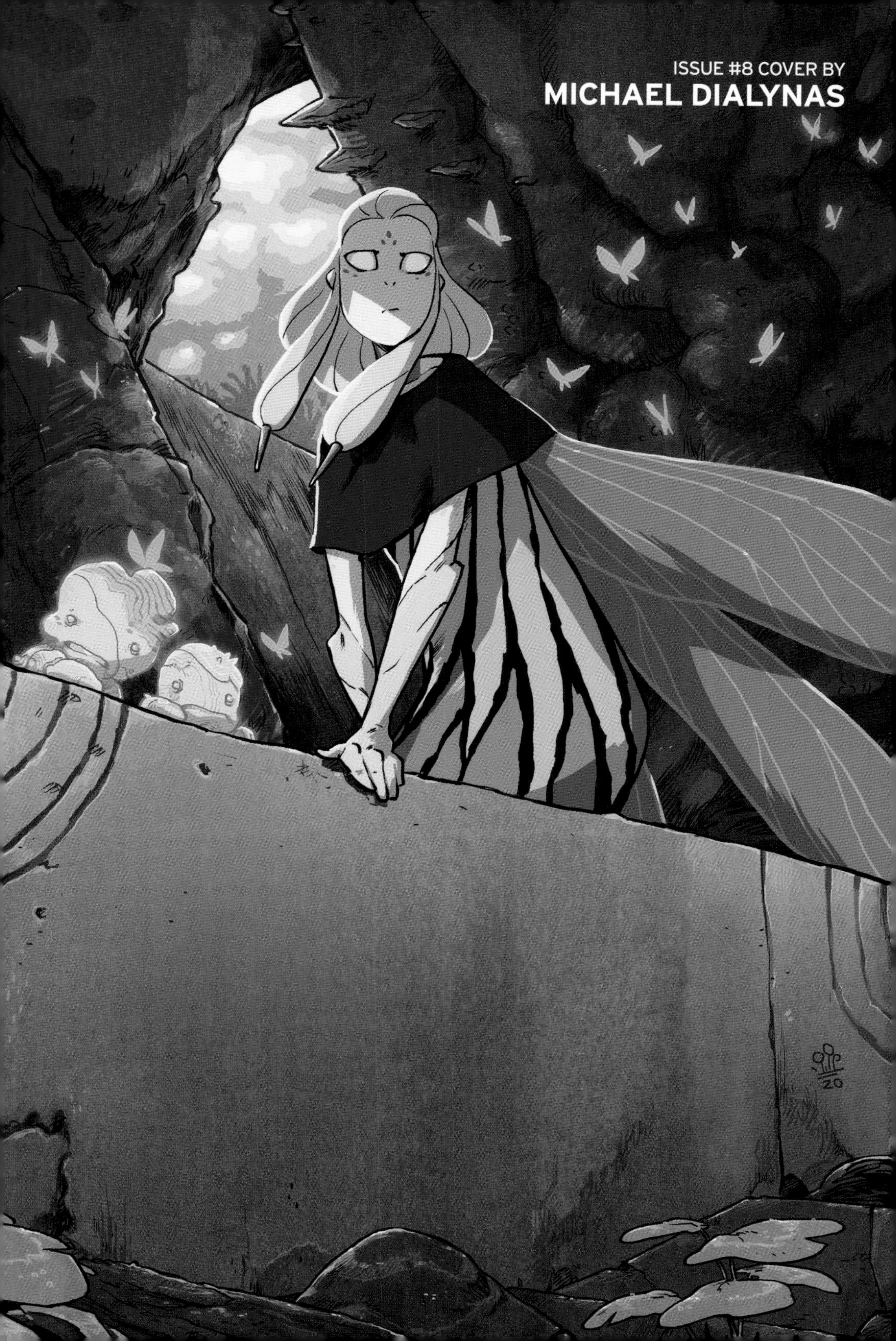

ISSUE #8 COVER BY
MICHAEL DIALYNAS

ISSUE #9 COVER BY
MICHAEL DIALYNAS

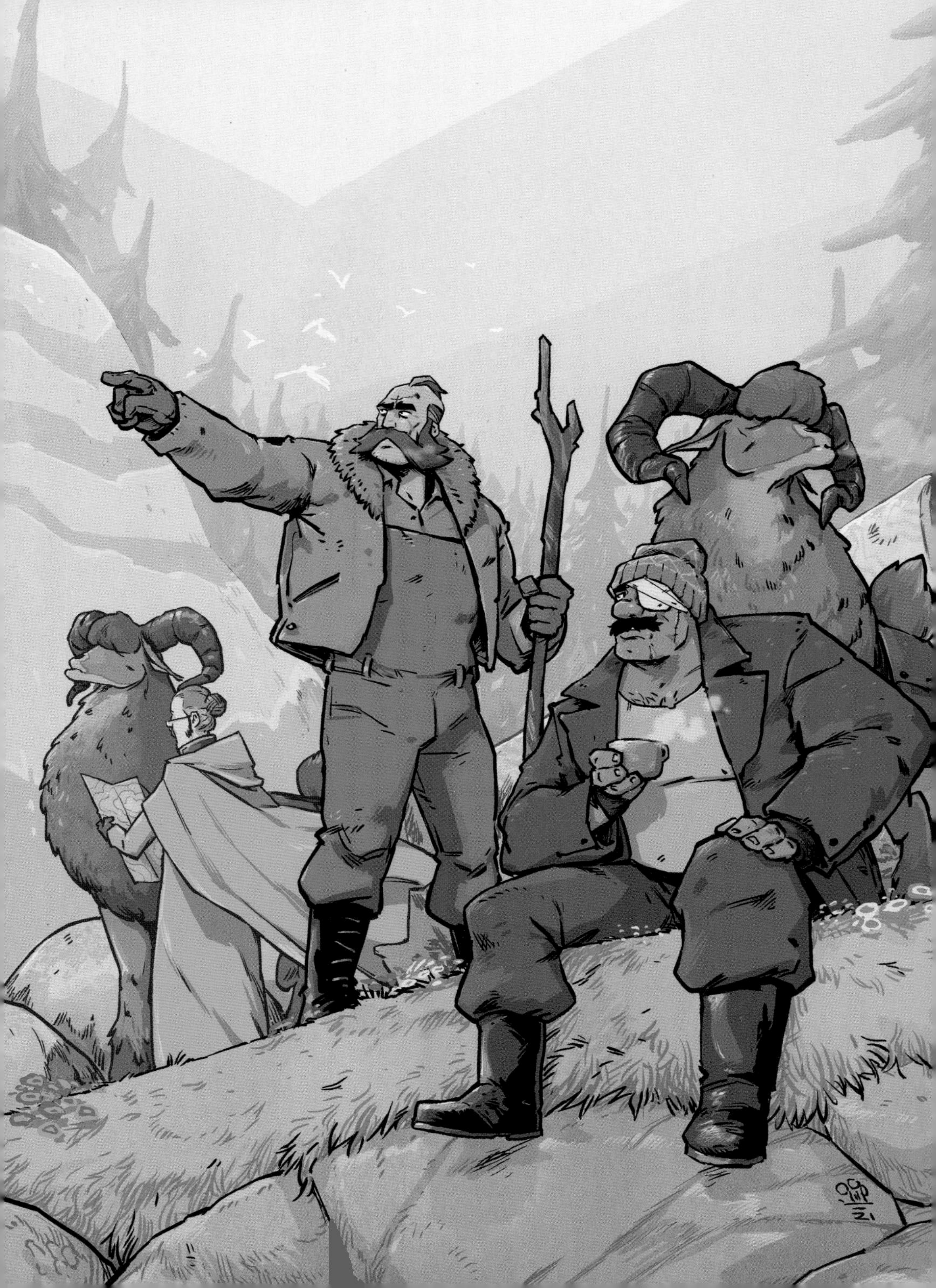

ISSUE #10 COVER BY
MICHAEL DIALYNAS

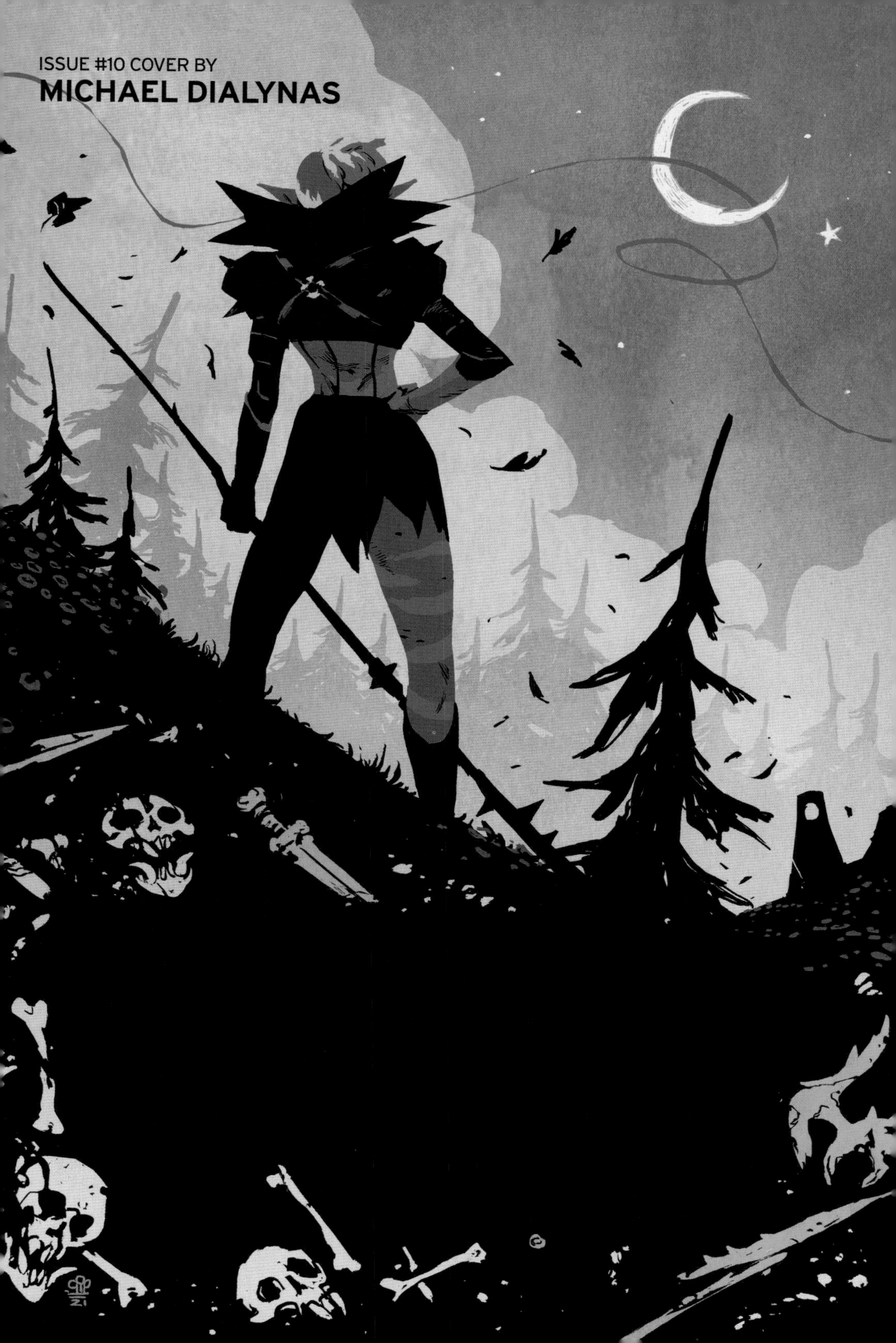

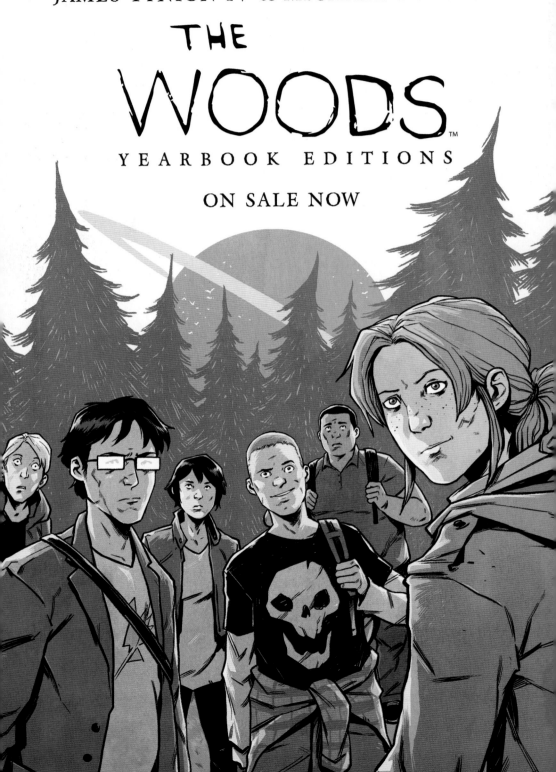

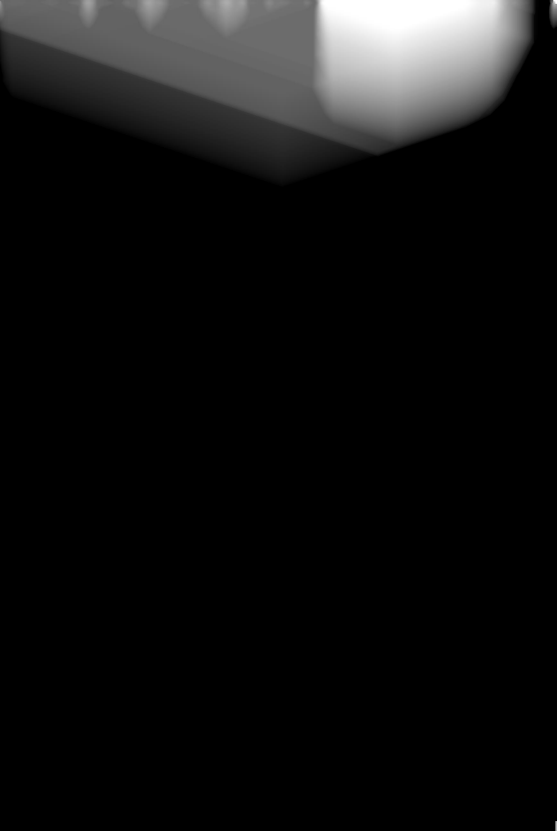

JAMES TYNION IV is a comic book writer, best known as the writer for DC Comics' flagship series, *Batman*. In addition to the 2017 GLAAD Media Award-winning series *The Woods* with Michael Dialynas, James has also penned the critical successes *Something is Killing the Children* with Werther Dell'Edera, *Memetic*, *Cognetic*, and *Eugenic* with Eryk Donovan, *The Backstagers* with Rian Sygh, and *Ufology* with Noah J. Yuenkel and Matthew Fox from BOOM! Studios, as well as *The Department of Truth* with Martin Simmonds from Image Comics. An alumni of Sarah Lawrence College, Tynion now lives and works in New York, NY.

MICHAEL DIALYNAS is a comic artist and mini-beast wrangler that resides in Athens, Greece. He is most known for his work on the GLAAD Award-winning series *The Woods* with James Tynion IV, *Lucy Dreaming* with Max Bemis, and *Spera* from BOOM! Studios, *Teenage Mutant Ninja Turtles* from IDW, *Gotham Academy* from DC Comics, and *Amala's Blade* from Dark Horse. When he's not chained to the desk drawing comics, he tries to live a normal life and see the Earth's yellow sun every now and then. WoodenCrown.com